HARD AS IT GETS

Becca went hot all over, like the sun had hung itself in the stairwell above them.

Nick leaned closer, closer, his free arm bracing on the wall above her shoulder. The warm puff of his breath caressed her lips as his gaze bore into hers. She couldn't move, couldn't blink, couldn't breathe.

He kissed her on a groan so needful it made her dizzy and wet. His mouth devoured hers, his big hand cupped the back of her head, his body completely surrounded and trapped hers against the bricks. It was a full-body onslaught, with every part of him engaged in the act of claiming and seducing.

Becca clutched at his coat, his shoulders, his back, his hair. Anything to bring him closer, deeper. His lips pulled and tugged, his tongue stroked and twisted. He smelled of leather and mint and tasted like sin.

The harder he came at her, the more her conscious mind let go. Her aches, the stitches, her house, even Charlie—for a few minutes, just a few precious minutes, Becca let it all go.

By Laura Kaye

Hard As It Gets

Coming Soon

Hard As You Can

LAURA KAYE

HARD AS IT GETS

A Hard Ink Novel

AVON

An Imprint of HarperCollinsPublishers

AVON BOOKS
An Imprint of HarperCollins*Publishers*
10 East 53rd Street
New York, New York 10022-5299

Copyright © 2013 by Laura Kaye
ISBN 978-0-06-226788-7
www.avonromance.com

First Avon Books mass market printing: December 2013
First Avon Books mass market special printing: July 2013

Avon Trademark Reg. U.S. Pat. Off. and in Other Countries, Marca Registrada, Hecho en U.S.A.
HarperCollins® is a registered trademark of HarperCollins Publishers.

Printed in the U.S.A.

10 9 8 7 6 5 4 3 2

To Jenn, who started it all.
To my peeps in the vault, who are the best friends
a girl could ever have.
To Brian, whose incredible devotion made it possible.
To Christi, who went way, way above and beyond.
Thank you from the bottom of my heart.

Chapter 1

*B*ecca Merritt stepped through the heavy industrial door and into another world. A buzzer screeched above her head, sending her heart into quick palpitations somewhere in the neighborhood of her throat. Compared to the late April warmth, the indoor air was like a meat locker, thick and intensely cold—or maybe that was just the draining weight of her anxiety these past days. She hugged herself and rubbed her arms.

"Be with you in a minute," a gruff voice called from the back. The driving bass beat of a hard-edged rock song echoed from the same direction.

Gripping her purse more tightly under her arm, Becca's gaze scanned the colorful images covering every inch of wall space. Tribal birds, winged hearts, dagger-eyed skulls, full-faced roses, crosses, and cartoon characters were some of the designs she noticed at first glance. Playful, gory, beautiful, haunting, many of the images were objectively artistic and oddly compelling.

Becca found tattoos intriguing, and she saw a lot of them on patients that came through the emergency department. She'd never really considered getting one for herself, though. Her father would've flipped out, and she'd always valued his opinion too much to rock the boat. With her dad gone now, she supposed there was nothing stopping her besides not knowing what image she'd want permanently drawn on her skin.

Like nails on a chalkboard, the buzzer sounded again and the door banged shut behind her. Becca whirled, expecting . . . she didn't even know what. Strange as the past few days had been, anything seemed possible right now. But it was just a woman. A totally fascinating woman. Despite wearing all black, she was a riot of color, from the dark red highlights in her shoulder-length black hair, held back in sloppy-but-cute pigtails, to the dramatic eye makeup, to the colorful ink running the length of both arms. She was the Goth yin to Becca's Plain Jane yang.

The woman juggled a stack of huge pizza boxes and a plastic grocery bag of canned sodas. "Sorry if you've been waiting a while."

"Oh, no." Becca rushed to her. "Can I help you with that?"

"Aw, you're a doll. Yes, please, before my wrist breaks off." The woman twisted her hand out. Becca unlooped the plastic handle from her arm, revealing angry red grooves in her skin from bearing the weight of it. "It's a good thing I like these guys so much." A quick grin as she dropped the two pizza boxes on the counter, which nearly reached to her chest she was so short. She heaved a deep breath and braced her hands on her hips. "Now, how can I help you?"

Becca's stomach flip-flopped. Would she finally start

getting some answers today? "I'm looking for a Mr. Rixey."

The woman arched a pierced brow. "*Mr.* Rixey? Don't hear him called that often." She chuckled and winked. Between her vibrancy and the mischievous sparkle in her dark eyes, she gave off such self-assurance that her presence dominated the room, making her seem much bigger than her petite stature. "And may I tell him who's asking?"

"My name is Becca Merritt. I don't have an appointment or anything." The rich, spicy smell of the pizza made her stomach clench. When had she last eaten, anyway?

"I think he's finishing up with someone, but I'll make sure he knows you're waiting. Have a seat, if you like." The woman gestured to the Naugahyde couch behind Becca, the one that had probably been new when bell bottoms were fashionable, if the pea green color was any guide.

"Thanks," Becca said. The cushion creaked as she sat.

The woman scooped the pies off the counter and disappeared behind a dividing wall. "Oh, Mr. Rixey, your presence is requested," she said in a singsong voice. The response was muffled by an outburst of exclamations over the arrival of their dinner.

The strangers behind the wall hurled playful insults and sarcastic retorts at one another. Becca smiled, reminded of Charlie, her younger brother. The one she'd always felt motherly toward, despite only being a year older. The quiet one, who'd been withdrawing into himself more and more with each loss her family had experienced over the years. The one she hadn't seen or been able to contact for almost a week—ever since their fight—not even through the private channels he'd set up just for the two of them.

And the one communication she'd received from him had ratcheted up her worry so much that she found herself sitting here. A ball of guilt and fear took up residence in her stomach and steamrolled right over those hunger pangs.

Five minutes passed. Ten. Fifteen. Becca mindlessly fingered the silver charms on her bracelet, a quirky collection of bars and circles, then spotted an album of photographs featuring satisfied customers with their finished tattoos. She flipped through the pages of colored ink, silently debating which ones she would've actually considered getting. Sighing, she returned the book to the table.

Damn, if coming to a tattoo shop with hopes of finding someone who could figure out what kind of trouble they were in wasn't a sign of desperation, she didn't know what was.

Footsteps approached from the back. Becca rose just as a man rounded the corner and stepped into the space behind the counter. The beat-up gray T-shirt he wore had an interstate sign that read ROUTE 69. Becca stared at it a minute and felt her eyes go wide when she realized what it said. Tattoos peeked out above his collar and down the lengths of both arms to his wrists. He was young and had emo hair, long and dark and disheveled in a totally sexy way. Two little rings of silver hung at the corner of his right eyebrow. She gaped for a moment, unsure what or who she'd been expecting. A flock of butterflies whipped through her abdomen.

He braced his hands on the counter. "Hi. Sorry to keep you waiting. You need to see me?"

Pull yourself together, Bec. Unable to sleep the previous night, Becca was already five cups of coffee into a possible nervous breakdown. She forced a deep breath. "Uh, yes. You're Mr. Rixey?"

He smirked and flicked his tongue against the piercing on the side of his bottom lip. "Yeah. What can I do for you?"

Becca approached the counter, suddenly uncertain where to start. So she went with the basics. "I need your help." The man frowned, but Becca pushed on. "Look, I'm sorry to just barge in here, but I might be in trouble, and I'm pretty sure my brother already is. He sent me this." She rifled through her purse, removed the folded printout, and offered it to him.

His frown deepened as he unfolded the rumpled paper. She knew the words by heart—

"You've got the wrong man."

Panic tripped her heart into a sprint. "No, my brother sent me here. He wouldn't have done that unless he thought you could help."

He shook his head, his odd yellow-green eyes filled with relief and sympathy. "It's not that. You gotta be looking for my brother, Nick. I'm Jeremy."

A headache bloomed behind Becca's eyes. She pressed her fingers into her temple and rubbed a small circle. "Oh."

He spun the sheet around on the counter and tapped his finger against the paper. "See, I've never heard of your brother, and I don't know any colonels. But I'm guessing that's some sort of a reference to the Army. Which was my brother's thing. Me? Not so much." He smiled, an expression that managed to be aw-shucks cute and flirtatiously sexy at the same time.

Becca accepted the printout of her last private message from Charlie, the one that had directed her to "Find Rixey, the Colonel's team, Hard Ink Tattoo," and sagged against the counter. "Do you know where Nick is? It's really important I find him."

"I'm Nick Rixey. Who wants to know?"

Becca jumped at the deep sound of the man's voice. Geez. How long had he been standing there? And, big as he was, how had she not heard him approach? It was like he'd materialized out of thin air.

The surprise of his appearance pounded adrenaline through her system. Her racing pulse had absolutely nothing to do with the bulge of his impressive biceps straining the sleeves of his black T-shirt, the hints of ink just visible on his upper arms, nor with his harsh yet darkly handsome face. And definitely not with the way his jeans hung on those lean hips. Right. Definitely not.

Given who her father was, or had been, *this* was the type of man she'd expected to find at the end of Charlie's cryptic note. His dark hair was a little on the long side, but the hard edges and leashed strength of his body clearly read ex-military. "I'm Becca," she finally managed. "I think something's happened to my brother, and his last message told me to find you." She held the printout toward him, her bracelet jingling.

Arms crossed over his chest, leaning against the wall that led to the back of the business, Nick Rixey appeared for all the world to be nonchalant and unaffected. So then why did he remind her of a jungle cat poised to strike, all tense muscles and killer menace? His gaze held hers, and there was something so icy and calculating about it. She felt . . . *observed* and . . . *evaluated*. The color of his eyes was the same as Jeremy's, but with none of the warmth. Becca had to make a point of not squirming under the intensity.

Just when she was certain he wasn't going to take it, he slipped the paper from her fingers, his gaze never leaving hers until he finally glanced at the message. His eyebrows sank into an angry slash. "Got a last name, Becca?" he asked in a deadly calm tone.

She restrained from verbalizing the *no* that parked itself on the tip of her tongue. But after the week she'd had—hell, the whole *year* she'd had—Becca was in no mood to play, even with Mr. Tall, Dark, and Dangerously Sexy. So she swallowed the sarcasm and made nice. After all, she *was* there to ask him for help. "Merritt. My name is Becca Merritt."

His jaw ticked and his narrowed gaze went arctic. "I can't help you."

Becca glanced to Jeremy, still standing at the counter watching their little drama unfold, then back to Nick. "But my brother—"

"If your brother's in trouble, you should go to the police." He tossed Charlie's message on the counter in front of her.

"I have. They aren't helping us." Her stomach dropped into her sneakers. She knew little about Nick, except that this man was the only solid lead she had for help.

He shrugged. *Shrugged!* "Don't know what else to say."

Blood roared through her ears. Anger, fear, and desperation swamped her. "Charlie wouldn't have sent me here without a good reason. I don't know what else to do, where else to go," she gritted out, hating the pleading in her voice.

"Sorry," he said in a tone that didn't sound regretful at all.

Becca stared at him, stared at the impassive expression on the face she'd found so incredibly attractive just a few minutes before. Now she wanted to haul off and deck him. Just to make him react. Just to make him care about something.

She was *so done* with the vortex of mystery and anxiety and uncertainty swirling around the edges of her life. Ever since their father died, Charlie had grown paranoid, distant, and reclusive, especially lately—and that was saying something for a guy who never met a conspiracy theory he didn't like. Becca had loved and admired her father, but she was so angry at him for getting himself killed and for never making things right with Charlie before he died. And she was equal parts sick with worry about her brother and pissed at herself for shutting him down when he'd tried to tell her about the supposed conspiracy he'd uncovered. Because, now that he was missing, maybe it wasn't so crazy after all. But what it had to do with this Rixey guy, she couldn't begin to imagine.

And now, another brick wall—this one made of six foot three inches of stubborn asshole. Clearly she'd put too much unwarranted hope into this stranger. She was as mad at herself for that as she was at him.

Grabbing the paper and stuffing it haphazardly into her purse, Becca heaved a deep breath. "I am, too. Sorry to have bothered you." She lifted her gaze to Jeremy, wanting to thank him for being willing to listen, but she was unable to voice the words. "I like your shirt" came out instead. Awesome.

Without waiting for a reply or meeting the other Rixey brother's gaze, she turned, walked past the wall of colorful images, and left Hard Ink Tattoo.

Fine. She'd figure this out on her own. Somehow. She just prayed Charlie was okay until she did.

Because no way was she losing another member of her family. Not again. He was all she had left.

"DUDE, THAT WAS harsh," Jeremy said.

Resisting the urge to go after her, Rixey pulled his gaze away from the spot where Becca had stood and glared. His conscience was doing enough of a number on him without his brother starting in. "Don't you have something to do?"

The younger man crossed his arms and returned the cold stare they'd both inherited from their father. "Nope. Seriously, man, why wouldn't you even hear her out?"

Find Rixey, the Colonel's team, Hard Ink Tattoo.

Because that message brought to the fore all kinds of bullshit he didn't really want to deal with. He'd experienced enough trouble at the hands of a Merritt, thank you very much. No way he was signing up for more. Been there. Done that. Got the scars. And the discharge papers. No matter that he couldn't ignore the way the woman's pleading blue eyes had sliced into him. Or that a part of him wanted to put the hope she'd worn as she'd first looked at him back on her expressive face. He pushed off the wall. "Gonna grab some chow."

Jeremy followed him into the back. "Fine. Play it that way. But it was a dick move, and you know it."

Rixey passed the three tattoo rooms, the piercing room, and the shop's office that comprised Hard Ink's inner sanctum before stepping into the wide lounge, with its two tables in the center, a couch along one wall, and a wall-mounted TV in one corner. "When I want your opinion, I'll give it to you."

"Yeah, and how's that been working out for you?" Jeremy followed him in.

Jess looked up from her pizza. "Oh, look, it's the Bickersons. I swear you two revert to twelve-year-olds in one another's presence."

"Shut up," Jeremy said, smiling at Jess, his piercer, part-time artist, receptionist, and general Jill-of-all-trades. Nick's little brother loved the girl like she was a sister, having saved her life a few years before. Rixey didn't know the details, and he didn't need to know. But he respected Jessica for the deep loyalty with which she repaid Jeremy. She'd more than earned the second chance he'd given her here.

Laughing, Taz rose and threw his plate in the trash. "Thanks for the grub, Jer. I'll head out."

Jeremy clasped hands with the man who was one of his oldest, regular customers. "You got it. See you in a few weeks and we'll start coloring that bad boy in."

"Sounds like a plan." They exchanged good-byes and

Taz left. Jeremy and Rixey sat at the table and accepted paper plates and drinks from Jess.

"Thanks," Rixey said as he plated himself two slices. He took a big bite—

"So what did that cute woman want?" Jess asked.

Rixey managed to force the pizza down his throat without choking on it.

Cute? Cute didn't begin to cut it. Becca Merritt was the all-American girl personified, with her fierce blue eyes and wavy hair the rich color of honey. Bet she tasted as sweet, too. And, damn, that body. It was all he'd been able to do not to gawk at the curves her fitted T-shirt hugged, or trace his eyes over the lace just visible through the thin cotton. It was like the sun had strolled through their front door, casting heat and light all over him. Only the haunted dark circles under her eyes ruined the analogy.

A part of him had felt twice as cold and dark when the door had closed behind her. She'd done just as he'd asked and split, so he didn't understand the ache of emptiness ballooning inside his chest. No way he was examining it too closely, either.

"Something about her brother being in trouble." Jeremy's voice pulled Rixey out of his head. "But she wasn't here to see me, she was here for Nick. But Nick refused to talk to her, even though she had great taste in T-shirts."

Jess glanced between them and frowned as she ate. Her arched black eyebrow told Nick everything he needed to know about her opinion on the subject.

Rixey sighed and pushed up from the table, Becca's hurt and disappointment playing on a loop in his mind's eye. He grabbed his plate and an extra slice. Seeing her had brought the whole friggin' mess with her father to the front of his brain. He was shit for company now. The loss of your friends, your career, and your honor did that to a man. Aw, sonofabitch. "I'm gonna take this upstairs."

He tuned out their voices as he retreated through the back of the shop to the industrial stairwell that led to the upper floors. Jeremy had bought the three-story building with the money their parents left him, and Nick had given him most of his share, too, becoming a silent partner and occasional tattooist in his brother's business. Not having been there to help Jeremy with everything that went down when their parents died in a car accident four years ago . . . Yeah, it was the least he could do. Literally.

Shit. He was on a roll with the bad memories.

On the second-floor landing, he turned right and keyed in a code. A metallic click sounded, and Rixey pulled open the heavy door to the warehouse-style apartment he shared with his brother. It was supposed to have been a temporary arrangement, but ten months later, he was no damn closer to getting a life because he couldn't think of anything that came close to replacing the one he'd lost.

Inside, the space still possessed an industrial character, with its brick walls, exposed I beams, high, wide windows, and fifteen-foot ceilings. But Jeremy had done a phenomenal job refurbishing the place and installing modern amenities. Whether it was graphic art, tattoos, or building the interior architecture of their place, the boy had a pair of hands like you hear about. As much of a pain in the ass as Jer could be, Rixey had to give him that.

He crossed the wide living room, with its enormous leather sofa and pair of well-broken-in recliners claimed from their parents' house, and headed down the hall to his office. He parked himself at his desk, booted up the laptop, and chowed on a slice of pizza while he waited for the login screen to load.

When the thing came to life, Rixey pulled up an internet browser and typed in Becca's name. He wasn't sure exactly what he was looking for, but something she'd said had dug its talons into his frontal lobe and refused to let go. *They're not helping us.* Not *me* but *us.* Who the hell was the "us"? Just the brother she'd mentioned? A husband? A kid? Man, two of the three of them gave him a real gut check he had no business feeling.

More distracting was the niggling question of how and why the Merritts would come to *him,* of all people. He didn't expect them to know that bad blood flowed like a river after a hard rain between him and their father's fabricated fallen-hero memory—they'd have no reason to, since the Army prettied that sitch up real good for public consumption. The bigger question was how they knew about Rixey at all. Or why they thought he was the best person to help.

None of it made any friggin' sense.

And, so what? Why the hell did he care? He owed Frank Merritt absolutely nothing. And his daughter even less.

True. But Rixey couldn't deny a kind of morbid curiosity about how the daughter of the man who'd ruined his life came to stand in his shop and ask him—of *all* people—for help.

Scrolling through the search results, listings appeared for Merritts by both the names of Becca and Rebecca. He ruled out the ones who lived too far away or had pictures that clearly weren't his Becca. *His?* No. Not at all what he meant. For fuck's sake.

In the end, he narrowed it down to one of two possibilities. The Becca who was an emergency department nurse at University Medical Center, or the Rebecca who was a kindergarten teacher at a private day school in the city. The woman he'd met seemed the sweet, nurturing type, the kind who brought warmth and comfort to others, so both jobs fit the bill. Rixey opened up the people search page and gathered some possibilities for address.

Why was he doing this again? He didn't need her address if he had no intention of tracking her down, seeing her . . . helping her.

No. He just needed to convince himself she was safe. He'd devoted a dozen years of his life to Mother Army because he wanted to help people—and something about Becca had resurrected that desire after nearly a year of lying dormant. Once, he'd idolized Colonel Merritt, his former commander, before it had all gone to shit. So, fine. It wasn't any skin off his nose to spend an evening checking things out. It wouldn't be like the process server jobs he did where confrontation was part of the gig. For this, he'd stay on the periphery, out of sight. Rixey excelled at not being seen unless he wanted to be seen. What the hell else did he have to do anyway?

And wasn't that cheery thought just par for the mothereffing course?

Whatever. It was just a little surveillance to make sure his curiosity didn't keep him up all night—like he needed one more thing.

Printouts in hand, Rixey stalked into his bedroom and changed into a pair of black cargo pants. He secured his ankle carrier and sheathed a blade, then shrugged the holster onto his left shoulder over his tee. He knelt in front of the open closet door and entered the code on his gun safe. The M9 felt like an old friend in his grip. He inspected the piece, holstered it, and slipped a spare magazine into the pocket on his thigh. Jacket, keys, phone, and addresses in hand, he made his way through the apartment and out the back entrance of the building. Last thing he wanted was to play twenty questions with Jeremy and Jess.

The gravel of the parking lot crunched under his boots. The last light of day held on for everything it was worth, casting bright pinks and dark purples across the twilight sky. But the old warehouse veiled the lot in thick shadows, making the black Challenger, except for its silver racing stripes, nearly fade into the dusky murk. Man, he loved that car. After a dozen years of humping it around in armored vehicles built for stability, not comfort, he'd promised himself something sleek, fast, and kind to the ass once he joined the ranks of the civilians.

He'd just never expected that to happen quite so soon. Or against his will.

Goddamnit.

Rixey dropped into the driver's seat and took all kinds of satisfaction in the growling rumble of the car's engine. Small pleasures, man, but these days, he'd take 'em where he found 'em.

Now, to find Becca and prove to himself all was well. And then he could say good-bye to the Merritts once and for fucking all.

Chapter 2

*T*hree hours later, Rixey found himself waiting in the dark on a quiet street wondering for the tenth time what the hell he was doing. The first address on his list had taken him into affluent Roland Park in the northwestern part of Baltimore. The woman of the house had had short black hair, so he'd headed crosstown to the second address located in the more middle-class neighborhood of Patterson Park. He'd been sitting there ever since, staring at her dark row house and hoping to get visual confirmation that Becca Merritt was doing just fine without him. Thank you very much.

The later it got, the more he became convinced he was just chasing ghosts. And that took his head to all kinds of places he didn't want it to go.

Before his ass fell all the way asleep, Rixey pushed out

of the car and sucked in a groan at the stabbing spasm the movement unleashed low on his left side. He might've been thirty-three, but, courtesy of two bullet wounds, he had the lower back of a seventy-five-year-old. At least, that's how it felt sometimes.

Gritting his teeth, he crossed the narrow one-way street, his muscles slowly relaxing as he worked them. He'd do his due diligence—walk the property, check things out, and then get the hell out of there. Let the past stay in the fucking past.

Talking to Becca would've been the easiest way to gather intel, of course, but the little two-story row house was as dark and quiet as a tomb. Had been all night. So he ignored the front door and made for the cramped covered passageway that cut from the front sidewalk to the backyard. The rectangle of darkness was a mugger's wet dream and seemed to swallow up any and all light.

Rixey paused at the edge of the pass-through and palmed the grip of the M9. All his senses came on line as he peered around the corner into the impenetrable darkness. Quiet. Still. Empty. He stepped into the shadows and let them swallow him up.

The far end opened onto a sidewalk the adjoined row houses shared. He scanned the visible landscape before stepping out of the passageway, then rescanned the full one-eighty from the back of the neighbor's house to the back of Becca's. A car passed by on the street, and Rixey crouched lower, moved quicker. The rear perimeter of the property met an alley, and he stole to the fence there and scanned again.

Clear and quiet. Just as it should be.

Time to bug out.

A dim light became visible toward the front of the house. In quick succession, lights illuminated the interior from front to back. And then Becca—the very same bright ray of sunshine he'd met earlier in the day—stepped into the window of the back door.

Heart suddenly double timing it in his chest, Rixey melded into the shadows of a tree at the corner of the yard.

Silhouetted as she was against the kitchen light, he couldn't make out her features, just the gold of her hair pulled back from her face. She pressed close enough to the glass to peer right and left, then yanked a pair of curtains across the glass. At the next window, she repeated the maneuver—right, left, closed.

Rixey frowned. What was she looking for? Maybe she was just cautious. Or paranoid. She was the colonel's daughter, after all. Surely some of the SOB's traits had been passed down the Merritt family tree. *Or, maybe something is* making *her paranoid.* She had asked for help, after all.

She was home now. And, as far as he could tell, everything was fine. He should get the hell out of there. Now. Right. So why couldn't he pull himself away from watching over her?

For a few moments, her silhouette moved around, then disappeared from sight. Soon after, a low glow fell upon both of the upstairs windows. And then the light came on in the bathroom, judging by the wavy glass blocks that comprised the window and obscured the view. Nothing happened for maybe another fifteen minutes, when lamplight illuminated the room next to the bathroom and Becca stepped into the open space between the window curtains. In a robe. Hair down and wet, if the darker color was any guide.

Tension ripped through Rixey's body and settled in places it had no goddamned business settling. She repeated the right, left, closed routine one more time, and the heavy, opaque fabric put an end to the show.

Forcing himself to focus, Rixey did another three-sixty

sweep of his location, then replanted himself against the bark of the tree and got comfortable with the idea of keeping lookout for a while. Just until she settled in for the night.

It took about an hour. She made a pass through the house, shutting off lights from bottom to top and ending with her bedroom. And then the place was dark again. Becca all tucked in her bed. Was her hair still damp? And was she an ancient-threadbare-T-shirt or sexy-pajamas kinda woman? He thunked his skull against the rough bark of the tree to divert his thoughts from imagining how both answers might look on her tight little body.

Shit on a shingle, what the hell was wrong with him?

Something else he was better off not thinking about right now.

Enough time passed that the moon shifted position in the sky, and Rixey gave the all clear. Nothing troubling going on here. Trying to relieve his screaming back, he rolled his shoulders and twisted at the waist, giving his traps, lats, and obliques a hi-how-are-ya before making his soundless way back to the Charger.

His baby came to life on a metallic purr. As he pulled a U-ey, the LED of his dashboard clock caught his gaze. 12:22 a.m.

Aw, hell, he was gonna hate himself in the morning. Seven-thirty chiropractor appointment—probably fortuitously timed, given how he'd spent his evening—followed by a day of being on call to serve papers to whichever poor bastards found themselves summoned, subpoenaed, ordered, evicted, divorced, or otherwise within the crosshairs of the law. Rixey specialized in what they called difficult services, which might find him doing witness or defendant location investigation—or skip tracing, dodging an angry fist, or chasing a soon-to-be-served asshole down a street. Good times.

At least Eastern Avenue was quiet at this hour of the night. Rixey sped along the strip usually bustling with business for the liquor stores and check-cashing joints located cheek by jowl next to storefront churches and generations-old ethnic restaurants. Hard Ink sat a few blocks off the main drag, between the run-down strip and one of the city's industrial areas.

The long, low building hunkered down on a corner, two brick arms stretching a half block down each street, with a square gravel lot in the crook of the L shape out back. Jeremy had grand plans to gather tenants for some of the unused space on the ground floor and had slowly but surely worked at rehabbing it. Generously put, except for the shop and their loft, the building was a work in progress. But Hard Ink had a loyal clientele and did a steady business, thanks to Jeremy's growing reputation. It suited them just fine.

The Charger came to rest where it had started the evening, oh, six hours earlier. Rixey dragged himself out of the car and crossed through the cool night air to the lamp-lit back door. A five-digit code popped the lock on the thick industrial number with a metallic *clank,* and he secured it behind him before hauling his ass up the steps. Inside the dark, quiet apartment, his brain shifted to auto-pilot. Weapons. Clothes. Bathroom. Bed.

He pulled the covers over himself, a twinge in his back reminding him to take some meds. Despite the darkness, his hand found the bottle of ibuprofen with no problem, and he downed four with the remains of a bottle of water he kept there for just that purpose.

His body sank into the mattress. His aches floated away. And his mind drifted . . . to the image of Becca Merritt standing in a loose robe in her bedroom window. She ran her fingers through her wet hair, coaxing it to air dry and causing the neckline of the white terry cloth to gape, hinting at the swells of her breasts. After a few moments, she pressed her palms to the glass and scanned to the right and left.

As if she knew he was there, her gaze landed on him. For a moment, it was white hot, and the scorch of it reached down his throat and settled into his balls. Blood flowed to his groin, waking up a part of his anatomy that hadn't seen action in more months than he wanted to count. But then the fierce blue of her gaze changed. Dark circles settled under wide eyes that looked at him with abject desperation. Her lips moved. *"I don't know what else to do, where else to go."*

Sleep fell away in a rush.

Blood pounding in his ears, Rixey stared up at the dark ceiling, its pattern of pipes, beams, and ductwork becoming discernible the longer he lay there, unconsciousness eluding him, guilt weighing him down.

Goddamnit.

Frank Merritt had stolen his career, his reputation, six of his best friends, and his fucking ability to sit or stand for any length of time without wanting to whimper like a little girl. What the hell more was he supposed to give? When would it be enough?

Even as he asked himself the questions, icy tendrils of dread snaked down his spine. And Rixey's internal *oh-shit-ometer* went on full alert.

That sixth sense he had—that uncanny instinct that had kept him alive and unharmed on more ops than he could name—was telling him Becca Merritt had brought bad news to his doorstep. The kind that reached out from the grave, grabbed you by the throat, and did everything it could to lay you six feet under.

BECCA KNEW THE key wouldn't work. Before she even slid it in the lock, she knew. Just to be sure, though, she pulled it out and slid it in again. It fit but wouldn't turn.

Charlie had changed the locks. Again.

He didn't like her to come to his apartment. He sorta hated having anyone mess with his space, especially with his equipment. But his message, which she could only interpret as a call for help in light of her inability to find him, was a game changer. She had to figure out where he'd gone and why. And his apartment made the most sense as a starting point.

She sighed and braced her hands on her hips. Nowhere in this small stairwell to hide a key, either.

Oh, Charlie, what the hell is going on with you?

Maybe whoever lived upstairs could help. She jogged up the narrow cement steps, whipped around the railing to the front porch, and knocked three times on the door.

Nothing. Three more raps still didn't get a response.

If she wanted a way into Charlie's cramped basement apartment, that only left the windows.

As she stepped off the stoop, she immediately ruled out the front basement window. A cracked plastic cap screwed into the sidewalk ensured no one fell into the below-ground window well. Not that her brother appreciated the light—one of the first things he'd done was tape several layers of newspaper over the glass.

Hoping she'd have more luck with his bedroom window, Becca circled the block on foot and made her way down the alley that ought to lead to the back of his house. Her sneakers scuffed on the debris-strewn cracked pavement, the sound loud in the otherwise quiet pass-through. For the umpteenth time, she looked over her shoulder, feeling conspicuous in her scrubs and suspicious all at the same time.

From out of nowhere, the memory of the night their mom died of an aneurysm slammed into her brain. When the ambulance had driven away, Charlie had hidden. She,

Scott, and their dad had searched for over a half hour before Scott had found Charlie sitting in the dark in their tree house out back. Her thirteen-year-old heart had been sure she was going to lose her mom and her little brother all in the same night. The relief of finding him had unleashed her grief.

That night was why she'd become a nurse. She wanted to know how to help if something like that ever happened again. Without question, she'd played a role in saving so many people's lives, doing what she did. Just never the lives of the people in her own family. And Charlie was her last chance.

Becca counted to the back of the fifth row house and groaned. Freaking perfect. The rusted gate that sat at one end of the chain-link fence separating the property from the alley was chained and padlocked.

I can't believe I'm doing this. It was like an episode of Nurses Gone Wild. If such a show existed. Which it probably did.

Toe in one square, she grabbed the rusted fence top and hiked herself over. She dropped to the overgrown grass and darted up the length of the narrow yard, her gaze flashing to the windows of each of the surrounding houses. It was a Thursday, so most people were probably at work, right? Still, Charlie's paranoia must've worn off on her, because her skin absolutely crawled with the sensation of being watched. But maybe that was normal when you were about to perpetrate a breaking and entering. Or at least try to. This wasn't the kind of thing with which she had a lot of experience.

Unlike out front, the back half-window was neither covered nor below ground. She knelt in the tall grass and leaned in close, shielding her eyes to block the glare of the afternoon sun. A set of yellowed blinds hung over the window, allowing her a view only where they were bent or askew. But it was so dark—

A door rattled and squeaked. "Hey! What the hell you think you're doing?"

Becca wrenched into a kneeling position, scraping her temple on the brick molding above the window in her haste. She gasped hard and fell back on her butt, gaping up as a man flew out onto the rear stoop above her. Had he been home the whole time? "I'm . . . I . . ." She swallowed, struggling for even a little bit of moisture in her suddenly arid mouth, and shook her head. The freckles covering the old man's brown cheeks might've given him a friendly appearance if he hadn't been glaring at her. Or wielding a bat. "The guy that lives here is my brother. I haven't heard from him in days," she blurted.

He lowered the Louisville, thoughts of slugging apparently fading away, and the tension drained out of his sloped shoulders. He pressed his fingers to his ear and adjusted a hearing aid. Guess that explained the no-answer when she'd knocked. "Charlie's sister, you say? You got some ID or something?"

The lanyard holding her UMC credentials still hung around her neck. She lifted it and rose to her feet. "Becca Merritt."

"Hmm," he said, his light brown eyes flipping from the plastic card to the green scrubs she hadn't bothered to change at the end of her shift. "You a doctor?"

"Nurse. Have you seen Charlie? He's not answering his phone or returning any of my messages."

He swiped his fingers against his temple. "You're bleeding there."

The sting had already told her as much. "It's okay. Have you seen him? Please."

The man rested the bat against the door and shook his

head. "I don't think he's been staying here. Ain't seen him coming and going, ain't seen no lights, haven't heard that music he likes to play."

Becca's stomach prepped for a three-story drop. "How long has this been going on?"

He gripped the rusted iron railing. "I'd say . . . a week. Maybe two. He's current, though."

Hope held her stomach in place. "Are you the landlord? Can you let me in?"

"He's in some kinda trouble, ain't he? Boy's too damn smart on a computer for his own good."

"What do you mean?" she asked, suspicion curling in her belly.

"Let's just say my son had a little parking ticket problem, and now he don't." His eyebrows arched on his forehead and let her come to a conclusion all on her own.

Typical Charlie. He'd gone from obsessively studying software and web code as a kid to hacking into websites when he was a teenager just because he could. All self-taught. Luckily, he'd parlayed his hacking skills into a legitimate job as a computer security consultant—a fancy way of saying big companies paid him a boatload of money to hack into their security systems as a way of testing and evaluating them. But he still occasionally wandered on the wrong side of the cyber law. Just for fun. "Sounds like him," she said.

He fished a set of keys out of his pocket and waved her up the steps. "I'll let you in, Miss Becca. Come on."

"Thank you," she said, following him. Uncertainty fluttered through her as she approached the door, but she pushed through it and latched onto the affection she'd heard in the man's voice when he'd spoken of Charlie.

Inside, the kitchen was like time traveling to the 1970s, with its mix of green and gold appliances. But the room was tidy and smelled of fresh, strong coffee. The assemblage of roosters on one wall gave the space a sort of out-dated charm and hinted at the presence, at one time at least, of a woman's touch. The living room was more of the same.

A cascade of reds and blues fell over the worn hardwood of the foyer, cast by the sun shining through the colored glass of the fan-shaped transom so typical of Baltimore row houses. She followed the man out the front door and down into the cement stairwell where she'd started this little adventure not long before.

His key went right in. He pushed the door open but held himself back, gesturing for her to go first.

"Thank you, Mr.—"

"Call me Walt. Everyone does."

She smiled and stepped past him. "Thank you, Walt."

Inside, murky gloom shrouded the apartment, the slice of filtered daylight from the open door the only illumination. "Let me get the lights," he said.

Becca walked forward, her foot coming down on something—

The overhead light came on.

The place was a disaster. Books and magazines shoved off shelves, the contents of drawers spilled every which way over the floor, clothing strewn about, the remains of cardboard boxes lying caved in here and there.

Her heart flew into her throat, and she charged forward. Charlie!

A hand clamped on her arm. "Wait. Let me check things out," Walt said, urging her toward the still open door. "Got a cell phone?"

Becca nodded, her mind reeling. He didn't need to tell her what to do with it. "Maybe we should both wait," she said. Last thing she wanted was for this old man to get hurt on her account.

"I'll be all right," he said, his brows an angry slash over his eyes. "Somebody did this in *my* house."

She dialed 911 as she watched the old man prowl around. When the dispatcher answered her call, she told him who she was and what had happened.

"Charlie's not here," Walt called from the back room, and relief surged through her. "No one is."

She relayed that information as well. All she could do now was wait for the police to show. Walt returned to her side at the door, shaking his head and making a bewildered sound low in his throat.

A few minutes passed, and she couldn't stand still anymore.

Careful not to disturb anything, curiosity born of anxiety dragged her through the apartment and into the small bedroom at the rear. Well, it was supposed to be the bedroom. An office was far more important to her brother. He slept on the couch and reserved this dedicated space for his huge L-shaped desk and computer equipment.

The damage was even greater here. Normally, a row of laptops covered one part of the desk, and countless other gizmos she couldn't begin to name or understand filled the shelves above. Paper, overturned containers of discs, haphazard piles of cable, empty pizza boxes, and other debris covered the desk and floor. The chair was overturned. The file cabinet had been emptied out, and all the desk drawers stood open.

The computers were all gone.

All she could do was shake her head in disbelief. It was surreal. Totally freaking surreal.

And it meant her internal gauges had been reading just right. Ultrasensitive was the perfect frickin' setting. Because Charlie *was* in trouble. Goose bumps erupted over her whole body.

Somebody had tossed this place upside down and over again. What were they looking for? Had they found it? And was Charlie here when they came looking?

The little choked noise she made was completely involuntary. The hand she pressed against her lips shook. *Don't go there. Don't go there until you have to. Oh, God, please not again.*

Sirens sounded in the distance and got louder—closer—fast.

"Miss Becca, the police are here," Walt said, placing the emphasis on the *po.*

Not sure of her voice, she nodded to the empty space and carefully picked her steps back through the overturned piles of her brother's life.

Walt waited at the door for her with kind, sympathetic eyes. How far they'd come in such a short time. For all she knew, he might've been the last person to see Charlie. *Alive,* her brain added, giving silent voice to her worst fears and raising an image of her older brother, Scott, in her mind's eye. He'd died of a drug overdose a few weeks after his college graduation, and it had shocked the hell out of all of them. They'd gone to different colleges, and she'd had no idea Scott even used. She couldn't live through the nightmare of burying a brother again. She wouldn't.

Tears pricked at the backs of her eyes. No. No way she was falling apart. Or assuming the worst. She *would* find Charlie and figure out what the hell was going on—and who was behind it. With both their parents gone, they were each other's only remaining family. And she refused to let her little brother down. She'd done enough by refusing to listen to him last week.

Becca shifted into crisis management mode, sliding into the cool, dispassionate discipline the most critical cases in her emergency department required—the one that helped make sure lives got saved, not lost.

A pair of light green eyes flashed into her mind's eye, and the rest of the man's face—the angled jaw, blade of a nose, and grim set of his lips—filled in around that cold stare. Nick Rixey. If Charlie's note meant he'd been a member of her father's Special Forces team, he would've had training and skills she really could've used right about now. If her meeting with him yesterday had gone differently. If he'd just heard her out. *Woulda, coulda, shoulda*. A blaze of anger flooded through her veins. No use yearning after what wasn't and would never be.

Car doors slammed out front. Becca stepped out the door, the transition between Charlie's cave and the late afternoon sun making her eyes squint and water.

Would they take her more seriously than they had when she'd filed the missing persons report? *Please, God, let them actually help me this time*. But if not, she'd damn well figure this thing out.

One way or another.

Charlie's life might very well depend on it.

Chapter 3

$\mathcal{R}$ixey's mind was still standing in the back corner of Becca's yard, keeping watch and waiting for the shit to hit the fan. Had been all damn day. The distraction was making him sloppy.

And sloppy pissed him off.

Sloppy meant mistakes. Like missing the perfect opportunity to intercept the witness in an assault case he'd been tracking all afternoon. It was like his brain needed a frickin' tune-up, because he sure as hell wasn't firing on all cylinders.

As he sat at his desk completing the affidavits for the three sets of papers he'd managed to successfully serve, he had no illusions about why that was.

His instincts refused to let go of this thing with the woman. It was like a fucking stone in his shoe, rolling around and jabbing at him. Normally, he was all about paying attention to instinct—sometimes it was all a man had on his side. And, generally, he trusted his instincts. They almost never failed him.

Almost.

The one glaring exception had been a spectacular crash and burn of a failure that had left men dead, injured, and changed forever. Himself included.

And it had involved a Merritt.

Now he didn't know whether the instinct rubbing his hide raw over Becca should be trusted or if his recent history was mindfucking him.

The forms chugged from the printer and Rixey scrawled his signature in all the appropriate places.

He leaned back and stretched, the reclining desk chair supporting his weight, then scrubbed his hands through his hair. The light in the room dimmed considerably, drawing his gaze to the window. Clouds were rolling in, blotting out the remains of the evening sun.

Too quiet. Too still. Too alone.

Story of his mothereffing life these days. *Goddamnit,* he missed the guys. The ones who'd died and the ones who hadn't.

Nope. Not gonna go there.

Becca . . .

Rixey was up and out of the chair before he'd even thought to move.

In his bedroom, he suited up just as he had the night before, a whole lotta déjà vu filling the space between his ears.

Only one way to un-fuck his head. He had to put boots on the ground and eyes on the subject. Shit. And he needed more intel, which meant he was gonna have to talk to her this time.

Keys, phone, and jacket in hand, he made for the living room.

His brother walked in the apartment door just as Rixey reached for it. Jeremy's gaze dropped to the holstered gun under Nick's left arm, and he frowned. "You're going out serving tonight?"

"Nah," Nick said. He usually had sufficient turnaround time on a service to avoid working at night, when things were more likely to get dicey quick. "Got something else."

"Something that requires your gun?" Jeremy's pierced eyebrow arched.

Not wanting to open up an inquisition about what he was doing—especially since even he didn't really know—Nick ignored the question. "All done downstairs?" Rixey asked. Hard Ink didn't usually close 'til nine.

Jeremy shook his head, longish hair tumbling into his eyes. He swept it back. "Grabbing some food before my next appointment. And that wasn't subtle at all, Mr. Spook."

Hand on the metal door latch, Rixey smirked. "Never a spook. That's CIA."

"Whatevs." Jeremy tugged the fridge door open, casting a yellow glow over that corner of the kitchen.

Rixey stepped out into the hall.

"Hey, Nick?" He ducked back in. Jer looked at him over the top of the refrigerator door, an unusually serious expression on his face. "Be careful."

The civilian version of *Don't get shot.* Roger that. "Yup," Nick said and closed the door behind him.

As he turned onto Becca's street for the second time in as many nights, he was struck by how close she lived to Hard Ink. Between the crosstown jaunt from the wrong Rebecca Merritt's house and his brain-dead trip home the previous night, the observation hadn't really sunk in before. Twelve minutes driving time was all that separated them.

Oh, no, it was a helluva lot more than that physical distance.

Lucky for him, the parking space directly across from Becca's place was open. He eased the Charger into it, not worrying about stealth since he planned to talk to her. Somewhere nearby, a dog unleashed a series of high-pitched barks as Rixey shrugged into his jacket, cut across the street, and climbed onto the little stoop.

He knocked—three solid raps. From the porch, he surveyed the street in both directions. The last gray light of day clung to the sky, casting shadows in front of buildings and under trees. He turned his gaze back to Becca's house. Flowerless rectangular planters hung from the sills of both front windows. The door was solid wood, black with white trim, and had a Schlage dead bolt, he noted with approval.

Rixey knocked again and looked down. The *Baltimore Sun* sat rolled up in a clear plastic wrapper on the little porch's edge. Not home yet?

Fine. He'd wait.

Back in the Charger, he pulled out his cell phone and scrolled through his contacts. Without any real intention, he swiped the entry for Shane McCallan. Once, one of his closest friends. After they'd all been discharged and sent packing to the real world, his former teammate had called and emailed more times than Rixey wanted to remember. He'd been too buried in his own physical and emotional morass, though, and had ignored every one of them. Shit. Now it felt like too much time had passed. A pansy-ass excuse if he'd ever heard one. Coward.

As the second in command, though, Rixey should've known. Should've predicted. Should've stopped the shit before it had come raining down all over them. If only he'd trusted his instincts. But he hadn't. He'd trusted Merritt implicitly and dismissed the things that hadn't made sense. No way Shane and the others didn't resent the hell out of him for that.

Fucking coward, more like it.

He didn't begrudge them whatever resentment they sent his way. It couldn't possibly be more than he directed at himself.

From across the street, a car door closed with a *thunk*. Rixey thumbed out of his contacts and dropped the phone to his lap as he glanced out the driver's side window.

A woman made her way up the sidewalk, an overhead streetlamp confirming it was Becca. His gaze tracked back to the car that hadn't been parked there before. A recent-model silver Prius, which seemed to suit her just fine.

Becca jogged up the front steps, swooping down in a weary-looking movement to retrieve the newspaper. She pulled the mail out of a wall-mounted box and unlocked the door. For a moment, the interior darkness obscured her, pushing blood through Rixey's veins at a faster clip. But then the front hall light came on and her silhouette moved behind one of the windows.

At the same time a movement darted past the darkened window immediately above her.

Not sure what he'd seen, Rixey went totally still, his gaze fixed hard and steady on the rectangular expanse of glass.

There it was again. A nearly imperceptible shifting of shadows in the dark.

Instinct flooded adrenaline through his system and he shot out of the car.

Because Becca Merritt was not alone in that house.

THE POLICE WERE going to file reports for illegal trespassing and criminal property damage. It was a giant step past the dismissiveness Becca had received when she'd gone down to the station days before to file the missing persons report, but neither was going to attract much in the way of manpower or resources. The cops had pretty much admitted that to her face before they'd left Charlie's.

Becca passed through the first floor of her row house, turning on lights as she went. She needed food and a shower. And then she could sit down and figure out where to start and what to do. She flipped on the kitchen light and dumped her purse and keys on the counter.

As she turned, her gaze went to the doormat in front of the back door. It was crooked and sat several inches out from the door. It hadn't been crooked when she'd left this morning, had it? She stepped closer, carefully, as if the hooked fibers might spring up and bite her. With her toe, she nudged it back into place, flush against the frame.

Her scalp prickled, all the hairs rising so high they threatened takeoff.

She blew out a breath. What'd happened to Charlie's apartment had rattled her. And no wonder. Whoever had tossed his place hadn't left a single thing untouched. Just the thought of that kind of violation made her skin crawl. A lump of sadness slid into her belly. Charlie was going to flip out. Maybe she could clean it up before he saw it. Only problem was, the boy knew *exactly* where everything was supposed to be. No matter how neat it looked to her eyes, his would see a thousand things wrong. Either way, she couldn't save him the grief of dealing with it.

Not to mention the fact that until she figured out what kind of trouble Charlie had stumbled into, she probably shouldn't be hanging out over there. His place clearly wasn't safe.

Becca stepped to the window covering the top half of the back door and scanned the yard, then she tugged the pale green cotton over the glass, shutting out the night's black gaze. She shuddered. Tonight wasn't the first time she'd found something she was initially *sure* wasn't how she'd left it. But usually she managed to come down on the side of sanity and convince herself she was imagining things.

After all, who really paid attention to the exact position of a throw rug? Or the exact angle of a stack of papers in relation to the corner of the desk on which they sat? Not her, until lately.

Enough. Time for food before her stomach ate itself.

She'd no more than taken a step in the direction of the fridge when she heard a soft thump. Becca froze, listened. The neighbor? Their houses were adjoined, after all. Except the noise had come from the front of the house, not the side wall.

Pull it together, Bec. She shook her head and reached for the fridge handle. Maybe she'd scramble some eggs. Or throw together a bowl of cold cereal. Low key was all she had energy for.

Squeak.

Goose bumps erupted across her skin, and her heart flew into her throat. She knew that squeak. Staircase to the second floor. Top step just right of center.

Someone was in the house. Coming down her front stairs. And he had to have heard her arrive home a few minutes before. Adrenaline spiked, sharpening her senses and kicking her heart rate into a sprint.

Hide? Flee out the back door? Grab a knife? Confront? Was squeaky-stairs-guy alone? Were there others? Her gun taunted her from its storage box in her bedroom upstairs. It had been a housewarming gift from her overprotective father upon the purchase of the row house—but it might as well have been in Bangkok for all the good it was doing her right now.

Thoughts ricocheted through her brain, the rapid fire momentarily freezing her between the options.

Then she was in motion. Wincing at every little noise she made, she picked up the landline and dialed 911. Afraid to risk even a whisper, she sat the receiver speaker down on the counter to muffle the operator's voice. When she didn't respond, they'd dispatch the police and an ambulance to the address associated with the phone number.

With help hopefully on the way, she tiptoed toward the back door. As she passed the butcher block, she eased a thick blade from the wood and prayed to any and every god that might be listening that she didn't have to use it. Because the only way she could was if she were within arm's reach of her intruder—which also meant she'd be within reach of *his* arms, too. Though he probably had something better than a knife.

Shit, shit, shit. So not helpful, Bec.

But likely true.

Squeeeeak.

Oh, God. That's the fourth step from the top. Get out now!

Holding her breath, she slipped her cell into her pocket and approached the door. The minute she opened it, the noise would tell the intruder exactly what was going on. In case he pursued, she'd have to move fast and not look back. A plan took shape—out the door, down the steps, run to the sidewalk and then back toward the alley. Then she'd just keep running until she found a place to hide or heard sirens.

It was possible she was going to have a heart attack first, the way the damn thing was booming against her sternum.

She reached for the doorknob.

It started turning on its own.

For a split second, her brain couldn't process the information.

And then it did. Someone was coming in the back door. She was trapped.

It all happened in a blur.

The door eased open. A man all in black stepped out of the darkness with a gun.

Becca swallowed her scream and lunged with the knife.

Chapter 4

*L*ight reflecting off steel.

That was all the notice Rixey had that something sharp and bladed was coming his way.

He holstered his gun with his right hand and reared back as he caught her striking wrist in his left. He forced her hand backward over her shoulder, the position bending her over the sink. The pressure on her joints loosened her grip, and he whipped the knife from her fingers and clamped a hand down on her mouth, his body holding hers in place.

"Sshh, Becca, it's Nick Rixey. Someone's in your house," he whispered, lips against her ear. Her pulse beat against his skin everywhere they touched. "I'm gonna let you go, but stay quiet."

She nodded, her breath puffing fast over his knuckles.

Dropping his hands, he eased off her. Her eyes were

wide blue saucers in her face, and her pulse visibly jumped on the side of her throat. Distrust poured from her gaze as it raked over his face, but then she pointed a shaking finger toward the arch that led to the next room and mouthed, *On the steps.*

"Stay here," he whispered, pushing the knife back into her palm to give her a sense of security. He was going to do his best to make sure she didn't need it. Gun in hand, he sidled up to the wall where the kitchen met the dining room. In a smooth set of motions, he swept his gaze and his gun over the room, clearing it.

A *snick* sounded ahead of him, followed by a rattle. The door.

Leading with his gun, Rixey followed the sound in time to see someone jet out the front door. He bolted in pursuit. He reached the stoop just as a body dove into the back of a dark-colored sedan sans lights. Tires squealing, the car sped down the one-way street, ignored the stop sign, and careened around the corner.

Sonofabitch.

Rixey secured the front door, eyeballed the dark stairs, and hustled back to the kitchen. "It's Nick," he said before he turned the corner. Didn't want to have to dodge that butcher knife again.

Air whooshed out of her as she lowered her hands, her knuckles white around the hilt of the weapon. "Gone?" she said, her voice little more than breath.

"Someone left out the front door, but I haven't cleared the rest of the house." She smoothed back wisps of hair that had fallen loose from her ponytail. The movement drew his gaze to a mark on her temple, and ice crawled down his spine. "What happened to your face?"

She fingered the angry red scrape, barely touching it, as if it was as tender as it looked. "Long story."

Later. Becca would tell him that story later. Along with

the rest of it. Everything he *hadn't* let her say when she'd first come to him at Hard Ink yesterday. Guilt flooded acid into his gut. Jeremy's assessment was right. He *was* a dick. And worse. Had he given Becca a chance, she wouldn't have been standing there hurt, scared, and clutching a knife like it was the only thing that stood between her and the great white beyond.

She blew out another breath, and her muscles went all loose. She turned, dropped the blade, and bent her toned body over the counter, elbows on the laminate surface and shaking hands holding her head. "Holy shit," she rasped. "Okay. Okay."

His gaze skated down the arch of her back and landed on the round swell of her ass, jutting out toward him. The thin material of the green scrubs left little of her curves to the imagination. His fingers twitched and his cock stirred with interest.

Which was wrong on about forty-seven levels.

"How is it that you arrived to my house right when the intruder was here?" she asked, looking over her shoulder.

Rixey didn't blame her for the distrust he saw in her still-wide gaze. "I should've listened yesterday, and I'm sorry I didn't. I decided to keep an eye out for a day or two. Make sure you were safe." Which, of course, she wasn't. Had something happened, that would've been on him.

A series of emotions flitted over her expression. "So, you've been . . . watching me?"

Aw shit, in for a pound . . . "Basic surveillance. But, generally, yeah."

For a long moment, she didn't say anything, just seemed to study his face. Would be perfectly within her rights to come at him with all kinds of accusations, and he'd have to take that shit lying down. "You were on my dad's Special Forces team?"

Rixey schooled his expression. "For five years."

After another moment, she nodded. "Well, thank you. I'm glad you're here."

Twin reactions coursed through him. Admiration that she'd taken the high road when no one would've begrudged her a bitch fit, including him. And irritation that she'd apparently just used her father as a way of measuring his trustworthiness. The fucking irony. "Look, I should clear the house. The way he bugged out, probably no one else here, but I should make sure."

She stood, hands braced on the counter, and nodded. "Okay. What do you want me to do? I have a gun, but it's up in my bedroom."

Sweet, innocent-looking Becca had a gun?

Sirens echoed off the buildings in the distance. Becca's eyes went wide, and she shot to the other counter and grabbed the phone receiver lying beside its base. "Hello? Hello?" She sagged and lowered it to its cradle. A shrill screech sounded right out front, and red lights flickered off the dim dining room walls. "I called nine-one-one. When I first realized someone else was here."

"That's good." Rixey holstered his weapon and zipped his jacket.

She'd called for help. Armed and defended herself. And held it together when help arrived. *Smart fucking girl.* Becca clasped her hands on top of her head, heaving another deep breath that drew his gaze to the lift and fall of her breasts. *Make that woman. Jesus.*

"Come on," he said, leading the way to the door just as the knocking commenced. He glared up the steps, his nerves rankling to have uncleared spaces at his back, as Becca jogged to the door and pulled it open.

"Thank you for coming," she said to the pair of uniforms standing on the other side. "There was an intruder, but he ran out this door just a few minutes ago." The cops urged them outside onto the stoop as a second squad car arrived. The new uniforms went through the house to secure the scene and ensure no one else remained inside. She answered the officers' basic questions about her identity and the incident.

Rixey eyeballed the street in both directions. Realizing they weren't needed, the EMTs were reloading their equipment onto the back of their rig. Here and there, neighbors gawked on stoops.

"And who are you?" one of the cops asked.

He turned his attention to the conversation. "Nick Rixey. Friend of the family," he said, managing not to choke on the word *friend*. Once, it had been damn true. Frank Merritt had been more than a mentor; he'd become a friend and confidant. Right before the old man had violated every principle they'd ever held dear: loyalty, trust, integrity, honor.

"Nick's a friend of my late father's. They fought in Afghanistan together," Becca said, the casual familiarity of her words aggravating him. She didn't know shit about him or what had happened in Afghanistan. The Army had made damn sure of that.

"Oh, yeah? I was there in '06 and '07. Marines. Reserves, now. You?" Cop was late twenties. Stocky. Hair high and tight. Shoulda guessed he was a jarhead.

"Army Special Forces. Whoever broke in picked the lock on the back door," Nick said, steering the conversation back where it belonged.

"Crime scene techs will be here soon. They'll give the place a full once-over," the Marine-cop said.

"Soon" turned out to be thirty minutes later. Two more uniforms carrying briefcases of gear disappeared inside. Nick's gut said Becca shouldn't be standing out there in the open, but there was little they could do but wait to be readmitted to her house, which surprisingly only took another fifteen minutes.

"Okay, Miss Merritt, why don't we walk through and see if you can tell if anything was stolen," one of the uniforms said.

Inside, Becca made for the upstairs first. Apparently nothing was off in the bathroom at the top of the steps or in the neighboring bedroom, but her gasp in the front bedroom-turned-office brought Rixey right to her side.

Several desk drawers stood open, and papers protruded from one file cabinet drawer as if the guy hadn't wanted to take the time to right his handiwork. So, he'd been rifling through her drawers and files. What the hell for?

"It doesn't look like anything's been stolen," she said, bewilderment plain in her voice. "At least nothing valuable." She turned to the officers who had followed her upstairs. "This can't be a coincidence, though, can it?"

"What's that, ma'am?" the older cop asked.

"I filed another report this afternoon. I went to my brother's house looking for him. I haven't heard from him for a few days. And his apartment had been completely ransacked."

Rixey heard the words as if she'd spoken them through a tunnel. What in the everliving fuck was going on? His instincts lit up all over the place and pointed to one undeniable fact: Becca Merritt was in some sort of worst-case-scenario trouble. And so was her brother, by the sound of the story she was telling the police.

Goddamnit.

Another fifteen minutes passed with Becca answering questions and getting some damn-near useless advice from the cops. *Keep your doors locked. Call a locksmith in the morning and get the locks changed. Ever consider a home-security system? Or a dog?*

Man's best friend aside, that back door had been unlocked when Nick had tried it. Knob hadn't been damaged. Glass hadn't been broken. And she sure as shit hadn't left it open, not with the paranoid behavior he'd observed the previous night. Someone had picked the sonofabitch. Bad guy wanted in again, a new lock wasn't likely to keep him out. Not unless she seriously stepped up the quality of the hardware.

And someone clearly wanted something from the Merritts.

The cops left Becca with some vague pronouncements about what would happen next. If anything. The eighth most dangerous city in America, Baltimore had fourteen hundred violent crimes and nearly nine thousand property crimes, burglaries, and thefts a year—statistics that kept Nick busy serving papers five days a week. And statistics that also meant Becca's seemingly victimless B&E wouldn't get a lot of attention from the authorities.

The despairing expression on her face told him she knew it, too. As she thanked the police, Rixey took stock of his late commanding officer's daughter. Weariness had settled onto her shoulders and dampened the light in those baby blues. Wisps of hair had fallen haphazardly from her ponytail, and exhaustion painted dark circles under her eyes. But Becca Merritt was still a looker—a real sweetheart of a face, curves in all the places women were supposed to have curves, toned but real. And he found her even more appealing for the fact that some seriously stressful shit had gone down here and she'd held it together better than most civilians would.

Nothing was happening to her, not on his watch. And at the moment, his was all the help she was gonna get.

Wasn't that a pisser.

She closed the front door and flipped the dead bolt, then turned to him.

Before she said a word, he gestured toward the steps. "Go pack a bag. Enough for a coupla nights, at least. I'm getting you the hell out of here. Now."

BECCA BLINKED. NICK'S expression was dead serious, the intensity of those pale green eyes daring her to argue. God, he'd looked like her worst nightmare as he'd come through her back door earlier—tall, muscled, and armed. A lethal menace all in black. But he'd helped her. And her father must've trusted him if they'd fought side by side for so long. Still, she wasn't going to be ordered around. "Where would I go? This is my home. Besides, I don't really know you to be going anywhere with you. No offense." She couldn't run scared. No matter how frightened she was right now. And she was. Her joints ached from trying to hold it together.

His expression didn't register any response to her refusal, but his tone turned frosty. "Wasting time, Becca. Go get some things together."

Screw being scared. Somebody had invaded *her* space. Anger flooded in behind the fear. She planted her hands on her hips. "I'm not letting some asshole chase me out of my own damn house."

The skin around his right eye ticked, just the littlest bit. "And what if that asshole comes back in the middle of the night? He didn't force entry. He picked the lock. Which he can easily do again. And next time, he might not stop at digging through papers."

She frowned, a dozen weak defenses against his logic springing up even as his words trickled ice down her spine.

Nick rushed in to fill the silence her hesitation created. "Pack a bag. Now. Everything else we can figure out later."

We? She crossed her arms. "What, so, *now* you're helping me?"

He gave a single tight nod.

Yesterday, he refused to even talk to her. Now he wanted to call the shots? What happened in twenty-four hours to bring about this one-eighty? Could she really count on him? "Why? What's changed?"

He stepped closer, close enough that she could make out the gold flecks in his eyes. "You, being in danger." His deep voice emphasizing the word *you,* combined with his intense gaze, spread warmth throughout her tired body. With a sideways nod to the stairs, he said, "Go pack a bag. Or I will."

The image of those big hands rooting through her panty drawer sprang into her mind's eye. Butterflies made a quick loop around her stomach. "Fine." She couldn't help Charlie if anything happened to her, so she walked past Nick toward the bottom step, hoping he didn't see the pink she suspected colored her cheeks. Three steps up, she felt movement behind her. She stopped and looked over her shoulder.

He was *right there.*

She hadn't heard him move. Just . . . sensed his presence. Her gaze flicked over him. The man had some damn broad shoulders under that black jacket. "We're doing the buddy system?"

"I'm going to do a quick sweep for bugs while you're packing."

"Oh. As in . . . Oh." Unease shivered over her. Becca hadn't even thought of that. At the top, she broke left into her bedroom and turned on the lights. Her gaze scanned over the place where she'd slept the past four years—the dresser, the bed, the night tables. Had the intruder come in here? The idea made her want to strip her unmade bedclothes and throw everything in the wash. She shuddered.

"I'll start in here," he said, following her in. "And then you can pack while I sweep the office."

Nodding, she watched him go to work, starting with the disassembly of the handset on her phone. Detached and methodical, he worked quickly, confidently. Though he seemed to be paying no attention to her personal things lying around the room, she couldn't help but wonder what he thought.

The guitar Scott had prized sat on a stand in one corner. Paperback books and framed pictures of her family crowded the nightstand along with her alarm clock. A crystal dish dominated the center of her dresser, filled with seashells she'd collected over the years—one for each trip to the beach she'd ever taken going all the way back to her childhood. Pieces of jewelry she hadn't bothered to put away lay loose on the dresser near her mother's jewelry box—hers now. She never gave these things a second thought. Did he wonder what kind of woman they added up to?

He checked each of the lamps, then crouched next to her nightstand. Using a tool he produced from his pocket, he removed the plate from the outlet. He poked around for a moment, screwed the cover back on, then repeated this process on the only other accessible outlet and the light switch box. Competence rolled off him in oddly appealing and tangible waves that kept the threatening anxiety from washing over her.

"Just pack essentials for tonight, okay?" Nick said as he made for the hall.

She blew out the breath she didn't realize she'd been holding. "Yeah, okay." From the bottom of her closet, she retrieved an overnight bag and tossed it on her bed. Moving around her room, she gathered clothes, scrubs, a couple of favorite sleep shirts, and a few days' worth of panties and bras, including her favorite pale yellow satin and white lace matching set. Just because wearing it made her feel good, and pretty. Had absolutely nothing to do with the hard-bodied warrior prowling around her house right now. Because that would just be *crazy*.

Right.

After piling everything on the bed, she pushed her door closed. She'd been in these scrubs so long she was about ready to burn them. As she stripped, her pulse kicked up. Nick was ten feet away in the next room. What if he barged in? Ridiculous heat rushed over her skin, like her body didn't think that was a completely bad idea. She tugged on a pair of jeans and grabbed a yellow Henley. There. More human already.

She chucked the dirties into a basket in her closet and made for the bathroom.

Nick's gaze landed on her the moment she opened the door. Man, those light eyes with the chocolate brown hair made a killer combination.

"Find anything?"

"Looks clean. Need more equipment to know for sure."

Small victories. But, after the day she'd had, it was better than nothing. "Okay, well, I'm almost done," she said, feeling like she needed to say something as she passed him in the hall. The bathroom light revealed the toll the day had taken. She leaned into the mirror. A dark red scrape filled the space between the end of her left eyebrow and her hairline, just above her temple. She soaped up a washcloth and cleaned the injury, wincing at the tender sting. Antibiotic cream went on next. The rest could wait. With Charlie missing, it hardly mattered how messy her hair was or how bad she yearned for a hot shower.

The feeling of being observed skittered over her skin, pulling her gaze to the right. Nick's big body seemed to take up the entire landing at the top of the steps. The black jacket, cargo pants, and boots—not to mention knowing he had a holster strapped around those big shoulders—gave off a paramilitary vibe, making him look like the soldier he'd once been. He wasn't obviously watching her, though her father had always had the ability to see out of the back of his head. No doubt Nick was the same.

Shaking off the sensation, she packed her toiletries and rushed back to her bedroom. Nothing about Nick's demeanor made her think he was getting impatient, but there was something in his silence that made her feel she should rush. None too carefully, she stuffed everything in her bag.

"Becca, can you think of any reason why someone broke into your house? And your brother's? What they might've been looking for?"

She paused with her hand on the zipper. Those questions had been driving her crazy since she'd first seen the disaster at Charlie's place. She thought back to their fight last week, to his insistence that their dad wasn't who she thought he was—and that he could prove it. How could that be relevant, though? "A few days ago I'd have guessed that the break-in at Charlie's had to do with his computer security consulting work. That someone was trying to steal secrets or something. But now? With the note, and tonight? I have no freaking clue." And her confusion about why this was all happening was giving her a grade-A headache. Becca shouldered her bag, grabbed her favorite pillow, and stepped out into the hall again.

Nick's gaze was narrow and sharp as a blade. "Does Charlie go missing a lot? Has anything like this happened before?"

"No. He's a bit of a homebody. Always was, even as a kid. Our mom died when we were young, and Charlie withdrew into himself and his computers. But he never just disappears like this."

"Does he have any friends? Anywhere he might go?"

Becca shook her head. "That I know of, most of his friends have always been online. He does corporate security consulting, and even most of his business meetings are calls or Skypes he does from home. I'm not even sure which companies he works for. Apparently he has to sign nondisclosure agreements as part of his contract work, so he can't say."

Something dark flashed over Nick's expression, and his jaw ticked. "We'll figure it out," he said, reaching for her bag. His fingers touched hers on the strap, warm and strong.

The *we* in his words shouldn't have been as comforting as it was. "Oh, you don't have to—"

"I got it." He slipped the bag from her shoulder to his.

"Uh, okay. Look, I have to say this. I appreciate your help very much. But please don't confuse my needing help with being helpless." She squeezed the pillow against her stomach.

He gave her an appraising look and nodded. "Fair enough." His gaze dropped to her flower-covered pillow.

"What? It's essential. I hate hotel pillows." She hugged it tighter.

"Well, you're in luck then." Nick gestured her toward the steps.

"Why's that?" she asked, starting down.

"No hotels."

"What? Where else would I go?" She paused at the bottom and watched him make his way down. Big as he was, he not only came quietly but also didn't hit a single one of the squeaks, like he knew where they were and how to avoid them. "How'd you do that?"

"What?"

"The stairs." God, it was like being around her father. Her heart gave a little tug. Not that the comparison was all bad. "Never mind. Back to this hotel situation."

He shook his head. "No hotels. My place is safer."

His place? Her stomach flip-flopped. "Uh . . ." was the

sum total of her intelligent response. Where would she sleep at his place? And would she be able to sleep at all knowing he was so close? "I wouldn't want to inconvenience you."

"You won't," he said, going from window to window and pulling all the curtains closed. "We'll leave the lights on. Hopefully that'll discourage anyone from another attempt tonight until we can get more serious hardware on these doors."

A shiver raced over her skin. There was that *we* again. "Do you think they'll be back?"

He paused at the last window and looked her way, his expression unreadable.

"Truth," she said.

He closed the curtain and returned to her, his eyes softer than she'd yet seen them, but no less serious. "I think they'll be back. But next time, we'll be ready for them."

Chapter 5

*W*ait. You live here?" Becca asked, recognizing the brick warehouse-style building she'd visited the day before despite the dark. The whole neighborhood was a collection of empty-looking brick warehouses located just a few blocks from the business end of the harbor.

"Yep," he said.

She stared at him, waiting for more. But Nick remained quiet as he turned into a gravel lot at the side of the building, big hands gripping the wheel, console lights casting shadows over his strong profile.

Nick cut the engine and glanced her way. "Home, sweet home."

She peered out the window at the dark brick building. "You mean tattoo parlor, sweet tattoo parlor."

He winked and pushed out of the car. "That's only the one part." The back door opened and he retrieved her bag.

What the hell was happening to her life? Charlie missing and maybe taken. Chased from her home. Now, taking shelter in a run-down warehouse in a not-great part of town. "Good to know, I guess," she murmured. Grabbing her pillow and her purse, she opened her door and stepped out. And almost walked right into Nick, who'd apparently come around to open her door. Warmth filled her chest, though she couldn't say why the polite gesture should affect her after everything else he'd done for her tonight. "Sorry," she murmured.

He placed his hand at the small of her back, and his heat seeped into her skin through the thin shirt. "This way." She wasn't a small woman, but he almost made her feel it walking next to him. And it wasn't just his height, though he had a good seven or eight inches on her five-foot-seven-inch frame. It was the breadth of his shoulders, the almost defensive way he moved next to her, his general presence.

On the brick by the back door, he flipped up a metal covering and entered a code into a backlit panel. The door disengaged with a snap and a low buzz. He opened it and gestured for her to go first.

The inside was pretty much what she'd expected. Brick walls, gray-painted cement steps, and a gray, metal railing. A wall-mounted light with grating over the bulb cast a dull illumination over the entryway, as did another at the bottom of the steps.

"Hard Ink's through there," Nick said, pointing at a door adjacent to the staircase. "In fact—" He tugged the door open and stepped through, holding it for her to follow. She braced it with her back but didn't enter. She was holding a pillow, for God's sake. Wouldn't whoever was here think that was weird? "Hey," he said to someone inside. He waved her in.

Oh, what the hell. Maybe it was good that someone else knew she was here. Though, truly, no part of her thought the sense of safety she felt around him was misplaced.

Was that because he'd known and fought with her father? Or because he'd shown up to help exactly when she'd needed him? She propped the pillow against the wall and rounded the corner to join him.

The room was large and airy, surrounded on three sides by warm brick walls. On the longest wall, a large graffiti-like painting read, "Bleed with me and you will forever be my brother." It was a striking design, a jagged cursive with reds and grays and blacks blending through the words.

Nick's brother, Jeremy, sat at a round table in the middle working on an intricate abstract drawing, a sketch pad, printed pictures, and a book on modern art in front of him. "Hey," he said, glancing up. He did a double take, shook his hair out of his eyes, and straightened in his chair. "Oh, hey. Uh, uh . . ."

"Becca," she and Nick said at the same time. Yeah, this wasn't awkward at all.

"Hi, Becca. Good to see you again." Smiling, he glanced from her to Nick and back again.

"What are you working on?" Nick asked, ignoring Jeremy's unasked but obvious questions.

The younger Rixey glanced down at the drawing. "Oh, an abstract tat I have to start tomorrow."

Nick walked over to the table. "That's a monster."

"Guy already has ink, but I've never worked on him before. This is easily four or five hours' work. Might take two sittings. Speaking of which . . ." He flipped to another page in his pad. "This dude came in right before closing and asked for a design along these lines, about this size."

Curious, Becca stepped closer. Jeremy had black letters in a block font on the backs of each of his fingers, but she couldn't make out what they read.

Nick glanced to the page and frowned. "And?"

"This one's totally yours, man." He smiled up at his

brother, clearly undeterred by the volume with which *hell no* radiated off Nick's body and expression. Becca couldn't help but compare the two men. Though they shared the same dark hair and light green eyes, Jeremy was lean where Nick had bulk, and he had tattoos everywhere she could see, except for his face. And it wasn't just their appearances that differed. Jeremy seemed to have an inherent playfulness that was so different from Nick's hard-edged seriousness.

"I'm busy," Nick said.

Wait, Nick did tattoos?

Jeremy laughed. "You don't even know when I want you to do it."

Uh, apparently. Well, that was . . . unexpected.

Becca got about a hundred times more curious to see someone get a tattoo. His big hands creating art on skin. What would that be like? She imagined the skin was hers, and her stomach did this completely maddening flippy thing. "You're a tattoo artist?" The question was out of her mouth before she thought to voice it.

Both men looked at her. "Yes," Jeremy said at the same time Nick said, "Not really."

Jeremy winked. "Ignore him. He's good. When I can get him to do it. He's especially good at people and faces. Which is why this one's yours." He turned the paper so she could get a better look.

The image was only roughed out on the page. A dynamic drawing of a man: half firefighter, half soldier. The man's face was tilted down, showing off his headgear, with the fireman carrying an axe on his shoulder, and the soldier resting an automatic weapon on his. One man, two identities. Very cool. And Nick could do this? Becca could barely draw a stick figure.

"Get Ike to do it," Nick said, eyes still on the drawing, as if he was studying it.

"Ike's off until Monday. Guy wants it done this weekend. Besides, doing this would give you an even fifty-five."

Fifty-five what? she wondered, but she didn't want to interrupt their negotiations.

Nick glanced at her, like he was uncomfortable with all the focused attention. "When?"

"Told him I'd call him. Any time this weekend. You tell me."

He pursed his lips for a long moment. "Saturday, then. First thing in the morning or late evening."

Jeremy slapped his hand to the sketch. "Done." He leaned back in his chair and crossed his arms, clearly pleased with himself. "So, you kids hanging, or what?"

The innuendo in the question flooded heat into Becca's cheeks.

"Becca will be here for a few days. I'm going to put her in Katherine's room."

Who the heck was Katherine? Becca's level of discomfort ratcheted up another notch, creating an odd emptiness in the pit of her stomach. Or maybe that was just the fact she hadn't eaten since . . . hmm. The piece of coffee cake she'd nibbled on in the break room this morning?

"Okay, well, welcome to the Hard Ink Hotel," Jeremy said with a smile and a bowed flourish. "Stay as long as you like. I'll try not to walk around naked while you're here."

"Thanks, I think."

Nick smacked him on the back of the head, which only made Jeremy laugh and strike out with a punch that missed. "Come on," Nick said, guiding her toward the door. "Don't worry about him. He doesn't do that. Much."

"See ya later, Becca," Jeremy called, amusement coloring his voice.

"Bye," she said, scooping her pillow from the floor, unsure whether to laugh or cry.

"Apartment's this way." Nick started up the steps. "We

own the whole building, so you don't have to worry about anyone else coming or going."

She nodded, and her heart hitched up toward her throat as they reached the landing bracketed by two more non-descript industrial doors. Another electronic code got them into the one on the right.

Unlike the hallway, the apartment wasn't what she expected at all. With its dark kitchen cabinetry, distressed plank flooring, and chic-but-industrial fixtures, it could easily have been a warehouse loft in one of the upscale rehab developments along the expensive Fells Point waterfront. "This is really nice." A long, narrow island with a stove and a black granite breakfast bar was all that separated the open, airy kitchen from the spacious living room. Less surprising in the home of two men was the huge plasma TV that hung on the opposite wall in front of a giant brown leather couch and two well-worn, over-stuffed recliners. An overflowing bookshelf spanned the short wall before the back hallway.

Nick looked around the space, as if seeing it for the first time. "Yeah. Can't take any credit for it, though. All Jer's doing." He crossed the room and led her down a long hall-way, giving her the guided tour. "Jeremy's room is here. Bathroom here. Mine's back there. And this"—he turned a corner and flipped on a light—"will be yours. It's nicer than the guest room we have." He settled her bag on the wide-plank floor.

Becca leaned against the jamb, discomfort at invading another woman's space giving her pause. Although, as she glanced in, there was nothing particularly feminine or personal about the room. A queen bed with a sturdy oak headboard and a plain maroon comforter sat against the lone brick wall, and a long oak dresser with a mirror filled an adjacent space. The warm coffee color on the other three walls tied it all together. "Who's Katherine?"

He cut his gaze to her. "Our little sister. She's a lawyer in D.C., so she's rarely ever here, but when she comes, this is where she stays."

Sister. So, two brothers and a sister, just like her family. Well, just like it had once been.

Before their mom died, she, Charlie, and Scott had been tight—Batman, Robin, and Batgirl had been Charlie's favorite game for them. After their mom died, things started to change. Their aunt came to stay with them whenever their dad deployed, and age and disparate interests took them in different directions. But the thread of loss and grief kept the three of them tied together enough that they could slip into that old closeness when they wanted it or needed it. Man, what she wouldn't give for Scott to be here now. With their dad often away, he'd always been so protective of her and Charlie. He would know what to do, where to start. What if she couldn't figure this out by herself?

Nick shifted beside her, making her realize she'd just been hanging in the doorway. And that, just maybe, she wasn't as alone as she felt.

Becca stepped into the room and dropped her pillow onto the bed, and a growl roared out of her stomach so loud it nearly echoed among the exposed beams and duct-work of the tall ceiling. She clamped a hand to her belly and chanced a glance at Nick.

The corners of his lips tipped up. "Guess it would be redundant to ask if you're hungry."

She couldn't help but chuckle. "Yeah, I didn't realize how much."

"Well, that's a problem I can solve. Tell me you eat meat."

Nick was going to cook her dinner? Or, er, meat at least? Now she was curious. "Uh, what if I don't?"

His bottom lip almost pouted, and the expression was

as unexpected as it was cute on his masculine face. "Well, that would be a shame, because it would mean I can't cook you my specialty."

"You have a specialty?"

He crossed his arms. "Of course I have a specialty."

She just bet he did. A soldier who carried her bag, tried to open the car door for her, put her up in his house to protect her, and now offered to cook her dinner. This guy was ten kinds of dangerous. And in more ways than she'd expected when she'd come to him for help. "Well, then, I eat meat."

The left side of his mouth pulled up in a crooked smile, hinting at a dimple on his cheek.

A freaking dimple. A single spot of softness on a man otherwise built of hard planes and rough edges. Becca tried not to stare, she really did. But she found herself wanting to press her lips to the little indent. For starters.

"Good. Take whatever time you need to get settled in. There's towels and stuff in the bathroom next door. Come out to the kitchen when you're ready."

She shook the ludicrous urge away. "You really don't have to go to any trouble. We could just order a pizza. I already feel bad enough—"

He stepped in close, his heat and masculine scent, all leather and clean spice, invading her space. "It's no trouble, Becca."

Awareness raced from her head to her toes. For a split second, she couldn't breathe, and the urge to lean into him, to lay her head against that big chest, to fist her hands in his clothes, had her nearly swaying on her feet. Would his body feel as hard and strong as it looked? Would his arms hold her tight, or lay loosely at the small of her back, his fingers interlaced? A rush of heat threaded through her veins. She forced herself to take a step back. "Need help?"

His eyes narrowed the smallest bit as they ran over her face. Had he felt the same pull? "Nope. I got this."

She smiled, wondering what the heck he planned to make but satisfied to let it be a surprise. "Okey dokey."

"Yell if you need anything," he said, then stepped out the door and pulled it closed with a soft click.

For a moment, she stared at the back of the door. And then the day caught up with her and she sagged to the bed. Letting her back collapse onto the firm mattress, her eyes traced a random pattern over the exposed architectural elements above her.

But her mind stayed firmly on Nick Rixey. He was just . . . really freaking gorgeous. And he was making her dinner. And, tonight, he'd be sleeping down the hall.

Between the way he'd reacted to her plea for help the day before and his general history as a Special Forces soldier, Becca had no doubt: Nick Rixey was the walking personification of "complication."

And Charlie going missing was all the complication she could handle.

Charlie was out there somewhere in trouble. He was the only thing that mattered right now. Not how hot Nick was, or how he tempted her body with desires she hadn't felt in a really long time, or how safe she felt with him. She blew out a deep breath. Soon her eyelids grew heavy and her body melted into the soft comforter.

Get up, get up, get up, she told herself. Yes, that was totally what she should do. Get up, go out there, and see what the sexy soldier man was cooking her for dinner. The thought made her smile, although she was far too drowsy to know if her cheeks actually managed to move in response. So, right. She was totally going to get up. In just a minute, or ten . . .

Chapter 6

$\mathcal{N}$ick slid the large skillet off the hot burner, hoping a little food would ease the anxiety that had been rolling off Becca since she'd first settled into the passenger seat of his car. She'd been a champ at holding it together, but it didn't take a genius to see that the night's events hung around her neck like an anchor, threatening to pull her under the surface. And who could blame her?

When she'd asked who Katherine was, his brain had imagined his sister in Becca's situation. And the momentary mental exercise had both twisted his gut and lit up every protective instinct he possessed.

So, here he was cooking sloppy joes—his favorite meal, the one his mother had always made to cheer one of them up—for his dead CO's daughter.

What a cluster.

He set out everything they'd need to eat and poured a

couple of glasses of water. Then he made his way back down the hall and knocked softly at her door. No answer.

"Becca? No rush. Just wanted to let you know dinner's ready." Frowning at the silence on the other side, Rixey hesitated, then cracked open the door. "Hey, Becca?"

She was sound asleep at the bottom of the bed, her face turned to the side, her feet still on the floor. It was like she'd just fallen over from exhaustion. And, given the dark circles under her eyes, that probably wasn't far from the truth.

Standing at the threshold to the room, he debated whether to just bug out or wake her. Her body had clearly been craving some sustenance, but maybe she needed sleep more. His indecision annoyed him, so finally he pushed into the room and crossed to the side of the bed. "Becca? Hey, Becca, wake up." No response. Out cold.

He eased the covers back from the top of the bed so he could slip her between them. Crouching by her legs, he removed her sneakers, then he leaned in over her.

God, she was pretty, with her soft, pale skin and her full, pink lips. The yellow shirt nearly matched her long hair, still pulled back in a ponytail. She just had a light about her he found so appealing. Because, these days, he didn't have much light in his own life. Everything was dark and heavy, saddling him with the bone-crushing weight of guilt and regret and wants never to be fulfilled. But Becca was just . . . sunshine, warm and life-giving.

His gut clenched. What if she'd gone upstairs when she'd gotten home earlier? What if the guy rooting through her office had been armed? What if Rixey hadn't arrived when he had?

He couldn't know the answers, of course, but he knew enough to know he didn't like any of the likelies.

He slid his arms under her shoulders and knees and lifted her up. Her warmth soaked into his skin, making him crave more of it, especially when she turned her face into his chest. God, when was the last time a woman had touched him?

"Charlie," she whispered.

A sharp wave of jealousy speared through him for a split second, until his brain's cognitive function pushed through the possessive urges and reminded him that Charlie was her brother's name. Jesus. Where the hell had *that* come from? What right did he have feeling jealous over her?

Refusing to examine those questions too closely, he laid her against the cool sheet and pulled the covers over her. She stirred, mumbling a little and pushing her bottom lip into a pout, and then she stilled again.

His body tight with all kinds of desires he'd no business having, Rixey turned on his heel, killed the lights, and closed the door behind him.

Back in the kitchen, he braced his hands against the counter and stared at the paper plates, napkins, and drinks he'd laid out on the breakfast bar. Probably better dinner hadn't happened, after all. She didn't have much insight into who might've broken into her place, and he had some things to look into before deciding how best to approach her brother's alleged disappearance. What the hell else did that leave them to talk about?

So, did you know your father's lies and betrayal led to the deaths of six of my friends, impugned my honor, and ended my military career? Can you pass me another bun?

Yeah, not happening. Ever. First, why would she believe him over the official Army line? Especially when the powers that be had gone out of their way to make sure no one would believe anything he or the others had to say about what had happened. Second, the Army had made his and his team's freedom contingent on the signing of a nondisclosure agreement, so he couldn't let that news pass between his lips even if he wanted to. Which he didn't. Frank Merritt deserved everything he got. But no kid deserved to find out that their father was anything but the decorated military hero the Army made him out to be. Rixey was a lot of things, but spiteful SOB wasn't one of them. Still, it chafed his hide to do anything that benefited the man responsible for pulling his life out from under him.

A door clicked open down the back hall, and Rixey's muscles tensed. Socked feet scuffed against the wood floors. "I'm so sorry," she said. "How long was I asleep?"

Rixey turned and found her standing at the edge of the kitchen, sleep still clinging to her features and making her look young, innocent. "Not long. Don't worry about it," he said, hoping his suddenly dark mood didn't bleed into his words.

She hugged herself and met his gaze. "You put me in bed."

He had no response that wouldn't leave him feeling exposed, so he shrugged. A trickle of embarrassment mixed inside him with the flash fire of anger set off by thoughts of her father. "So, you wanna eat or what?"

She frowned and looked away, her arms squeezing tighter across her chest. She took half a step back the way she'd come.

Damnit. She's not her father, asshole. "Wait. I'm sorry. I'm a moody bastard sometimes. Come sit down."

Becca hesitated for a moment, then slowly approached a stool at the breakfast bar. She eased herself onto it, and her gaze flicked to the stove. The hint of a smile played around her lips. "You made sloppy joes."

He crossed his arms and nodded, discomfort crawling down his spine. Why the hell did this woman tie him up in knots like this? And exactly why had he cooked for her?

"Sloppy joes are your specialty?" She glanced up at

him, her expression two seconds away from breaking into a grin.

He didn't know what to say that wouldn't sound defensive or insecure. Fucking sloppy joes. He clawed a hand through his hair. "It's not filet mignon, I know—"

"It's perfect. Sloppy joes are on my top five comfort foods list, *ever*."

Nick eased onto a stool at the bar, her words quieting some of the bullshit in his head. "Yeah?"

"Yes, they're awesome. So, thank you."

Side by side, they made their sandwiches—him two, her one—and then she took a bite.

Her eyes flew wide. "Mmm. This is so good. This isn't just Manwich sauce, is it?"

Manwich? "Hell, no. How would it be my specialty if all I'd done was open a can?"

Her laughter was full and deep, easing the tension in his shoulders. She returned her sandwich to her plate as her humor turned into an outright belly laugh and she covered her mouth with her napkin. "Sorry," she finally said. "Didn't mean to insult the chef."

Warm satisfaction flowed through him at her obvious enjoyment of what he'd made. No need for her to know it was one of about four things he could cook. "Manwich." He shook his head and took a bite.

"Oh, come on. Manwich is good. *I* make Manwiches."

"Now you're just being difficult."

She laughed again, just like he'd hoped she would, and, oddly, he felt it right in the middle of his chest. Now this, *this* was what he'd been hoping to do for her when he'd offered to make her dinner in the first place. Put her at ease. Take her mind off her problems. If he could just keep a lid on his inner asshole, though knowing who her father was taunted that motherfucker like nobody's business.

Taking another bite, he glanced her way. And found her sideways gaze focused on his arm, where a band of ink circled his bicep. Six soldiers in black silhouette connected by the dark ground on which they walked. One soldier for each of the men—each of the *brothers*—he'd lost in what had been an ambush meant to kill the whole team of twelve. Hindsight was always fucking twenty-twenty. Now when he replayed that day in his head, the setup was so damn obvious that he never failed to wake up in a cold sweat, yelling at his dream self not to go forward. But that ship had sailed and crashed on the rocks of misguided trust. Later, he'd gotten the tat. A small way to commemorate those who had gone before him, who had died while he'd lived. His gut rolled.

Those baby blues lifted to look at his face, a furrow marring her brow, then cut away again. "So, um, do you have any idea why Charlie might've thought I should come to you for help?" She sat the uneaten half of her sandwich down and shifted in the seat toward him.

"No. I was going to ask you the same thing."

She sighed. "He told me almost nothing, which is my own fault."

The sadness in her eyes filled him with the urge to make this all better. No way it was that simple, though. "Why don't you tell me everything from the beginning."

"Well, I mentioned that Charlie is a computer security consultant. He got into that by being a hacker. A really good one, apparently. He mostly stays on the right side of the law these days, but because he's played on the wrong side and has seen things people aren't generally supposed to see, he's prone to conspiracy theories."

"Probably part of the job description."

She twisted her napkin and nodded. "Probably. Lately, we'd only been communicating through this online chat program he created. He wouldn't talk on the phone, and he hadn't been staying at his house. Last week, we had a fight because he started in on my father, how he wasn't the man I thought he was, that he'd found something that proved it. This wasn't new ground for Charlie. He and Dad didn't get along, and—"

"Why? If you don't mind my asking." All of this made Rixey's instincts prickle with awareness. What the hell did Charlie find? Given the trouble the Army had gone to prettying up Merritt's story, Nick was surprised to think they'd missed a loose end somewhere. Was it possible that trouble had followed the colonel's casket home from Afghanistan?

Becca cut her glance to him, her expression wary. "Charlie's gay. Dad didn't react well when Charlie came out, and he never made it right before he died."

Rixey frowned. *Sonofabitch.* The news soured his stomach and stripped away another part of the heroic veneer her father had worn. Given Jeremy's inclination to play both sides of the field, Rixey had no tolerance for homophobic bullshit. That Rixey knew of, Jer had never been serious about a man, but that was his business and no one else's.

"Some of the things they said to each other . . ." She blew out a breath and shook her head. "It wasn't unusual for Charlie to go off on a rant. Last week when it happened, I cut him off and told him it was time to move on. Dad was dead and nothing good could come from continuing to dwell on the past." She dropped her gaze to the counter, and Rixey studied her as his brain chewed on her story. "He disconnected the chat, and I couldn't get in touch with him after that. Day before I came to see you, I found he'd posted the message I showed you about finding you at Hard Ink."

Damn, there was a lot to process in all that. Not the least of which was the fact that the last time Becca spoke to her brother, or chatted, whatever, they'd fought. And now he was missing. Why and how had Charlie connected whatever he'd supposedly found out about Frank Merritt to Nick, to a member of "the Colonel's team"? Why would Charlie have thought Rixey relevant for helping them? And how did any of it relate to the guy's disappearance?

"God, it's really not much to go on, is it?" The pleading he recalled from the day before returned to her gaze and sliced into him all over again.

"It's a start. We'll figure something out. I have a friend who's a private investigator that I'll talk to first thing in the morning. Okay?" The little furrow between her brows eased and she nodded. He finished his first sandwich and wiped his mouth. No way he could fix this tonight, but maybe he could take her mind off the situation. "So, what else is on that top five list?" he asked, latching onto her earlier comment.

She nibbled at a piece of her bun. "What do you mean?"

"Of comfort foods."

"Oh. Let's see." She picked up her sandwich again. "Sloppy joes, of course. And, hmm, lasagna, chicken pot pie. Uh, macaroni and cheese. And maybe pot roast. Or meat loaf and mashed potatoes. Aw, or red beans and rice."

"That's seven," he said, enjoying her enthusiasm, not to mention the way talking to her pulled him out of the darkness of his own head. "And no chili and corn bread is a huge oversight."

"Hmm . . . chili's a good one. As you can see, I'm not picky." And he damn well liked that. She finished the rest of her sandwich and reached for another bun, then stretched to scoop more sloppy joe from the pan. After she got it all fixed the way she wanted it, she lifted it to her mouth and glanced at him. "What?"

Rixey shook his head and hoped the distraction had worked. Even if only a little. "Nothing. Eat up."

They'd just finished their seconds and carried their dirties to the sink when Jeremy walked in. "Dude. You made sloppy joes and didn't tell me? You better've saved me some." He stepped up to the stove and peered into the pan. "Aw, yeah."

Becca chuckled.

Jeremy's gaze cut to her and froze, then he looked at Rixey. Shit, Nick recognized that glint in his brother's eyes. Jer was about to be a pain in the ass. Since Nick had returned to the real world, he hadn't once brought a woman here, let alone cooked for her. No doubt his dipshit brother was reading all kinds of significance into that.

"So, Becca, did *you* enjoy the sloppy joes Nick made for you?"

"Yeah," she said, leaning against the counter. "They were great." She didn't seem to hear the innuendo dripping from the guy's words.

But Rixey did. And he knew his smart-ass brother enough to know he was like a dog with a bone. Wouldn't stop until they were squirming. Which would undo the relaxed rapport he'd finally managed to achieve with Becca. "Jeremy," he said, lacing the syllables with a warning his brother sure as hell would recognize.

Grinning, Jeremy started in. "Wow, that was really nice of Nick to—"

Rixey swiped the pan out from under Jeremy's nose and crossed to the trash can. His foot depressed the pedal and the metal lid flipped up.

"Hey!" Jeremy whirled, following Nick's quick movements.

Nick tilted the skillet at a forty-five-degree angle and paused, ready to scoop the leftovers into the trash. "You were saying?"

Jeremy gasped and threw his hands out. "What the hell are you doing, man? You can't . . . that's sloppy joe!" Mouth agape, eyes wide, his expression was almost comical.

Becca glanced between them, a confused smile on her face.

Nick winked at her, then arched a brow at Jeremy. Boy damn well knew what this was for.

Jer rolled his eyes. "All right, all right. Just"—he gestured to the stove—"step away from the trash. Slowly."

Settling the pan back on the burner, Nick glared, then finally let go of the handle. Jeremy pulled it close and shielded it with his body like it was his firstborn child. Rixey snickered.

"If I hadn't known you two were brothers before this moment, I would know now." Becca grinned.

Building his sandwich, Jeremy glared out from under his long hair. "Why? Because he's such an asshole?"

She laughed, but then her smile turned sad. "No, because just then you reminded me of my brothers."

"You have more than one?" Rixey asked, not remembering Frank ever mentioning a third kid. Rixey had known her father for five years, though Frank had never been the most verbose when it came to his personal life. Wasn't unusual. A lot of guys compartmentalized their real-world lives while they were in the field. Thinking about everything and everyone you were missing back home was exactly the kind of distraction that got you injured or killed.

"I did. My older brother, Scott, died eight years ago this summer. He was twenty-one. Heroin overdose." She blinked up at him. "Anyway, Scott and Charlie were in a perpetual competition to annoy one another. I just tried to keep out of the way." She lifted one shoulder in a small shrug, a faraway look in her eyes.

"I'm sorry to hear that, Becca." Damn if the sadness in her voice didn't cut right into him.

"Thanks," she said.

Jeremy slid around to the bar and pushed onto a stool. He bit into his sloppy joe with a loud moan. When Becca chuckled, Rixey found himself glad his brother was there. Losing his parents had been horrific enough. He sure as hell couldn't imagine losing his kid brother.

Pain in the ass or not, Jeremy was a good guy through and through. Would do anything for a person, and often did. Which meant Nick had been remiss in not explaining Becca's presence. "So, Jer, I should've mentioned it earlier, but Becca's here because someone broke into her house today."

Jeremy's gaze cut to hers, his eyes scanning over her face and landing on the scratch. He frowned. "Shit, seriously? I'm sorry. That sucks. Does this have something to do with your brother?"

Becca sank onto the stool next to him, as if Jeremy's outrage on her behalf put her at ease. And it probably did. Jer had that way about him. "I don't know. But we're going to find out." Her blue eyes cut to Nick, filled with equal parts determination and question.

Rixey nodded. He'd do everything he could to keep the darkness from closing in over her.

Her expression brightened, and some of the stress seemed to bleed out of her shoulders. She cast a sideways glance at Jeremy. "Can I have a bite?" He jerked his sandwich to the side, away from her, and she gave a soft laugh. "Just kidding."

He mock-scowled at her, then smiled when she bumped her shoulder into his.

"So, you like sloppy joes, bacon, and walking around naked. What else do I need to know about you?" Becca asked.

Jeremy frowned. "Bacon?"

She pointed. "Your shirt."

He looked down at himself and chuckled. "Oooh. Right." Damn boy and his funny-ass T-shirts. This one read, "This Guy Loves BACON" with two hands pointing their thumbs back at himself. After that, they fell into an easy conversation.

As Rixey watched the two of them together, resolve threaded through his very bones. Becca had lost one brother to tragedy. No one should have to go through that once, let alone twice—even if she was related to the man who'd ruined so much for him. But she wasn't responsible for the sins of her old man. So he was going to do everything he could to make sure it didn't happen again.

Chapter 7

$\mathcal{B}$ecca couldn't sleep. Despite being more exhausted than she'd maybe ever been in her life, she'd tossed and turned for hours. She couldn't get her mind to stop racing from one question to the next. *Where is Charlie? Is he okay? Could he have run, or was he taken? Who ransacked his apartment? Who broke into my house? How are we going to figure all this out?*

We. As in, her and Nick.

God, the man kept her on edge. One minute polite and helpful, the next cold and moody. As if her head wasn't spinning enough from the mystery of Charlie's disappearance.

Sighing, she turned on her side. She'd wanted Nick's help—no, more than that, she needed it. Still, she couldn't help but feel like she was getting in way over her head.

The image of the soldiers inked on his right bicep

came into her mind's eye, their silhouettes dark and still. Six soldiers. Why six? *Seven* men on her father's team had been killed in that enemy ambush. Maybe it wasn't the memorial she'd first thought? Or maybe it was just symbolic of those who'd gone before him? The thought touched her heart. That day, she'd lost her father, but Nick had lost a whole family of people who no doubt meant the world to him. In that moment, sitting at the bar eating the meal he'd made for them, she'd realized they were connected in the grief born from the events of that day, and it had made her feel they weren't strangers after all.

Except, really, what did she know about Nick? Ex-Special Forces. Had been with her father when he died—which made her eyes sting if she thought on it too much. Lived with his brother. Did occasional tattoos. Made kick-ass sloppy joes. Had a dimple on his left cheek and at least one tattoo. Helped her when he didn't have to.

Actually, she supposed she knew more than a little.

And, geez, she'd come at him with a butcher knife.

He'd disarmed her in a flash of movement and muscle. In her terror, she hadn't fully registered that moment, but her mind went back to it now. Replayed it. Resurrected the feel of his tense, hard body trapping hers against the counter, his masculine heat and the soft caress of his breath washing over her.

And now that hard body lay sleeping just down the hall.

A flush ran over her skin, and Becca tossed back the covers.

Sitting up, she reached for the lamp and squinted against the light when she turned it on. Lying there was no use. Her brain felt like that of a kid who'd consumed too much sugar, bouncing from one thing to the next, and her body was wired to the point of being jittery. There wasn't much she could be doing for Charlie in the middle of the night, but that didn't stop the urge from flooding through her.

Out of bed, she slipped on some sleep shorts under her old tee and stepped to the door. It opened with a click that revealed nothing but quiet darkness on the other side.

Keeping one hand on the wall to guide herself, she made her way to the big open kitchen and living room. At a panel of switches she'd noticed earlier, she tried each one until she turned on the cool, industrial fixture over the breakfast bar. It threw a wedge of gold on each side, casting illumination over both the kitchen and the closest edge of the living room.

She opened the fridge and surveyed the shelves and drawers. After all, the last thing Nick had said to her before they'd gone their separate ways at bedtime was "Make yourself at home. What's mine is yours." Which had left her mind churning on exactly what the full practical application of that principle might include . . . But, at the very least, she assumed it included midnight raids on his fridge. One of her worst and most favorite habits.

But the contents primarily fell into one of four categories: beer, other drinks, restaurant takeout and general leftovers, and meat.

Wrinkling her nose, she closed the lower door and opened the upper one. Icy air blasted out as her gaze landed on a two-deep stack of ice cream tubs, the double chocolate fudge brownie catching her eye in particular. "That's more like it."

She pushed the door shut and turned to the counter. And screamed.

Nick was standing like a silent phantom at the edge of the dim light. The half-gallon container flipped out of her hands and did a triple somersault in the air before she dove for it at the same time Nick did.

They crashed and she shrieked, her hands flush against a mountain of bare, hard flesh, and the tub of ice cream fell at their feet. His arms came around her, his greater weight nearly knocking her over and making them stumble until he'd all but pinned her against the counter.

Time froze for an instant, then Becca burst out laughing, the ridiculousness of the past ten seconds growing in hilarity the more she thought about what had just happened. She covered her mouth with one hand as her head fell back and her laughter devolved into a series of choked chortles she couldn't control. She gasped for breath, her forehead falling against Nick's chest.

His chest. Holy crap, the man was half naked and she was touching him. Her hand. Her face. Her stomach against his. The details of their position finally registered in her sleep-deprived brain.

He was all over her.

She lifted her gaze over the hard planes of his chest, getting snagged for a long moment on the swirling tribal pattern of black ink that ran over the bulge of his shoulder and down his arm. Finally she met the light green of his eyes. Nick stared down at her, one eyebrow arched, one corner of his mouth lifting enough to bring his dimple out to play.

"Hi," she whispered, the release of the laughing fit making her shoulders lighter, less tense.

"Hi," he said. He didn't move away or drop his arms from caging her against the counter.

Heat bloomed over her skin. Becca released a shaky breath, one that emphasized just how close they were. Her hands, lying flat on the pads of his pecs, itched to move and explore. And her tongue volunteered to follow close behind.

What was it about this guy that made her brain shut off and her body turn on? *Way* on. Her nipples went tight, liquid heat gathered low in her belly, and her hips were a breath away from grinding against his. Wanting this man—and acting on that desire in any way—was a really bad idea. All her energy needed to be focused on finding Charlie. But when she was around Nick, need vibrated through her veins and lust became a living thing inside her. And, oh, how she wanted to let herself go.

As if he'd picked up on the shift in her mood, Nick's gaze went molten and he leaned in, just the smallest bit, his line of sight zeroing in on her lips. *Oh, God, he's going to kiss me.* She swallowed hard, her mouth going dry.

"Hey, is everything okay—oh. Oh, shit. Sorry. Carry on." Jeremy's voice retreated as quickly as it had appeared. Down the hall, his door clicked shut.

Nick wrenched back, leaving Becca frozen and breathless and hungry against the granite. As much as part of her absolutely loathed the distance between them, his position several feet away allowed her to soak in the whole of him. The broad, muscled shoulders, the cut definition of his chest and abdomen, the way his unbuttoned jeans hung on his lean hips. Unbuttoned. Like he'd just pulled them on. And, with how low they sat, no way he was wearing anything underneath. Even his bare feet, sticking out beneath the ragged hem of the denim, were sexy.

"Becca, what are you doing?"

Busted. Her gaze whipped up to his. The heat absolutely blazing in his eyes did nothing to help pull herself together. She bent down and retrieved the fumbled ice cream. What she really needed was a cold shower. With a handheld showerhead. And really good water pressure. The thought was so not helpful.

"Midnight snack," she said as she placed the tub on the counter's edge, hoping he believed the rasp in her voice was left over from sleep. "Want some?"

He remained silent until she looked at him. "Maybe I do."

The words hung in the air between them, seeming to answer a question she hadn't asked. Or maybe she had. If they were playing chicken, she definitely lost, because she was the first one to turn away.

A moment later, he stepped to the counter, then leaned onto his elbows next to her. The position bunched his biceps, pulling her attention to another piece of ink he wore there. Toward his shoulder, above the band of fallen soldiers, a silver knife lay atop a pair of crossed arrows. The inner part of the Special Forces crest, readily familiar to her from her father's service—except this was different. A black circle surrounded the weapons like a shroud.

"Trouble sleeping?" he finally said.

She dragged her finger through a bit of condensation on the ice cream's lid. "Yeah. I'm wired. Too much nervous energy. Didn't mean to wake you, though."

He shook his head. "Wasn't asleep."

"Oh." She wondered why, but since he hadn't offered, she didn't want to push. She blew out a long breath, trying to get her body to settle down. His proximity wasn't helping. Heat poured off his arm into hers.

"I might have a better way to blow off some steam."

Her heart tripped in her chest. His expression was serious, challenging. "Better than chocolate ice cream?"

"Yep. You game?"

She pushed the container of ice cream away. "Depends on exactly what it is you're proposing." Her mind reeled with the possibilities. Anticipation spread a shiver over her skin.

The smile he unleashed was a complete killer, part smirk, part smolder. Twin urges coursed through her—to smack it off him or kiss it off him. Just then, both urges ran neck and neck.

Rixey grabbed the double chocolate fudge brownie and chucked it in the freezer. "I'll show you." He made for the front door.

Becca frowned. "Uh, where are you going?"

"Come find out."

Gesturing to herself, she stepped around the counter. "I'm not exactly dressed for a middle-of-the-night stroll."

His gaze dragged over her, and she felt it like a physical caress. "You're fine. Except, um—" He cleared his throat. "You might want to put on a bra."

Put on a bra? Hands on her hips, she watched him attempt to keep a straight face, then she turned on her heel. "Not what I expected you to say."

"What's that?" he called.

"Nothing," she muttered. *Put on a bra. Hmph.* Apparently their ideas about good ways to blow off steam differed. Clearly, she was way more affected by him than he was by her. And just as well. In her room, she slipped a bra on under her sleep shirt. Shouldn't even be thinking of anything else while Charlie was missing. No matter that Nick made her feel more like a woman than any other man ever had. *Selfish much, Bec?* Guilt settled over her like a lead blanket.

From the moment she returned to the hall, Nick's gaze was on her. Leaning against the front door, he watched her walk the straight line to him. And, damn, even though she was trying like hell to ignore it, he was sex on a freaking stick, his folded arms emphasizing the inked and stacked muscles of his biceps and shoulders, and leaving bare the trail of dark hair that disappeared into his now-buttoned jeans.

"All right, lay it on me. What kind of big surprise requires a bra at two o'clock in the morning?"

"This way," he said, holding the door for her. He followed her out and gestured to the door opposite their apartment, where he entered a code into another electrical panel.

"What's with all the keypads?" she asked.

"Secure. Easily changeable. Not easily picked." A

metallic *click* sounded and he stepped inside, into the yawning darkness. He reached to the wall, flipped some switches, and light illuminated a mostly unfinished, cavernous space. One they used as a gym, judging by the machines, free weights, and other equipment within.

But Becca couldn't focus on the details of the huge space. Because all she could see was the magnificent expanse of Nick's bare back.

Running almost the whole length of his spine, a dragon wrapped itself around a deadly black sword, hilt just below his neck, point at his lower back, ending near a mass of scars that traveled outward toward his hip and disappeared below the waistband of his jeans. The dragon's wings spanned his shoulder blades, and the movement of his muscles made it appear alive, actually struggling to hold its perch on the steel. The red of the beast's eyes looked out from the image, holding her gaze.

Surrounding his left shoulder, the tribal tattoo looped and jagged in a lighter shade of black than the dragon. A reach for something off a shelf revealed lines of writing on his rib cage beneath his right arm, but Becca couldn't make out what they said.

Tattoos had never looked better than they did on this man. She was absofreakinglutely sure of it.

"Put these on."

A pair of fat white boxing gloves fell into her hands. "We're gonna box?"

He smirked. "Figured you'd enjoy taking a swing at me."

Her mouth dropped open. "What? I don't want to—"

"Relax." He grabbed a smaller pair of black gloves for himself and slid one on. They left the tips of his fingers exposed. With a smirk, he pointed. "We'll use the heavy bag."

Becca's gaze cut across the room, where an oblong

vinyl bag hung suspended from a beam. "Oh." Actually, beating the crap out of something *did* sound like a good way to work off some nervous energy. "Cool."

"Here. Let me help you with those." He tucked one of her white gloves under his arm and held up the other. The padding that encased her hand was cool and stiff, and the Velcro band that secured it was tight around her wrist.

"These fit perfectly."

They repeated the process with her other glove. "They're Katherine's. Figured they'd work for you."

"Katherine boxes?"

Tugging his other glove on, he nodded. "Yeah. My sister is tiny, like five foot two. Before she left for college, I made sure she knew how to take care of herself. Now she's hell on wheels."

Becca smiled at the image of this apparently petite yet kick-ass woman, but also at the obvious affection in Nick's voice. "You were a totally crazy overprotective big brother, weren't you?"

"No more than necessary."

She knocked her gloves together. "Ha. According to you or her?" His scowl made her laugh. "Uh-huh. That's what I thought. I think I'd like to meet your sister."

He crossed to the heavy bag. "I'm sure that would be tons of fun for me. You ever hit a bag like this before?"

Becca stopped a few feet away. "Er, no. You don't just hit it?"

"Not if you don't want to hurt yourself. Hit it wrong and you could sprain or break your wrist. Watch, and then I'll walk you through it." Nick stepped about an arm's length away, his body at an angle to the black vinyl, right foot, hip, and shoulder back. He brought his arms up, elbows in tight and gloved fists in front of his chest. As he explained, he demonstrated in slow motion a few times, twisting his body into the fake punch. "Your goal is to make solid contact with the bag, not to push it or make it bounce. Like this."

He unleashed a series of right punches, the muscles rippling under his skin. His movements were precise and efficient.

With a gloved hand, he stilled the bag and turned to her. "Now I'll show you how to do a one-two punch, and then you're up."

"Okay," she said, half of her eager to try, because smashing something right now would probably feel great, half of her perfectly content to grab a tub of popcorn and a drink and watch him as long as he wanted to do it.

He got back into position and demonstrated again. Using his full power, Nick attacked the bag. *Smack-smack, smack-smack, smack-smack.* Light on his bare feet, the dragon absolutely alive underneath his powerful movements, he hammered his punches into the firm surface for a full minute.

Becca picked her jaw up off the floor before he saw. But . . . just . . . wow. He was beautiful to watch, all controlled strength and purposeful movement.

He stilled the bag. "Your turn."

She swallowed hard. No way she was going to look like *that,* but the idea of being able to direct her strength that way had her stepping up without reservation.

He moved behind her, and heat radiated off him. "Hold your arm out so you know how far away to stand. Good. Right foot back, hip and shoulder angled away." Becca followed his instructions. "Okay, arms up." His big hands fell on her shoulders and gently squeezed. A tingle of nerves and heat shot through her. "Relax your muscles. Only thing you want to keep tense is your wrist. No floppy wrists."

"Okay. Floppy wrists bad. Got it." She let her shoulders go loose under his grip.

"Good. Now, start out in slow motion so you can get the feel for the movements." She twisted her body, bringing her arm out straight against the bag. He stepped in close to her extended arm. "If you weren't wearing the glove, what part of your hand would be touching the bag right now?"

Becca concentrated on her position. "The middle knuckles of my fingers."

He adjusted the angle downward. "You want to hit with the knuckles closest to your hand. Try again. Slow." Becca did it a half dozen more times under his intense observation. "Good. That looks good."

Despite the chilly air, warmth rolled over her skin. Since she really hadn't exerted herself yet, it was hard to deny that he was the cause, his bare muscles and patient, encouraging words. "I want to hit it for real now."

He stepped back. "Go for it. Just take your time."

Staring at the bag, Becca released a deep breath. Her right fist shot out, made contact, and retracted. A wave of giddiness flashed through her. Position, breathe, punch. She did it three more times, then grinned at Nick.

Liquid heat filled his gaze. He nodded. "Good. Again." Was she just imagining it, or did his voice sound deeper?

Her heart pounded in her chest. She threw four more punches, lifting a light sheen of sweat from her skin. "I don't feel like I'm hitting it very hard, though."

Nick moved to her right side. "Do it in slow-mo again. Just a right punch."

She did.

His hand fell on her hip, stirring up a nest of butterflies in her stomach. "When you punch, make sure you're involving your hip. The power is coming from your back foot. Let it move your body with the punch. Slow-mo again." He pushed her hip further into the movement. "Now, do it."

Concentrating, Becca threw a punch. She threw her gloved hands into the air. "That was harder."

Nick nodded. "Again."

Becca pounded the bag in slow repetitions. She'd have to figure out how to add this to her regular exercise routine, which mostly consisted of running a few miles around the park by her house. Because, damn, it felt good. The movements required her concentration, shutting out all the crap that had been bombarding her brain.

"I think you're ready for more," he said after a while. "Try the one-two." For a moment, she shook out her arms, then got back into position. "Only small steps with your feet, and twist your body into the bag. Try it slow first."

Demonstrating the one-two, she liked the way the fluid action made her body feel, especially when Nick stepped behind her and placed his hands on her hips, encouraging her to turn more into the punches. She shuddered, her mind conjuring all kinds of really distracting images. Him, gripping her hips from behind while he—

"Okay, give it a go."

She blew out a breath. Heaving her mind out of the gutter, she directed the pressure cooker of her lust and anxiety at the vinyl and struck out. Left-right. Left-right. Left-right. "Feels . . . freaking . . . awesome," she gritted in between punches. And it really did. She pictured Charlie's apartment, thought of someone breaking into her house, recalled the precise moment she'd learned that her mom had died of an aneurysm when she'd been thirteen. And Scott of a totally mind-boggling overdose. And her father of an enemy attack. *Smack-smack, smack-smack, smack-smack.* Her fists pounded harder.

Sweat dripped down her face and her mind raced. *Where the hell is Charlie? God, if somebody took him, hurt him . . .* She punched faster. *What else can I do? There's got to be something. Why didn't I listen to him? What if I never see him again?* A moan echoed from somewhere, but all she wanted to think about was the amazing release pummeling the heavy bag brought.

"Becca. Becca, stop." Hard arms banded around her upper body and hauled her back. "Becca, it's all right."

Without the exertion to distract herself, she came slamming back into her body. It wasn't sweat alone that covered her face but tears as well. A sob worked up her throat. Nick turned her into his body, cradling her head against his chest as best he could with the thick gloves. "Sshh, it's okay. I've got you."

She shook her head and gulped down the jagged ball of emotion, afraid that if she started letting go, she might never stop. "I'm okay. I'm all right," she rasped against his hard chest.

"I know," he murmured against her hair.

Becca's breathing hitched, and she sucked Nick's masculine scent—all clean sweat and spicy soap and leather—down deep. After that, the rest of her senses came online in sequence. The feel of his hard chest against her cheek, warm and pulsing with life. The heady sight of his inked shoulder, bringing his arms around to hold her. The sound of his heart, picking up steam beneath her ear. That only left taste . . .

Out of nowhere, her emotions lurched in a new direction. Her tears dried up, but just the thought of acting on the urge to press her lips, her tongue to his skin had her body growing damp elsewhere. God, as wrong as it probably was, she had no doubt she could lose herself in him, that being with him would take away all the crap filling her head and weighing on her chest. Even if only for a little while.

Heart slamming against her breastbone, panting breaths

falling against his pecs, she looked out over the edge of the responsible thing she *should* do and leapt. "I want to kiss you," she whispered, the room spinning around her at the admission. If he hadn't been holding her, she was sure she would've fallen.

On the outside, he didn't seem to react, but their position gave him away. His chest rose and fell more quickly, his heartbeat thundered. The pressure of his growing cock nudged her belly.

The thrill of arousing him made her bold.

She pressed her lips to his chest, once, twice. On the third kiss, she let her tongue drag against his skin, drawing the salt of his sweat into her mouth. His taste—the very fact that this was happening—blew her mind, especially as his thick erection grew harder against her. Her hands yearned to clutch him, to feel every ridge and cut of muscle, but the gloves made it impossible.

"Becca," he growled. A warning.

The need to have him inundated her. She couldn't deny it. Didn't want to. Her mouth came down on his nipple.

The groan that ripped out of his throat shot right between her legs and filled her with an empty ache that begged for relief.

Hands tight on her upper arms, he shoved them apart but didn't let go. Mouth open, breathing hard, muscles rigid everywhere, he glared down at her with a lethal look that did absolutely nothing to deter her lust.

He ripped off his gloves and threw them to the floor, blazing eyes never leaving hers. And then he was on her.

Hands in her hair, he tilted her head back and devoured her in a kiss. Hot. Hard. Commanding. Her lips fell open on a gasping moan and his tongue slipped between, stroking against her own. He tasted of mint and man and sinful promise, and Becca couldn't get enough.

The room spinning around her, she grasped at his

shoulders—and groaned at the gloves. "Off, off," she rasped around the edges of the kiss.

Nick pulled back, his face a dark mask of desire. He removed her gloves in about two seconds and tugged her into his chest, holding her tighter than before, kissing her more deeply.

Becca's hands were immediately in heaven, caressing and grasping at the bunched muscles of his chest, his shoulders, his back. He was hard everywhere, and the strong, aroused feel of him curled heat low in her stomach.

One hand holding her head, his other hand slid down her body and cupped her breast. She moaned as he massaged her through the layers of her clothing, his thumb stroking over and over against the hard nub of her nipple. Her hands found his hair, soft and thick, and grasped and tugged at it as he tormented her with his mouth and fingers.

His hips rocked against her belly, and Becca gasped and shifted against him. Groaning, he dropped the hand from her hair to her ass and urged them more tightly together. Wetness created a maddening need for friction between her legs. God, this was crazy, but she wanted him like she'd never wanted another man. She dragged her fingertips over his chest, slipped her hand between their bodies, and grasped his cock through the denim. Oh, he was a delicious handful. She couldn't wait—

"Stop." He pulled back and grasped her wrists.

"Why?" she asked, missing his heat against her.

Chest heaving, he rolled his tongue over his bottom lip, like he was tasting her there. "Because you're upset and vulnerable. And I shouldn't take advantage. I won't."

"It's hardly taking advantage if I want it." And she did. She just wanted to lose herself in his body, his intensity, his strength, for a long while.

His fingers dug into her wrists, just shy of painful. "It's not a good idea."

Her gaze dropped to the bulge filling out the left front of his jeans. Jesus, if he straightened himself out, she had a sneaking suspicion the rise of the denim might not cover the whole of him. Her mouth watered. "Looks like a pretty good idea to me."

"Damnit, woman." The percussive blast of his curse drew her gaze back to his face. "I'm trying to do the right thing here."

"Why? If I don't want you to—"

"Because I want to make you hold onto that bag while I bury myself in you so hard and so deep you don't know your own name. But then tomorrow, in the light of day, when your brother's still missing and we're still trying to figure out the mystery of who broke into your house, getting fucked by a stranger in a warehouse will be just one more thing you have to deal with. And I won't do that to you."

The words absolutely stole her breath. She tugged out of his grip. His words dragged Charlie back to the center of her thoughts, where he should've been all along. Guilt sloshed over her arousal and pricked at the backs of her eyes.

"Fine." She scooped her gloves off the floor and crossed the room to return them to their shelf, then made for the door. "What's the code to your apartment?"

"Becca," he called, a note of regret in his voice.

She lifted her gaze to him, and his face was all shadows and hard angles. Harsh, but beautiful. "No, I should thank you. You're right. The code?"

He braced his hands on his lean hips. "Zero-five-zero-one-two. But Becca—"

"I enjoyed the boxing, Nick. You're a good teacher." She pulled open the door and decided to just leave it all out on the floor. With everything he was doing for her, he deserved the truth from her. One last time, she looked his way. "But you should know. You fought beside my father. And you're helping me when you don't have to. You don't feel like a stranger to me."

Without waiting for his reaction, she stepped into the hall and closed the door behind her.

Chapter 8

$\mathcal{W}$ay to fucking go, Rixey." He blew out a long breath, eyes still glued to the door through which Becca had just departed. "No matter which way you have to march, it's always uphill. Shit." He stalked across the room and slammed his gloves down on a shelf.

He thought about going after her but quickly dismissed the idea, because he wasn't sure he could resist finishing what they'd started.

Watching her punch that bag, her eyes blue diamonds of concentration, her curves moving and flexing under that thin T-shirt, small grunts of exertion spilling from her open lips. It had been about as much as he'd been able to bear. Then, when he'd realized she'd been crying, that she'd literally been beating the emotions out of herself, a surge of protective possessiveness had run through him so swift and potent all he'd known was the need to get her in his arms.

And then she'd kissed him. Licked him. Sucked on his skin.

All those urges he'd had while she'd boxed had grown darker, needier, irresistible. Between his injuries and the ginormous mindfuck he'd been grappling with since his discharge, it had been more than a year since his body had last known the tight pleasure of a woman. And she'd stirred up a freight train of lust he hadn't been able to hold back.

Jesus, her taste, her heat, the feel of her lush curves in his hands. Sweet fucking perfection.

When her hand had fallen on his cock, the touch had jolted a measure of awareness into his brain. He hadn't been kidding about what he wanted to do to her. Even now, the mental image of her hanging onto the heavy bag while he took her kept him hard and aching.

But there were too many reasons to shut that shit down before things went balls to the wall, not the least of which was the fact that her father had torn apart his life, killed six of his closest friends, and turned him into a man he barely recognized anymore. A jagged hole of guilt and loss opened up in the center of his chest. Why hadn't he seen Merritt's lies sooner? Seen them for what they were? He shook his head and rubbed against the squeezing ache under his sternum. Given who she was, he should stay away from anything physical. Besides, with all the ways he'd failed—himself and his men—he didn't deserve the comfort of her warmth and light anyway.

Not to mention the fact that after what had been done to the team, he hated lies. And the NDA meant he couldn't tell Becca the truth. Another good reason to keep his dick in line. He scrubbed his hands roughly over his face.

With a last look around the gym he'd slowly but surely assembled since his return to the real world, Rixey killed the lights, crossed to his place, and made his way to the back of the quiet, still loft to his office. No sense going through the façade of lying down to sleep. The land of nod wasn't on his current radar, not with how cranked his body was.

He fell heavily into his desk chair and pulled his drawing into his lap. Following from Jeremy's rough sketch, the half fireman, half soldier tattoo was nearly done, though that didn't mean he understood why he kept letting his brother talk him into doing this. Part of it was that art had always been the one thing he and Jer had in common. Well, that and video games. That was about where it ended. Only a year separated them, but Rixey had been sports, and his brother had been books. Rixey had been parties and drinking and hell-raising of the usual teenage variety, and Jeremy had been quiet around everyone but his small circle of Goth and punk friends.

But there was more to it, and Rixey knew it. He continued to do these tats and apprentice toward a license he didn't really want and had no intention of using in the long term because he was fucking floating through life. No purpose. No plan. No mission.

For a dozen years, *all* he'd worried about was completing the mission and getting everyone home safe. In Afghanistan, his team had done counterinsurgency work, counternarcotics work, which had often been the same thing, and local police force training. It had been challenging, dangerous, and sometimes frustratingly thankless work, but it had given him the sense of purpose in life he'd been lacking as a younger man.

Now? Wish in one hand, shit in the other. See which one fills up the fastest. He chucked the pad to the desk.

The Army had given him more than just a purpose. It

had made him part of something much bigger than himself, placed him in the middle of a brotherhood who understood him implicitly. Nearly a year later, he still mourned the loss of the six good men gunned down in the ambush. Eric Zane, Carlos Escobal, Jake Harlow, Walker Axton, Marcus Rimes, Colin Kemmerer. Their memory was a weight on his shoulders he was privileged to carry. But in not doing more with his life, he wasn't doing enough to honor their memory. His survival should've *meant* something, shouldn't it?

You do *have a mission, shithead. Keep Becca safe. Find her brother. Get whoever is harassing them to back the fuck off. Maybe* that's *why you're still here.*

Fair enough. It was a worthy mission. And if it filled the void for a few days, all the better.

A kind of peace settled over his shoulders—well, as close as he freaking got to anything in the same zip code as peace. And it was enough. Really, it had to be, didn't it? With a last glance at his soldier-fireman, Rixey pushed up from the chair and made for his bed.

What was on the other side of his soldier identity? Someday soon, he'd have to figure out the fubar of his career and find his own next mission. Wasn't anybody going to drop that shit in his lap. But, damn, oh stupid thirty in the mothereffing morning was too early to put his brain cells to work on that particular conundrum.

Not even bothering to shed his jeans, Rixey sprawled facedown on the bed, wincing as his jacked-up back reminded him it no longer appreciated that position. He flopped to his side, tugged the sheet up over his hips, and punched the pillow.

Jesus, he was tired.

Knock, knock, knock.

He whipped his head up, alertness crashing through the haze of sleep. Light shone into the room. No way was it morning already. No. Fucking. Way. Felt like he'd fallen asleep about thirty-six seconds ago.

"Building better be on fire," he groused.

Jeremy leaned into the room, looking a helluva lot more awake and together than Rixey felt. "Becca needs to be to work in forty-five minutes. Her car's not here?"

Shit. No, it wasn't. He'd wanted to clear it for any kind of tracking devices before she drove it again. "Okay. Gimme ten."

"I wouldn't mind taking her."

"No," he said. "I got it." The door clicked shut behind Jeremy. Rixey pushed out of bed, his back raising hell and his cock hard as steel, and his brain went right to the events of the previous night. Kissing, touching, groping. *Sonofabitch.* Hopefully, they'd make some major headway on figuring out Becca and Charlie's situations today. The sooner she was back at her own place and out of his life, the better for both of them.

In the meantime, he'd keep his hands and his dick to himself. It shouldn't be that fucking hard.

"SORRY I DIDN'T think to ask about your schedule last night," Nick said in a gravelly voice as he entered the kitchen and went right to the coffeepot. He poured a cup and turned to her, his butt leaning against the counter.

Becca swallowed a bite of cereal. Oh, man, he was as beautiful in the light of day as he was in the shadows of night. He'd clearly showered, and the dampness made his hair darker. His gray T-shirt clung to his skin, wet spots showing through here and there like he hadn't dried all the way. The gun holster emphasized the bulk of his shoulders.

She cleared her throat, hoping things weren't going to be awkward between them. They were adults, after all; they should be able to handle a kiss. Okay, a make-out. A really hot make-out. "It's fine. We have a little time. And Jeremy was keeping me entertained with a description of his T-shirt collection."

Jeremy grinned and nodded around a big dripping bite of Cocoa Puffs. The shirt he had on today was black with the words *Orgasm Donor* centered around a red cross. The guy was a flirt and a total smart-ass, and she kinda adored both about him.

Rixey shook his head. "I don't think there's a dirty shirt he doesn't own."

His brother sat his bowl in the sink with a *clunk*. "It's my mission to make sure that's true."

Becca smiled. "Do you have any of the Big Johnson shirts from down at the shore?"

"Do I have . . . I'm wearing one tomorrow just for you."

"Oh, God," she said. "That was a dumb question, wasn't it?" She slipped off the stool with her empty bowl.

"Told ya." Rixey held out his hand. "Here, I'll take it."

"Thanks," she said, meeting the light green of his eyes, like the sea glass she sometimes found at the beach. He held her gaze for a moment, silently asking if they were okay. She smiled, relief flooding through her. "I'll be ready in five." She dashed to the bathroom and brushed her teeth, then grabbed her purse and rejoined them in the kitchen.

Jeremy winked. "*Adiós, muchacha.*"

She winked back. "*Hasta luego.*"

"Oh, well played."

She chuckled and followed Nick to the door.

"Later," he called to Jeremy, guiding Becca out. "Remember the apartment code?" She nodded. "In case you need it, the exterior code is six-eight-zero-one-three."

She repeated the number out loud, twice. "Got it."

Outside, the morning air was cool and damp. Puddles settled here and there in the gravel, as if it had stopped raining not long before. They walked to his car in silence, and he followed her around to the passenger side, where he opened the door.

How he could be such a hard-ass and have such good manners, she didn't know. Probably a military thing. Definitely a sexy thing.

A moment later, Rixey settled into the driver's seat. "Where to?" he asked as he brought the engine to life on a low growl.

"University Medical Center. Greene and Lombard. I wish I didn't even have to work today, but I'm covering for someone who couldn't find anyone else. If I bail, they'll be shorthanded. And Fridays are always crazy. But I'm going to arrange to take a leave until we find Charlie."

"Well, I need to put some plans into place anyway. So you won't miss anything."

She nodded, and they made their way through the early morning traffic in silence.

"While you're at work today," he finally said, "if you'd be comfortable giving me your keys, I'd like to check your house and car out more thoroughly. If you'll call a locksmith and let me know what time they're coming, I'll meet the guy and get your locks changed."

"Are you still going to visit the private investigator?"

He nodded. "Yeah. He has the bug detection equipment I need, actually. And he'll know the best way to organize the search."

She frowned, hating that she had to do this last shift. "I wish I could go with you."

"We can see him again when you're free. Whatever makes you comfortable."

Warm pressure filled her chest. "Thank you. I just want to know what's going on." She glanced out the window, worry for Charlie gripping her like quicksand.

"I don't blame you one bit, Becca."

The empathy in his voice drew her gaze. His expression was full of compassion. Man, she was lucky to have him helping her, though she felt bad derailing his whole day. "Are you really sure you want to do all this? I don't want to wreck your schedule."

His eyes flashed toward her. "I wanna help. Let me. And, anyway, I can set my own work hours, so it's no problem."

"Oh. Tattooing?" Amazing to think he had an artistic side. She'd love to see him draw something sometime. Maybe after they found Charlie and all this was over. She refused to believe it would end any other way.

He frowned. "What?"

"You work tattooing?"

Nick gave a rueful laugh. "No. I meant it when I said I'm not really a tattoo artist. Most of the time I'm a process server."

"Oh." *That* job, she totally got for him. "Is it dangerous?" she asked.

"Not most of the time."

She heard what he hadn't said. "Hmm. But sometimes it is." The thought that he put himself in harm's way even now that he was back in the States made her stomach drop. And now he was putting himself in even more danger for her. "I want you to know I appreciate what you're doing, Nick. No matter what." She couldn't finish the sentence. She wouldn't.

"Hey." His warm hand curled around hers. She squeezed back, so grateful for the show of support. "Try not to worry. I'm going to do everything I can."

When her eyes pricked, she pretended to get real interested in the passing scenery again. "Okay."

A moment later, she gave him another squeeze and eased her fingers out from under his, then retrieved her smartphone and opened the internet browser. Soon after, she was explaining to a locksmith what had happened at her house. Angling the phone away from her mouth, she whispered, "Two thirty okay?" He nodded, and she made the appointment. "All set," she said when she hung up. It took a big worry off her mind to know he was doing this for her. "When this is done, do you think it'll be safe for me to stay there again?"

"Probably. We'll get you squared away. Don't you worry about it."

"Thank you. And I get off at three, so I'll be able to help you later." Despite the morning rush, they sailed crosstown on Lombard, arriving at the hospital in what seemed like no time at all. "Drop me off anywhere," she said.

He pulled to the curb. "Pick you up at three, then?"

She blinked at him. "If you're gonna be at my house this afternoon already, I'll just take the bus home. It's what I usually do anyway."

Nick frowned, like he disapproved, but then nodded. "You sure?"

She gave him a small smile. "Yeah. I'll be home by four at the latest."

"Good. Let me see your phone." He made quick work of adding his info to her contacts and calling his phone from hers so he had her number, too. "Call me if you need me before then."

"Okay." She handed him her keys, opened the door, and got out, then stuck her head back in. "Thanks for everything, Nick." At least if she had to be at work, she could take comfort knowing he was out there working on Charlie's behalf until she got off.

"Hey, Becca?" he called right before she closed the door. She leaned back in. "Be careful."

"I will. Thanks." She closed the door and threaded through the stream of pedestrians toward the hospital's tall glass entrance. At the door, she glanced back. Nick sat in his car at the curb, watching her. And the fact that he was still there blew away some of the cobwebs of loneliness that hung here and there inside her. She wasn't in this alone. She and Nick were in this together. Gratitude made her smile and wave. And then she pushed through the doors into the chaos of the emergency department.

Chapter 9

*R*ixey knocked softly on the doorjamb and leaned a shoulder against the wood.

Phone braced between his ear and his shoulder, Miguel Olivero looked up with a smile and waved him in, then lifted a finger in a just-a-minute gesture. His salt-and-pepper hair revealed his sixties-ish age, but he was so animated—his expressions, his gestures, his volume—that you never thought of him as an old man.

Dragging the chair to the left so his back wouldn't be to the door, Rixey dropped his ass onto the pleather and scanned his gaze around the office space that probably hadn't been fashionable when it was new in the 1980s. The dark wood paneling made it feel like the walls were closing in, bug carcasses collected in the rectangular fluorescent light fixtures above their heads, and the veneer of the particleboard office furniture had peeled off here and there, exposing the pressed yellow wood beneath. But Rixey still liked visiting here because of the man behind the desk.

Miguel slammed the receiver back in its cradle. "Look what the cat dragged in," he boomed with his usual over-the-top joviality. "How the hell are ya, kid?"

Rixey couldn't help but smile around the guy. "Same old, same old."

"How's work?" Miguel said, tugging the knot of his striped tie loose like it was strangling him.

"Keeping me busy." Rixey had met Miguel through the man's nephew, who was one of Jeremy's regulars. As a former cop and private investigator, Olivero had a lot of contacts in the law enforcement world, and he'd hooked Rixey up with the process serving gig nearly a year ago. Now the man had become something of a friend.

"How's the back?" he said, firing through his usual list of catching-up questions.

"About as good as it's gonna get, probably. But fine." It was close enough to the truth, and griping about it just reminded Nick he wasn't the man he used to be.

Miguel's bushy eyebrows slashed down. "Bah. Still doing PT? Don't let them docs throw you out before you're ready."

Rixey gave a small smile. "Don't worry. I'm taking care of myself."

"Y'better. How's your brother?"

"He's good. Got a good head on his shoulders. What's new with you?" Nick asked, hoping to shift the focus away from the soup sandwich his life had become.

Miguel leaned back in his chair and laced his hands over the swell of his stomach with a satisfied smile. "My son's making me a grandfather again."

Rixey sat forward. "Congratulations. That's great news." He ignored the small ache that planted itself in his chest. As twisted up inside as the last year had left him, he wasn't sure he'd ever have that for himself. And, if by some act of God he did, he'd never be able to see his father's pride in becoming a grandfather.

"Yeah. Number three. Nothing new with me, though. Insurance fraud, adultery, tracking down deadbeats. You know how it is. Eh." He gave an exaggerated shrug. "So, what is it you need help with?"

"A friend of mine's in trouble. Her brother is missing. Took off or taken, we don't know yet. But his house was tossed. Then, last night, someone broke into her place, too. Seems like someone's looking for something. But she's got no clue."

Olivero's whole face frowned. "Police doing anything?"

Nick shrugged. "Reports filed. Nothing stolen that we can tell. Got any thoughts on where and how to start tracking him down?"

Miguel rubbed his jaw. "Wonder if the police pulled any prints. Hmm. I'll call my guy and see if I can get a copy of whatever they've gathered so far. Beyond that, start at the scene and work out. Interview neighbors, take the brother's picture around, go to any frequent hangouts, check his credit card statements. How time sensitive is all this?"

Similar approach as the skip tracing Rixey sometimes did to serve papers, though that was predicated on the idea that the person disappeared himself, rather than being taken against his will. Either option seemed viable here until ruled out, but Rixey hoped for Becca's sake that Charlie had just gotten a scare and gone to ground. "Moderate to high. Becca's pretty upset, as you can imagine."

"Becca's the friend, I take it?" Mischief danced in Miguel's brown eyes.

Chuffing out a laugh, Rixey shook his head. "Yes, she's the friend." Although maybe that was too strong a word.

Only circumstance and a dead man had brought them to-gether, so it was doubtful they'd be hanging when they got this mess sorted out. A boulder of pressure settled itself on his chest, but Rixey refused to examine that sense of constriction too closely. It had started when she'd asked about returning to her house, then gotten heavier when he'd had to leave her at the hospital unprotected.

"Let me talk to my contact at BPD. That'll probably give us the best starting point."

Nick nodded. "Thanks. One other thing. I wondered if I could borrow some equipment to sweep her house for electronic surveillance devices. I'm meeting a locksmith over there in about an hour, so I could kill two birds with one stone if I could borrow it this afternoon."

Miguel steepled his fingers. "Where does she live?"

"A block off Patterson Park."

"I'll do ya one better," Miguel said, sitting up and plac-ing his arms on top of the desk blotter. "I'll come with ya. I could use some fresh air. Two pair of hands can sweep a house faster than one."

It was just like him to offer. "I'm gonna take you up on that."

Miguel slapped his hands on the desk. "Good. We're gonna make a full-blown PI out of you before it's all said and done." He winked, and Nick gave a rueful smile. Miguel had been after him about this for a few months, but he couldn't help feeling like it was something else he'd fall into, rather than choosing it for himself.

Forty-five minutes later, Rixey pulled onto Becca's street, Miguel following behind in his nondescript dark sedan—affectionately known as the stakeoutmobile. They parked, and Rixey met Miguel at his trunk.

Three pieces of equipment sat within. A briefcase-sized plastic box held a non linear junction detector, which looked a lot like the metal detectors people used at the beach and could sense radio signals or transmitters inside walls, baseboards, and ceilings. A smaller case held an electronic field detector, a handheld device that identified audio and video signals. The third kit held a thermal imager that could read heat signatures thrown off by electronics hidden in walls and ceilings. Olivero had other pieces for cases specifically focused on countersurveillance, but he thought these would likely do the job. And Rixey trusted his judgment.

Rixey retrieved all three cases into his arms.

"You don't have to be such a hotshot," Miguel said, slamming the trunk with a wink.

"The grunt work's the least I can do." Nick led their way to Becca's front door.

"Let's put the stuff inside and then we'll do an exterior sweep to start."

Nodding, Rixey fished the keys from his pocket. Finding the right one took him a few tries, but then the key finally turned and he pushed the door open. He stepped back to let Miguel through.

"Holy Mary, Mother of God."

Frowning, Rixey stepped into the little foyer behind him. "Sonofafuck." Brazen assholes had come back after all.

The place had been tossed. Nick dropped the cases to the floor and drew his gun. Olivero was right there with him, gun drawn and at the ready. The older man nodded, and they moved in unison to clear the first floor and the small basement.

Making their way back through, Rixey saw that the rear door stood open a crack. He resecured it. Heart thundering in his chest and adrenaline flying through his veins, all Nick could think was *thank fuck* he'd made Becca leave last night. Shit, the thought that she might've been there when someone did *this* . . .

Drawers dumped out, books knocked off shelves, cushions tossed and torn. Destructive, but about what you'd expect if someone was looking for something. It was the other damage that filled his gut with dread. Pictures and figurines smashed, plants knocked over, the dirt spilled everywhere and then tracked through the carpet. Looked like two, maybe three guys by the different-sized prints. Seemed like a lot of damage for the sake of damage.

Rixey nodded toward the stairs. Weapon at the ready, he leaned into the stairwell, gave a quick looksee, then hightailed it up. A clear sight into the bathroom told him the room directly ahead was clear. He signaled to Miguel to cover him and darted across to Becca's room.

Jesus.

The floor was a veritable debris field, with clothing and books and jewelry and seashells underfoot. Fuckers had smashed her guitar and emptied out her drawers and closet.

All this damage made no God-given sense. It had taken time and potentially risked the stealth of their actions—and the intent seemed punitive, terroristic. His gut dropped to his boots when he imagined Becca's reaction. And that he was going to have to be the one to break her heart with the news.

He rejoined Miguel in the hall and made quick work of ascertaining the last room was also clear.

"As a crime scene, this place makes no friggin' sense, Nick," Miguel growled, echoing Rixey's own thoughts as he looked over the disheveled piles of papers covering every surface of Becca's office. The full weight of Miguel's gaze lifted to Rixey's, and the man didn't have to say a word. This wasn't any ordinary B&E. And it wasn't any typical missing persons situation. This was something organized, deadly serious, and royally pissed off, by the looks of this place. Way too much emotion involved in all this destruction to read it any other way.

Becca. Jesus Christ, she was out in the open, completely unprotected—and unsuspecting. "I have to go get Becca." Nick backed to the door. "I don't know what this means, but no way I'm letting her take the bus home by herself."

Miguel nodded. "I'll stay here and handle this."

"Locksmith should be here soon. Tell him to install the highest-grade locks on every exterior door," Rixey said, alarm pounding against the inside of his skull. "Windows, too. I don't care what it costs. And thank you, Miguel."

"Go get your girl, son."

Rixey turned and jogged down the steps, already pulling his phone from his pocket. The crap-ton of *oh shit* parked on his chest made it impossible to analyze what all this meant, how it was all connected. He just couldn't see the forest for the trees, and he wouldn't be able to until Becca Merritt was back in his presence and under his protection, safe and sound.

BECCA SAT DOWN on a bench in the small outdoor courtyard with a diet Coke and a pack of peanut butter crackers. Not because she was hungry but because she hoped they would settle the upset stomach she'd had all day.

As she nibbled at a cracker, her gaze traced over the open rectangular space. Surrounded on three sides by the towering hospital, it was a favorite hangout for staff seeking a bit of fresh air and a short reprieve from the demanding pace inside the hospital. Here and there, people filled benches, talked on cell phones, or clustered around the one corner where smoking was permitted.

Just another hour left to go. Which was good, because being at work instead of out looking for Charlie was making her crazy. With everything that was going on, her brain had struggled all day to remain present. And being distracted was always a bad thing to be in the ER.

She cracked open the soda and took a sip. Thank God

she didn't have to stay into the evening. Weekend nights were always the worst. By 5:00 p.m., the crap would really start hitting the fan, but she'd be long gone by then. Maybe Nick would take her to meet his PI friend, or they could go talk to Charlie's neighbors. She just needed to do *something*. Anything, really. Then later, would she be staying at her house or Nick's? She'd have thought her preference would've been clear, but she found herself thinking about how nice it was to eat dinner with someone, and have somebody with whom to share the day ahead over breakfast.

It had been a long time since she'd had anything close to that in her life. Becca dated occasionally, when she had the time, energy, and inclination—which hadn't happened often since her father died, truth be told. But even before then, she just hadn't met anyone who really made her *feel*.

I want to make you hold onto that bag while I bury myself in you so hard and so deep you don't know your own name.

The erotic promise of his words slammed her into the memory of being pressed against Nick's body, both of them sweating and breathing hard, the undeniable urge to have him coursing through her, the taste of his skin in her mouth, the strong grip of his hands on her skin. The feelings had been so overwhelming because she'd truly never felt anything that emotionally and physically intoxicating before.

Not until Nick freaking Rixey.

And, God help her, she would've entertained Nick's desires if what he'd said afterward hadn't overwhelmed her with guilt.

After hours of trying to balance her worry for Charlie against the needs that her unfulfilled arousal demanded, she felt more than a little strung out.

A long yawn rolled out of her, the result of the restless

night's sleep and a crazy day. Around eleven o'clock this morning, someone made the cardinal mistake of saying it looked like a quiet day. Like clockwork, the emergency department got slammed.

Two multi-victim MVAs. A kid with a 105 temp. An overdose. A GI bleed. Several cases of garden-variety chest and abdominal pain. And those were just the ones she remembered off the top of her head.

"I don't usually get to see you, girl. How you been?" Her pink scrubs bringing out the warm tones in her brown skin, Janeese Evans plunked down on the bench.

Becca managed a small smile at the nurse she'd gone through orientation with years before. Now they tended to work different shifts, but with Becca covering for someone, their paths had crossed. "I'm so-so. How are you?" she asked, resisting venting her fear and frustration at the woman. For the thousandth time, she found herself wishing her best friend, Cassie, still lived in Baltimore. It would've been nice to have someone to talk to about all this, but Cassie had moved to Chicago with her new husband right after their wedding two years ago. Now they Skyped every couple of weeks when life didn't get in the way. Becca didn't feel close enough to any of her other friends to dump something this serious on them, and wasn't that a sad statement.

Once they got Charlie back, Becca vowed to pull her life together. Spend more time with Charlie. Take a class. Volunteer for a charity. She'd been doing a little too much going through the motions lately, and that was a damn shame. If anyone knew how fleeting life could be, it was her.

"I'm good. Tyler just turned two." Janeese beamed, and an empty ache took up residence in Becca's chest.

"No way. How the heck did that happen already?" Becca didn't begrudge her friend an iota of happiness, but if Becca was honest, she was lonely. It wasn't something she dwelled on or let herself feel sorry about, but there was no denying that the past year or two had sorta kicked her butt. Joking around with Nick and Jeremy in their kitchen last night had been a stark contrast to her usual solo routine. Even though she didn't know them well, it had felt nice to be a part of a family for a few hours, even if from the periphery.

"I know. It's crazy. He's so big and never stops talking and chasing the dog. Hey, are you okay?" She leaned forward. "What happened to your face?" The woman arched a questioning brow.

"My house got broken into last night—"

"Shit, really? You okay? Is that what that's from?" Janeese gestured to Becca's temple.

Becca shook her head. She couldn't talk about Charlie, not if she expected to finish out her shift. "I'm okay. I've got a friend helping me. It's just that the intruder picked the lock, so I need to get new ones installed before I can stay there." She supposed "friend" was a fair description for what she and Nick were.

"Police doing anything?" Janeese asked.

"They filed a report." Which wasn't going to get Becca much. Especially in Baltimore, where the crime rate was sky high.

Janeese seemed to agree. "Hmph."

"Want one?" Becca asked, tilting the package of crackers toward her. They weren't helping her stomach after all. God, it felt like the clock was ticking backward.

"Sure," Janeese said, taking one. They munched crackers in silence for a few minutes. "Hey, look at that."

Becca followed her friend's gaze to the open end of the courtyard, where a sidewalk veered around to the ambulance bay. A little dog sniffed a trash can. As he came around the other side, Becca sucked in a breath. He only had three legs. One of his hind legs was gone. She rose to her feet. "Have you seen him before? He looks like a puppy." Becca's heart squeezed.

"Uh-uh."

"Aw, let's go see him." They crossed the grass, passing several other hospital staff who were watching the little guy, too. When Becca got close, she crouched down and held out her hand. "Hey, buddy."

The dog—a German shepherd, she guessed—paused and tilted his head her way.

"Oh, my God, he's all ears." His sweet face and over-sized ears were mostly black, while his chest and paws were a warm, caramel brown. The puppy's coloring reminded her so much of Wyatt, their family dog, who was already an old man when they were all kids. Wyatt had followed Charlie around like he'd thought he couldn't let the youngest Merritt out of his sight. The mutt had even slept with Charlie.

"Wonder how it lost its leg," Janeese said.

And so young, too. He couldn't have been more than a few months old. "Come here, boy."

After a moment, the shepherd hobbled over on enormous paws. He was surprisingly stable and wore no collar or tags, which could have explained why he was a bit scruffy around the edges. "Hi, boy. Er, oh, girl."

She licked and nipped at Becca's fingers with her sharp puppy teeth, then flopped over and offered her stomach.

Becca laughed. "Silly little thing, aren't you?"

Janeese crouched down beside them. "Must be a stray. Shame on whoever would dump a puppy like this." She got lured into the belly scratch, too.

The shepherd rolled onto her paws and toddled around them. Becca scratched her back, the cuteness and memories of Wyatt wrapping tendrils of temptation around her heart. With everything going on, could she really take on another responsibility right now? But the puppy was all on her own, and so was Becca. "Maybe I could take her home," she said, trying out the idea and giving Janeese a sideways glance.

She laughed. "You're getting sucked in, aren't you?"

Becca chuckled. "Kinda. Yeah."

"Well, she seems friendly enough. And shepherds are good guard dogs. Police use 'em. Might give you some peace of mind after what happened."

Well, that was true, and it certainly gave Becca a logical argument for considering this craziness. The puppy laid down by Becca's feet and found one of her shoestrings to snack on. Her big ears were so silky. "I guess I could take her to the vet and see if she's okay. And then, maybe . . ." She left the rest of the thought unspoken, but even so, the idea was planting deep roots in her mind and her heart. This sweet girl needed a home, and Becca wouldn't mind the company. "Come here, you."

The puppy was a chunky sack of potatoes in her arms, all paws and snout and ears, but so, so cute. And warm. And cuddly. An enormous pink tongue sideswiped her cheek, making Becca laugh as she stood up. She was going to have to change shirts after this, but she couldn't find it in herself to regret holding the dog.

"Aw, you've gone and done it now. Picked her up. You are *doomed*."

Janeese was right. The more Becca entertained the idea of keeping her, the more she wanted to. "Yeah, I think I am." Smiling, she glanced around. "But what am I going to do with her for the rest of my shift?" Oh, and she couldn't take the dog on the bus. "Do you think—" Her phone vibrated against her hip. "Oh, hold on." She fished the cell from her pocket, swiped to answer the call, and put it to her ear all while dodging more wet puppy kisses. Laughing, she said, "Hello?"

"Becca, it's Nick."

It's a sign! Maybe he can still take me home. "Oh, hey. You know, I was just thinking about asking you for a ride after all—"

"Becca, listen to me. I'm on my way to you right now. You need to stay in a safe place. Stay inside and off the street. I'll come into the ER for you when I get there." His car motor revved in the background.

Tingly goose bumps broke out over her body. "Why? What happened?"

"I'll explain when I get there. Just do what I'm telling you." His tone was stone cold and tight.

"Okay." Dread flooded ice along her nerve endings, and tears stung the backs of her eyes. "Is it Charlie?" she whispered.

"No. You stay somewhere secure, you hear? Becca?"

"Yeah. I will."

The line went dead.

Chapter 10

As she lowered the phone, Becca glanced around the courtyard. The sunny spring day suddenly seemed so out of place, almost sinister in perpetuating the lie that everything was good, nice, pleasant.

"What's the matter?" Janeese asked, frowning.

"I don't know. My friend's on his way to get me, but he wouldn't say why." Becca ran her hand over the puppy's ears and neck, the soft texture of her coat giving Becca something else to think about. Something besides the bad news Nick was bringing her way. It had to be Charlie. Didn't it? But Nick said it wasn't, and he wouldn't lie to her. *What else could it be? Maybe my house is bugged after all?* "He told me to stay inside, to stay somewhere safe. Maybe it has to do with the break-in?"

"Holy shit, girl. Well, let's go in the break room, then."

Janeese wrapped her arm around Becca's shoulders and guided her. "Should you call the police?"

"I wouldn't know what to say." Not yet, anyway. A sour taste rose up the back of Becca's throat. She swallowed, hard, but it wasn't enough to wash away the rising tide of panic. "I can't take the dog inside, though."

"Don't even worry about that. You stay in the room with her until your friend comes, and it'll be fine."

Becca nodded, and so many worst-case scenarios paraded through her mind that they accumulated into a deafening rush of white noise that left her feeling strangely detached. In fact, the only thing she could really feel was the dog's warmth and softness, the gentle rise and fall of her breathing.

Janeese swiped her ID and opened the exterior door to the break room, and Becca was relieved to find the room empty. "You wait here. I'll go find Donna and send her back," Janeese said.

That was good. Becca needed to talk to the head nurse anyway about taking some time off. "Thanks. Oh, my friend's name is Nick Rixey. Can you buzz him in when he gets here?"

"Yeah. Be right back." Janeese slipped into the hallway, the hustle and bustle of the emergency department spilling in through the open door.

When it shut, Becca put the puppy on the floor. "Want some water, pretty girl?" The answer was an enthusiastic yes, if the speed with which the puppy drank was any indication. Whatever was going on, at least this whole area was secure. No one could get back into the ER without being admitted by the desk nurse or swiping a UMC badge. *Just hang on for a few minutes, Bec. Nick will be here soon.* She heaved a breath. "Stay here for a minute, 'kay?"

The dog looked up, cocked her big ears, then dove back into the dish Becca had set down for her.

Becca slipped into the adjoining locker room and wound her way to the second row. It was a good thing she'd had this lock so long, or the fog hovering around her brain would've kept her from remembering the combination. She removed the lock, grabbed her purse, and resecured the door.

Woof!

Jogging back to the break room, she hoped no one else had heard the animal. No doubt the puppy would be a big hit with the other nurses, but Becca didn't want to disturb any of the patients. She pulled open the door to find her new best friend sitting and waiting right on the other side.

"Don't worry, I'm here," Becca said, crouching down and petting the scruff of her neck. "You need a name. What am I going to call you?" The dog tilted her head to the side as if trying to decipher the words.

The door to the hall opened, and Becca cut her gaze across the room.

A bald-headed man in a facilities uniform stood in the breach. "'Scuse me," he said.

For a moment, she braced for trouble, but then she saw the badge clipped to his shirt pocket. "Can I help you?" Becca said, standing.

He looked around the space. "Doing a check for lightbulbs that need to be replaced." He pointed to the fluorescent ceiling fixture in the corner by the exterior door, dark where all the others were illuminated.

"Oh, of course." She hefted her purse up on her shoulder and shooed the puppy away from chewing on her fingers. Mouthy thing.

The man crossed to the closest table and set his toolbox down. The dark skin of his arms was covered in raised scars and ink, and she wondered if her brain would've even registered the latter before she'd walked into Hard Ink a few days ago.

Becca picked up the dog so it didn't bother the maintenance man and crossed to the door. Maybe Janeese had gotten snagged on a code and Nick was out there but didn't know where to find her?

Her fingers brushed the doorknob, and something grabbed her from behind. The rough contact was so unexpected that she didn't realize what was happening until a hand clamped over her mouth and an arm banded around her chest.

With a strangled cry, she grasped at the hand nearly smothering her, forgetting about the dog in her panic and dropping her to the floor. The puppy yelped and scrambled to her feet.

The man hauled her backward toward the courtyard door. Becca dragged her Crocs, losing both in the process, and tugged and scratched at her attacker's arms. Victory flared through her when he released her chest. Until something sharp jabbed into the side of her ribs.

Cold fingers dug into her face, demanding her attention. "When we step outside, you're going to walk beside me. No screaming, no more fighting. Or else I'm going to slide this blade in nice and deep." He poked it harder for good measure, and Becca gasped into his palm at the sting.

A rolling growl drew Becca's wide-eyed gaze back to the dog, whose show of teeth, braced posture, and downward tail all read aggression.

Metal clanked and cool air blew from behind her. The man slowed up, like maybe he was scoping the scene first. "Real friendly now, Miss Merritt," he rasped, way too close to her ear. He knew her name? "I'd hate to have to hurt any witnesses who saw me shank you."

Dread crawled over her skin. *God, Nick, where are you? Please be here.* Every instinct inside screamed that she'd be lost for good if this guy got her out the door.

The puppy's growls crescendoed in volume.

"Here we go," the man said.

White-hot terror washed over every inch of her, and in an instant she decided she'd rather take her chances getting stabbed than abducted to God only knew where. Becca gripped the molding around the door with both hands and braced for the slicing pain.

"What'd I tell you, bitch?" The knife jabbed.

She cried out, losing her grip with one hand, and the dog went crazy barking. It charged and attacked the man's leg, but a kick sent the puppy sprawling with a whimper. She didn't stay down. Wobbly legs back under her, she barked and lunged again.

The door across the room exploded open.

Nick burst in, weapon raised, stance ready, expression absolutely deadly. "Let her go, and I'll consider not planting some lead in your eye socket."

The bad guy's knife twitched, and Becca clasped her hands together and wrenched back with her left elbow with all her might. Whatever she'd connected with earned her a satisfying grunt and had the desired effect of diverting whatever plans he'd been making with the blade. Suddenly, she was free, and a hard shove to her back sent her sprawling face-first to the floor. Trying to catch herself, she landed funny on one hand, and her forehead glanced off the floor.

Her attacker fled out the open door as Nick called her name.

Footsteps crossed the room, then stopped at the sound of a long, low growl.

Groaning, Becca pushed onto her elbows. Her little guardian had placed herself between Becca's prone form and Nick's advance.

His expression managed to be livid and bewildered at the same time.

Making a little calling sound with her mouth, Becca caught the puppy's attention. "'Sokay, girl. He's a good guy." She held out her hand. After a moment's hesitation, the shepherd whined and lay down by Becca's shoulder.

Nick holstered his weapon and came around to her back. Easing his hands under Becca's arms, he said, "Can you sit up?"

"Yeah," she rasped, holding her breath as every joint protested the movement. "Thank you," she managed. "For getting here in time."

Metal scraped along the floor. "Chair right behind you. On three." He counted off and lifted her into the chair.

Her whole body sagged into the plastic.

"Becca?" a voice asked from the doorway, where a slack-jawed crowd had gathered. Janeese. Donna. Alison, the nurse she'd been subbing for. Others whose names she couldn't immediately bring to mind in the moment. Becca nodded.

They poured into the room, a momentary shocked silence followed by everyone talking at once.

"What the hell happened?" Janeese asked.

"A maintenance man grabbed me," Becca said. "Nick scared him off and he fled out the door."

"Did you recognize him?" Donna asked.

Becca shook her head just as Barry, one of the hospital security officers, pushed into the room, followed a few minutes later by Tomás and Mike, two BPD officers she knew pretty well. They'd been hanging in the ER waiting to take witness statements. She groaned inside, especially as Nick's silent agitation became more pronounced in the tension of his muscles and ticking of his jaw.

"Becca, are you cut somewhere?" Janeese pointed and knelt next to her. "Honey, you're bleeding."

She twisted to the left. A line of crimson was soaking into the green of her scrubs. Lifting her ripped shirt, she frowned. How did she not feel that gash? "Oh," she said. Her gaze lifted to Nick, standing next to her, his eyes trained on her wound and absolutely on fire. That blazing glare lit onto her face next. As reserved as he looked on the outside, she doubted anyone else in the room realized that he was an active volcano on the inside.

The next ninety minutes passed with her giving a statement to the officers, being admitted, and getting stitches—the cut wasn't too deep, so she only needed four—winning an argument about keeping Nick and the puppy in the room with her, and failing to get Nick to tell her why he'd come racing to the hospital in the first place. If all that wasn't enough, she also had a visit from the hospital lawyer, who was clearly trying to feel out whether she was going to sue, but on the upside they told her to take off as much paid time as she needed to recover. And given the situation with Charlie, that was a godsend.

By the time she was discharged, the adrenaline letdown had kicked in with a vengeance, leaving her tired, shaky, and feeling a whole lot like she'd been hit by a Mack truck.

Carrying the puppy like a football under his left arm, Nick guided her out to his car. He kept her a half step in front of him, his big body shielding hers from the side and back as they crossed to the sidewalk and paused at the curb.

He opened the car door and eased her down. Carefully, Becca lowered into the passenger seat and accepted the dog into her lap.

The door slammed so hard it shook the car. Nick stalked around the hood, very clearly still on full alert. He ripped a parking ticket from under the wiper and sank into the driver's seat. Another slam. And then the car came to life on an exaggerated roar of the engine.

The puppy shrank into her chest, and Becca eyeballed

Nick. Everything about the rigid discipline of his movements and the deafening volume of his silence screamed rankly pissed off.

Shifting in her seat, she reached across and placed her hand on his arm. His muscles locked up tight under her touch and his posture and expression painted a billboard for *Back the hell off,* but Becca couldn't wait another moment.

"Nick, I need to know. What happened?"

AFTER EVERYTHING ELSE this day had thrown at him, it was her touch that threatened to break him. Because it made Rixey want to haul her into his lap and prove with his mouth and his hands and his cock that she was okay.

It was the adrenaline high talking. He knew it and had experienced it before—the need to grab onto life with both hands and not let go. After all, he hadn't known Becca Merritt long enough to explain those urges any other way. Right?

Shy of a good, long fuck to even him out, Rixey would settle for punching something. Hard. And repeatedly.

So close. He'd come so close to losing Becca. When he'd opened the door and seen that asshole yanking her out the other side, his paws touching her skin, Rixey'd yearned to lay that motherfucker *out.* Even now, lethal intent surged through his veins until he could barely breathe. No way he could examine all of the whys of that right this second.

"Nick?"

Her voice wrenched him from his thoughts, but not out of the dark, violent headspace. "Not now. I can't talk to you right now," he managed. His emotions were too volatile. Anger roiled too close to the surface. Aggression surged through him. "Let's just get home."

Not waiting for a reply, he veered out into traffic, his

gaze making a constant circuit from the windshield to the rearview mirror to the side-view mirrors. He bet dollars to donuts they'd pick up a tail. Sure enough, within a block he was certain the gray van five cars back was following them. Just in case, he made a few choice last-minute turns and gunned it through the dying breaths of every yellow light he encountered. Either he lost the van, or paranoia had gotten the best of him and it'd never been in pursuit in the first place.

Sonofabitch.

As they hit the eastern side of town, Nick chanced a look Becca's way. Her expression was absolutely bleak, one tiny push away from shattered, and her skin was pale as snow—except for the swollen goose egg above her left eyebrow from when the lowlife had shoved her to the floor. That was bright fucking red.

Say something, asshole. Throw her a goddamned rope. "What's, uh, what's with the dog?" *Outstanding, Nick, truly.*

She tilted her face and rubbed her cheek against its big ear. "I found her."

"She has three legs." Rixey winced at the idiocy of the observation.

"Uh, yeah." Her gaze slid out the passenger window, making it crystal clear she wasn't in any more of a mood to chitchat than he'd been before. And fine. Until he got her off the road, situational awareness was his top priority. Everything else could wait. He cut in and out of traffic on Eastern Avenue, eager to get her home. Eager to get her safe. A few moments later, Becca's posture straightened and she leaned forward, like she was looking for something. Her gaze whipped toward him. "This isn't the way to my house."

Icy slush slid into his gut. As if she wasn't already dealing with enough, he was going to have to find the words to tell her what had been done to her home. "Not going to your house."

"But I thought—"

"It's a new ball game, Becca."

"Because someone tried to grab me."

Her tone was way too fucking nonchalant for his taste. He glared. "Because someone tried to *abduct* you and stabbed you. For starters."

"And? Why else?"

Shit. He really didn't want to have this conversation in the car. But she was going to think him a royal asshole if he refused to answer. The words tasted like acid as he gathered them on his tongue.

His phone rang, the vibration skittering against his hip from within his coat pocket. "Hold on a minute." He fished it out, read Miguel's name on the screen, and put the cell to his ear. "This is Nick."

"Did you find her?" Miguel said by way of greeting.

"Yeah, about thirty seconds before some lowlife nabbed her from a staff break room."

"Jesus, Mary, and Joseph. Is she okay? Did you get a look at the perp?" Nick could tell from the cadence of Miguel's breathing that the man was pacing.

"For whatever good it'll do me, yeah, I got an eyeful. Becca's a little banged up, but she's a trooper." Which, honestly, was a goddamned understatement. She'd resisted her assailant, gotten in an elbow to the guy's kidney that had probably ensured Nick wouldn't have to make good on his threat to shoot, and dealt with a frenzy of well-wishers and questions and general ER chaos with patience and grace. She was more than a little like her old man—in all the best ways. Rixey glanced her way and found her blatantly listening in on the conversation. Not that he blamed her. "Listen, things wrapped up over there yet? I think you should clear out until I get a better handle on this. That location is too hot."

"Door locks are changed. The guy's doing the sliding window locks now."

"Good. Did the police come?" Silence. "Miguel?"

"That's not an option right now. But I'd rather explain in person."

Aw, for fuck sake. Not an option to call the police? The whys behind a statement like that could not possibly be good. "You know where to find me. My door's open."

"Yup. I'll come as soon as I can."

"Okay. Listen, watch your six on the way out."

"You got a tail?" Miguel asked.

The question had Nick doing the mirror-mirror-windshield circuit one more time. "Not anymore. But maybe earlier."

"Will do. Stay safe, Nick."

"Right back atcha." They disconnected.

Instinct was telling him they hadn't yet hit bottom on this situation, whatever the fuck it actually was. And figuring that out was job one. Because right now he was running blind in the middle of a shit storm he hadn't seen coming. How he was going to come up with the who, what, when, where, and why all on his own was a whole other problem.

You can get help if you ask for it.

It wasn't just the men who'd been killed that he'd lost last year, it was the other four survivors, too. Because he'd been too fucked in the head to find a way to get right with his role in what'd happened to them. How could they possibly want to stay friends with someone who'd failed them so spectacularly? But, goddamnit, they'd be the world's best ace in the hole to bring in on this situation.

"Who was that?" Becca asked.

"Friend named Miguel Olivero. Private investigator I

told you about. Ex-cop. He was helping me out at your place earlier."

Rixey purposely passed the road that led most conveniently to Hard Ink and drove four blocks out of his way. His rear still looked clear, but this situation had proved again and again that he couldn't be too careful. And it was driving him crazy, because he felt like he was missing pieces to a puzzle that he somehow found himself in the middle of.

"You think someone's following us?" she asked, twisting to look out the rear window.

"Just a precaution. Someone obviously knew to find you at the hospital. They knew what you looked like to make the grab." A right turn to double back. "And whatever this is, Becca, they want you." He glanced in his rearview. Still clear. "Can you think of anything else Charlie might've said that could be relevant?"

Becca was silent for a long moment, a frown of concentration on her face. She shook her head. "No. Although I keep wondering what kind of information would make him say he could prove Dad had been involved in something bad."

"It's a good question. And figuring that out might lead us to Charlie." Two more turns and Rixey eased the Charger into the lot behind the shop, his mind churning on the situation.

He backed into a spot, wanting an easy out in case he found himself needing to leave quick. Suddenly he was looking at everything differently. Now he saw a situation that needed a whole host of plan As and Bs. A security problem that required planning and redundancies and fail-safes. An operation that necessitated a team if it had a prayer in hell of being successful.

A mission that needed to be completed—with everyone

getting home safe and whole. At one time he'd committed his whole life to that very ideal.

Killing the engine, he was up and out of the car immediately, gun in hand, eyes working a three-sixty sweep. He opened Becca's door and offered her his palm.

She lifted the puppy to him, and Rixey made quick work of depositing her onto the ground.

Becca gasped. "She'll run away."

Helping her stand, he shook his head. "She defended you. Twice. She won't leave your side."

Flinching, Becca rose to her feet. "Man, I think I'm gonna need a fistful of ibuprofen and a bottle of wine for dinner."

He hated that she was hurting, but he was also glad she wasn't one of those people who refused to admit their limits. It took strength and courage to know when you were at the outside of what you could handle. It was a lesson Rixey wasn't sure he'd fully learned, so hell if he didn't find himself admiring that about her. Just one more thing in a growing list. "I think that can be arranged."

She reached the panel first and entered the code with no hesitation. The mechanism clicked free and they stepped inside, the fur ball rushing in ahead of them.

In the shade and security of the hallway, he managed to get the first deep draw of oxygen his lungs had had in hours. He holstered his weapon.

Becca whirled, almost pinning him against the door. Eyes of blue fire threatened to scorch him and held him captive. "All right, Nick. Enough. We're here. Start talking. Now."

Chapter 11

$\mathcal{B}$ecca's insides nearly vibrated with the need to know what the hell Nick wasn't telling her. She'd hit the edge of her tolerance for any more mystery, even of the tall, dark, and achingly handsome kind.

His lips pressed into a grim line and his eyes flashed. "Becca, let's just—"

"No." She stepped right into his space and jabbed a finger into the granite of his chest. "Don't put me off anymore. I deserve to know. I *need* to know," she said, hating the strained pitch of her voice.

His expression went dark and his jaw ticked. She saw it in his eyes the minute he made the decision to spill. Her stomach plummeted to the floor. It was bad. He didn't need to tell her that much. Everything inside her braced for the onslaught of bad news.

When he spoke, the words were even, straightforward,

factual. "Someone ransacked your house. Picked the back door lock again. Went through just about every room."

The brick walls bent and warped around her, but she shook off the dizziness and forced herself to focus on Nick's face. His presence was the only thing grounding her. "Why would they do that? Could you tell if anything was missing?"

He shook his head. "The why of it I intend to figure out. I promise you. But the place was too much of a mess to—"

"Take me." Becca pushed past him and hit the handle on the door.

Arms wrapped around her from behind. "Becca, we—"

"No!" She threw off the hold and scrambled away, her back coming up hard against the wall.

Nick's expression was a roiling sea of emotion. Surprise. Fear. Anger. Concern. "I'm sorry. What just—"

"That was how he grabbed me." She swallowed hard and shuddered at the remembered press of the man's flesh against hers. "I'm sorry," she rasped, embarrassment heating her face, despair and exhaustion sucking the fight out of her.

He came forward slowly. "Don't apologize," he said, his voice cranked tight. "And don't cry." His thumb swiped under her eye, once, twice, and then his knuckles caressed her cheekbone. The little touches were comforting, sweet, and she thought maybe he needed to give them as much as she needed to feel them. He tucked the loose strands of her destroyed ponytail behind her ear.

"I'm not crying," she said despite the wetness plain on her face. She shook her aching head, then pressed her cheek into his hand. "I'm not."

"I know."

Peering up at him, her breath caught.

The moment their gazes connected, his expression shifted from sympathetic concern to uncontrollable desire. His mouth fell open. His chest rose and fell against hers. His fingers burrowed into her hair.

Becca went hot all over, like the sun had hung itself in the stairwell above them.

He leaned closer, closer, his free arm bracing on the wall above her shoulder. The warm puff of his breath caressed her lips as his gaze bore into hers. She couldn't move, couldn't blink, couldn't breathe.

He kissed her on a groan so needful it made her dizzy and wet. His mouth devoured hers, his big hand cupped the back of her head, his body completely surrounded and trapped hers against the bricks. It was a full-body onslaught, with every part of him engaged in the act of claiming and seducing.

Becca clutched at his coat, his shoulders, his back, his hair. Anything to bring him closer, deeper. His lips pulled and tugged, his tongue stroked and twisted. He smelled of leather and mint and tasted like sin.

The harder he came at her, the more her conscious mind let go. Her aches, the stitches, her house, even Charlie—for a few minutes, just a few precious minutes, Becca let it all go.

The surrender was euphoric. It rushed through her blood and sent her flying.

"That was so close, Becca. Too close," he rasped, kissing her jaw, her ear, her neck, and sending her heart flying. His fingers stroked down over her breasts and found the hem of her shirt. And then those warm, calloused hands snaked up her stomach, pulled down the cups of her bra, and caressed her breasts skin to skin. He massaged her, teased her with roughened fingertips, and tormented her nipples until she was panting.

She gripped the collar of his coat, half afraid her knees would go soft and give out. Nick pulled his body away just enough to tear the coat off his arms and throw it to the floor. Geez, the gun holster was sexy hugging tight over his shirt, but he slipped out of it, too, and eased it to the floor with a *thunk*. Then his hands were back on her breasts and his tongue was back in her mouth, stealing her breath and convincing her she could live without it.

God, this kiss. It was the kind she'd remember forever, that would invade her dreams and haunt her in quiet moments. The kind her older self could look back on and know, once, she'd really lived. The kind that, no matter what, she could never, ever regret.

And it made a part of herself bloom with affection for the man who'd made her feel that way.

She snaked her hands under his shirt, moaning when her palm smoothed over the hard planes and muscled ridges of his abdomen, his sides, his chest. Her fingers swirled through the light covering of hair on his chest and swiped light, teasing brushes over his nipples. The low growls he released into the kiss as they explored each other thrilled her, made her yearn for the opportunity to bring a man as powerful and deadly as him to his knees in ecstasy.

"Closer," he ground out. With one arm, he ripped the cotton over his head, revealing a body that was no doubt capable of inflicting pleasure and pain in equal measure. Desire roared off his skin and his hands were everywhere, plucking at her nipples, kneading at the swell of her ass, pulling them harder together.

The heat of his demanding touches ripped through her and settled a pressing ache low in her abdomen. She squeezed her thighs together in response, emphasizing the wetness of her arousal against her panties.

"I want you, Becca. I'm not gonna lie." He spoke in low tones against her cheek, but pulled back to meet her gaze. "But I think—"

She placed three fingers over his mouth. "Don't think."

His eyes flared and his mouth dropped open. He caught her middle finger with his teeth and ran his tongue in tight circles over the tip, making it perfectly clear how good that particular action would feel if applied elsewhere. With a groan, he released her finger and dragged his hand around to cup the space between her legs. "Are you wet for me?"

Becca nodded, her heart doing its best imitation of a jackrabbit.

One of his eyebrows arched. "Yeah?" He slipped his hand into her scrub bottoms and under her panties. He kicked one of her feet to the side, opening her thighs to his touch. "Oh, fuck, sunshine, you are so wet." His fingers stroked through her folds, and her heart skipped a whole stanza of beats. Did he just call her—

His mouth came down on hers at the same time his thick middle finger penetrated her. He swallowed her moan as he mimicked the act they were barreling toward. "I am wound too tight, Becca. Do you understand? In about ten seconds, I'm going to be all over you. And I'm not going to be able to go slow. It's gonna be hard and fast and rough."

He meant it as a warning, but Becca heard it as an engraved invitation on fine linen paper. That was a party she sooo wanted to attend. "Good," she said, groaning as he removed his hand.

Green eyes blazing, Nick slipped his visibly wet finger between his lips and sucked. It was one of the most erotic things she'd ever seen.

With a sound that was nearly a growl, he retrieved his wallet from his back pocket and removed a condom. His gaze trapped her against the wall as if she couldn't move unless he told her to.

Suddenly, the floor went wavy under her feet, challenging her hold on reality. Was this really happening? Would someone see them? Did she care? Her headache flared behind her eyes and Nick went blurry, and then a rush of white noise shoved the questions away.

OUT OF NOWHERE, Becca swayed to the right.

Rixey grabbed her by the ribs, holding her steady. "Whoa, you okay?"

She sucked in a harsh breath and flinched away from his right hand, eyes flying wide, her pretty mouth shifting into a grimace.

Ice trickled down his spine and extinguished his arousal. "Shit, your stitches. I'm sorry." He dropped his righty to her hip, afraid she wasn't yet steady. What a fucking dog he was, crawling all over her when she was this vulnerable. Exactly what he'd said he wouldn't do. No matter how hard his body craved the connection. And not with just anyone. With *her*. But not like this. And not with everything that was going on. "I'm sorry," he said again, a wave of self-loathing turning his voice to gravel.

"It's okay," she said with a small, embarrassed smile.

He gave a humorless laugh. "It's about a million miles from okay. I shouldn't have—" The words stuck in his throat, because so many failures competed to flesh out the sentence. *I shouldn't have let you go to work this morning. I shouldn't have sent you away that first day. I shouldn't have tasted your juices on my tongue, because now I'll never be able to forget just how sweet you are.* "Something about you Merritts screws with my judgment every time."

"What? What's that supposed to mean?" she asked, that little frown of hers filling the space between her eyes.

Smooth, Rixey. "Nothing. You steady?" Because he really needed to stop touching her.

"Steadier. It's just a headache. But I want to know what you meant." She fixed her bra and crossed her arms over her breasts. Fierce animation roared back into her eyes.

"Not a goddamned thing, Becca." Giving her a last, searching look, he dropped his hands and bent for his T-shirt. He tugged it back on, failing to force away the re-membered feeling of her hands on his skin, then grabbed his jacket and slung his holster loosely over one shoulder. "I'll take you upstairs. You should rest."

"I'll go upstairs, but I'm not resting. We still haven't finished talking, you and I. If someone broke into my house, I should go there. Call the police. *Something*. This can't all be coincidence." A flush on her cheeks replaced the pallor from moments before.

"I know, but we can't."

She froze. "Why the hell not?"

He heaved a weary sigh, not sure what he was going to do if she insisted. "On the phone earlier, Miguel made it sound like there's a reason we shouldn't report the second break-in. He wanted to tell us in person. I trust him im-plicitly, so I'd like to wait to hear what he says. He'll be over as soon as he can. But it is your decision."

She rubbed the skin above her eye, bringing his gaze to the bruise forming on her forehead. "You really think it's better to wait?"

"I don't think Miguel would advise that unless he had a good reason."

"God. What now?" Her shoulders sagged and she rubbed her forehead again. "Okay. I'll hear him out. And thank you for being straight with me." She sighed and turned, then crossed the stairwell to where the puppy lay curled in a ball by the door to Hard Ink. "You've been waiting patiently, haven't you?" she said.

Rixey caught up with her, hollow pressure expanding in his chest at the sadness saddling her shoulders and dimming the lightness he'd admired about her from the start. He wanted that back. For her. For himself. "Wanna see something funny?" he asked, hoping his idea might replace the anger and hurt in her expression. She shrugged, her guard back up again. "Open the door and let—what's her name?"

"I don't know yet," she said. "Maybe Sadie. Or Georgia."

"What about Cujo?"

Her disapproving expression was almost comical, and it was a lot better than what she'd worn a moment before. "Cujo is a boy's name, and he was a crazy killing menace. Plus Cujo was a Saint Bernard."

Rixey winked, and she rolled her eyes. "Well, then, open the door and let Sadie-or-Georgia in by herself. We'll hang back and see what happens." All right, it was probably stupid, but if it made her smile, he was all for it. No plan was stupid if it worked . . .

She glanced from him to the puppy, who was now sitting up and watching the two of them talk like she knew the conversation was about her.

Nick opened the door from the private stairwell, and Sadie-or-Georgia loped in. He and Becca followed, and she now wore an amused expression. They peeked around the corner and watched as the puppy sauntered around the empty lounge for a few minutes before making its way up the hall between the tattoo rooms toward the front.

"What in the hell?" came Jeremy's voice out of one. "Hey, Jess, what is walking—"

A shriek sounded from the lobby. "Holy shit." Jess's laughter followed a moment later. "Somebody lost a tripod," she snickered.

Becca had her hand pressed to her mouth, and the rise in her cheeks told him she was enjoying the show.

"Hey! No! Gimme that back," Jess yelled.

The puppy trotted down the hall again, something red

in its mouth. Jessica barreled after her with a scowl on her made-up face.

"Is that a dog?" Jeremy yelled. "Why is there a dog?"

Beside Nick, Becca was giggling.

And then the dance started. The puppy rounded one of the tables with its prize clutched tight between its teeth. Jess chased her to the right, and the puppy dashed left. Then Jess veered to the left, and the puppy ran right. "C'mere, you little thief!"

Becca snorted. "I should help her." They stepped out from their hiding place and Jess glared. "I'm sorry," Becca said, humor coloring her voice. "I'll help."

Jess waved her away. "No, no. I'll get it. It's fine."

"Come here, puppy," Becca called and snapped her fingers. "Come here, girl."

Jess hiked herself up on the table, scooted her butt across, and dropped down on the other side, surprising the dog by changing the rules of the game. The puppy growled and took off like a cartoon, her legs taking a minute to find purchase before she shot around the other table. "You little fucker, c'mere!"

Rixey stood with his arms crossed and watched the circus unfold. Much as she tried, Becca couldn't stop laughing. This was even better than he'd hoped for.

Jess got in a swipe at the dog's tail and the shepherd barked around the scrap of fabric in her mouth.

Jeremy stepped out of the tattoo room wearing his mask and gloves. "What in the holy hell is going on out here?" The dog shot toward him and Jeremy crouched and caught her in a body hold. "Uh, hello." He looked up. "We have a dog now?"

Becca smiled. "She's mine."

Jess stepped forward. "Um, Jeremy."

Wagging her tail, Sadie-or-Georgia deposited its prize on Jeremy's knee. He set the dog down and looped his gloved finger under a string. Holding it up, he pulled his mask off and arched a brow at Jess.

It was a thong.

Jess dove for it.

Jeremy rose in a flash and held it above his head. Short as Jessica was, she didn't have a prayer.

"Jeremy Rixey, I will kill you."

He hugged her tight against his chest and cocked his gaze up toward the panties. There was writing. *If you can read this, it's your lucky day.* He barked out a laugh.

Becca grinned, her expression halfway between sympathy for Jess and hysterics. Nick should've known that between Jeremy and Jessica, letting the dog in here would lead to some sort of slapstick antics.

"I have to ask why you have panties here and how the hell the mutt got 'em."

Jess stomped her knee-high black boot. "Just give them to me."

Jeremy reached up with his other hand and held the thong so it hung straight, all except for one loose string. "Why are they—?" His eyebrows flew up under his long hair. "Are these *ripped*?"

The phone rang, the ringer echoing between the office and the front desk.

Jess braced her hands on her hips and tapped her toe. "Give. Them."

"Not until you tell me why they're—"

"Because, unlike *you,* I had sex last night and the guy ripped my thong off. Are you satisfied?"

Jeremy's expression froze.

"Probably not as well as you are," Becca said. Despite her bright red cheeks, she met all three sets of eyes that whipped her way. Damn, she wore that mixture of embarrassment and daring so well it shot right to Rixey's cock.

Jeremy burst out laughing, and even Jess gave her a

begrudging chuckle right before she punched Jer in the stomach. He grunted and handed over her panties. With a flip of red and black pigtails, she marched toward the front desk.

Through it all, Rixey couldn't stop watching Becca. The way she laughed and smiled, the ease with which she teased and joked with Jeremy. Rixey remembered back to when she'd first walked through Hard Ink's front door. He'd thought her sweet and innocent. The girl next door. And maybe a part of her was those things. But she was also the woman who'd come at him with a knife, who'd resisted a significantly bigger man attempting to abduct her, who'd tried her hand at boxing without any self-consciousness. The woman who'd kissed him. The first woman he'd kissed in over a year. And the woman who made him want so much more.

Too bad he didn't deserve any of it, though that didn't stop him from wanting her comforting touch, her warm body, her light chasing away his dark. Selfish bastard.

"Hey, Nicholas," Jess called, knowing he disliked his full name. "Miguel's on the phone."

Becca turned to him with a grin. "Nicholas?"

He arched a brow and made for the office. "It's Nick. Or Rixey. Or 'Hey you.' "

"Or asshole," Jeremy offered, stripping off his now dirty gloves and returning to his client.

"Preferable to Nicholas," Rixey said over his shoulder. As he turned into the office and lifted the receiver, he wondered why the hell Miguel was calling him on the landline. "Hey, Miguel."

"Hi, Nick. Wanted to let you know I got held up with an issue with one of my clients. I'm still coming over, it'll just be a while."

"That's fine, but why are you—"

"Calling on the landline? Because I didn't want to delay

getting you some information before I can get over there and fill in the details. And this is more secure."

If someone was so inclined, it was much easier to pick up a conversation from a cell phone. The fact that Miguel was taking precautions against that meant he was worried. Rixey pushed the office door closed. "Okay. What's going on?"

"I called my guy at BPD to report the break-in and find out who'd covered the scene the day before. Report hadn't been filed yet. He couldn't even readily put his hands on who the lead investigator was. And none of the evidence was in the database. So I asked about the missing persons investigation on Charlie Merritt—"

"Let me guess. They're not taking it seriously." Rixey sank into the desk chair.

"No. That one hadn't been filed either."

Rixey sat forward, suspicion prickling over his skin. "Are you shitting me?"

Miguel heaved a breath that made its way down the line. "I wish I were. I don't want to speculate about what this means before checking out a few more things. Speaking of which, do you know if Becca called nine-one-one during any of this?"

"Twice that I know of. When she found the break-in at her brother's and last night when she realized there was an intruder in her house. Why?"

"I want to look into something. I found her home number online, but do you have her cell, too?"

"Yeah. Hold on." Rixey fished through the recent dials on his cell and recited the number.

"Listen, just hold tight. I'll help you work this if that's what it comes to."

"Thanks, Miguel. See you when you get here." Nick replaced the receiver and sank heavily against the backrest.

This snafu was spinning out of control. One missing

person, three break-ins, a kidnapping, and, at best, nonco-
operative police? All of which might also have something
to do with Frank Merritt? Way more than he could handle
on his own, even with Miguel's help.

Rixey knew what he had to do.

But it was gonna suck ass to make the ask. At this point,
his former Special Forces teammates owed him a whole
lotta nothing. It was possible they wouldn't even listen.
But if they did, it was shit to call needing a favor after
falling out of touch. He was going to have to own that,
though, and choke down whatever grief they wanted to
give him.

And, damn it all to hell, if they agreed to help, they
might very well have to do this outside the technical con-
fines of the law.

That was a fucking lot to ask from anyone.

But if Frank Merritt *was* at the bottom of this mess,
he and his men might have a shot at not only protecting
Charlie and Becca but also restoring the honor of everyone on the team. And Rixey would give just about anything to make that happen.

He just hoped he wasn't alone.

Chapter 12

The first one Rixey had to talk to was Shane McCallan, not just because they'd been close but also because Shane had made so many attempts to reach out. The intelligence specialist could curse you out in more languages than you'd ever heard of and had medic training to boot. He and Nick had served together in the Army Special Forces for six years, much of that time in Afghanistan. Until the day their A-Team's convoy was ambushed under highly suspicious circumstances and they were all blamed for the deaths of seven men in a cover-up of mind-boggling proportions.

Now Shane worked for a defense contractor in Northern Virginia. He had landed a lot more squarely on his feet than Rixey, and Nick was truly glad that his onetime best friend seemed to be doing a helluva lot more than getting by.

Nick placed the call.

Each ring reverberated against his innards, making him shift in his office chair. These conversations were likely to be as comfortable as an eyeful of sand, which should have the upside at least of distracting him from the fact that Becca had decided to soak in a hot bath down the hall—

Someone picked up. Then there was a long pause that made Rixey press the phone more firmly to his ear. "Nick," Shane finally said. "Long time." There was nothing welcoming in the man's voice. His words were clipped so tight they even hid his usual hint of a southern drawl.

Rixey expected nothing less. "Shane. I know. And I'm sorry for that—"

"Save it."

Shit. Rixey blew out a breath. "I fucked up."

"You calling to walk down memory lane?"

In for a penny . . . "No. I got a situation."

Shane's humorless laugh was like a fist to the gut. "You calling me for a favor, Nick Rixey?"

No sense beating around the bush, not when the damn thing was on fire and throwing off sparks all over the place. "Yeah, I am."

"Son of a bitch."

"Pretty much. Will you at least hear me out?"

"You're seriously asking *me* that question?" Rixey had to pull the cell away from his ear. "After months of refusing to answer a single one of my phone calls or shoot back an email? Hell, a message saying 'Fuck you very much' would've been better than the friggin' silent treatment."

"You're right."

"Damn straight I am."

Shane was entitled to every bit of his anger, but Nick didn't have time for the kind of venting his friend would require before they could ever have a chance to be squared away. Time to cut to the chase. "My situation has some-thing to do with Merritt's extracurricular activities." At least that was the conclusion his brain kept coming back to when he tried to make sense of what Charlie'd told Becca. And now with Becca's police reports conveniently disappearing from record? Man, that took him right back to the cover-ups after the ambush.

An arctic blast made its way down the line. "I'm listen-ing. For now."

It was enough of an opening. The rest of the story should blow it wide. "Fair enough. Somehow that shit spilled stateside and landed on Merritt's kids. Son's missing. Daughter came to me for help and was nearly kidnapped today. Both their houses have been tossed. Someone's looking for something."

"And I should care about the old man's kids why?"

Rixey thought about this for a moment, shoving down the knee-jerk responses and really chewing on what he thought could possibly be at stake. Finally, he said, "Be-cause my gut's telling me what our bad guys are looking for is somehow connected to what happened to us. And there just might be an opportunity here to get our hands on some intel that would allow us to prove our innocence, to prove that we were railroaded right out of the damn Army. I'm talking about a chance to reclaim our honor. For the five of us—*and* for the six who never made it off the road that day." He never counted Merritt among the losses, not when he'd caused them. Was the same reason the tat on his arm only commemorated six soldiers.

"Shit," Shane said, the southern lilt returning to his words. "Just how far out on a limb are you with that bit of speculation?"

"Possibly pretty far. Maybe all the way." But Rixey had heard the consideration in his friend's voice. "But maybe closer than I think, too."

"Your gut's a fucking burr on my balls."

The corner of Rixey's mouth twitched. *Come on, Shane.*

"When do you want me?"

On Becca's behalf, relief had Nick easing against the chair's backrest to let his head fall back. He stared at the ceiling. "As soon as you can get here. Tonight."

"Course you do. Fucker." Rixey could almost hear the wheels turning in McCallan's brain. "Fine. I'll throw some things in a bag and hit the road. You still at your brother's?"

"Yeah."

"With rush hour, it'll probably take me an hour and a half to get there."

"Roger that. And thanks."

Shane disconnected without a reply.

Pulling the phone from his ear, Rixey prepared to eat his next big helping of crow. His next of three. Only question was whether Beckett Murda, Edward Cantrell, and Derek DiMarzio would give him the same chance as Shane.

And there was only one way to find out.

BECCA CAME AWAKE on a gasp, the sensation of being watched sending her heart into an immediate sprint. After her bath, which she'd had to keep on the shallow side because of the stitches, she'd curled up on the couch and turned the TV on for background noise while she'd waited for Nick to finish with his calls and his friend Miguel to arrive. But the combination of her recent lack of sleep and the aftereffects of the attack at the hospital had made it impossible to keep her eyes open. Her nap hadn't been particularly restful, though, as nightmares kept jolting her into bleary-eyed consciousness. She pushed up onto her elbow and found Nick standing at the foot of the sofa.

"Sorry," he said.

She shook her head and slid into a sitting position in the corner, her knees tucked up underneath her. The puppy was curled on the floor in front of her, and she only opened her eyes long enough to make sure Becca was still there. "Everything okay?" she asked. Nick's expression was like a storm, dark and turbulent, but she had no idea what could've caused it. Before her bath, he'd seemed quiet, almost pensive, but not agitated the way he did now.

"Everything's fine." His hands curled into fists.

She wished she knew how to help him, how to lighten whatever load he carried. Oh, who was she kidding? The load she'd pretty much dropped on top of him. Becca patted the leather cushion. "Sit with me?"

On a tired exhale, Nick settled into the far end of the leather sofa. He braced a still-booted foot against his knee. After hours of being in his own home, he still hadn't fully relaxed. She was half surprised he wasn't wearing his holster.

For a moment, she allowed herself to admire him— the strong profile, the curl of dark hair at his neckline, the band of ink around his thick bicep, the way the black denim clung to the bulk of his thigh muscles. He was so freaking gorgeous, it was hard *not* to look at him.

But it wasn't just the physical, impressive as that was, that drew Becca in. He wore weariness like a second skin, maybe one he didn't even realize he'd donned. She saw it in the tense set of his broad shoulders, like they bore an unseen weight. In the shadows of his yellow-green eyes, which never quite reflected humor or happiness even in those rare instances when he smiled. As someone who'd experienced way too much loss, Becca knew what grief felt like, the way it both hollowed you out and weighed you down. As a nurse, she was used to seeing people in pain. She knew what it looked like. The loss, the grief, the pain—it was sitting right in front of her. And it made her feel closer to him, or at least it made her *want* to be closer.

"I'm sorry about all this," she said.

He looked her way. "What?"

Becca shifted toward him. "I pretty much just crash-landed into your life."

He studied her for a long moment, something dark flashing behind his eyes, then he nodded. "I just hope I can help."

"You already have."

Without the least attempt to shield it, Nick ran his gaze over Becca's body, clad in a plain lavender shirt and jeans. She shivered under his avid interest, as if it had been his fingers responsible for the exploration. Heat ran over her flesh, remembering all too well how good his touch felt. God, they'd come so close to having se—

"Are you okay, Becca? When I came into that room, and he had you halfway out that door, a blade in your side . . ." His hand gripped tight around his ankle and he looked away.

She scooted herself onto the middle cushion but stopped shy of touching him. His body almost vibrated with tension. "Nick, look at me." When he did, she smiled. "We don't know each other well, right? But I promise to be honest with you." His brow furrowed, and she rushed to explain her words. "I want you to know that, especially with everything you're doing for me. So, in the spirit of honesty, I'm ready to crawl out of my skin over Charlie, my joints ache, these damn stitches sting like crazy, and my headache still hasn't gone away. And I'm pissed as *hell* about . . . all of it." She reached out and placed her palm on his forearm, stroking her thumb over the corded muscle. "But I'm okay. By morning, the worst of the aches will be gone. Until then, ibuprofen is my friend."

His jaw ticked and his gaze fell to her hand. "I don't know all the details yet, but I think Miguel's worried we can't trust the police."

Can't trust the police? Blood rushed through her ears until it thumped out an echo of the quickening pace of her heart. She forced herself to take a calming breath, not that it really worked. "Then how can we—"

"I called some friends, the remains of my team. Your father's team," he said, an odd tenor to his voice.

Her mouth dropped open. She'd never met any of the men on her dad's A-Team. Heard a few stories, but that was about it. By the time she became an adult, her father's deployment averaged over three hundred days a year. Sometimes she thought the other SF guys were more his family than she was. "The other four." Without meaning to, her gaze dropped to his tattoo. With the *six* soldiers.

He nodded. "They're all on their way. Three of them will be here tonight." He looked at the chunky black watch on his wrist. "Probably within the next hour or so. The fourth is flying in tomorrow morning. These guys are the best. We'll come up with a plan to figure this thing out."

The news was good, a relief even, and prickled over Becca's skin. "Wow. That's . . . amazing." But didn't it also mean that . . . "Wait. If you guys are going to go after whoever has Charlie, whoever attacked me . . ." She searched his gaze. "Without the police . . ."

"If Miguel's suspicions pan out, there's no other way to do this now but off the grid."

Becca's stomach dropped. "But you could get in trouble. If something happened, you guys could—"

"*You're* already in trouble, Becca. We can handle it."

"I don't doubt that." She shook her head. "But why would they do this for us? Me and Charlie, I mean." Why were these strangers dropping what they were doing and coming here? And how could she ask these men who'd already sacrificed so much to give even more? She frowned, guilt making her head throb harder.

"Because I asked them to. Simple as." Something dark and protective flashed behind his eyes.

It's for Charlie, Bec.

Becca latched onto that thought and hugged it tight. Maybe their camaraderie with her father drew them to this, the desire to help their fallen commander's family? "Okay," she said, finally. "I don't know how I'm ever going to thank you. Any of you. I don't think this is the kind of thing where a case of your favorite beer suffices."

"Don't thank us yet. Come on, why don't we go downstairs?" He rose, scaring the puppy awake. "I'll introduce you to everyone when they get here. In the meantime, you can harass Jeremy."

Becca smiled. "Well, with an offer like that." She scooped the shepherd into her arms and stood, her muscles protesting the movement after lying there so long. "What do you think of Phoebe?" When he frowned, she nodded to the dog.

He grimaced. "Too . . . dainty. Or something. And the 'ph' is weird. How 'bout Spike? After those ears." He rounded the couch and headed toward the door.

She followed after. "I'm not sure you get this whole naming concept. Boys get boy names. Girls get girl names. *She* can't be a Spike."

He shrugged as he opened and closed the door for her. "Better than Phoebe." They made their way downstairs, where, much to Nick's consternation, they had to pause to let the puppy out back to do some business.

The evening air had a chill to it as they stood in the gravel watching the dog sniff every blade of grass around the edge of the lot. *Where are you, Charlie?*

"I need to get a leash and a collar for her. And food. And all the other stuff a dog needs," Becca said, trying to distract herself. Jess had run up to the convenience store and bought a small bag of food earlier, but it wouldn't last long. "You know, when I decided to keep her this afternoon, I thought I'd be going home again."

His gaze cut to hers. "It's no trouble." He shrugged and watched the dog's dark silhouette. "We always had dogs growing up."

She hugged herself. "Yeah? Us, too. What kind?"

"Just mutts. But they were awesome."

Becca nodded and pressed her lips together to keep from uttering the *awww* that nearly slipped out. Something told her Nick wouldn't love being thought of as sweet. "Come on, puppy," she called, clapping her hands. The dog loped out of the darkness toward them.

"What about Killer?" he said as he opened the back door. "That's gender neutral."

They crossed the stairwell hallway, and Becca couldn't decide whether to laugh at Nick or ask if he'd been dropped on his head as a small child.

Inside Hard Ink's lounge, Jeremy sat at one of the tables drawing against a sheet of dark purple tracing paper. "What are you crazy kids doing?"

"I'm trying to pick a name for the puppy, and your brother isn't helping."

Smiling up at her, Jer said, "You can put her down if you want."

"I don't know. Last time I did that she ended up uncovering sex secrets."

Jeremy barked out a laugh as Jess called from one of the tattoo rooms, "I heard that!"

Joining Jer at the table where he was tracing a large cross with a banner and flowers around it, Becca put the dog on the ground. "What are you doing?"

"Creating a stencil that will transfer the outline of the design to a client's skin."

"Oh. So you don't just freehand it?"

"There is a style of tattooing called freehand, but that refers to drawing with markers directly on a person's skin instead of stenciling on the design. Either way, the tattooist has a guideline on the skin. You really gotta know what you're doing to freehand without any lines. I'd never do it. The skin's just too pliable."

"Oh."

Flicking at his lip piercing, he looked up at her. "You got any tattoos, Becca?"

"No."

He grinned. "Want one?"

"Oh, I don't know." She glanced at Nick, who was studying her, like he was waiting for her answer, too. Man, the thought of his hands drawing on her . . .

"Well, you just ask, darling, and I'm your man."

Nick unleashed a sigh that was almost a growl, and Jer just laughed. Most of the time, Nick was so reserved. She kinda adored his brother's ability to get under his skin, not to mention Nick's apparent displeasure at Jeremy's flirting.

"So, I have another question," she said, changing the topic. "What do you think of Phoebe for the dog's name?"

He finished tracing a line and glanced up at her, his face thoughtful. "How the hell do you spell it?"

Nick held out his hands. "See."

She rolled her eyes but couldn't help smiling. "Yeah, yeah."

Jess stuck her head out of her room, her shoulder-length black and red hair braided to the side. "I still vote for Tripod."

Becca chuckled. "That's . . . terrible."

Jeremy snickered. "Or Hopalong."

"You guys!"

"Skippy," Nick said, a smirk forming on his sexy lips.

"Three-Speed," Jeremy said in a completely serious voice.

Both the guys burst out laughing.

"Hey, what about Trinity?" Jess called.

Becca glared at the idiot men. "Thank you! A semi-serious name, finally." She held her hand out to the dog, who came over and gave a few wet kisses. "You guys be nice or I will totally sic her on you. Look at her, you'd never even know she was missing a leg the way she gets around." And it was true. She was mostly pretty steady on her feet.

The older Rixey finally managed to pull himself together, though it was hard to really be mad at him when he almost never laughed like that. He leaned his elbows on the table and looked her way. "Becca? I'd like to catch Jeremy up on everything if you don't mind."

She glanced between them. "Oh, yeah. Sure."

Jeremy paused from his drawing. "What's up?"

Nick recounted the day's events, from the attempted abduction to the damage at her house—which dropped a bucket of jagged rocks in her stomach every time she imagined how bad it could be. Then he explained that his Army buddies were going to be congregating at their place for the weekend, but he was vague about the why of their visit. Listening to the recounting of her day, Becca found it really damn hard to believe he was talking about her life.

When Nick was done, Jeremy sat, drop-jawed, looking at her, his gaze lingering on the bump on her forehead. He dragged his hand through his dark hair. "Are you okay?"

She shrugged. "Yeah. I kinda want to see my house, though."

Nick pressed his lips into a firm line. "It's not safe. Not yet. Maybe once we have a plan and the guys are all here?"

It *wasn't* safe. It didn't take a brain surgeon to figure that out after the house had been broken into twice in twenty-four hours, but not knowing how bad and what was broken and whether anything had been taken made every worst-case scenario larger than life in her mind. *Stuff* was all she had left of most of her family members, so it was hard not to worry about it. Still, figuring out how to track down Charlie was far more important than whatever had been done at her house. "Okay."

Jess and her client walked out of the tattoo room, and the twenties-ish woman was all smiles over the colorful stars-and-flowers design that now covered her wrist under a wrap of plastic. It was pretty. *I could do something like that. Though I'd want it to mean something.* Becca glanced at Rixey's hands, sending an odd flutter through her stomach.

The buzzer screeched in the front lobby.

"Probably my client," Jeremy said, rising.

"I'll get him checked in," Jess said, leading the girl to the front. A moment later, Jess ducked back around the corner. "Uh, guys," she stage whispered. "There's a big-ass male model out here."

Becca grinned, but Nick flew out of his chair. "Don't call him that, Jess. It'll go right to his frickin' head."

"Which one?" she asked with a grin as he stepped around her and went out front.

"Have you met any of these guys?" Becca asked Jeremy, who had turned to watch Nick leave.

Flicking at the piercing on his bottom lip, he shook his head. "No. He's pretty tight-lipped about them. Not the kind to tell war stories or anything." Her dad had pretty much been the same way. She could really only say she knew one of his military colleagues well, and that was because her father and General Landon Kaine had been friends since their days at West Point. He'd visited their house from time to time.

Just when Becca thought Nick had been gone a really long time, he and another man made their way toward the lounge. And, holy wow, if men could be pretty, this guy was. Tall and lean, his light brown hair was short on the sides and longer on top, where the blond-tipped ends stuck up this way and that like he'd run his hands through it a million times. His steel gray eyes held a natural smile in their depths, and if God had ever used a chisel on a man's jaw, it was this guy's.

"Everyone, this is Shane McCallan," Nick said in a tone of voice that seemed reserved, even for him. "Shane, this is my brother, Jeremy."

"The smarter Rixey, I presume," Shane said with a hint of a southern accent.

They shook and Jeremy smiled. "I like you already."

"You already met Jess." Shane shook her hand with a wink, and Becca swore the normally kick-ass woman went weak in the knees. *The Shane Effect,* she thought, twisting her lips to hide her smile. "And this is Becca Merritt," Nick said.

Those gray eyes locked onto hers for a long moment, but apparently his secret swoon power didn't work on her. Instead, she found herself looking away to wonder at the shadows that'd settled over Nick's expression. "I'm sorry to hear about your brother," Shane finally said, offering his hand.

She returned the shake. "Thanks. And thanks for coming."

The man cut his steely gaze at Nick and jammed his hands in the pockets of his slacks. "Well, when a brother asks for something, it's only right to step up." The room went frosty as the two stared at each other.

The buzzer sounded out front again.

"I'll get it," Nick said.

He returned a few minutes later with a giant of a man who had a noticeable limp. A blue-eyed blond with a warrior's face, serious and utterly masculine. Scars marred the skin all around his right eye, making her wonder if whatever had caused them had affected his sight. Taller than Nick or Shane, and broader, too. The guy might've been a linebacker from the size of his neck and shoulders under the dark sports coat.

Linebacker did the hand-clasp-one-shoulder-bump greeting with Shane like the old friends they were, and while he repeated the action with Nick, there was a hesitation there that niggled at her stomach. Nick introduced him as Beckett Murda, and, as the greetings went around again, a feeling of protectiveness for Nick crawled up Becca's spine.

Beckett stepped forward and extended his bear mitt of a hand to her. "Miss Merritt," he said as they shook. She gave her thanks once again and he nodded. While he didn't go at Nick with the outward sarcasm Shane had exhibited, Becca watched for and saw the two of them throw icy sideways glances at each other.

Where was the camaraderie and brotherhood she'd expected from soldiers who'd been where they'd been and done all that they'd done? Not here, that was for damn sure. Tension pulsed off the three former teammates, but Becca kept her questions to herself. For now.

Thank God for Jeremy. The guy could ease anyone into a conversation, she was sure of it. Before long, she'd learned that Shane worked for a defense contractor in Northern Virginia and had grown up outside of Richmond. And, while Beckett proved a harder sell on conversational chitchat, he shared a little about his work doing private security. Becca mostly hung on the sidelines, preferring to listen and get the lay of the land about who these men were who'd be helping her and Charlie.

Odder was that Nick stayed on the periphery, too. Even Jess participated more.

Becca wasn't sure how much time had passed when the front buzzer went off.

"I'll go see who it is," Nick offered again, disappearing from the group. "Jeremy, it's your client," he called. Jer excused himself just as the front door set off the buzzer one more time. A few minutes later, Nick led another man down the hall—the last expected arrival for the night, according to what he'd told Becca earlier.

This guy was about Nick's height, with skin so dark it was almost black. He had a killer smile and a bald head, and the form-fitting, long-sleeved shirt he wore didn't make her guess at all about how cut he was underneath. But what Becca most appreciated was that he seemed more relaxed, less hostile around Nick.

"Everyone, this is Edward Cantrell," Nick said, introducing Jeremy, Jess, and her in turn.

"Becca," Edward said. Was she imagining it, or was his smile not quite as bright when he said hello to her?

Nick took a deep breath, as if steeling himself. "Well, you all have come a long way, and it's late. Let's head upstairs."

As the men made for the door, Nick avoided Becca's gaze. At the back door to Hard Ink, he directed them up the stairs and gave them the code to the apartment. Then he came back to her.

Becca arched an eyebrow, already bracing for a fight. The *you're-not-invited* vibe had been loud and clear, which was stirring up a hornet's nest in her brain.

And he knew it, too. He gently took her by the shoulders. "Wait. Before you go off, hear me out. There's no way you didn't pick up on the tension. Let me hash some things out with them and catch them up on the basics. We won't make any plans without you."

She studied his eyes and could see only sincerity there. The urge to fight dialed back a notch. "Okay, but what's with all the cold shoulders?"

He shook his head. "Just gimme a while with them, okay?"

When she nodded, he turned to go. From the stairwell, his boots echoed as he pounded up the steps.

"Damn," Jess said, plopping onto one of the couches. "I think I should've joined the Army. Cause I would ride that convoy all day long." Her face squinched up. "Not Nick, I mean. Just, you know, the other three."

Becca laughed and crossed to sit with Jess. The puppy curled into a ball on the floor in between their feet. Jess launched into a running commentary on Nick's team-mates, and, outwardly, Becca laughed and smiled in all the right places. But on the inside all she could think about was the ringing of her internal alarm system that said the arrival of these men somehow made everything a lot more complicated.

Chapter 13

$\mathcal{R}$ixey stepped into his apartment, and three sets of eyes swung toward him. Man, this was gonna suck before it got better.

Almost a year ago, they'd barely limped back to base when it had become clear someone had been spinning the ambush in a way that had buried the knives so deep in their backs they weren't ever coming out. From that moment, they'd existed in a state of collective outraged pissed off—one in which Rixey still lived. As if their friends' deaths and their own injuries hadn't been bad enough, the realization that the commander they'd respected and admired had lied to them and betrayed them for a little green had poured salt on the wounds.

Worse, when the shit had hit the fan, Mother Army hadn't had their backs. No one had believed their version of the ambush, that it had been the result of some sort of underhanded black op gone bad on Merritt's part. No fucking sir. Instead, their fitness reports had suddenly included marks for "needs improvement" and low ratings that hadn't been there before. Records of fighting and disorderly conduct and other disciplinary infractions had materialized out of thin air in the personnel files of the team's survivors, discrediting them piece by piece until blame for the ambush had stuck to them like white on rice. It had been like falling down a fucking rabbit hole. The only way to stop the free fall had been to choose between a dishonorable discharge, which had included an all-expenses-paid vacation to Leavenworth, or an other than honorable discharge, where they might live to fight another day.

They'd packed up their corroded reputations—because that shit wasn't just *tarnished*—and chosen the latter. Not because they'd feared a trial but because some brass inside the Army—or possibly higher—*had* to have been pulling strings, making prison all but a done deal. The who and why of it was a complete mystery. And the NDA the Army had required as part of the deal had made it so they couldn't talk to anyone outside the team without risking their freedom. But maybe, *just maybe,* Charlie had found a string they could pull to unravel that motherfucker once and for all.

It could be the chance he'd been yearning for all these long months to restore his name, his reputation, his honor. He just hoped the team saw it that way, too.

As Rixey approached the group, a part of himself flickered back online. He'd missed the company of these guys the way an amputee missed an appendage. Being with them again both eased the phantom ache and worsened it, because they could never really be whole again. Not with six of them cold in the ground. Seven, if you included their commander. Nick didn't.

Beckett and Easy—Edward's nickname after his initials, E.C.—sat on stools at the breakfast bar making small talk. Shane stood at the far end, arms crossed, his expression a stone wall.

"Thanks for coming," Nick said, mirroring Shane's position at the opposite end of the bar. The metaphor was a kick in the ass—them facing off instead of standing together as they had for so many years.

"What happened to Merritt's daughter's face?" Beckett asked, being his usual hard-ass self. He knew her first name, and Rixey had no doubt he'd phrased it that way to keep their CO front and center in everyone's minds. Like they could ever forget. And like Beckett wasn't convinced he wanted to help her.

Then again, hadn't his own first reaction been the same? "Attempted abduction today. She fought the guy off. Got the goose egg on her forehead and four stitches from a stab wound to the ribs for her troubles. The scratches by her eye were an accident."

Beckett stared at him a long moment, surprise and appreciation flickering through his gaze. Second to appealing to their bone-deep desire to redeem their honor, Becca was probably his strongest asset in getting through to these guys. They were pissed and wary—and rightly so. But the urge to help, serve, and do the right thing was also stamped into their DNA.

"Why don't you start from the beginning," Shane said.

Nick gave a tight nod and resisted the memories of how many other times he'd given briefings and orders to these men. This wasn't the Army. He wasn't their second in command. And he wasn't the same man he'd been then. *Goddamnit.* "Becca came to me two days ago. Her brother was missing, and the last communication she'd received from him told her to find me. I turned her away." That got their attention. Shane uncrossed his arms and braced himself against the counter. Easy sat up straighter on his stool. "I didn't want anything to do with the Merritts or whatever trouble they had. But I couldn't shake wondering why her brother Charlie, who I'd never met, would tell her to seek my help. Why he'd specifically tell her in a note that I was a member of their father's Special Forces team."

"How'd he know who you were?" Beck asked.

"Not sure. Maybe Merritt talked shop with them at some point? Or something in his personal effects?" Nick shrugged, and the small movement revealed how much tension had settled into his shoulders. The air was heavy with it. "What was even more interesting was why, once he found me, Charlie thought I'd be able to help with whatever trouble he's in." He still couldn't shake the feeling there was something there. "So I kept an eye on Becca to see if there was really anything going on. Last night, I chased an intruder out of her house. He'd been digging around in her office, by the looks of things. That's when she told me Charlie's house had been tossed a few days before."

Easy clasped his big hands in front of him. "Sounds like some bad juju, but I'm not seeing a connection." Around the bar, heads nodded.

Rixey glanced between the men and hoped his next information was the same money shot for them as it'd been for him. "After the break-in, Becca mentioned that she and Charlie fought before he went missing. He's a hacker, and he told her he'd found something that proved their father wasn't who she thought he was." Rixey paused, giving that a beat to sink in. "Since he said that, he's gone missing, someone's broken into and searched both their houses, and someone tried to grab her today. Whoever this is came back and took a second swing at Becca's place sometime last night. Turned the place upside down.

Somebody's clearly looking for something from the Merritts and not finding it. Yet."

"Jesus," Shane bit out.

"Merritt wasn't who any of us thought he was," Easy said. His tight monotone belied the white-hot anger flashing behind the man's dark eyes. Rixey wasn't the only one still existing in that state of outraged pissed off, apparently. But that's what happened when someone tried to strip a man of his honor.

Nick met each of their gazes, looking for the smallest evidence that he was getting their buy-in on this. So far, that was about as clear as mud. "Exactly. So, the sixty-four-thousand-dollar question is, what did Merritt's son find that led him to the same conclusion?"

"Any idea how good a hacker he is?" Beckett asked in a low, calculating voice.

"Good enough that companies pay him to test their cybersecurity measures by attempting to hack in. Beyond that, dunno."

Shane heaved a deep breath. "There's a lot of circumstantial bullshit here, Nick. It's like *if* times *maybe* divided by *could be* to the hundredth power. *If* Charlie found something that related to Merritt's black op, and *if* someone found the info had leaked, and *if* they nabbed Charlie and were actively investigating what he found and how he'd found it, then *maybe* there's a connection to what happened to us."

"Easiest way to know if all that's true is to find Charlie. He sounds like the key to all this." Beckett shrugged. "That's a job for the police or a PI."

"Yeah. Why not let Baltimore's finest handle this sitch?" Easy asked, looking between them.

Rixey's cell buzzed in his pocket. "Hold on," he said, pulling it out and hoping it was Miguel. Bingo. "Miguel?"

"Yep. I'm at the back door."

Rixey gave him the code and disconnected. "Gimme a minute. I have someone who can answer that question better than me." He crossed to the apartment door and opened it. Miguel's footsteps echoed in the stairwell as he made his way up. "Thanks for coming out so late," Nick said when the older man hit the landing, a leather case in hand.

"Sorry I got hung up."

"Don't worry about it. Come on in. Got some people I want you to meet."

"Hold up, Nick. Something you need to see before we're in mixed company," Miguel said, hanging back in the hall. Rixey let the door fall shut as his friend popped open his case. "After you left, I made some calls from Becca's office while I waited for the locksmith. I found this partly buried under a pile of papers and files that had toppled over on the desk." He handed Nick a brown paper bag.

Frowning, Nick opened it and peered in. He pulled out the first item, a black-handled military knife with a nasty curved blade in a plastic bag. The second plastic bag was lighter, smaller. Nick lifted it out. "What the everliving fuck? Is this a finger?" His hackles raised so high they were barely attached to his body.

"Yeah. Pinkie, judging by the size. Nail's been torn off. Cut was nowhere near clean. When I saw it . . ." Miguel shook his head. "Times like that I wish I'd never given up the cigs."

"This was on Becca's desk?"

The older man nodded, concern etching into the lines on his face. "Knife had it pinned to the surface. Think maybe the papers fell over later, because this was meant to be seen."

Rixey stared at the severed finger. Jesus. Didn't take two guesses to surmise who it likely belonged to. And if he was right, it answered the question of whether Charlie had been kidnapped or gone on the run. Ice ran down his spine. How the hell was he going to tell Becca? "Was there a note or a ransom demand?"

"Nothing." Miguel snapped his case closed.

"What's the fucking message, then?" Just general threatening menace? Together with the level of destruction at her house, it all seemed aimed at terrorizing. If Charlie *had* found information related to Merritt's extracurriculars, maybe it all meant his captors were frustrated they couldn't get the intel out of him? Or maybe this was meant as a diversion from their efforts to capture Becca, too? Damn, and was it coincidence that the blade was military grade?

"Good question. And I've got more intel, too."

Rixey blew out a long breath. "Come on in. I invited a few of my Army buddies over in case we needed more boots on the ground on this, which seems pretty frickin' obvious now. They should hear whatever you have to say."

Miguel nodded and followed him in. "Oh, here's the new keys to your girl's house." Rixey mentally refuted the words *your girl* as he pocketed the ring of three keys.

As soon as he learned what other shit was raining down on them, he'd have to let Becca know what'd happened. But how the hell was he going to tell her the fuckers who destroyed her house and tried to kidnap her had—assuming all three incidents were connected—also dismembered her brother? Especially when he couldn't say what the calling card was supposed to mean. Was Charlie dead? The attempted abduction could play either way—either they'd killed Charlie and needed Becca for . . . something, or Charlie wouldn't talk and they wanted leverage. Both soured Rixey's gut.

His teammates all turned to see who Rixey was bringing into the fold. He and Miguel stepped up to the bar. "This is Miguel Olivero. Ex-BPD. Now a private investigator.

He's a good friend and trustworthy." The guys nodded to the older man. "Miguel was helping me at Becca's today when we found it'd been tossed. After I left to get her, he found this stabbed into her desk." He settled the bagged knife and finger onto the counter in front of him.

Sitting closest, Beckett lifted the smaller bag to examine it.

"Well, fuck me running," Shane said. "Her brother's?"

"Presumed," Nick said. "He's the only one that makes sense, anyway. I'll have to see if Becca can ID it." Man, he'd do anything to keep her from having to see this, from having to bear the weight of it. "Apparently, this isn't all Miguel learned today." He turned to his friend and nodded.

Miguel braced his hands on the counter. "You guys don't know me from Jack, but I used to be a Baltimore City cop. Still got friends on the force. Sticks in my craw to say it, but something's way off with how this case is being handled. No reports have been filed, despite three separate incidents and dispatches. Did crime scene techs come to Becca's after the first break-in?" Nick nodded. "Well, no evidence in the system, either. My contact couldn't even find who the lead investigators were for any of it. On a hunch, I had a dispatcher friend run Becca's phone numbers against the nine-one-one logs."

The arrow on Nick's *oh-shit-ometer* pushed hard into the red.

"There's no record of her *ever* calling nine-one-one from either her house or cell phone numbers."

"Sonofabitch," Rixey bit out, the blood heating in his veins. "I know she called nine-one-one after the first break-in, because police and ambulance responded to the call."

"I'm not questioning you or her."

Miguel let the statement hang there, his meaning clear. Miguel Olivero, decorated veteran of the BPD, thought the police were dirty on this. Rixey had to agree. He looked from Beckett to Easy to Shane. "This is why we can't hand Charlie's disappearance over to the authorities. This stinks of a cover-up." And damn if that smell wasn't too fucking familiar.

Miguel nodded, his whole face frowning, an unusual look for the usually gregarious man. "You said someone tried to grab Becca from a staff break room at the hospital?" Rixey nodded. "That means uniforms, credentials, knowing schedules. Operation like that requires planning, resources, know-how, and brass balls." Murmurs of agreement rose up around the bar. "Add that to all these missing records, and this is big time."

Shane tugged his fingers through the top of his hair. "So, you're talking about running a kidnapping investigation and hostage rescue operation? Completely off the books."

Rixey braced, his stomach muscles going tight. "Yeah."

"We don't even know whose yard we'd be pissing in," Shane said. Despite the negativity of the words, there was a note of consideration in the man's voice. "But I guess that's where we'd start."

Nick's gaze flashed to Shane's, hope surging that he was on board. From the expressions on everyone's faces, he wasn't the only one looking at the numbers and seeing that one plus one plus one seemed to add up to five, too. Didn't matter if that shit didn't make any sense. It just meant they didn't have all the factors relevant to the equation. Yet. "Does that mean you're in?"

Shane stared at him a long moment. "This whole thing is nuttier than a squirrel turd, but my gut's telling me that yours just might be right. And if that's true"—he glanced to Miguel like he didn't want to say too much in front of an outsider—"we might find some other useful info, too. So, yes, I'm in."

Rixey nodded, when inside he was fist pumping all over the place.

Easy scrubbed his hands roughly over his bald head, then looked up. "If there's a chance here to clear our names, you can be damn sure I'm in." He was obviously less concerned with what Miguel heard.

"Beckett?" Rixey asked.

The man's cold blue eyes glared at him. "I sure as hell ain't letting you three get yourselves killed or arrested without me, and Easy's right. This could be our best shot at setting things right. I'm not missing out on that. So, let's do this."

Relief melted the tension out of Rixey's neck. "Okay, good. And thank you for hearing us out." Heads nodded around the bar. "First, goes without saying, but I'll say it anyway as a reminder: Becca's on a need-to-know on the backstory of all this, *right*?" Knowing glances flashed back at him. No way any of them could forget about the goddamned NDA. "Okay, so, Shane's correct. The first step would be finding out who we're up against. We can start by searching both their houses for clues and canvassing Charlie's last known whereabouts for witnesses."

"What did the perp at the hospital look like?" Miguel asked. "Any identifying features?"

Rixey tried to resurrect the man's image in his mind's eye, but the clearest details were of his hand over Becca's mouth and his knife in her side. "Tall, African American, early twenties, lots of tats and brands on his arms."

"Get a good look at any of the ink?"

Rixey shook his head. "No, but Becca might've."

"Well if the guy was any kind of organized crime—mafia, jailhouse, or local gang—there are some online databases of tattoo identifications. These won't help if he's a lone wolf, but if he's running with any of these outfits, there's a chance. I might be able to get her a look-see at some mug shots, too, and I got a friend who's a genius sketch artist," Miguel added.

Nick nodded. "Good. Plus whatever computer magic Marz can work when he gets here tomorrow." Derek Di-Marzio was a god among men on all things computers. Maybe he could even trace Charlie's digital trail.

Beck's gaze whipped up. "You invited Marz?"

Aw, shit, here we go. "Fuckin' A, I invited him," Nick replied, his tone making it clear he thought this a no-brainer.

A storm rolled in over Beck's features. He swung off the stool and rounded the bar toward Rixey. "Christ, Nick, the guys's got a—"

"He's part of the team, Murda. Simple as."

Fact that the man had lost the bottom half of his leg to a grenade made no friggin' difference to Rixey. Marz deserved to be part of this gagglefuck of a reunion if he wanted to be. And he did. Of all of them, he'd been the most readily receptive to the meeting and the mission. The man's amputation was no different than Rixey's back being shot to hell or the loss of acuity in Beck's right eye. It wasn't just about Marz's amputation, though, and Rixey knew it. It was more the fact that he'd lost the leg saving Beck's life that day.

Limp aside, Beckett was up in Rixey's face in about two point six seconds. It was like an eighteen-wheeler barreling down on him. "You really think *you,* of all people, should be talking about our team?"

The unresolved agitation from the day's events banked in Rixey's gut caught fire, heating his blood and sending him another half step closer to a man common sense generally told you not to antagonize. Huge, grim-faced, and lethal beyond measure, Murda was the kind of guy instinct had you crossing the street to avoid. But Nick had his own killer arsenal to draw from, fueled by a sea of rage that roiled just below the surface. "I fought for it. I bled for it. Damn straight I can talk about this team."

Just when Nick was sure Murda wasn't gonna back down, he did. Shaking his head, he turned and scoffed on a laugh. "Right. You just didn't care about it enough to keep us together."

A flash fire ripped through Nick's veins. He'd agonized every goddamned day of the past ten months over what had happened to these men. "What the fuck did you just say?"

"You heard me, Rixey. You *acted* all gung ho brotherhood when things were good, but five minutes after we were stateside"—Beckett shoved him—"it was out of sight, out of mind."

It was the contact that did it. Something inside Nick's brain snapped and sent a roar of aggression flooding through him, deadening his hearing and dulling every sense that wasn't focused on defending his honor against the accusation.

Rixey charged.

They clashed in a wall of muscle and a battle of wills. Nick took an uppercut to the gut that rearranged more than a few of his organs, and he dished out a jab to the throat that had Beckett choking and rasping for breath. Rixey's conscience dripped acidic shame into his chest cavity over the fact that he *had* withdrawn from the team once they'd all returned stateside, but his sense of loyalty and honor infused his spine with steel because, while he might've been fucked in the head—he'd own that every day of the week and twice on Sunday—he'd never once given up on any of them or surrendered to the bullshit that had so unjustly stripped them of everything they'd once been. *Out of sight, out of mind?* Jesus, there were times he would've gotten on his knees for five minutes of reprieve from the guilt and the loss.

Another hit landed against the kidney on his bad side

and he flew back against the steel doors of the fridge, his head glancing off the metal and his lower back screaming at the jarring impacts.

Beckett came at him swinging, brute strength his biggest asset. But Rixey had speed and agility, and a carefully timed dodge earned Murda's knuckles a *hi-how-are-ya* with the immovable freezer door.

Raised voices sounded and tugging hands touched as if from a distance, but he and Beck were caught up in an exorcism of demons that had to play out to its brutal end.

"Stop it! Oh, my God, stop!" Becca.

Her voice hauled his conscious brain out of the fog of war and he rebounded into himself. Struggling to focus, he blinked and scanned the kitchen, looking for her. His gaze finally latched onto hers at the precise moment Beckett's elbow connected with his face.

BECCA FLINCHED AND gasped at the force of the impact. Nick's head whipped to the side, sending his whole body careening into the edge of the breakfast bar. The groan that ripped out of him when his side hit the granite had her struggling out of Shane's grip and lunging toward Nick.

She wrapped her arms around his back and shoulders, hunched over the bar. "Jesus, Nick, are you okay?" Beckett hovered just behind them, his face twisted with anger. She nailed him with a glare and said, "Whatever the hell this was is over. Back off. Now."

"Fuuck," Nick groaned under his breath as he forced himself upright. Bleary eyes cut to Beckett's retreating form and made a circuit around the room before turning to her. He grimaced, and the muscles down his left side spasmed, judging by the way he held himself.

Fierce protectiveness squeezed her heart and bloomed into outright fury. But taking care of Nick was all that mattered right now.

"Come sit down," she said, tugging an empty stool closer and guiding him onto it. His face. God, his right cheekbone was split wide, blood streaming from the cut and the skin already puffing up the whole way to his eye. "You got a first-aid kit?"

"Under the sink in my bathroom," he said, his words sounding like they'd been dipped in sandpaper.

"Would someone see if you can find it? His room is the last door at the end of the hall."

"Sure, kid." The older man—Nick's PI friend?—double-timed it out of there.

Shane grabbed the roll of paper towels, wet a few, and laid out a stack of damps and dries on the bar next to her.

"Thanks," she said, angry as hell at the lot of them but appreciating the gesture.

Nick pushed her hands away from his face. "I'm fine," he said in a voice that told her he still wasn't drawing full, deep breaths.

"You're about a million miles from fine." She purposely echoed words from earlier in the day. His pale green eyes cut to hers and she arched an eyebrow. "Honesty, remember?" When her point registered in his gaze, she let it go. "Take your shirt off."

"Why?"

"Because I want to examine you. Your breathing's shallow and you're protecting your side."

His face went a shade paler as he removed the cotton over his head, and she didn't miss for a moment that he performed most of the action with his right hand, his left still shielding whatever was hurting him.

"Turn," she said, gesturing for him to swing his knees around so his left side was in front of her. "Can you hold your arm out of the way, please?"

The puppy whined and paced at Becca's feet.

"Go lay down, baby. Go on," she said. The dog curled

up a short distance away, her eyes locked on them. Becca's gaze scanned over Nick's ribs and lats, down to where a mass of scars disappeared under his waistband. Her hands gently followed. "Tell me where it hurts." Man, you could've heard a pin drop as quiet as the room had gotten. And, good. 'Cause if one of them uttered a single smart-ass comment, she was likely to lose her shit. Sparing about four seconds, she took a moment to glare at his so-called teammates, all collected around the far end of the bar watching her. Shane and Edward's expressions were somber and serious, and Beckett's head was hanging on his shoulders. "Somebody get some ice for Beckett's knuckles."

The big guy's head whipped up, and he studied her as Shane made for the fridge.

Softening her touch, Becca palpitated the edge of the scar tissue. Nick sucked in a breath through his nose, and his muscles flinched and clenched.

"What happened here?"

"Gunshot wounds times two, one penetrating, one not. Fractured pelvis and perforated bowel that healed. Lingering nerve damage," he said as if by rote. And she guessed it was. "It'll be okay."

She nodded, swallowing down the heartache and stream of comments that might embarrass him in front of his guys. *You don't look okay. You can't even take a deep breath. I'm so sorry you got hurt*. And, geez, not just hurt. That litany of injuries would've required multiple surgeries, a lot of pain, and a difficult rehabilitation. "Just gonna clean up your face." At the sink, she scrubbed her hands thoroughly.

Shane found a plastic bag, filled it with ice, and tossed it to Beckett, who caught it in the hand that hadn't had a head-on collision with a steel box.

The older man returned with a white metal kit in hand. "Found it," he said.

Drying her hands, she gestured to the bar. Miguel set it down and opened it for her. "Thanks," she said. "Are you Miguel?" Average height, he was a bit full in the middle, with graying dark hair and warm-toned skin.

"Yeah. I'm sure sorry about this whole situation, Becca," he said, a kindness about him that drew her in.

If Nick trusted the man, so did she. "Me, too. But I appreciate that you helped Nick today."

Unexpectedly, Shane stepped up and laid out everything she'd need—gauze, alcohol wipes, and a few packages of Steri-Strips. He opened a package of gloves for her and held it out. "Thanks," she said, donning the gloves and appreciating that his actions allowed her to keep her hands sterile. Way he was looking between the supplies and Nick's blood, it was like he wanted to help.

As she got to work, the weight of everyone's observation pressed in on her, but she couldn't think of them right now, or how badly she wanted to take a few heads off—Beckett's, because he'd hurt Nick, and the others', because they hadn't done anything to intervene. Which was just as bad in her book.

In front of Nick again, she held his handsome, tired face with one hand while she cleaned it with the other. His gaze lit on her face, and she knew he was watching her work, but she kept her eyes on the task at hand.

She hadn't really expected to say the words when they started coming out, but once they began, she felt their rightness down deep. "Nick asked you guys here as a favor to me. He apparently did so knowing some sort of tension existed between you. Had I known *this* would be the cost to him, I would've insisted he tell you not to come." She opened the alcohol wipes and slipped them from their sleeves. "Gonna sting." Her gaze flickered to his eyes, which bored into hers with blazing intensity.

He didn't react to the application of the alcohol.

Once it was clean and dry, Becca gently pulled the split skin together and applied the butterflies. Seething, she shook her head. "I don't know what the problem is between all of you. That's your business. But my brother's safety? That's my business. So if you guys can't keep your shit together, then feel free to go. Because we need more of this like we need more holes in our heads." She pressed two strips over the ends of the three holding the wound closed. "There." Ripping off her gloves, she stepped away.

Nick grasped her arm, the *thank you* clear in his expression.

She nodded and crossed to the sink to wash her hands again. On a long sigh, she turned in search of the trash can. "Hey, Nick, where's the . . ."

As she approached the breakfast bar, something in the middle of the granite captured her attention. With all the excitement of the fight, she'd been entirely focused on Nick. But now . . . She stepped closer.

"Becca."

Time slowed to a crawl, and her gaze became laser-focused. She reached out, her hand passing over a bagged black knife to a second bag. Cold prickles broke out over her skin.

Nick whipped off the stool. "Becca, don't."

But her fingers were already on the plastic, grasping it, lifting it. Her stomach rolled viciously.

A severed pinkie finger sat within. At one point, it had been broken at the middle knuckle and had healed badly, creating a hooked shape to the digit. Becca knew exactly when that had happened. They'd been building a tree house in the backyard with their dad. Scott had been hammering and had missed, finding nine-year-old Charlie's pinkie instead of the head of the nail. Afterward, Charlie kept taking the splint off, and the joint had healed crooked.

The fingernail was missing. The edge of the amputation was jagged.

Oh, God, they're torturing him, maiming him.

In a blinding flash, Becca's blood pressure bottomed out and a tingly sweat covered her skin. She dropped the bag and clamped her lips together, hoping to hold back the surging vomit long enough to—

The trash can appeared in front of her. Becca stomped on the pedal to raise the lid, bent over, threw up everything she'd eaten for the past ten days. Or, at least, that's what it felt like. Long after her stomach had expelled its contents, she continued to heave until tears streamed down her face and she gasped for breath. Someone held her hair. A hand rubbed her back.

She gagged and shuddered as the dry heaves eased, her muscles no more than wrung-out dishrags, her head and body aches roaring back with a vengeance. Wet paper towels appeared in her peripheral vision, and she used them to wipe her mouth and cool her brow and cheeks.

Joining her abject terror over Charlie were new emotions—embarrassment and humiliation. *I just threw up in front of Nick, in front of four war-hardened ex-Green Berets. Shit, shit, shit.*

Becca forced herself into a standing position, one that revealed that, of all people, hard-ass Beckett had been holding her hair while Nick had been rubbing her back. Equilibrium eluding her, she sagged against the row of cabinets behind her and pressed her hands to her mouth. "Sorry," she whispered.

"Nothing to apologize for, Becca," Miguel said. Low murmurs of agreement echoed the sentiment.

With bleary eyes, she watched Beckett pull the trash can away and knot the bag.

"So," Miguel said in a careful voice, "does your reaction mean you recognize it as your brother's?"

She nodded and accepted a glass of water from Shane. "Thanks," she said, and took a few small sips. "I'd know that crooked knuckle anywhere." Her brain was an absolute whirlwind of when, where, who, and what, but one question rooted itself deep. She dragged her gaze away from the baggy, refusing to let herself imagine for a *single second* how much pain Charlie must've experienced, and glared at Nick. "How long have you had this?" she asked, voice raspy, throat sore.

His expression was an ashen mask of *Oh, shit*. "Bec—"

She thrust out her finger toward the bar. "How long have you known about this? Oh, my God, did you find this at my house before you came to the hospital? Is that why you were so upset when you called me?" A knot of emotion lodged in her raw throat. That was hours ago. For *hours* he'd let her kiss him and joke about the puppy's name and nap on the couch and talk tattoos with Jeremy while he'd sat on the information that someone had chopped off Charlie's freaking finger? Rising hysteria made her jittery, and then a boomerang of delayed reaction clotheslined her, making her light-headed.

"No. I didn't know until a few minutes ago. I swear." Sincerity rang through his words as Nick slipped the glass from her hand, grasped her arms, and forced her to turn toward him. "Miguel found it after I left to come get you."

Miguel nodded. "It's the truth, Becca. I'm sorry I didn't get over here sooner to fill you in. I wasn't comfortable fleshing out the details over the phone, not with everything . . ."

"Meaning what?" she asked.

Nick's hands slid up and cupped the sides of her neck. "We think the police are dirty. None of the reports you filed exist, and neither do the records of your nine-one-one calls."

The room went a little spinny around her. "What? How is that possible?"

"We don't know. But everyone's on board to find out," Nick said, gesturing to the assembled group.

She nodded, the baggy drawing her gaze against her will. "Does this mean Charlie's dead?" she said, her voice breathy and high. At the very least, it definitely meant he'd been kidnapped, not just run away.

"Not necessarily." Nick gently squeezed her muscles. "But we don't know. There was no note, no instruction, no ransom demand. Miguel found it on your desk with the knife. That's all we know for sure. Don't assume the worst." His big hand cupped her cheek and he leaned in. "If it helps at all, where Charlie's investigation or our plans are concerned, I promise I won't keep anything from you."

"Thank you. And I'm sorry I jumped to conclusions." She blew out a shaky breath. "I far prefer to handle things head-on rather than not know and get blindsided." She waved her hand toward the counter. "Puking aside, I'm not fragile. I'm not going to break. I deal with blood and guts and crisis and tragedy every day of my life. I *can* handle this."

"I don't doubt that for a minute, Becca." Eyes blazing with emotion she didn't dare guess at, Nick seemed to be looking into her very soul, judging her strength, evaluating her mettle.

She held his gaze for a long moment, letting him look his fill. "Good. Then, what's the plan?"

Chapter 14

After another hour of restrained arguing, they had a multipronged plan in place for tomorrow, and Becca could barely resist the dangerous tide of hope rising inside her. *Finally* she could see some forward progress.

But just one thought of Charlie's severed finger took care of that. *Jesus, they cut off his finger. What kind of animals . . . ?* She forced herself not to think about it—not because Charlie didn't deserve every bit of her sympathy and concern but because if she focused on it she just might dissolve into a puddle of despair.

Sitting around the living room as the hour approached midnight, weariness covered all of them like it was an element in the air they breathed. To a man, these guys were big, strong, tough—capable of doing some serious damage if necessary. But the more she got to know Nick's former teammates, the more she noticed that they had some other interesting things in common with him—shadowed eyes, Grand Canyon-sized chips on their shoulders, and a demeanor that always seemed just shy of producing a true smile or a full laugh. Like they'd all been through something together, something that had not only marked their skin and their hearts but also touched them all the way to the depths of their souls. And not in a good way.

"All right, come to my office first thing in the morning, and we can do the forensic drawing and go through the databases," Miguel said.

Nick shook his hand. "Will do. Thanks for everything."

The man nodded. "We'll figure this out," he said.

They might've just been platitudes, but Miguel's words went right to her heart. She stepped in front of him. "What you're doing means a lot to me. I hope I can repay you some day."

"I'm a dad. Got kids your age. I couldn't not help. Don't you worry about it." He squeezed her arm. "Get some sleep."

Before the door even shut behind Miguel, Becca asked, "Can't we at least search Charlie's and my place tonight? Get a jump on tomorrow's to-do list?"

With his hand on the small of her back, Nick guided her to the grouping of chairs in the living room. "Both those locations have proven unsecure, Becca. We need to compile equipment, and the guys need intel on the locations so they're not going in blind. This isn't something to start at midnight, especially when we don't know who or what we're fighting. Except, possibly, someone on the inside of the police."

She sighed. His words made sense. They did. But the urge to find Charlie, to *save* him, agitated through her all the way down to her cells, especially now that they *knew* he'd been kidnapped. "Okay. I get it."

He squeezed her arm. "For sleeping arrangements," he

said to the guys, "someone can take the guest room in the back. Someone can take my bed, and the couch out here pulls out. I'll grab some blankets."

"Wait. Somebody else should have Katherine's room. I generally sleep for crap and end up walking around or watching TV. So I'll sleep out here," Becca said. "I don't mind."

He frowned and shook his head. "That's okay."

"No, really. Besides, I'll be more comfortable on a couch than any of you guys." She rounded the counter. "Let me just grab my stuff." Without waiting for his response, she made her way down the hall. Truth be told, the day had left her achy and beyond exhausted, but her brain was still going a million miles a minute. Sleep wasn't likely.

After she threw her bag on the bed, she quickly gathered her things, rolled them up, and stuffed them inside. She grabbed her pillow and straightened the bedding, then turned to leave.

Nick stood in the doorway, muscled arms braced on each side of the molding. "You should keep your bed."

For a moment, she was too dumbstruck by the sliver of skin that appeared between the bottom of his shirt and the top of his jeans to respond. She'd seen the full glory of his chest, of course, so why she found that strip of abdomen so alluring, she didn't know. Maybe because it tempted her to lift the rest of the cotton away? "Um, why?" she managed. "It's fine."

Something flickered behind his eyes. "You've been through a helluva lot today, Becca. Whatever this is, it's only just begun. You need rest to deal with it."

His concern made her smile. She crossed the room to him, pushed up onto tiptoes, and pressed her lips to his jaw. "Thank you for wanting to take care of me. I'll be fine on the couch, though. Promise."

"I do." His gaze connected with hers, warm and intense, and he lowered his arms.

"What?" she asked, hiking the strap of her bag higher on her shoulder.

Nick's brow furrowed, and for a moment he looked away, like he was grappling with the words. Finally, his eyes were back on hers. "Want to take care of you." His jaw ticked. "When that guy had you . . . and then you were bleeding . . ." He shook his head.

Her heart squeezed with affection for him. No, not just affection, something bigger, deeper. How could she have known him for only a few days, when it felt like it had surely been so much longer? Becca cupped the hard angle of his jaw. "I don't like seeing you hurt, either." Her thumb stroked over his cheek, just south of the red swelling around his busted cheekbone. Tape on his face, the skin around his right eye bruising, stubble covering his jaw and chin . . . God, he was beautiful in all his rough edges, utterly appealing. Suddenly, it was too much, and she was too close. Dropping her hand, she stepped back. "Between your cheek and my forehead, we're a pair, aren't we?"

The corner of his mouth twitched. "Yeah." Then his expression went serious again. "If you won't sleep here, then take my bed."

His bed? "Uh, but I—"

"It'll give you more privacy. I saw what you slept in the other night, remember? And I'd rather these meatheads didn't."

The tone of his voice might've sounded playful if it hadn't been for the dark glint in his eyes. Was that jealousy? Protectiveness? Both had her heart kicking up in her chest. "Where were you planning to sleep, anyway?"

"Couch in my office."

"Oh." Why did that news unleash a flicker of disappointment inside her? "But I was trying to give one of the guys a bed. You know, maybe make them a little less cranky."

His lips twitched again. "I know you were. But they could sleep standing up if they had to. They'll be fine. I'm not worried about them."

But he was worried about her. She wanted to wrap her arms around him, but instead she just shrugged. "Just tell me where you want me, then."

"In my bed." His eyes went molten.

So boldly stated, the words dragged over her skin and heated her blood. "I set myself up for that one, didn't I?"

It was the closest thing to a real smile she'd seen from him. And it was lethally sexy. He just nodded.

A few moments later, she made her way to Nick's connected office and bedroom. Curiosity flowed through her as she stepped inside. An overstuffed dark blue couch, the kind that sucked you right into its cushiness, filled one wall, and a flat-screen TV hung opposite. Magazines were stacked on top of a small bookshelf packed with titles she couldn't make out. The desk had an organizer full of forms and files, and a laptop sat open but dark in the center. A sketchbook lay on the corner, some sort of line drawing just visible in the diffuse glow of the hall light.

Turning on the desk lamp revealed what looked to be the finished drawing of the soldier-fireman tattoo he was supposed to do tomorrow. It was . . . really freaking good, like the man was walking off the page toward her. Was he still going to be able to do this for Jeremy? God, she really had just taken over his life, hadn't she?

A narrow hallway extended from one corner of the room, and Becca headed that way. A wall switch threw light onto a set of open sliding closet doors on the one side, the bathroom door on the other, and presumably the bedroom door at the far end. She set her bag on the floor outside the bathroom as her gaze landed on a series of black garment bags pushed flush against one wall of Nick's closet. Her gaze dropped to the floor, where a set of shiny black dress shoes and a pair of well-abused combat boots were tucked beneath the hanging bags. Two military-issue duffels filled the shelf above. Aside from his tattoo of the Special Forces crest, these were the first things she'd seen that proved he'd once served in the U.S. military. It was like he'd packed that part of himself away.

Suddenly feeling like she was snooping, Becca grabbed her things, stepped into the bathroom, and closed the door behind her.

When she came out a few minutes later, Nick was in his bedroom chucking dirty clothes into a hamper. Well, except the lone sock the puppy was chewing on next to the bed. Other than his big bed with its plain dark green comforter dominating the center, the nightstand on one side with the only lamp, and the long dresser against the opposite wall, the room was pretty empty. There weren't even curtains on his windows, just drawn blinds. Two stacks of cardboard boxes sat in the far corner. More parts of his life packed away, she guessed.

Was she imagining it, or was he limping? For a long moment, she studied him. Sure enough . . . Protectiveness flooded through her. "You don't have to pick up, Nick," she said, leaning against the doorjamb. "It's been a long day for you, too."

His gaze cut across the room toward her. "It's no problem. I changed the sheets," he said, raking his fingers through his dark hair.

Becca's fingers twitched in response. His hair was soft and thick, just long enough to grab when they kissed . . . "You didn't have to do that, but thanks. I really wouldn't mind sleeping on the couch. I don't want to disturb you if I can't sleep."

"No. Bed's all yours." At the door, he paused and looked down at her, his normally bright eyes dark in the low light. His nearness made her skin tingle. "G'night."

The sudden urge to hug him, to hold him, to ask him to stay surged through her. She didn't fight it. Stepping into him, she slid her arms around his back and laid her head against his chest. "Thank you," she said.

When his arms finally came around her, she released a breath. God, he was warm and strong, and it felt *right* holding him like this.

He kissed the top of her head.

The soft, sweet touch sent her heart flying. She tilted her head back, wanting, hoping.

Eyes locked on hers, Nick leaned down slowly. Becca's lips fell open, hungry for him. His breath caressed her skin, and his nose rubbed against hers. Anticipation of the kiss had her nearly breathless, and she fisted her hands in his shirt. His lips claimed hers gently, almost reverently. He lingered for another moment, then withdrew. "I hope you can get some sleep." He stepped around her and pulled the door closed with a click.

NICK HEAVED A breath and forced himself to walk away from his bedroom. Because, Jesus Christ, Becca was going to be sleeping in his bed tonight, those long legs sliding between his sheets, that silky golden hair sprawled against his pillows, the sweet perfume of her skin soaking into his blankets.

But he'd been right to suggest she sleep back here, no matter how much ache settled into his balls for wanting her, because her little sleep shorts were *so* not fit for public consumption. At least not if he had anything to say about it.

Maybe she wasn't his to protect and shield from other men's eyes. Okay, she wasn't. But that didn't make his possessive instincts any less real or any less strong. Whatever that meant.

In the bathroom, he gulped down some ibuprofen with a few handfuls of water, then grabbed a cover from the top shelf of his closet and tossed it to the couch. Having spent more than a few nights sleeping there, he knew it was comfortable enough. Something caught his eye, and he did a double take at the desk.

Aw, shit. The tattoo he was supposed to do tomorrow morning.

In the chaos of the day, he'd forgotten to touch base with Jeremy about canceling. And once the guys had arrived, he hadn't had a chance to talk to him. Jeremy was smart enough to know when to keep his head down and his mouth shut, and after slipping through the apartment in the midst of a tense discussion that had gone suddenly quiet, he'd holed up in his bedroom.

Which was just as well. Much as possible, Rixey wanted to keep his kid brother out of this in case the whole thing went south. No way he was letting any of Merritt's bullshit rain down on another innocent person, especially not his own blood.

So Jeremy would have to be on a need-to-know.

A click turned off his desk light, plunging the room into darkness. He wasn't gonna sweat the tattoo. It was the least of the problems he'd have tomorrow. *Take a frickin' number.*

On a deep sigh, he sank to the edge of the couch, made quick work of removing his boots and socks, and tugged off his shirt. The action brought to mind Becca's voice. *Take your shirt off.*

Her hands had been soothing against his skin, adding

a dose of solace to the seizing ache of his side and lower back after Murda's dirty kidney hit and his little run-in with the counter. Her touch had gentled as she'd examined the area around his scars, like she'd known he hurt there. And she had. She'd known he hadn't been taking regular breaths, she'd observed his posture and understood what it had meant. They'd known each other but a few days. Either she was a damn good nurse or she could read his body and his tells already. Probably both. He didn't know whether to be horrified or to take her into his arms and never let her go.

'Cause that thought was really fucking helpful right now.

Maybe it wasn't. But he couldn't deny that Becca's hands had touched him in places that lay deeper than his skin.

On a sigh, he undid his jeans and added those to the pile of clothes, but he left the cotton boxers on so Becca didn't find him lying bare-assed out here in the morning.

Stretching out, Rixey threw the cover over himself. No matter how he lay, his back screamed. Finally, he turned into a position in the neighborhood of tolerable and closed his eyes. And found himself looking at the picture of that jackhole jamming a knife into Becca's ribs.

Jesus.

He blinked the image away and tried again.

And this time saw the horror on her face as she stared at Charlie's finger. The blood had literally drained from her skin. If Beckett hadn't hauled the garbage can in front of her . . . well, it was a good thing he had. And then the guy had held her hair out of her face—all Rixey had felt toward that touch was gratitude for the man's compassion and help. In that moment, every bit of anger he'd been holding onto from the fight had fizzled out of him. Murda was a good man. They all were.

But the rage they felt had the power to turn them into loose cannons. He'd need to remember that. Direct it. Find a way to use it as an advantage.

The image playing against the inside of his eyelids shifted again. He saw Becca, coolly calm as she'd taken care of him after the fight. If he hadn't found her competence and focus sexy enough, she'd had the guts to order Beckett to back off, to dress down his men, to stand up for him when it was pretty frickin' clear a whole lot of aggression was aimed his way. When was the last time someone had stood up for him that way? He might not deserve it, but the fact that she'd done it lit him up in places that were usually deep dark.

Rixey blew out a long breath. Sleep was about as likely as stepping into a time machine, traveling back a year, and undoing the hell his life had become.

At some point, his brain miraculously and finally stopped churning, and Rixey dozed off.

Click. Click.

Rixey's eyes popped open at the soft sounds, and his brain surfaced from the haze of sleeping. Staring into the darkness, he listened and realized what he'd heard was the bathroom door closing. A few moments later, he heard the door again just before a dark silhouette crossed the far end of his office, moving slowly and silently along the wall.

"You okay?" he said, his voice ragged in his own ears.

She gasped. "Shit, you scared me. I'm sorry. I didn't mean to wake you."

"It's okay. What time is it?"

"About one."

"Can't sleep?" he asked, pushing up onto an elbow. That made the second night in a row.

"No."

There was something in the tone of her voice . . . He

needed to see her. "Shield your eyes," he said, stretching for the lamp next to the couch. He squinted against the glow and found her standing by the door, hugging herself like she was cold. "You all right?"

"Yeah."

"I'm happy to report you're a lousy liar." He winked and eased into a sitting position, moving slowly because his back was still being a pain in the ass. Literally. Better than earlier, though that wasn't saying much.

She shrugged with one shoulder. "Took me a long time to nod off," she said, "and then I had a nightmare. So . . ."

The sadness in her words and the fear in her eyes drew him off the couch. A sudden need filled his chest. He wanted her to lean on him. He grimaced, his muscles not appreciating the too-quick movement. "Uh, sorry," he said, grabbing and stepping into his jeans.

"Your back still feeling bad?" she said, eyes on the floor.

Forcing himself not to limp, he stepped in front of her and studied her face for a long moment. With her soft blond hair and her wide blue eyes and her alluring feminine curves, Becca was so very pretty. The marks on her face did nothing to detract from her appeal. Instead, they made him want to kiss her to make sure she wouldn't feel their discomfort. But he shouldn't. He really fucking shouldn't. After all the ways he'd failed the men sleeping down the hall, he didn't deserve the spot of lightness she'd bring to his life, even for just a short time.

And it was clear his men agreed. Jesus, it had been downright frosty between them most of the night. Maybe too much time had passed to try to fix all the ways he'd failed them. If so, it was his own damn fault. Again.

Becca peered up at him, those worried eyes so open and honest. That honesty appealed right to the heart of him and had him unthinkingly sliding his hands over her shoulders and under her hair to cup the slim column of her neck. She wasn't her father, damnit. She didn't play games. She didn't hold back. Time and again, she'd come right out with the truth, even when it couldn't have been easy to say. "What was your nightmare about?" he said in a low voice, ignoring the internal alarms telling him to keep his distance.

She twisted her lips and stared up at him. He felt like he was willing the words out of her, he wanted them so bad. "Charlie being tortured." Her eyes went glassy, but she straightened her spine like she refused to let the undoubtedly terrifying images bow her.

Nick's gut clenched and he softly squeezed her neck. Nothing he could say to make that ugly reality any better. "I'll do everything I can." *Everything I can to make sure you don't lose your last remaining family.* But he couldn't say that part out loud. He refused to make a promise he didn't know he could keep.

She nodded. "I know." She closed her eyes and rolled her head in response to his fingers. That little expression of comfort and pleasure shot straight to his cock. Eyes still shut, she said, "On a scale of one to ten, how bad's your back?"

He couldn't keep his lip from twitching. Apparently her sharing came with a quid pro quo requirement. And fair enough. "Three." Her eyes flew open, filled with skepticism. "Three if I remain absolutely still and don't breathe." She arched an eyebrow, but he'd almost eked out a smile. "Okay, a six."

"Does it hurt all the time?"

"Nuh uh. My turn."

"Oh, I didn't realize we were . . . Well, be my guest." That time, she smiled.

Field was wide open. What did he want to know? If he wanted her to understand he was there for her, there was one place that made sense to start—really making the effort to get to know her. "Are you and Charlie close?"

She tilted her face and brushed her cheek against his forearm. "Yes, but in our own way. Charlie's hard to get close to. He's introverted and more comfortable talking to people online than in person. But he's loyal and kind and has a hilarious, dry sense of humor." Big eyes looked up at him. "And he's my little brother, you know?"

Nick nodded. Sounded like Charlie was the exact opposite of Jeremy, but he got exactly what she was saying. "I do know."

"Are you doing physical therapy for your back?" she asked. Under his fingers, the muscles in her neck and shoulders began to relax.

"I did PT for six months after I got home. Now I see a chiropractor who's also damn good at therapeutic massage. My turn, and I'm going back to my first question again. Are you okay?"

She looked him right in the eye. "I'm scared."

He wondered if she knew how brave it was to just admit her fear that way. She might not have her father's size or training, but she'd clearly inherited a healthy dose of his warrior's spirit.

"Of what?" he finally said.

"Of not finding Charlie. That they're hurting him. That, after our fight, he doesn't know how much I love him." Nick drew his hands from her neck and caressed her hair, his fingers pushing through the thick layers to lightly scratch her scalp. She sighed. "I'm scared one of you will get hurt. Or all of you will get in trouble." Releasing a shaky breath, her gaze dropped down to his chest. Lingered. "Does it hurt your back to lay on your stomach?" she asked.

He frowned at the out-of-left-fielder. "Uh, yeah. Why?"

Becca pulled his hand to her mouth and kissed the center of his palm. "Sit down facing backward." She rolled the desk chair closer.

Rixey stared at the chair like it was speaking in a foreign language. Well, one he didn't speak anyway.

She laughed. "Don't be so suspicious. Just sit your butt down already."

"Well, since you put it that way." He straddled the chair and rested his forearms on the back. She knelt on the floor behind him, and every nerve ending in his body took note.

"Undo the button," she said in a low voice, tugging on the waistband of his jeans, her fingers skimming the skin of his lower back.

"Uh, Becca." Her command sent his brain to places it had no business going.

"Were you always this bad at taking orders?"

He undid the button, his zipper coming down a little in the process, and he wondered what the hell he was doing as his erection was tempted to life.

"Tell me if it hurts or if it's too hard." She smoothed her palms straight up his spine, out over his shoulder blades, and down his sides, her fingers almost tickling along his lats. The first few passes were soft and gentle, but soon her fingertips pressed in and her thumbs rubbed deep circles into his sore muscles.

He had to bite back more than one groan. At his shoulders, she worked out from his spine, her surprisingly strong grip working knots out of his traps. When she walked her massaging fingers up his neck, he dropped his head forward on a groan he couldn't restrain.

"Okay?" she asked, her breath floating over his skin.

"Feels fucking phenomenal." He felt her soft laughter puff against his back. And now he was all the way hard.

"Good."

She continued until his upper back was purring and his

cock was punching at the open fly of his jeans, begging to be released. Despite the relaxation of, well, *some* of his muscles, the pace of his breathing slowly but surely picked up, his libido making plans his brain hadn't agreed to. Yet.

"This dragon is beautiful, Nick."

"Yeah?" he said into the space between the chair's backrest and his chest, picturing in his mind's eye the beast wrapped around a sword spanning the length and breadth of his back.

"Must've taken a long time."

"Three sittings. Jeremy did it." He'd gotten his first tat at eighteen, a tribal on his shoulder which he'd since added to. But in the months after he'd returned home, he'd gotten quite a few new pieces. He prized them for their ability to memorialize and to temporarily replace the never-ending mental anguish with the sting of the tattoo gun on his body. The dragon had given him several days' worth of blissful quiet in his head while the needles had run over his skin.

There was a pause, like maybe she was examining it more closely. His head conjured up all kinds of unhelpful images, like her leaning in, brushing her face against his skin, her lips . . . "He's really good."

"Jeremy? The best."

"Does it have a meaning?"

The answer to that could be too damn revealing. "Dragons are protectors of valuable and sacred things. They're fierce and powerful defenders," he said, choosing his words carefully.

She stroked a finger straight down the blade of the sword. Nick shuddered. "What is he protecting for you?"

Hesitating for only a moment, Nick rotated the chair forty-five degrees and lifted his right arm. He knew the column of words inked there by heart:

LOYALTY
DUTY
RESPECT
SELFLESS SERVICE
HONOR
INTEGRITY
COURAGE

The core values of the United States Army. Words that defined what being a soldier was all about and words that he'd personally striven to uphold for nearly his entire adult life. To Nick, these weren't platitudes or pretty concepts to trot out at ceremonies or in speeches. They formed the basis of a code at the heart of the brotherhood of arms. They formed the foundation upon which soldiers lived and died. Live up to them, and anything was possible.

Violate them the way Merritt had and it all went to shit. He should know. He was living the goddamned consequences.

Her hand settled over the words, just rested there, like Becca was holding the ink to his skin. Like she, too, was protecting it. A knot lodged in his throat, and he forced that fucker right on down. He'd grieved enough over everything he'd lost, especially when others had made far greater sacrifices. Enough was enough was efucking-nough.

He shifted the chair so his back faced her again. Regret at telling her about the dragon, about the words, settled into his gut. It left him feeling too exposed, like his nerves sat atop his skin.

But she said no more about it. Instead, her thumbs worked into the small of his back. Her touch was pleasure and pain all at once, the pain of working out the muscles required before the pleasure of relief could come. Slowly, she kneaded toward his left side, the massage gentling as she neared the mass of scars from his injuries and multiple surgeries. Her fingers curled around his side and swept into his pants.

He flinched and sucked in a breath, not because she'd hurt him but because her fingertips had been so damn close to his cock. Though not nearly close enough . . .

His side was sore, and even the light touch was a little uncomfortable, but the longer her warm hands brushed softly over his skin, the more his muscles eased.

"Okay?" she said, her voice soft and breathy. Or maybe that was just wishful thinking caused by the heat roaring over his body at the way she was taking care of him.

"Yeah."

Just above his hip bone, she settled into a rhythm using both hands, her thumbs swiping low in the back, her fingers rubbing under the loose denim in the front.

"Do I want to know why you and Beckett were fighting?"

A few ins and outs of his breath passed before he decided whether to answer. "He's pissed I haven't been a better friend, and he's right."

"Well, no matter what you did, you didn't deserve to be attacked in your own home. I meant what I said to them, Nick. You're going so far out of your way for me. I'm not letting anyone abuse you for it."

There she goes again. As if each massage, each squeeze, and each soothing caress weren't ratcheting up his arousal enough, her rising to his defense had him absolutely throbbing for her. Her warmth was all over his back from her hands and her breath and her nearness. It was too much. It wasn't nearly enough.

Goddamnit, he wanted her.

It wasn't just her hands on his body, or the relief flooding through him, or the lateness of the hour, although all three played a role. It was more the bone-deep solace he felt in her presence as her light and her warmth seeped into him. The way she seemed to anticipate what he needed, even if he would've been the last one to acknowledge it for himself. How she'd given him a purpose again after all these long months, one he hadn't realized how badly he needed. And it all made him *want*.

Nick wanted to claim her and possess her and climb so far inside her heat that he'd forget about all the shit in his head. He wanted her writhing under him and boneless with pleasure and crying his name out loud. He wanted her seeking safety in his arms and comfort from his hands.

He spun the chair around to face her. She reared back on her knees and her gaze flew up to his. He shook his head, competing desires warring inside him. To possess her and protect her. To be honest and shield her from hurt. To do the right thing and do what *felt* right.

Damnit, he needed her.

On a groan, he reached out, grasped her neck, and hauled her up to him.

Rixey consumed her with the kiss, pouring every bit of his gratitude and desire into the movement of his lips, his tongue, his hands. She moaned in surprise, and he devoured that, too. God, she smelled of warm vanilla and tasted of mint. Little needful whimpers and sighs and gasps spilled out around their lips, and he reveled in every last note of her pleasure, of her desire. He pulled her closer and penetrated her more deeply with his tongue. The damn backrest separated them, but he couldn't let her go long enough to rectify the problem.

"God, sunshine, what are you doing to me?" he rasped around the edge of a kiss.

Her fingers dug into his hair, pulling, grasping. He loved the bites of pain against his scalp, evidence of her loss of control.

If he didn't stop soon, he was going to lift her into his

arms, lay her out on his bed, and cover her with his body. And there would be no going back.

Get a friggin' grip, Rixey. Now.

Panting, he pulled his lips away from hers, his hands cupping her cheeks so she didn't dive back in for more. Foreheads together, he let himself bask in a moment more of her heat, her scent, her touch. He kissed the corner of her mouth, because *he* was the one struggling to resist, and stroked his hands over her hair. Finally, he pulled away. "It's late," he said, hating the words but needing them.

Her fingers played with the hair at the nape of his neck. "I know," she whispered, peering up at him with midnight blue eyes.

"Come on." He pushed up from the chair and gave her a hand at the same time. Miraculously, his muscle aches were more diffuse than before her massage. As if he needed another reason to want to kiss her. "You should—"

"I don't want to be alone, Nick." She shook her head and ducked her chin. "Can I just . . . maybe, stay out here with you?"

"Becca—"

"Please?"

The pleading slayed him. He grasped her hand and led her to his dark bedroom.

"Get in," he said at the side of the bed. "You need sleep, and you're not going to get it sitting up out there."

"But—"

"I'll sleep here, too."

"Really?"

The obvious relief did a number on him. It felt damned good to be needed—too damned good, so he played it off. "It's a hardship, but for you, I'll make the sacrifice." He swatted her butt, and his cock rose up and took notice. "Get in."

"Nicholas Rixey, did you just . . . smack me?" The sounds of the mattress accepting her weight and the covers shifting followed her into the bed.

He lay down on the very edge, his mind still spinning on the fact that he'd just spanked her, when a new realization hit home. *Shit, I'm in bed with Becca.* "Why, did you like it?" he said, forcing nonchalance into his voice when he felt anything but.

Her non-answer was a real kick in the ass, because he'd bet his right nut she was laying over there debating how to answer. And now his cock wanted back in the game. *Fuck.*

Yes, please.

Jesus, when your brain started talking to your cock, you were on some fucking really thin ice. "And don't call me Nicholas," he groused.

She chuckled and shifted positions, judging by the movement of the mattress.

"Lying on your back can't be much better than lying on your stomach."

He grunted, but it was true. But if he rolled on his right side, he'd be that much closer to her, and right now he swore she must be throwing off solar heat, he felt her presence so intensely.

"Nick?"

He tensed, unsure what the hell she was going to come at him with next. "Yeah?"

"Thank you."

Oh. The tension ebbed out of him. "You're welcome."

Gingerly, he turned onto his side, easing his back and restoring the relief she'd given to him with the gift of her touch.

"Nick?"

"Hmm?"

"I feel like I've known you a lot longer than a few days."

So do I. But nothing good would come from making *that* admission. "Becca?"

"Yeah?"

"It's time to stop talking now."

She laughed, the sound warm and sunny in the darkness. The metaphor wasn't lost on him.

Becca was the light to his dark.

Her honesty, her touch, her very presence settled a blanket of comfort around him like nothing else had this past year. And he wanted to wrap himself up in it and never let go. How the hell that worked without her getting hurt at his hands, without his bitterness and anger weighing her down, he didn't know.

And he wasn't sure it was good for either of them for him to figure it out.

Chapter 15

$\mathcal{T}$he warm weight was the first thing Becca noticed. All along her side, on her shoulder, covering her thigh. She didn't want to open her eyes and chase away the dream of lying so close to Nick, because there was no way it was real.

Except the more she woke up, the more she realized she wasn't imagining it. His jeans, his skin, his heartbeat all truly pressed against her. Sometime during the night, Nick Rixey had made himself into a blanket, and she was the beneficiary of his covering heat.

Judging by the numbness of her arm, his head had been resting on her shoulder for a while. She turned her face toward him and her cheek found the soft unruliness of his hair. A smile crept over her face. Here he'd insisted on clinging to the edge of the mattress when they'd gotten in bed, but he'd sought her out in his sleep and curled up against her.

And curled up was the right way to describe it. His head on her shoulder, his leg over her thigh, his arm stretched over her stomach and his big hand tucked under her hip. Like he wanted to make sure she didn't go anywhere.

It was actually kinda sweet. Not at all a description she'd usually apply to Nick, with all his rough edges and gruff moods and serious intensity.

Opening her eyes to the gray light of early morning skirting in around the blinds, Becca soaked in the amazing image of Nick's body sprawled all over hers. Man, that gave her some ideas she wouldn't mind bringing to reality. Him, over her, moving, taking, claiming.

The way she wanted him was crazy. She knew it was. After all, she'd only known him a few days. But that didn't make it any less real. At twenty-eight, she'd never felt anything like the passionate urges he seemed to wring out of her with just a look or a touch, and who knew if she'd find another man capable of making her feel this way again. He was quintessentially masculine and quietly powerful and arrogantly commanding—sometimes to the point where she wanted to throttle him. But mostly, her body reacted to these qualities as if they were a gypsy healer's most potent aphrodisiac, mysterious and irresistible and maybe a little dangerous, too.

Becca rubbed her hand over her face, hoping the coolness of her palm might ease the sudden heat flooding her cheeks, not to mention elsewhere. It was no use, though, because as long as this much of him was touching this much of her, desire and lust would rush through her until she was nearly mad with the aching need for him to fill her up in any and every way he could.

Maybe that should embarrass her. But it didn't. Even

if it had been a while since she'd last had it, she'd always liked sex. And there wasn't a part of her that doubted that sex with Nick Rixey would be absolutely mind-blowing. The only question was why he kept pulling back, when it seemed clear he was interested.

If there was one thing all the losses in her life had taught her it was that life was short, fleeting, and way too precious to waste waiting around for happiness to hit you over the head and make itself known. Happiness wasn't something you *found,* happiness was something you *made*—by living in the moment, by cherishing the people in your life right now, by finding the courage to change those things you didn't like. She hadn't always gotten it right the last year or two, and that had to change. Starting now.

As these thoughts raced through her mind, a familiar pang of guilt settled in her heart for Charlie. But they *would* find him. She absolutely refused to entertain any other outcome. And, then, maybe after . . .

Yeah. After.

Nick shifted, rolling closer, if that was possible, and her just barely restrained lust broke free. The change in his position brought his erection against her hip. And, *Jesus,* he was big. Imagining taking all that masculine flesh into her hands, her mouth, her core had her suddenly light-headed, despite lying down. As if that weren't enough, when he'd moved closer, the thick cords of his thigh had pressed squarely against the junction of her legs. Summoning all her willpower, she forced herself to lie perfectly still. Because if she lifted her hips even an inch, the friction of his body pressing so intimately and deliciously against her clit would make her come.

He sniffed and murmured, and his breathing slowly changed from the slow, shallow draws of sleep to the deeper pattern of wakefulness. "What are you thinking so hard about?" he said, his voice a seductive, raw gravel.

"Nothing," she whispered.

"Bad liar, remember?"

She smiled. Not even awake and he was already a smart-ass. "You're laying on me."

He lifted his head, eyes still soft with sleep and oh so bright. "Er, oh, God, Bec—"

"Don't move, please? I wasn't complaining."

"Then what—"

"It's just . . ." The way he was looking at her, half concerned, half like he might make her every dream come true, had her spilling a fast stream of honesty that was about five point two light-years beyond oversharing. "I'm horny. And you're hot as hell. And we're clearly trying to be good. Although, I'm not sure why, exactly. And, anyway, I don't want you to move. Because I like the feel of you. And I—"

His mouth swallowed the rest of the nonsense spilling from her lips. The kiss was aggressive and needful, his tongue twining with hers, his hands in her hair, his chest atop her breasts. For a long moment, she was so stunned by the kiss that all she could do was give in to the sensual assault. His leg pressed between her legs, hard against her clit, the bunching and shifting of his muscles shoving her step by step closer to the edge of restraint. A stream of moans and whimpers worked their way up her throat until finally she couldn't stop her hips from dancing against his thigh.

"Nick," she rasped around the edge of a kiss. "Oh, God."

"What?" he said, pulling back. He stroked his nose over her cheek to her ear. "What's the matter?" He eased his thigh away.

Her whimper was full of protest for the loss of him. The sexy bastard chuckled. "Don't stop," she managed.

Tracing his tongue around the shell of her ear, he rocked his hips against her nice and slow. "Don't stop what?"

Becca swallowed roughly, arousal making it hard to breathe, hard to think. "You're teasing me."

He chuffed out another small laugh in her ear, casting shivers over her skin. "I am."

Digging her fingers into his hair, she grasped two handfuls and held tight. "Well, don't. I want . . ."

Nick's tongue was in her mouth again, exploring every wet corner and stealing her breath. He pulled back, panting. "What? What do you want, sunshine?"

The nickname tugged her heart into the action, too. Did he realize he said it? "I like when you call me that."

He bit her bottom lip and tugged, his gaze boring into hers, one eyebrow arched. "What do you want?"

She pulled his wrist from her face and guided his hand to the heat between her legs. With only her panties separating his skin from hers, no doubt he could feel it.

"Jesus," he ground out, his forehead falling upon hers and those bright green eyes absolutely on fire. "You want to come?"

"Yes."

Nodding against her face, he whispered, "Yeah. And I want you to come." He devoured her in a kiss and hooked a thumb in the lacy band of her panties. Slowly, he pushed them down to her knees, then she curled her legs and he pulled them the rest of the way off.

Nick kissed her again, and there was nothing tentative about the way he worked his mouth. The passion with which he tasted her with his lips and tongue, and nipped with his teeth, and caressed with his hands was all-consuming. Appreciative little grunts and moans worked up from the back of his throat, like he was eating the finest meal after a long fast. She was lost to him. "You need this, don't you?"

"So much, Nick." Emotion rose up within her, tightening around her throat and pricking at the back of her eyes. She wasn't sure exactly what caused it, but suddenly she was absolutely overwhelmed with sensation and desire. "I need you."

He kissed her jaw, her throat, her collarbones, and then he pulled her shirt up and off and exposed her breasts. More of those appreciative noises spilled from him as he drew himself atop her to kiss and lick and suck at her flesh.

His hand dragged downward and cupped her core. The sprinting beat of her heart made it hard to breathe. "Already so wet." He swiped his tongue over her bottom lip. "Is that for me?"

Jesus. "Yes."

"Yes, what?"

"Yes, for you."

"Damn straight." His middle finger sank deep. Throwing her head back into the pillow, she cried out, one hand fisting in the covers, the other digging into the muscles of his shoulder. He fingered her slow, letting her get used to his presence deep inside, and soon she rocked her hips to urge him to give her more. He did. For a moment, he pulled all the way out, then he slid back in with his middle and ring fingers together. The man had *big* freaking hands, and his fingers stretched and filled her until her blood hummed and raced. He flicked her clit with his thumb, once, twice, and an orgasm crashed over her, catching her off guard, contracting her muscles, sending her flying. She slammed her thighs closed around his hand and arm, hoping she could hold him there forever. He growled. "That one was too easy. Again."

Dizziness threatened. "I can't—"

"You will." Withdrawing his hand from inside her, he pushed her legs open and crawled between them. His big shoulders overflowed the space between her thighs. "I have to taste you."

He tilted her hips up with his hands and dragged his tongue through her folds. Becca cried out, one hand darting to his hair and holding tight. His tongue was relentless, licking, stroking, penetrating, circling until she was pure overloaded sensation. *Too much, too much, it's too much.* But it was like he was in charge of her body and it bent to his will. Arousal shot through her again, more intense, more demanding. He flicked and sucked at her clit and slid his fingers deep inside again. The combination shoved her toward the edge.

Panting and moaning, her body tightened, sensation gathered, and pressure built . . . but then she hung there. For a long moment, she was suspended until she was holding her breath and gritting her teeth.

"Come all over my fingers," he ordered against her lips. And then he focused on her clit with a series of fast, hard licks. She came in a flash of blinding light that momentarily sucked in on itself before exploding outward in a million pieces. She moaned and thrashed beneath him and finally tugged at his hair to get him to stop.

In a flash of movement, he rose up over her and claimed her mouth in a hard kiss. "I want you, Becca."

Elation roared through her. "Yes."

Rising out of bed, he kicked off his jeans and boxers. His cock jutted out, long and thick. His body was lean, strong, all hard planes and cut muscles. Ink marked his skin in more places than she'd previously seen, but then he was rolling on a condom and dragging her hips to the edge of the bed. "I want to be able to see you." He took himself in hand and dragged his tip through her folds, his face a gorgeous mask of lust and desire. "Sure this is okay?" he asked, his voice a raw scrape.

"More than okay. I want you, too."

He pushed inside, slowly filling her with a delicious pressure. She moaned, unable to look away from the roiling heat in his eyes. Finally, his gaze moved from her face to where he penetrated her, his eyes absolutely on fire. Something snapped inside him. Holding her hips in a tight grip, he withdrew and thrust, his rhythm hard, fast, almost frantic. The intensity was mind-blowing and sent her flying. She grasped the edge of the mattress to keep herself in place against the demanding pace.

On a groan, he fell forward, bracing himself above her with one hand and grabbing her shoulder with the other, his hips flying. The change in position pushed him deeper inside her and dragged his body tight and hard over her clit. God, the way he moved, like a great wave rolling up over her, covering her, claiming her. She was awash in sensation—the incredible fullness between her legs, his heat on her skin, his tight grip. "So fucking good," he said, meeting and holding her gaze. His face was all hard angles and utterly appealing. "I can't hold back."

She smiled. "Don't try to."

Holding her tight, he hammered into her, and then he unleashed a guttural shout and came. His muscles rigid, he moved through the orgasm, pulsing inside her, the ecstasy of his expression one of the most erotic things she'd ever seen.

His whole body went loose and he eased his chest atop hers, his forehead resting on hers with his eyes closed. For a moment, they lay like that, their breathing evening out, their bodies cooling. She stroked her hands over his sides and back.

She would hold him like this all day.

So much for waiting until after all this was over. But Becca couldn't bring herself to regret being with him, because it made her feel all the more that they were in this thing together.

He kissed her, a gentle show of appreciation, then he pushed himself up and withdrew.

Becca frowned. Because the withdrawal wasn't just physical. As he dealt with the condom and tugged his jeans on again, he didn't look at her, didn't talk to her, wouldn't meet her gaze. She pushed into a sitting position and hugged her knees in front of her. "Hey," she said.

"We should get moving. You want the shower first or should I?"

NICK AND BECCA sat on either side of the sketch artist in Miguel's office as the image of her attacker came to life in black and white. The guy was good—had to give him that. And, thank fuck, because at least something was going right for him so far today.

Rixey shifted in his seat and chanced a glance at Becca, who'd worn a frown on her pretty face ever since he'd shut down on her after they'd had sex. Damn incredible sex. But, *goddamnit*, he hadn't meant for that to happen. She'd just been so warm, and sexy, and honest about what she'd wanted, what she'd been feeling. It had felt so good not to be alone. He hadn't been able to hold back. And he'd done exactly what he'd said he wouldn't.

Too much stood between them, things he couldn't and shouldn't say. And he was far too fucked in the head with grief and loss and guilt. She deserved so much fucking better than that, than him. When his brain had come back online, he'd been so angry at himself he'd barely been able to breathe. Still was. And just like he'd said, Becca was paying the price by being hurt and confused. No fucking hero here, that was for sure.

Problem was, he wanted more with her. Maybe he even wanted it *all* with her. Bringing her pleasure and seeing her shatter in his arms had given him such satisfaction, like making her happy gave him some kind of meaning in what had become a meaningless existence. If he thought he'd felt close to her last night, it was nothing compared to what sharing her body made him feel.

Whole. Lighter. Not alone.

Sonofabitch. After all the ways he'd failed others he cared about, he wasn't worthy of feeling the solace she gave.

And if fucking up with Becca wasn't bad enough, the team had been as pissy with him this morning as they'd been last night. At least they'd gone their separate ways to put their plan into action, with Easy going to the airport to pick up Marz and Shane and Beckett canvassing Charlie's neighbors. So, until they all met up again, he had a short reprieve from the guys.

But Becca was a different story. He wasn't sure how he was going to make that snafu better, or whether he even should. It sucked ass to contemplate, but maybe he should just allow the discomfort to fester between them. It'd make it a helluva lot easier to keep his dick and his hands in check if she wasn't looking at him with those bright blue eyes so filled with invitation and interest. Now, when they looked at him at all, they were filled with hurt and regret.

And damn if that didn't give him a major check to the gut.

"All right," the artist said. "What do you think of him now? Any changes?"

They leaned in and Rixey looked to Becca. She returned the glance. It was the first time she'd met his eyes since she'd slid off his bed and walked naked out of his bedroom, her body still flush and so beautiful in the morning light. He nodded.

A moment later, her eyes pulled away from him and focused on the sketch. "That's him."

"I agree," Nick said. The bastard's face was clear in his mind. But little else. "Becca, what about tattoos? Any chance you remember any of the guy's tats?"

"He had a lot of them on his arms and neck." She closed her eyes for a long moment. That little frown took up residence between her brows. When her eyes opened again, she shook her head. "I first noticed him when he crossed the room. I saw the tattoos, but I wasn't really paying attention, you know?"

"Anything at all could be useful," Rixey said. "Don't worry about remembering everything."

"Okay." She fingered the pale blue shirt over her left bicep. "He had a scar or a brand here, but most of it was hidden beneath his sleeve. Um . . . Oh, on the back of his left hand he had a solid black square. This isn't very helpful, is it?"

"It's a start, Becca, and it's more than we had. What about when he was holding you? Did you get a closer look at his ink then?"

Her gaze went unfocused, and he hated that she was putting herself back in that place again, even if only mentally. She gasped. "He had a cross on his right arm, from inside his elbow down. The ends were pointed like arrowheads, and in the background there was a circle or a halo made of tiny circles, like a chain."

The artist started sketching and asking for any other details she might've noticed.

The image took form on the paper, and Becca nodded. "Yeah, that's it. As far as I can remember, that's pretty close."

"That was great, Becca," the man said. He quickly drew a square. "I'll include this image, too. Looking at this much of it might jog your memory."

When the artist departed, Miguel congregated them around his desk and pulled up the online crime identification database he'd mentioned the night before. For a frustrating hour he flipped through pages on known Maryland criminal outfits and gangs—mafia families of various ethnicities, street gangs, prison gangs, outlaw motorcycle gangs, gangs native to Baltimore and those that had spread their influence from other cities.

They came to the end of the data. "Nothing here connects this cross tattoo to any of these groups." She sagged back in her chair.

"Maybe not," Miguel said. "But between the sketch and the tats you remembered, at least you have a few things to show around and see if people recognize." He nailed Rixey with a serious stare. "Just remember, whoever he is and whoever he works for, asking questions could stir up a bee's nest."

"Yeah." Precisely why Nick felt like they were dealing with the tip of an iceberg, with a hulking mountain of killer ice hidden beneath the surface.

"Should we put both Charlie's picture and this man's sketch on the reward poster?" she asked. "I'm so mad at myself for not making one sooner."

"Couldn't hurt," Miguel said. "And, listen, don't do that to yourself. Way I understand it, you didn't have confirmation there was any foul play to Charlie's person until last night. Rewards offerings like this can be useful, but they also bring in a lot of false leads. You have the manpower to work through that now, but you didn't have it a few days ago."

Seeing an opening to rebuild a bridge, Nick grasped her hand. "I agree. You're doing great, Becca. Charlie's lucky to have you fighting for him."

Her eyes went glassy, but she managed a small smile. "Thank you." She nodded. "I needed that."

Guilt squeezed tight bands around Nick's heart. What she *didn't* need was him screwing with her emotions the way he had this morning.

Miguel turned to his computer, clearly giving them the privacy he could in his small office. After a moment he said, "All right, kids. Just tell me what you want on the flyer."

"What amount do you think would be effective?" she asked, her expression serious.

"Depends what you can afford," Miguel said. "Not unusual to see rewards for a hundred dollars on up."

"Five hundred? A thousand? Given what you found in my house, Charlie may not have a lot of time." She glanced between them. "Make it a thousand."

Thirty minutes later, they had half a ream of MISSING PERSON: REWARD FOR INFORMATION LEADING TO DISCOVERY OR ARREST flyers listing the number of a prepaid phone Miguel had given them for this purpose. Becca was chomping at the bit to start posting them.

"Before we do that," Nick said, "let's go back to Hard Ink and catch up with Derek. He should be here by now. Before we start inviting calls, I want his input on how to track the numbers the calls are coming from."

Her shoulders drooped, but she nodded. "Okay."

On the way back, Nick called the others and informed them of the rendezvous, but he and Becca were the first ones to return to the building, even after stopping to pick up some pizza. They ducked in the back of Hard Ink, Becca wanting to make sure the puppy wasn't causing any problems for Jeremy.

Both Jer and Jess were with clients, but Jeremy heard the door and popped out of his room, mask and gloves still on. "I rescheduled for eight o'clock tonight," he said, referring to the appointment Nick had had to move from this morning.

He'd felt bad about pushing it back, but he could hardly sit around and do tattoos while the rest of the team and Becca got to work. "Okay, thanks. And sorry."

Jeremy nodded.

"How's the puppy doing? Is she in your way?" Becca asked, bending down to pet her. Rixey had to admit the mutt was kinda cute with those monster ears and paws.

"No, she's awesome. She slept most of the morning directly between our doors like she didn't want to play favorites. Needs a name though."

"I know," Becca said. "What about Shiloh?"

Above his mask, Jeremy's eyebrows cranked down. "Like the Civil War battle?"

She laughed, and Nick was so drawn to the sound. He wished he'd been the one to cause it. "Just try it out for now. See how she likes it."

He winked. "I'll have a full report waiting for you. Hey, so, what do you think?" He gestured to the front of his shirt. "Told you I'd wear one for you."

"What's it say?" She walked closer, and it was crystal clear the moment she read his Big Johnson Tattoo Parlor shirt, with its iconic cartoon character tattooing a naked woman's back. Her mouth dropped open on a gasp. "I can't believe you wear that."

"Well"—he waggled his eyebrows over the mask—"it's only fair to warn people." The shirt read, "You're gonna feel more than a Little Prick."

She pressed her lips together like she was trying to hold back her laughter, but humor absolutely danced in those blue eyes. "I think you might be a bad influence on my baby." Becca leaned down and covered the dog's ears. The puppy tried to gnaw on her hand.

Jeremy scoffed. "You wound me. I may never recover." He retreated toward his room and pointed at Nick. "I gotta get back to it. Eight p.m. Don't forget."

"Yeah, yeah," Rixey said. *It's on the list.*

Becca ran Shiloh-for-now outside for a quick business trip, then they left the dog to nap and play in the shop while they went upstairs to wait for the others. Nick placed the pizza boxes, paper plates, and canned sodas on the bar.

"I'll be right back," she said, retreating down the hall without waiting for him to respond.

Bracing his hands on the counter, he watched her walk away, that boulder making its presence known on his chest again. Pissed at himself as he was, he didn't want her hurting. Before they had an audience, he followed her back to the room.

Not thinking, he pushed through the mostly closed office door and inhaled to speak her name, but the word died on his throat.

She stood in the bathroom doorway naked from the waist up, except for a pale yellow and white lace bra. The yellow looked so pretty against her skin, and the lace curving over the swells of her breasts tempted his fingers, his tongue.

He was immediately hard.

"Uh, sorry," he murmured, turning at a ninety-degree angle from her and diverting his gaze to the floor.

She gasped. "Shit. Do you realize you make, like, no noise when you move?"

He scrubbed his hand over his hair and willed his libido under control. This was the damn problem in a nutshell. "Sorry. Old habit." He caught movement in his peripheral vision but didn't let himself look.

"Yeah. My dad was the same freaking way."

And there went the erection.

"It's so nice out, I was worried I'd be too warm in long sleeves. Did you need something?" she asked, stepping into the office in a short-sleeved shirt. With a flash of her hands, she twisted her long hair up on top of her head and used a band to hold it up off her neck.

He gave a tight nod and forced himself to focus despite the fact that the lacy bra remained visible through the white V-neck. "I need to apologize."

Emotion flickered over her expression, but she just looked at him.

"I was an ass and I didn't mean—"

"Look—" She shook her head and stepped to the door. "Let's not do this. Okay? I'm not going to lie, you hurt my feelings. But, in the end, it was a good thing. Because you reminded me I need to stay focused on Charlie. I can't be distracted by anything else. So don't sweat it."

Voices sounded from the living room, and Nick frowned. The words should've given him relief. She'd let him off the hook and wanted bygones to be bygones. But there was that damn boulder again. "Okay," he said. "Come on."

Anticipation filled his gut as they entered the living room. Standing in the middle of Shane, Easy, and Beckett was Derek DiMarzio, looking about a hundred times better than the last time Nick had seen him. His brown hair had grown out to the length of his jaw, and his shoulders appeared bulkier under his shirt. Hell, he looked downright fit and healthy, maybe even like he had a bit of a tan. Most noticeably, he was standing on his own two feet. Or, presumably, his own foot and a prosthesis.

Nick walked right up to him and held out a hand. "Thanks for coming, man. You look great."

Marz wore his trademark smile, just one watt dimmer than a full-on grin, and returned the shake. "I feel great. Nice to see you. Thanks for giving us a reason to get back together."

Rixey felt the unspoken sarcasm radiating from the other three, but he let it go. Hard not to feel a healthy dose of positivity and gratitude in the face of someone like Marz, who had suffered the most catastrophic injuries of any of them yet seemed to have the best attitude.

"Come on in. Grab some slices and let us catch you up."

"I just dumped my gear there," he said, pointing to a stack of cases by the front door. "That kosher?"

"Yeah, no problem."

Marz crossed to the kitchen with barely a limp, and Rixey wasn't ashamed to admit that emotion threatened to choke him up. He looked at the other guys and realized they were watching Marz, too, and in that moment they were united in their admiration for the teammate they all remembered lying in pieces on the war-torn ground. Nick had been the closest to Marz and Murda when the grenade had shot into their position. Marz had seen the writing on the wall a split second before his teammate and had shoved him out of the way. The explosion had taken both men down, Murda's leg mangled and Marz's gone from below the knee.

By that time, Rixey had already taken two rounds in the lower back, but Marz's leg had fountained blood. So Nick had dragged himself over, torn the Afghani scarf he'd bought at a bazaar on base from around his neck, and balled it against the wound. Their medic had already been taken out, so Shane had gone to work on the pair of them while Nick had pitched in how he could. Easy, Axton, and Harlow had provided them cover, but only Easy had survived.

Man, Rixey had done them all a disservice by dropping off the face of the earth. All this time, they'd needed each other. They'd needed to know how everyone was doing and handling the multitude of shit hands they'd been dealt. They'd needed to draw strength and determination and resolve from the one place that had *always* given them those things—their team. Damnit all to hell and back. He *had* failed them.

When a man wore the Special Forces tab on his uniform, he held himself to a higher standard. Marz was clearly living up to it. Nick wasn't.

That changed now. No more excuses. No more burying his head in the friggin' sand. No more cutting himself off.

Marz opened a lid and grabbed two slices. He turned and looked at them all. "What?"

The question flipped a switch in the rest of them. Suddenly they were all making small talk and gathering around the chow.

"Nothing," Nick said, joining him at the bar. He handed plates to Becca and the other guys. "Marz, I want you to meet Becca Merritt. It's her brother, Charlie, we're looking for."

Nick saw the momentary calculus flash through Marz's gaze, but it was nothing Becca would pick up on. "Becca. Wish we were meeting under better circumstances," he said.

She smiled, right away more at ease around Derek than she'd been around the others so far. "You, too."

Once everyone had food, they took up spots around the living room, the guys filling the couches and chairs and Becca and Marz kneeling on the floor at the coffee table despite everyone's offers to give up their seats.

Rixey caught Marz up on the details of what'd happened before his arrival, then asked everyone to report on what they'd learned in the morning.

"We canvassed Charlie's street and talked to some neighbors, though the man who lives upstairs wasn't home," Shane said, looking at Becca. She nodded. "No witnesses, but one person told us Charlie cabbed everywhere. It's not a neighborhood where cabs regularly drive through looking for fares, so he would've had to call. There are a *lot* of taxi services in this city, but assuming he went with one of the bigger ones, we're talking about doing follow-up with eight to ten."

"He got rid of his car a few years ago. He didn't use it much and didn't like that it made his movement easy to track." Becca looked at Marz with a twist of her lips. "He could be a bit paranoid."

"Not unusual among hackers, especially good ones, which it sounds like he must be if he's making a decent living white hattin' it." She frowned, and Marz added, "Meaning hacking for nonmalicious reasons. Getting paid by corporations to do it for security testing." All this was right up Derek's alley. Computer security, surveillance, and investigations were some of his specialties. He liked tech and he liked toys and he liked to talk about them and explain them until your ears bled with an utter lack of understanding. But you went along with it because he was scary brilliant. "So, we need into phone records, dispatch records, what else? Credit card records? Any of his equipment available to scan?"

"No," Becca said. "All his machines were gone. Or taken."

Marz pursed his lips. "I brought some high-powered gear, but a lot of what we're talking about is usually sub-poena territory. What's the thinking?"

Rixey filled him in on what Miguel had learned and met Becca's fretful gaze, knowing she was worried about them on this point. But it couldn't be helped. "We're off the grid on this."

Derek nailed him with a stare, his brain clearly chewing on the idea behind his dark brown eyes. "Given everything that's at stake, I'm okay with that."

With Marz, things were always that easy. And it helped that he had the skills to make it happen, with or without permission.

But it also meant they were officially operating outside the law.

Nick filled Marz in on Becca's plan to post a reward, and the man scrambled up off the ground, crossed the room, and grabbed a bag off the pile. He knelt on the floor next to Becca and pulled a laptop free of the case. "I need to write all this down. Make a list of tasks and equipment." He rubbed his hands together and smiled at Becca as the machine booted up, enthusiasm pouring off him.

She grinned, then did a double take at something behind him.

When he'd taken a knee, his pants leg had ridden up, revealing the metal pylon of the prosthesis on his right leg. Marz glanced her way again and saw her looking.

"AK or BK?" she asked, diving right into the subject none of the men had yet broached. And damn if that didn't impress him.

"Below the knee." He patted the shank. "Got my own hardware now, complete with shocks and microprocessors. Actually, this is one of four."

"Why so many?"

He ticked off on his fingers. "One for running, one for rough terrain, one for street wear, a waterproof one for showering."

"You're running?" Beckett asked, his expression a careful mask.

"Dude, I'm running an eight-minute mile," he said. Pride in his friend flooded through Rixey. Marz was a damned inspiration. That much was sure. "All right, here we go." Marz's fingers flew over the keyboard.

Most of the time, Beckett kept things battened down inside, not showing much reaction one way or the other. It was part of the reason their fight had caught Nick off guard last night. But Nick saw emotion surface in the other man's eyes, guilt and grief warring with gratitude and admiration. Rixey didn't shy away from it, though. He held Beck's gaze and willed him to know he was there for him. *Damnit, Murda, it wasn't your fault.*

All of a sudden, Becca pushed up from the table. "Anyone want another slice?" she asked, skirting around Nick's chair as a few of the guys called out affirmatives. She went straight to the sink and turned on the faucet, but then she just stood there.

Rixey frowned as he watched her. And then he saw it. Her shoulders shaking, just the smallest bit. Was she crying?

Torn between giving her privacy and aching to know what had upset her, he eased out of his chair and grabbed another slice for himself, making plenty of noise with the box so she knew he was there. She stiffened and wiped at her face, then washed and dried her hands.

When she turned, he was right there. She tried to look away, but he grabbed her chin with his fingers. God, he wanted to kiss her, kiss away whatever had caused the sadness behind those baby blues. Emotion played over her face, like she didn't know what to say or maybe was afraid to say anything at all. And, okay. He'd really just wanted her to know he was there for her. He kissed her forehead, letting his lips linger for a moment so he could breathe her sweetness in, then stepped away. He grabbed his plate and returned to his seat.

A few minutes later, she was delivering slices to everyone who'd asked for more and resuming her place beside Marz. "What is all that?" she asked, looking over his shoulder.

"Equipment I might need."

She blew out a breath and surveyed the group. "Whatever any of this costs, none of it is coming out of your pockets. If you say we need it, we'll get it. And I'll figure that part of it out."

Nick frowned. He could guess what professional-grade computer and surveillance equipment might cost, and it wasn't chump change. Besides, if his suspicions were right, they were getting as much out of this as she and Charlie were. Maybe more. "Becca—"

"No, I mean it. I have a decent savings tucked away. This is more than a good enough reason to use it."

The men nodded, and Rixey let it go for now. He could tell in the looks they exchanged between themselves that she'd earned a notch of respect, first for addressing Marz's amputation head-on, and then for this. Damn, there was just so much to admire about this woman.

"You got a place for me to set up shop, Rix?" Marz asked. "I'm going to need workspace for several computers and some equipment, lots of outlets, and internet access."

Nick frowned, thinking the problem through, then nodded. "Probably not ideal, but I've got a gym across the hall. The whole back corner is totally open. It's all wired for cable and internet, otherwise the space is rough."

"Secure?"

"Completely."

Marz shrugged. "I'm easy."

"Hey, that's my line," Easy said.

"Heard that about both of you," Shane said.

Marz barked out a laugh. "Fucker." His head whipped toward Becca. "Oh, shit, sorry."

She smiled. "I'm pretty sure I can handle some 'fucks.'" And damn if she didn't wink, knowing full well what she'd just said. Didn't look his way, though.

"Well, fuck, then," Marz said, grinning. The guys laughed. Rixey shifted in his seat, her words sending his brain in all kinds of directions it did not need to go. "All right. I just emailed this list to myself. So let's go do some toy shopping and get this show on the road."

Chapter 16

There it is," Becca said, pointing over the front seat toward Charlie's house. After nearly three hours of shopping, carting several thousand dollars' worth of new equipment in, and helping Marz get everything relocated into the back corner of the gym, she, Nick, and Beckett had left Shane and Easy to help get his research station up and running while they'd headed out with the flyers. At least she had savings she could dip into. She'd tucked away most of her share of their father's life insurance, plus she always added to her savings first when she got paid. Net result was a bigger-than-average rainy day fund. And this situation was the equivalent of a downpour. "Wait. Why are you—"

"Making sure no one's watching the place," Nick said, driving by the row house.

"Oh." As she looked around, nothing appeared to be out of place or suspicious. It was a quiet, empty-feeling street in a run-down neighborhood. Despite the beautiful Saturday afternoon, no one was out walking a dog or playing or sitting on their stoop. Suddenly, the emptiness itself took on a sinister quality, and threat of danger lurked around every corner and behind every parked car. A shiver ran up her spine.

Two streets down, he turned and went around the block back to Charlie's. He pulled to the curb a few doors down from the house and killed the engine.

Beckett got out of the passenger seat and adjusted it forward for her, even going so far as to offer her his hand.

"Thanks," she said, grabbing her bag and the flyers and briefly meeting his intense gaze. The guy was downright intimidating, truth be told. But then she remembered he'd held her hair while she'd thrown up . . . A man who'd do that couldn't be all scary. "Let's see if Charlie's landlord is home now. He can let us in his place."

"That's fine," Nick said. "Just, whatever you do, have one of us with you. We're armed, and you're not. No going off on your own." Icy green eyes bored into her. At least he was looking at her and talking to her again. She still had no idea what had happened this morning, why he'd seemed so mad at her. What they'd shared had been amazing. The fact that he'd acted like he regretted it stung. Bad.

"I got it." In any other situation, she might've bristled at his tone, but someone *had* tried to grab her, after all. Even if he'd been a jerk this morning, a part of her insisted he cared. Why else would he be willing to go to all this risk and trouble for her?

Then there was that moment by the sink. Seeing Marz so full of life despite everything that'd happened to him had overwhelmed her with joy and pride, despite the fact that she'd just met him. And then a stray thought had slithered through her brain. *Why didn't Dad survive, too? Why isn't he here with me and these guys helping us figure this out? It's not fair.* She'd been so blindsided that tears had come to her eyes before she'd even realized she was going to cry. But no way had she wanted to break down in front of that group of men.

She hopped up the steps to Walt's door and knocked. Just as she raised her hand to knock again, someone released the locks from the inside and pulled it open.

"Miss Becca?" he said, his light brown eyes flying from her to the two men behind her. His brow furrowed as his gaze settled on the bruise on her forehead. At least the goose egg had gone down. Now she was just a walking dull ache.

"Hi, Walt. I'm sorry to drop in on you without calling, but I wondered if we could come in for a few minutes and talk. About Charlie." He eyeballed the guys again. "They're my friends."

"Yeah, okay. For you, Miss Becca. Come on in."

She smiled and stepped into the foyer. "How are you doing?"

He shrugged and sighed, watching Nick and Beckett like a hawk as they filed into the outdated-but-neat living room. "I'm getting by. You find your brother yet?"

"No, but Nick and Beckett are helping me." She made introductions and Walt shook their hands, still a little wary of them. "I'm going to hang these around," she said, handing him a flyer. "We have to figure out where he went when he left here."

"You cops?" he said, looking between the guys.

"No, sir," Beckett said.

"They fought wi—"

"Becca," Nick said sharply, cutting her off. She frowned at him, and he shook his head. "Sir, do you happen to know which cab company Charlie used? Was there one? Several?"

"Usually Yellow Cab," Walt said, frowning. "Had 'em pick him up down the block at the convenience store. Never here."

Becca's heart leapt. Maybe a store clerk knew Charlie and would remember when they'd seen him. "That could be really helpful. Thank you. Would you be willing to look at a drawing for me?"

"I suppose. Of what?"

She handed him the sketch. "A man who tried to kidnap me yesterday."

"What?" His eyes flew wide. This time, when he looked at Nick and Beckett, his expression was different, more open, like he was putting the pieces of a puzzle together and deciding he liked the picture they made. "That what happened to your forehead?"

"Yeah. Luckily, I got away." Well, luck and the incredible, sexy guy standing behind her. Becca had no idea how she'd repay him when this was all over, but she knew she'd owe him big. "But between that incident and the fact that someone did to my house what they did to Charlie's, I'm being extra careful. And we're trying to figure out who this man might be."

Walt held the picture some distance in front of him and looked down his nose studying it. "I don't know him. I'm sorry." He passed it back and pointed to the next sheet on her stack. "What's that?"

"A tattoo he had on his arm. Mean anything to you?"

"No." He rubbed his hand over his mouth, contemplation clear in his expression. "You got copies of these you could leave with me? I could show them to my son. He knows a lot of people. Maybe . . ." He shrugged.

She didn't know his son, but she wasn't going to refuse help. "That would be great. I'd appreciate any help."

Nick stepped closer. "Walt, have you seen anyone snooping around Charlie's place? Any cars sitting and watching it? Anyone on the block not usually here?"

"No, and after what happened the other day, I've been keeping an eye out. But if y'all leave me your number, I'll call if I see something. And when I hear from my son, too."

"Just use that number," Becca said, pointing to the reward flyer in his hands. "Right now, another friend named Derek is manning that phone. I'll let him know to get in touch with me right away if you call."

"All right," Walt said.

"One last thing. Would you let us into Charlie's apartment again?"

A few minutes later, they were down in Charlie's dungeonlike space. Everything still looked just as it had the other day. She hung with Walt at the door while the guys did a methodical sweep through the place, checking for bugs, looking for anything out of the ordinary. Nick called Marz and told him about the Yellow Cab lead and what kind of equipment was left in Charlie's office, but apparently nothing useful remained that Marz could investigate. The visit was a bust. Nick and Beckett met her back at the door, and they left.

"I'm sorry I can't do more to help," Walt said out on the sidewalk.

"You're doing plenty. And I appreciate it." Despite the whole near-miss-with-a-baseball-bat situation, she felt an affection for the man ever since he'd insisted on charging into Charlie's when they'd seen it'd been ransacked.

After Walt went back inside after promising he'd call later, Becca turned on Nick, wondering what she'd done wrong. "Hey, why did you cut me off before?"

"Sorry. I should've said something earlier. At this point, Becca, you have to assume you can't trust anyone outside our circle. Information equals advantage. We don't want to give away either if we don't have to."

"Oh. Okay. That makes sense. I guess I'm not used to thinking that way." She dug into her purse and grabbed the stapler she'd brought, then stepped to the nearest phone pole to tack up a flyer. The spring breeze made her wrestle to keep the paper flat.

"No reason you should. Normal people don't." Expression serious, his gaze did a constant scan over the street. The sunlight made his green eyes brighter than usual. It was such a striking contrast to his dark brown hair.

She glanced at him. "You're not normal?"

He smirked. "Not even a little. Come on, let's head toward the convenience store." He pulled his cell from his pocket.

"How many times do you think a Yellow Cab has picked someone up from that Handi-Mart in the past few weeks?" she asked.

"Good question. Hopefully not many."

Becca paused at another pole, where she struggled to get the staple in.

"Here," Beckett said. "Gonna hurt your hand." He took the stapler and pounded a little metal hook into each corner like he was cutting soft butter, revealing a mountain range of purple bruises across his knuckles from punching the fridge.

"Thanks. How's your hand doing?"

He frowned, then held up his righty and flexed his fingers. "I'll live," he said. Even though the words were abrupt, the expression on his face softened just a little.

She slid a flyer under the windshield wipers of each of the cars they passed. Maybe these wouldn't make any difference in the end, but it felt good to be *doing* something. At the intersection, Beckett walked the four corners, hanging a flyer on the poles all the way around. The man was hard as heck to engage in conversation, but his actions proved he was a good guy. She'd just remember not to take his gruffness personally.

Nick stayed close to her side, his muscles braced and his gaze doing a constant circuit. His nearness resurrected uninvited memories of their morning activities in his bed. God, he'd felt so good.

"Marz is a really cool guy," she said, not wanting to think about how amazing Nick had made her feel. Those orgasms had been so good they deserved to have a party thrown in their honor. Complete with confetti and noisemakers. Nor did she want to think about how he'd withdrawn and screwed it all up. "Not everyone would remain so positive after losing a leg."

Nick nodded, deep admiration sliding into his expression. "He's the best. Although he is possibly the worst singer you will ever hear in your lifetime."

Beckett rejoined them and laughed under his breath. "That's the damn truth."

"And there are times you would give anything for a roll of duct tape to get him to stop talking for five minutes. But he is loyal to a fault and cool in a crisis . . ." He glanced to her, then Beckett. "Know what he said while Shane was working on him? After the grenade went off?"

The big guy's head whipped toward him, eyebrows cranked into a sudden frown.

"What?" she said, feeling a little nervous about being between them. If they went at it again like last night, she was going to get squashed.

"He was flat on his back and losing blood like a sieve. I'd balled this scarf I had against the wound, and my hand was red in a matter of minutes. Shane asked him how he was doing. You know, trying to keep him talking to keep him conscious. And Derek said, 'I think my toenail clippers are going to last twice as long now.' "

"Oh, my God. That is horrible . . . and funny." She chuckled. Out of the corner of her eye, she saw Beckett turn away, like he was scanning behind them.

When they reached the convenience store parking lot, Beckett grabbed more flyers to hang. The ice had slipped back into his demeanor, and she couldn't help but wonder why. Becca and Nick went inside, and she looked around the guy in line in front of her to the store clerk, a middle-aged man with a name tag that read, "Prajeet."

"Can I help you?" he said when it was their turn.

Becca slid a flyer on the counter. "Do you recognize this man, by any chance? He's my brother, and he went missing. His neighbor told me he would catch cabs from here sometimes."

Prajeet lifted the paper. "Charlie. I know him. Doritos and Mountain Dew, just about every time."

Becca's heart flew into her throat. "Do you remember how long it's been since you last saw him?"

"Oh." Prajeet stared out the window in thought. "It's been at least a week. Maybe two. He came in to use the ATM. It was late, like after midnight. And, yes, he caught a cab."

Nick stepped in close to her, his hand on her lower back and his thumb stroking her skin through her thin shirt. "Is there any chance you remember what day that was?"

"No. I'm sorry. But I think maybe more like two weeks ago than one."

She held out her hand. "Thank you so much, Prajeet. I'm Becca. Would you please call that number if you think of anything else? Or if you see him again? It's really important."

"I will be happy to do that for you," he said, returning her shake. He grabbed a roll of clear tape from under the counter. "And I'll put this here, too." He taped the flyer to his counter.

Gratitude filled her chest. She wasn't sure how she'd expected people to act, but so far she felt like they were actually getting somewhere. Or maybe that was just wishful thinking? "That's wonderful. Thank you."

Outside, they made their way to the sidewalk and searched for Beckett, who was about half a block down in front of a gas station. She shifted her feet and looked around, suddenly filled with nervous energy and the desire to keep moving forward.

Nick's hand fell on her shoulder. "Hey."

Becca met his gaze. "What?"

"Everything's okay. Breathe," he said, squeezing gently.

Closing her eyes, she took a deep, cleansing breath. How did he know she really needed a little reassurance? "What if we're too late?" she said, voicing her worst fear as she looked up at him again.

He shook his head. "Stay positive until you have a solid reason to think otherwise, okay? You'll drive yourself crazy. Today's going to be a marathon, so you gotta pace yourself."

"Right. You're right. Okay."

Cupping her face, he studied her. "How are you feeling today, anyway? I didn't get a chance to ask earlier . . ."

Earlier . . . as in when they were having sex and then he was giving her the cold shoulder. And was she imagining it, or had there been more than a hint of guilt in his voice? "Mostly just achy. And my side hurts. But I took ibuprofen and it's manageable. You?"

The small smile brought out his dimple. "About the same." Man, the combination of those harshly handsome good looks and his sweet concern was a real heart-stealer. And the more time she spent with Nick Rixey, the clearer it became that he was stealing hers. It had started before the sex, but clearly their closeness this morning had amplified everything she was feeling for him. The admission made her stomach flip-flop and her heart race and her knees weak—it was just . . . overwhelming in the midst of all this other chaos.

"Learn anything?" Beckett asked when he rejoined them. Nick filled him in, and Beck nodded. "Marz might be able to find that ATM withdrawal."

"Good point," Nick said. He fired off a text.

She huffed. "If we could go to the cops, they could get a warrant or a subpoena or whatever it is they need and get the bank to just give them the information."

Nick frowned. "Yeah. It sucks, but until we know more, we gotta assume someone on the inside is helping the bad guys, which means for the time being we have to consider the police unfriendlies."

"I know. Where to now?" Hard to believe she and Charlie were caught in a situation where she couldn't trust the police. What the hell had Charlie found?

"I did the block up that way," Beckett said.

"All right. Let's head back the other way, then."

"Oh, did you put one in that bus stop shelter over there?" she asked, pointing.

Beckett held up the stapler. "This doesn't work in plastic or metal."

"Finally, a problem I can fix." She rooted in her purse and found the roll of clear tape she'd brought. "Ta-da!"

Beckett arched a brow. "You got a cold beer in there, too?"

She chuckled and passed him the tape. "Don't I wish."

Tape in hand, Beckett jogged across the street and taped a flyer to the inside and the outside of the shelter. For the next half hour, they hit up more cars, poles, and shelters. A barber agreed to tape the flyer in the window of his shop, and a pastor let them post it on the community bulletin board inside his church.

"Hold up," Nick said, his phone buzzing in his pocket. With a quick scan of the relatively empty street, he pulled it out and answered on speaker phone. "Marz, this is Nick. You're on speaker."

"Hey. I got something," Derek said. Becca looked between the men with wide eyes. "The ATM was a dead end. I managed to dial into it, and it was pretty easy to bypass the remote authentication system and override the machine's firmware, but that only lets me record current and future transactions, not past ones."

"Marz, I didn't understand half of that, but you're killing me here," Becca said.

The man chuckled. "Oh, sorry. I get carried away. I got into Yellow Cab's dispatch records. Man, their firewall was seriously weak. Anyway, there have been three pickups from that convenience store in the past two weeks. Two dropped off to residential addresses and one to a motel."

Nick nodded. "Text me the addresses?"

Pause. "Done. They're all near you, so it shouldn't take long to check them. Hey, you all have enough hands? I forgot something, and Easy said he'd get it."

"That should be fine, but send Shane our way." Becca met Nick's gaze, wondering why he'd asked for more help.

"Roger that." Marz hung up.

"Why did you ask him to send Shane?" she asked.

"Because we have specific addresses to check out now. If we happen upon the location where Charlie's being held, I want us to have more backup." His phone vibrated with an incoming text message. "Our first solid lead," he said. "Let's check them out."

Becca's stomach churned with equal parts dread, anticipation, and hope. *Wherever you are, Charlie, we're coming. Just hang in there a little while longer.*

BECCA'S HOPES WERE hanging on by a very thin thread with a frayed spot in the middle. After ruling out the two elderly ladies who lived at the residences on Marz's initial list, they were on their way to a third motel. Apparently Charlie had been moving around a lot. What the hell made him so afraid? Any other time, she might've written it off to his paranoia, but given that someone had kidnapped and tortured him, he'd clearly behaved completely rationally.

And she hadn't believed him the last time they'd chatted. Her stomach was a sour churning sea at the memory.

At the first seedy motel, it had taken the entire seventy-five dollars she'd had in her wallet to get the clerk to agree to look in their records to see when Charlie had checked in and out. He'd used the name Scott Charles—a combination of both her brothers' names, which made Becca's heart clench in her chest—and stayed for four days before he'd called a cab and left at the crack of dawn.

In case it took more bribes to track his movements, Becca made the maximum withdrawals from two different ATMs. In the meantime, Marz found what they needed in Yellow Cab's dispatch records to locate Charlie's second hotel, where he'd stayed only two days, and then his third.

Heading out Pulaski Highway, they crossed the city line into Baltimore County. With each hotel, Charlie had moved further away from his home. She couldn't begin to imagine why he'd moved when he had—or what he'd been running from. It was like she'd stepped into the middle of a nightmare where nothing made sense and the rules changed the moment something became clearer.

A few minutes later, Nick eased his car into the parking lot of a roadside motel. Two stories high and maybe fifteen rooms wide, the place screamed *cheap!* or, maybe, *rooms by the hour!* Shane pulled in behind them in his pickup, and they all met outside the lobby.

"Third time's a charm," she said, forcing positivity she didn't feel into her voice. The guys murmured words of encouragement she'd bet they didn't really feel, either. They stepped inside.

"Can I help you?" the woman behind the desk asked around a wad of gum. Probably in her fifties and the definition of haggard, she had a drawn, bored look to her expression.

"I hope you can. My brother Charlie is missing, and we know that a cab dropped him off here on Sunday." Six days ago. *Six days ago* Charlie might've been standing right where she stood now.

The desk phone let out a shrill buzz. "Excuse me a second." She cracked her gum as she answered.

Becca frowned at Nick, and he gave her a wink that told her to hang in there. Suddenly, a wave of gratitude washed over her. No way she could've done this without him, without all of them. Not just because they provided protection and know-how but because they gave her the confidence and the wherewithal to go out searching for Charlie, to talk to people, to *bribe* them to talk to her. She'd always been more of the straightlaced, follow-the-rules type, so she was pretty close to certain she never would've had the lady balls to do that on her own.

"Someone will bring that right up," the woman said and hung up the phone. "Marla?" She called the name twice, the second time nearly yelling. A slim woman in an outdated maid's uniform rushed into the lobby from a door marked Staff Only. "Take new towels to 203," she ordered.

With a quick glance at them, the housekeeper nodded and slipped back through the door.

"I'm sorry, what were you saying?" the woman droned.

Becca tamped down her annoyance and slid a flyer on the counter. "My brother Charlie is missing. We're looking for him. And we know from Yellow Cab that they dropped him off here last Sunday."

A *bang* sounded out behind her. Becca flinched and looked over her shoulder, noting that Nick had placed his body between her and the noise and the other guys had their hands in their jackets. The maid's brown face blanched, and the door she'd apparently opened too hard slowly eased back toward her. "Sorry," she said, bending to retrieve a pile of white terrycloth she'd dropped to the dingy tile floor.

The desk clerk rolled her eyes. "So, you think your brother stayed here?"

"Yes," Becca said, releasing a breath. "Can you tell us how long he was here or when he left?"

"Sorry, hon. It's against our policy to give out any information about our guests," she said in the most patronizing tone on earth.

But Becca wasn't dissuaded, since this was the same thing the other clerks had said, too. At first.

Checking over her shoulder, Becca waited for the maid to exit the lobby. Her gaze whipped back to the receptionist. "Is there anything I can do to convince you to help me? I have reason to believe Charlie's life is in danger."

The woman gave her a once-over and loudly chawed on her gum. "You're not suggesting I do something unethical, are you?"

"You call it unethical. I call it doing the right thing. I know he was here, and I know when he arrived. I only need your help with when he left." Frustration pricked at the back of her eyes.

"Sorry. If the police bring me a warrant, I'll be happy to share." She snapped her gum. Becca was ready to strangle her with it.

Nick leaned his hands on the counter. "We'll make it worth your while," he said with a nod toward her computer. "Can't you help us?"

Her eyebrows flew to her teased hairline. "I think y'all better get on out of here."

Becca's stomach dropped to her feet. "Ma'am, please—"

Nick grasped her arms from behind and squeezed. "It's okay. Come on," he whispered against her ear. He bustled her across the lobby and out the door to the parking lot.

"What are we going to do now?" she said, looking up at Nick.

"We'll figure it out. Don't worry." When he rubbed her hand, she realized she was shaking.

Anger roared through her. They were *so* close. She felt it, like Charlie'd left an echo behind she could still hear. She blew out a long breath and looked away.

At the far end of the row of exterior doors, the maid they'd seen in the lobby—Marla, the clerk had called her—came jogging down a set of concrete steps. Head lowered, shoulders curled in, walking fast, it was like she didn't want anyone to notice her . . .

On a gasp, Becca's gaze whipped to Nick's.

"I'm already with you," he said. "She looks like a scared rabbit, though. You comfortable asking?"

Becca was already heading toward her. "Miss? Marla?" she said, walking fast across the parking lot, flyers in hand. "Can I please ask you a question?"

The woman lifted her head, her gaze darting between Becca, the guys, and the lobby door.

"Please? I need your help."

Her shoulders sagging, Marla came to a stop, looked both ways, then waved Becca to follow her. She walked a few steps back the way she'd come and ducked into a dim hallway.

Becca followed at a jog. Nick called out after her, but she was too afraid the maid would slip away to wait for him. She crossed between two parked cars, hopped up onto the cracked sidewalk, and, heart a racehorse in her chest, stepped into the same hallway. At the end of a row of vending and ice machines, Marla stood with her arms crossed tight over her chest.

"Do you know something about my brother, Marla?" Becca asked, passing her a flyer.

Nick barreled into the hallway a moment later, a dark scowl on his face. He didn't say a word, though the cocked eyebrow said plenty.

Marla's brown eyes latched onto the sheet Becca held, though she didn't take it. "Yeah, I saw him. But I need money," she said, eyes on the floor like maybe she wasn't proud of the words. "I got kids, and this place don't pay enough." She shrugged her thin shoulders.

Becca dug into her purse and grabbed five twenties. Marla balled them in her fist. "My brother? When did you see him?"

Marla sniffed and lifted her gaze, working it back and forth between Becca and Nick. "He came on Sunday, like you said." Becca leaned in as if she could will the words from the woman's mouth. "On Monday morning, early . . . they took him off in a gray van."

Becca's heart tripped into a sprint. She knew the trail they'd been following probably ended in exactly this kind of story. Obviously, *someone* had taken Charlie against his will at some point, because he hadn't cut off his own finger and left it at her house. But hearing it . . . she had no words.

"Who's 'they'?" Nick took over, wrapping his arm around Becca's shoulders and pulling her in against him. Solid. Strong. Unwavering. She soaked him in and forced herself to calm down.

Marla played with a chain at her throat. "Bangers. Kind I left the city to get away from. Same types you see downtown selling heroin on street corners. Was three of 'em."

"Any of them this man?" Nick said, slipping the paper from Becca's tight grip and holding it up.

Marla shook her head. "I don't think so, but I wasn't trying to see them, either, if you know what I mean. Got a bad feeling the minute their van rolled into the lot. I was upstairs cleaning the room of an early checkout when I heard this loud bang. I peeked through the curtains, and sure enough the men from the van were breaking down a door. They put a hood over his head and dragged him out."

"Did you call the police?" Becca managed, incredulous. How had something like this happened in broad daylight?

Marla looked at her like she had three heads. "I wasn't risking narking on a gang for some addict with an unpaid debt."

Becca's jaw dropped. "Charlie's not an addict."

"Coulda fooled me," Marla said, flipping the pendant of her necklace between her fingers.

"What made you think that?" Nick asked.

"Dark circles, bloodshot eyes, all disheveled looking and acting paranoid. Plus, he paid with cash when he checked in, like he didn't want anyone to know he was here. Almost everyone uses plastic these days."

Becca whirled to Nick. "He's not a user. I promise you that. God, after Scott—" She shook her head. "There's no way."

"I believe you. All of that could easily be explained by him being on the run for so long."

Relief flooded through Becca's chest, making it easier to breathe. That he outright believed her—no debating, no questioning, no measuring—meant the world to her. She sagged against him.

"Well, believe what you want. That's what I saw." Marla dropped the necklace and crossed her arms. Becca frowned and stared at the oval pendant.

"One last question," Nick said. Marla rolled her eyes but nodded. "Was there anything left in his room after they left?"

"No, they cleaned it out. Now 'scuse me, I have to get back."

The pendant had an engraved cursive *C* in the middle of the silver. *C,* for Cathy. Becca's mother. Becca frowned, her heart nearly stopping cold, and stepped in front of Marla. "That's my mother's locket." Her gaze flashed to the woman's, who wouldn't meet it back. "That's my mother's locket," she said again, half disbelieving what she was seeing.

Marla shrugged. "I found it."

Nick moved in closer. "Where?"

"Doesn't matter."

"It does to us." He pulled another hundred out of his wallet. "Please give the lady back her family heirloom."

For a long moment, Becca thought Marla was going to fight them, but the power of the stack of twenties in Nick's hand apparently convinced her. She unhooked the necklace and almost threw it at Becca. "Was on the floor in his room. I didn't steal it. Now 'scuse me." They stepped to the side, and she darted past them.

Before Becca even had the chance to start freaking out—which she was well on her way to doing—Nick cupped her face in his hands and tilted it up. He kissed her forehead. "Knowing the details doesn't change anything about his situation. I know that wasn't easy to hear, but she gave some things to go on. At worst, this was net neutral. Okay?"

Neutral. Right. Charlie being kidnapped, hooded, and dragged away in a van. "I'm trying," she said, gripping her mom's locket tight.

"You're doing great, Becca. Don't doubt it for a minute. Oh, but unless you want to have a heart attack patient to care for, don't run into a dark space without letting me clear it first. She could've been leading you into a trap." That arched brow made a reappearance, and it was as sexy as it was stern, though he probably didn't intend the former.

"I'm sorry. All I could think about was losing her."

He kissed her forehead again. "I understand that. But I'm more worried about losing you."

The words overwhelmed her with emotion—gratitude for his concern, admiration that a hard-edged soldier could show such tenderness, and another feeling, too. One that created a warm, expansive pressure in her chest. "Okay," she managed. She opened her palm and showed the locket to Nick. "This was mine. It's from my mom's jewelry box in my room. I have no idea how Charlie would've gotten it."

Nick frowned. "When was the last time he was at your place?"

She shook her head. "He came over for Christmas. So, about four months ago?"

"Let's get you out of here and we can talk more about it." He grasped her hand and led her back to Beckett and Shane, who had been standing guard outside the hallway. As they all made for Nick's car, he said, "Street thugs grabbed him Monday morning. Emptied his room."

"Well, that nails down time of disappearance, but it only hints at who took him," Shane said. "Where to now?" He paused at the driver's door to his big charcoal gray pickup.

"Back to Hard Ink, I guess," Nick said.

"Wait." Becca leaned into the crook of steel created by her open car door. "Can we go to my house?" She knew she couldn't stay there, but there were some things she'd really like to check on and bring with her. And the morbid curiosity to see just how wrecked the place was had been crawling up her spine for the last day. She knew what Charlie's apartment looked like. Was hers better? Worse? Maybe it was stupid to fixate on it, but the unknown felt harder to deal with than just facing it.

Nick frowned. "That's a bad idea."

His words didn't surprise her at all, or deter her. "Just long enough to pick a few things up. While we have everyone with us?"

"Hold on," he said, pulling his buzzing phone out of his pocket and holding it out. "Marz? On speaker again. What's up?"

"Hey. Just relaying that a Walt Jackson called for Becca through the reward line. Asked if she could return to his place as soon as possible. That make sense to you?"

"Yeah," she and Nick said at the same time.

"Also, FYI, we're done with the cab trace. Charlie was grabbed from the Road Star Motel last Monday morning. Found a witness," Nick said. Another moment or two of small talk, and they hung up.

Torn between disappointment at not getting to go home and anticipation of what Walt might have to say, Becca nodded. "Let's go, then." She slid into the soft leather seat and settled into the corner. Man, she was tired, just bone weary. But no matter how bad she felt, it couldn't possibly come close to what Charlie was going through, and that's what she had to remember. With Nick and Beckett murmuring in the front seat, she almost gave in to the lull of the road noise and let herself drift off.

Becca wedged open the oval locket and frowned. The pictures that had always lived inside, one of her dad in uniform and another of the three kids, were gone. Marla had replaced them with pictures of her own, apparently.

Vibrating with anger, Becca tore the images out and snapped it shut.

Back at Walt's, Nick said, "Don't tell him anything about what we learned today, okay? It's great that he was willing to help, but we have no idea who his son is, and you don't really know Walt all that well."

Scrubbing her hands over her face, Becca nodded. "I feel like we can trust him, but I get your point. I won't say anything."

Nick led her over to Shane's truck. "The landlord's skittish. You mind keeping a lookout? Unless you'd rather head back?"

"No. I'll stay. I'm feeling a little like we're flappin' around in the wind. Makes sense to stay together," Shane said.

Nick tapped the open window. "Agreed. Won't be long."

They crossed to Walt's house, and he opened the door just before they reached his stoop. "Got the message, I see. Come in." He stepped into the light of the hallway, revealing a busted lip.

"Walt, what happened?" Becca said.

"He got jumped is what happened," a man said as he stepped into the foyer. Probably about forty, with Walt's coloring, eyes, and freckles, and a tattoo of a snake coiling around the length of his right forearm.

"Not their fault. Becca, this is my son, Louis Jackson."

"Hi," she said with a quick shake. Nick and Beckett followed. "What happened to you?" she asked again, fear mixing with her exhaustion and hunger and making her shaky.

"Had a visitor downstairs. About two hours ago. Masked. Caught him coming out of Charlie's. Chased him off but—"

"He got punched and knocked down for his trouble. Lucky it wasn't worse," Louis said, eyes flashing.

"Oh, my God. I'm so sorry. Are you hurt?" Guilt rushed through Becca's body. She couldn't believe whatever this was had spilled over on Walt, too.

He waved a hand. "Nothing that won't heal."

"You're lucky you didn't break a hip, Pop."

Walt scoffed.

"Why the hell would they come back?" Nick asked. "Can we borrow your key, Walt? I'd like to see if anything's changed since earlier."

The old man fished the key ring out of his pocket. "Bring it right back."

Nick turned to her. "Stay here and stay inside. We'll check it out."

Nodding, Becca watched them leave. She could just make out the sound of Charlie's door opening. What the hell was going on? She turned back to Walt. "God, I'm really sorry. Do you need me to check you over? I'm a nurse."

"No. Come on in and sit down," he said. "Just a banged-up elbow, mostly. Survived worse. Will survive this."

LOUIS SAT NEXT to her on the couch and pulled a stack of paper in front of him, including the sketch of her assailant's tattoos. "I didn't recognize the man, but I might know the tattoo," he said, his tone less angry now. "See . . ." He pointed to the solid square she'd seen on the back of her assailant's hand. "This by itself doesn't mean anything, but it *could* mean something if there was more to it." Grabbing a blank notepad he'd apparently brought for this purpose, he drew a series of symbols:

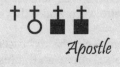

Apostle

"I'm sorry. Would you mind waiting until my friends return? I don't want to forget anything or miss asking a question."

Louis tapped his pen on the page. "Sure. I'm sorry about your brother, by the way."

Becca nodded. "Thank you."

Long minutes passed. Occasionally she heard a dull thump or the low murmur of a voice from downstairs. Still holding her mom's locket, she twisted the chain and turned the pendant in her hands. She flipped it open again, sadness filling her at the loss of the family photos. Why had Charlie taken the necklace? And when?

Becca leaned toward the lamp on the end table. There was something in the ovals where the pictures went. She gasped. A string of letters and numbers filled the two spaces, roughly engraved, as if by hand. She turned the silver to catch more light. The right side read, "WCE." The left side was a string of numbers: 754374329. Without saying a word, she snapped it shut and slid it into her jeans pocket, her heart suddenly beating fast. She'd show Nick when they got home.

A knock sounded at the front door, and Becca nearly jumped. She rose as Walt and Louis made their way to the foyer, and Nick and Beckett followed them back into the living room a moment later.

Tension and anger radiating off him, Nick held out his hand. Two rectangular pieces of what looked like metal filled his palm. "Bugs," he said. "That hadn't been there this afternoon."

"One audio and one video," Beckett said.

"That doesn't even make sense," Becca said. "They already have Charlie, why would they monitor his house now?"

" 'Monitor' is precisely the right word. I think they're watching for who's coming and going. Maybe they already know someone's searching for Charlie. Reward flyers have been up for a few hours, so it's possible. And the timing would make sense."

Beckett stepped to the coffee table. "Those are map symbols for churches."

"That's right." Louis stabbed his pencil point into a black square. "But they're also gang symbols. If this is what you saw, Becca, then the man who tried to abduct you is a member of the Church Organization, a prominent gang run by a crime lord named Jimmy Church." Looking up, he met her gaze, then looked at Nick and Beckett. "And surveillance like that is definitely within their capability."

"Okay," she said, sitting down again.

"See," he continued, "gangs are hierarchical institutions, and they have different ways of showing that. One is with tattoos. In the Church organization, the simple cross represents an affiliate member, almost like a prospective member. Youngsters. The cross and steeple symbol represents formal gang members. They're officially in the gang. These are the guys doing the street hustling of drugs and guns and prostitutes. The cross and tower symbol is for hard-core gang members, men in their twenties or thirties who have fully adopted gangs as their lifestyle and run crews of younger members, seeking to expand business and territory to earn status. At the next-to-top are the apostles, who hold the leadership positions, often running the gang's front businesses. They've earned their seniority with a lot of time on the streets and in prison, usually, and now they have the money and the influence to stay mostly clean of the illegal activities, all while directing them. At the top, of course, is Jimmy Church, the Messiah."

"Uh, wow," Becca managed, letting all that soak in. It was a whole other world. "Can I see?" He handed her the page. "I saw the square. That much I'm sure of. There wasn't any writing beneath it. But it's possible there was a cross atop it. I saw him from across the room, though, and I wasn't really paying attention." She looked up at Nick. "It's possible there was a cross. I know there was something above the square."

He nodded. "Louis, what kinds of drugs does this organization sell? Any specialties?"

"Well, everybody sells everything, but Church has been working to dominate the heroin trade for years. He inherited this organization from his grandfather, who back in the eighties sold most of the heroin in Baltimore. Church has probably built it back to about seventy-five percent dominance, so if someone's selling heroin, they're probably Church's men."

"Can I ask why you're willing to tell her all this?" Beckett asked, arms crossed, expression serious as a heart attack.

Not even a little flustered by Beckett's demeanor, Louis laced his fingers between his knees. "I did my time in a Baltimore gang, and I did my time in prison. Now I work on the city's gang task force and run a community program that gives kids alternatives to gangs and helps gang members transition to civilian life. I met Charlie a few times and liked him. Would hate to know he'd been caught up in something with Church. And now it seems my pop's in danger. I thought my expertise might be of some help."

"Thank you, it does help," Becca said, looking from Louis to Beckett, who gave a nod and eased off. For the first time, his abrasive intensity struck her as being more like big brother protectiveness than just being a hard-ass for hard-ass's sake. She even found it a little endearing.

"Good. Now, my turn for a question," Louis said. "Am I right in thinking that the three of you are here discussing this with me instead of the police because you're trying to find Charlie without them?"

Becca rose and glanced to Nick, unsure whether to answer.

"Why do you want to know?" Nick asked.

"Because you might not find the police as useful as you'd think on this. Church has people on the payroll everywhere. Deep pockets, man, and widespread influence."

Nick's expression was a brick wall, but Becca felt way too awkward to just pretend the question wasn't still hanging in the air. "Can we just say we're not sure who to trust yet?"

"Yeah, that's cool. Well"—he lifted a half-inch-thick spiral-bound report out of his green canvas messenger bag—"in case I'm right, this might be useful to you." The title appeared through the clear laminated cover: *Maryland Gang Survey: Church Organization*. "When you're done with it, just get it back to my dad."

Becca leafed through the pages. The organization's history, known membership, gang identifications, businesses, criminal records, and more fluttered through her vision.

"It's not everything there is to know, but it's a lot of what we do know," he said.

Overwhelmed by the threat an organization like this could pose to Charlie—hell, to them all—she let the booklet flip closed with a snap of pages. "I know I keep saying this, but thank you."

He rose and met each of their gazes. "Don't thank me yet. If Church has your brother, this situation is *real* serious. And it's likely to get worse before it gets better."

Chapter 17

*H*ey, Nick? I found something," Becca said when they got back in the Charger.

He and Beckett turned in his seat toward her. "What?" Nick asked.

She fished the necklace they'd retrieved from the maid out of her pocket and opened it. "Look at the inside surfaces in the light."

Nick turned on the overheads and held it up. Someone had carved letters and numbers into the silver. "Were these here before?"

"No. The pictures that were in there were mine, so I know there wasn't writing in there before. Charlie had to have done this after he took it. No idea what it means, though."

Beckett reached for the necklace. "You drive. I'll call

this in to Marz. He can start running searches on both strings."

Not long after, Rixey eased the Charger into a spot across the street from Becca's house. His gut told him bringing her here was a bad idea on about fifty-two levels—especially with what they'd just found at Charlie's. But if he was going to live up to his word, he had to be a partner and not a dictator, much as that sometimes sucked—not because he wanted to control her but because he wanted Becca safe and happy.

And her house was damn unlikely to achieve either of those goals right now.

He turned in the driver's seat and met her expectant gaze. God, even with everything the day had thrown at her, she was beautiful and brave and still clinging to hope. And with what they'd learned at Walt's tonight, holding onto any kind of positivity was a damned act of heroism.

"No more than ten minutes, Becca. You're not going to have time to tour the whole place. Find the things you want to take, throw them in a bag, and we're back out the door."

She nodded, clearly eager to go inside.

Shane was on the sidewalk, weapon drawn, methodically scanning the street.

"Okay, here we go." Nick unholstered his gun and nodded at Beckett, then the two men got out and Rixey released the seat forward for her. Bracing herself on his hand, she stepped onto the pavement, and Nick was on her like white on rice. He hustled her across the road, Shane and Beckett flanking them. Key in hand before they hit the steps, Rixey reached around her when they got to the door and slid the grooved metal home. Inside, he flicked the switches on the front wall and urged her in so the guys could enter behind them. Last in, Shane secured the door.

Nick was wishing they'd made this trip during the day so the interior lights wouldn't have advertised their presence when he heard her.

"Holy shit. Ho-ly shit. Holy freaking shit."

Standing in the middle of what looked like a tornado's debris, Becca surveyed the damage as she turned in a slow circle, her face pale with shock. When her eyes landed on him, it was like being sucker punched in the solar plexus—her pain and fear sucked the wind right out of his lungs.

He crossed the room and took her hands. "When this is all over, we'll make this right. Okay? Important thing is your safety. You weren't here when they did this, and I don't want you to be here should they decide to return."

She heaved a shaky breath. "Right. Okay. Um, I think everything I want is upstairs." A series of expressions played out over her pretty face, and he literally watched her shove back the panic and steel herself.

Shane and Beckett took up positions at the first-floor doors as Rixey followed her up the stairs. He felt her sense of loss like a jagged rock in his gut. And, man, he would've done anything to bear that burden for her. But sometimes life forced you to walk through the shit whether you had a good pair of boots or not—and it was apparently Becca's turn.

Sonofabitch.

From the steps, she made for the bathroom, but stopped abruptly with an "oh" when she turned on the light. The mirror was shattered, shards everywhere. "Jesus. I'll never get the glass out of the bottom of my shoes if I go in there. Who would *do* this?"

"Tell me what you need, and I'll get it."

"I've got a professional first-responders-type first-aid kit in that closet over there," she said. "Thought it might be good to have on hand."

Hanging onto the molding, Nick leaned in and grabbed a towel off the bar. He flipped out the fabric and settled it over most of the glass. The terry muted the sound of the crunching as he crossed the narrow room.

"It's a red backpack."

In the closet, the pack easily stood out. He slung it over his shoulder. "Anything else?" Something caught his eye and he grabbed and tossed it to her. "How 'bout that?"

Becca squeaked but caught the yellow rubber ducky in her hands. She laughed. They didn't have time to play around, but the thirty seconds it took to distract her from the horror that was her house was worth it. "Actually, Shiloh might like this. She doesn't have any toys."

He grimaced. "That's not a dog name. She's a guard dog. She needs a strong name." Under his feet, the glass crunched again as he made his way out. He dropped the backpack at the top of the steps.

"I know. I just need five concentrated minutes to really think about it," she said, stepping into her bedroom doorway. "Oh, God." She hit the overhead light switch and went utterly still as her gaze scanned over the room. The sudden gasp and sob ran ice down Rixey's spine. Becca bolted over the wreckage, her feet slipping.

"Becca?"

"No. No, no, no." She scrabbled on hands and knees over her bed and clutched at the fretboard of the destroyed guitar lying on the far side. She hugged it to her chest, shoulders shaking and gasping around suppressed sobs, and the wires dragged still-connected pieces of the guitar's bridge and body into her lap. She caved in over it, her back trembling and tense. "No, no," she rasped, tears choking off her voice.

Nick's throat went tight and he was beside her in an instant, wrapping himself around her and whispering soft shushes. "It's okay, sunshine. It's okay." The words felt like crushed glass in his mouth because, whatever this was, it wasn't in the same fucking zip code as okay.

"Is not . . . was . . . Sc-Scott's," she managed around hitches of breath. "Was all . . . all . . . I had . . . l-left."

Sinking onto the edge of the mattress, he pulled her whole body into his lap, settled her face into the crook of his neck, and held her close. Her hand fisted so tight into his shirt that it would probably never fit the same, but he didn't care. He'd bear anything if she didn't have to be going through this right now. She shook against him and held her breath in an effort to restrain the overflow of emotion, and Nick just rubbed her back and kissed her sweaty forehead and vowed on his dead parents' graves he would find the animals responsible for hurting her. Then he'd take those motherfuckers down.

Slowly, the shuddering became less severe and her breathing calmed. Rixey was acutely aware that they'd been at the house longer than they should, but he also didn't want to further upset her.

She slipped her hand between their bodies and wiped at her face.

He tugged up the bottom of his shirt and held it out. "Here. Use me."

A single sad, choked laugh escaped her, but she took him up on her offer, burying her face into his chest as she dried her eyes on the hem of his shirt. When she let it go, it was damp against his skin.

Still in his lap, she eased upright. "Do you . . . h-have . . . a knife?"

Holding her, he leaned over and retrieved the blade from his ankle sheath. "What do you need?"

"Will it cut these wires fr-free?" She blew out a breath, trying to calm herself. "Stupid, but I want to take this." Her knuckles were nearly white from gripping the fret-board so hard.

The blade made quick work of slicing through the metal wires. "It's not stupid at all." He returned the knife to its hiding place, then cupped her face in his hand. Eyes puffy, face red, damp hair sticking to the sides of her cheeks, she was still the most beautiful woman he'd ever seen. "I know it's not fair for me to rush you, but we—"

"I know." She pushed off his chest.

He held her tight another moment. When her sad blue eyes flipped up to his face, he leaned in slowly and kissed her on the lips. No pressure. No heat. Just a tender press of flesh on flesh to let her know he was there. "Whoever did this, Becca, I'm going to make them pay." He helped her to her feet.

When she got down, she moved quickly, almost mechanically, retrieving some clothing here, loose pictures there, and a handful of jewelry she was able to fish out of the mess on the floor. "My bracelet," she gasped, pulling a strand of silver charms out from under a pile of crushed seashells. "It was from my dad." She clipped it to her wrist.

"Careful, Becca," he said as she picked through the debris. Shattered glass and sharp-edged shells were everywhere.

"I will. This is my mom's jewelry box. Where the locket was." She lifted the wooden box, now mostly empty. "I wonder . . ." Pulling out the bottom drawer, she reached her hand in. Something clicked, and a drawer popped out on the back. A small sheet of paper sat within. She gasped.

Nick crouched beside her.

"Oh, my God," she said. "Charlie used to love to play with this when we were kids. He was absolutely fascinated with the hidden compartment. My mom would leave dollar bills in it for him to find." She unfolded the small, square sheet. It read, "WCE 754374329 United

Bank of Singapore 12M." What in the world? "Those are the same letters and numbers as in the locket. It's a bank account?"

"Looks that way. Good job, Becca. This could be a real lead." And not just for Charlie. If that *12M* stood for what he thought, it was a dollar amount. The kind one could make, say, from having a longtime hand in the heroin trade in Afghanistan. Determination settled in his gut, and a little hope, too. "We'll get Marz on this. See what he can make of it."

She nodded, then crossed to her closet, where she retrieved a big tote bag and dropped her treasures in, including the rubber duck. Rooting around in the loose clothes on the floor, she finally yanked a navy blue sweatshirt from the pile. She shook it and held it up. "Wonder if Jeremy would get it," she said, turning it toward him. It read, "There are 10 types of people in the world, those who understand binary, and those who don't."

"I don't get it," Nick said.

She gave a small smile. "It's a nerd joke. Charlie gave it to me." After adding it to the bag, she knelt and repacked a box of what looked like mostly papers and photos that had been dumped out. "I want to take these," she said, pushing the box and tote toward him as she rose. "One more thing." She rolled open the drawer to her nightstand. "Fuck."

"What?" he said, a murderous storm brewing in his gut on her behalf.

"They stole my goddamned gun. I should've taken it that first night, but I thought I'd be back . . ." Nick peered into the mostly empty drawer just before she slammed it shut on a growl. "I am so fucking . . . *mad.*"

He didn't blame her in the least. He was seething, and this hadn't even happened to him. "I'm sorry. I've got a piece at home that might be good for you."

"I don't want *your* gun, I want *my* gun," she said, tugging her fingers through the length of her hair. "I'm sorry. I don't mean to bite your head off. But I am . . ." Her hands clenched into fists, and she leaned her forehead against them. "I just wanna kill someone right now. Which is . . . a really fucking bad thing for a nurse to want to do."

Rixey bit back the kernel of humor her words unleashed. Truth be told, he admired her rage. She was hurt, she was overwhelmed, and she was no doubt scared out of her mind, but she wasn't letting it break her. Anger was good. Anger helped you fight. And, *Jesus,* but she was fierce and sexy when she was enraged.

He never thought he'd say it, but he had to give Frank Merritt credit for this one thing—he'd raised a strong, courageous daughter who could handle herself when the shit was hitting the fan. If Charlie was anything like her, they had a better-than-average shot at him being alive and making it out of this fubar.

She huffed and threw out her hands in a gesture of *Enough,* her bracelet jingling in emphasis. "There's only one thing I want from the office, and then I'm done. Promise." Retrieving the box and tote, he followed her into the hallway, reaching back in to douse the ceiling light. She made her way to the front room, then groaned and cursed and kicked paper around for a minute before returning with a stuffed bear in an Army uniform, complete with ID tags. "This stuff is all I have left of them, you know?"

"I get it. You don't have to justify it to me, Becca. Anything else you can think of, quick?"

She tucked the bear into the bag and shook her head. "No, I'm done. Let's get out of here before something else happens. Besides, this place is pissing me off."

RIXEY PREPARED TO get his head torn off as they stepped into his building's back door. In the midst of the scene at

Becca's house, he'd forgotten the appointment with his tattoo client. Jeremy had called as they were leaving her place, but Rixey had let it go to voice mail, wanting to keep his focus on her and making sure they weren't being watched or tailed. He'd sent Jer a text message saying he was en route, but without question, Jeremy was going to skin him alive. It wasn't undeserved. He was almost fifteen minutes late.

Her keepsakes filling his hands, he turned to Becca and apologized. "I forgot I have this tattoo to do. It's gonna take an hour. Maybe two. Go 'head up with the guys and grab some dinner. I'll be up later."

"You seriously do ink?" Shane asked, hiking Becca's medic kit on his shoulder.

Rixey braced. *Oh, goody, something else for him to ride me about.* "Yeah, I seriously do. Occasionally." He shrugged.

"You any good?"

"Bare some skin and find out."

Shane grinned, his expression making it clear he enjoyed harassing Nick. "If you wanna get me out of my clothes, lovah boy, you gotta wine and dine me first."

It was maybe the first smile Nick had cracked around Shane since the guy had arrived yesterday. And, damn, it felt good. Normal. Like before. "Asshole."

"That's southern fried asshole, to you."

"Only you would want a more descriptive version of asshole, and then consider it a compliment."

"We do everything bigger in the South." Shane winked at Becca, whose face brightened with the bit of levity. It was miles better than the despair she'd worn the whole way from her house. And Nick wanted to buy Shane a barbeque dinner for cheering her up. Even if for only a minute.

"Here." He jammed the box into Shane's gut, enjoying

the surprised "*Oof*" he earned, then dropped the tote bag on top of it. "Make yourself useful and carry this up for Becca, will ya?"

"Sonofabitch," Shane said, half laughing. He and Beckett turned toward the steps, but paused for Becca to go first.

Holding the sketches, the booklet on the gang, and the remainder of the flyers tight against her chest, she glanced between the guys waiting to go upstairs and Nick, standing with his hand on Hard Ink's doorknob. "Um," she finally said. "Mind if I stay with you?"

The uncertainty in her voice slayed him. Like he might actually say no. Guilt parked itself on his chest again for being an angst-ridden asshole this morning, because that was probably why she'd wonder if he wanted her around. "Of course. Just, uh, give that gang profile and Charlie's note to Beck to give to Marz. See what kind of sense he can make of those."

Murda slipped them from her pile of papers. "Probably speed read it in about fifteen minutes," he said, giving Becca what passed for a smile. "We'll take care of your stuff. Don't worry." Neither of his teammates had been upstairs when Becca had broken down, but Rixey suspected they'd both heard it. He also suspected that accounted for the big guy's gentleness with her now. There was a lot more beneath Beckett's hard-ass surface than met the eye. He just didn't like people to know it.

"Thanks," she said.

"What's this 'we' bullshit?" Shane said, starting up the steps. "I don't see your ass schlepping anything."

Beckett followed after, boots stomping out a rhythm on the concrete steps. "You that out of shape, McCallan?" The ribbing continued as they went up the stairs.

Becca smiled as she glanced at Nick. "Are you sure you don't mind?"

The words hauled him to her, and he leaned his forehead on hers. "I'd never mind having you with me. Come on. You get the fun of hearing Jeremy ream me out. Guard your eardrums." He tugged open the door and held it for her.

"I'm sorry I made you late," she said, twisting her lips. "I forgot about your appointment."

"Not your fault. What we were doing was important." Rixey entered the lounge with a *mea culpa* on his tongue. Whatever pile of pissed off he was about to step in, he totally deserved.

Jeremy leaned around the corner from the front desk, glared, and ducked back out. "Give us a few, Alek. We'll be right with you," Nick heard him say. Then his brother barreled down the hall toward him. "This might not be your thing. I get that. But it's my business. My livelihood. My reputation. And I don't appreciate you fucking with it."

"I know. I'm sorry." The anger he could deal with, but that look of disappointment in his brother's eyes was a real kick in the ass.

Becca stepped in close, her arm touching Nick's, providing a united front. "It was my fault, Jeremy. I'm sorry. We were looking for my brother."

"No. My commitment, my fault." Nick reached out and squeezed her shoulder in silent thanks.

Jer looked between them like he was at a tennis match. "Fine. Whatever. Got your head on straight?"

"Yeah. I'll take good care of the guy. Alek's his name?" Jeremy gave a tight nod. "I'll go meet him and get set up." Jeremy turned on his heel and stalked back toward the front. Rixey gave her a little smile. "Thanks for the help."

"It's the least I could do." She shifted her feet and tilted her head. "So, I don't suppose there's any way I could watch you, is there? Probably violates some kind of confidentiality, or something."

The thought of her being in the room with him stirred heat in his groin, both because she wanted to watch him work, and because it made him think of working on her. "It's up to the client. I'll ask." He crossed to the closet in the corner where he hung his jacket and gun holster. It was probably on the wrong side of paranoid, but given the situation, he felt better remaining armed, so he slipped the piece into the back of his jeans and made sure his T-shirt covered it.

"Do you think that's necessary?" she asked.

"What?" he said, turning. She gestured to his back. "Probably not. Have a seat for a few."

"Okay." She dropped her purse and the stack of papers onto one of the round tables and settled into the couch. The puppy loped over to her and hopped her front paws onto Becca's lap.

Grabbing his sketch from the desk in the office, Nick made for the reception area.

"Awwwww, you're in troubllllle," Jess said in a gratingly annoying voice when he passed her room.

"Yeah, yeah. I'm aware."

She snickered. Typical Jess. Good thing he liked her. Mostly. When she wasn't busting his balls. Then again, when was that?

Sitting on the big green couch, his client was a man probably in his mid-thirties, dark hair, tall by the length of the legs stretched out in front of him, crossed at the ankles. Nick approached and extended his hand. "Really sorry to keep you waiting. I'm Nick Rixey." For the next ten minutes, he talked to Alek about the tattoo, its placement, and his past experience getting inked, and he got permission for Becca to watch.

Nick grabbed his stencil from the office and leaned around the corner where Becca sat. "We're a go if you're still interested."

Becca smiled up at him. "Really? Yeah."

"You sure you wouldn't rather go up and have some grub? Lunch was a long time ago." If he hadn't had to do this tat, he'd have been three slices into some leftover pizza himself.

"I'll eat with you after."

He crossed to the fridge in the corner and grabbed two bottles of water. "Well, at least have something to drink. Come on." He led them into the rectangular tattoo room and gestured to the visitor chair often inhabited by a client's friend.

She sat and watched him as he prepared his workspace and tools. "How did you first learn to do this, anyway?"

He scrubbed his hands and forearms at the sink. "Jeremy. He got an apprenticeship his freshman year at the College of Art here in town, and by his junior year he was working almost full-time for the guy and doing some fantastic work. Along the way he taught me what he'd learned. I enjoyed it enough that Jer bought me a basic set of my own machines for Christmas one year, and I practiced a lot because at that point I was trying to decide what the hell I wanted to do with myself. I was in college but felt restless as hell. I figured, why not."

"How do you practice tattooing?"

Rixey chuckled. "Not on real people. They have this rubber practice skin you can use to get familiar with the tattoo machine, and some people practice on fruit and pig skin. Anyway, Jeremy wanted to drop out of college, but my parents had a shit fit."

"So he didn't?" she asked.

"No, he graduated. I was the one who dropped out."

Her eyes went wide. "Why?"

"September eleventh. I finally knew what I was supposed to be doing. Was like a light switch flipped. Six weeks into my senior year, I took a leave of absence and enlisted in the Army. Never looked back."

He cleaned his table and collected his ink, tools, and supplies.

"When I came home last year, I was still laid up with recovery for a few months, so Jer suggested I apprentice with him for real since I had the time to practice again. Once I was on my feet, I got the process service job to pay the bills, but I brushed up on my skills and then started doing clients in my off hours. Small pieces, mostly."

She was watching him like she didn't want to miss a step of what he was doing, and it made him slow down and remember the enjoyment he found in this art. "You okay?"

Becca grinned. "Yeah, this is fun."

"If you say so. I'll go get Alek." Rixey made for the lobby. Within another fifteen minutes, he was ready to tattoo. "Keep your arm positioned on the armrest like that and just relax," Rixey said, sliding on a mask and some eye protection.

Two hits of ink with the needle, he held the skin taut and outlined the bottom of the image first, the vibration of the machine familiar in his hand. He'd do a long line, then wipe away the excess ink the skin pushed back out. And repeat. "Doing okay, Alek?"

"Yup."

"Becca?" He finished a line and spared her a glance, and she appeared absolutely rapt.

She nodded. "Great."

"So you don't have any tattoos, Becca?" Alek asked.

"No. I like them, but I'd never thought seriously about it. Until recently."

Those last two words pinged around inside Rixey's skull for a few minutes.

"What would you get?" he asked. Nick was grateful Alek was asking the questions. Truth be told, he was damned curious, but it wasn't like he could focus on a conversation with her when he needed to pay attention to what he was doing.

"I'm not sure. I'd definitely want something with meaning. Maybe something to remember my older brother who died. His favorite thing in the world was playing the . . ." She gasped.

Forcing himself to finish out the line, Rixey resisted looking at what had caused her reaction. He pulled the machine away from Alek's skin and glanced at her. "You okay?" he asked, concern curling into his gut.

Her wide eyes cut to him. "The guitar. His favorite thing was playing the guitar. I could . . . maybe . . ." She looked to him with a small shrug, like that revelation hadn't just been the big fucking deal Rixey knew it was. A blush filled her cheeks. "I had his guitar, but it got broken."

"Definitely sounds meaningful, then," the guy said.

Rixey bored his gaze into her, wishing like hell they were alone so he could hold her and comfort her and paint a picture on her skin. Man, this woman had the ability to tie him up in knots like no one he'd ever known, and it was crystal fucking clear why. He was falling for her. Hard. Part of the reason he'd been so pissed at himself this morning was that he'd known being with her hadn't just been about the physical.

Damn, he hated that this stranger was in the room with them when she shared that idea for a first tattoo. It was too personal, too sentimental, and the thought that Alek might be sitting there imagining her naked with the dark lines of a fretboard running up her spine had the blood nearly boiling in his veins.

But Rixey couldn't say any of that right now, could he? He didn't have the time or the privacy to tell her how special he thought her idea was, how special he thought *she* was. Instead, he just said, "I think it sounds perfect, Becca." He bottled the rest of that shit up, took two more hits of ink, and dove back into outlining, shutting their occasional chitchat out.

Seventy-five minutes later, he was done, and Alek's soldier-fireman had come to life on the skin of the man's arm. "See what you think," Rixey said, pointing to the mirror. He leaned out of the doorway. "Hey, Jeremy? You out there?"

"Yo!" came his voice from the lounge. He appeared a moment later.

The guy examined it for a couple minutes. "Wow, man. It's . . . frickin' phenomenal."

"Damn, Nick, he's right," Jeremy said, stepping into the room. "That's some fine work. I *knew* this one was yours."

The piece *was* good. Maybe his best. "Mind if I take a picture of it for my portfolio?"

"Sure. Actually, would you take a shot with my phone, too?"

Rixey took a few snaps with the office camera and a few on Alek's smartphone. Jeremy clapped Nick on the back, then excused himself.

"What do you think?" Alek asked Becca, standing in front of her and flexing.

She smiled. "I think it's pretty fantastic. Looks great on you," she said, her gaze sliding to Nick. "Consider me impressed."

Man, the way she was looking at him did all kinds of bad things to his body. Her gaze was appraising, appreciative, as if she was seeing him in a whole new—and approving—way. Heat and arousal licked down his spine and brought his cock to life. He arched an eyebrow, but he still had work to do. He put a dressing on Alek's arm and secured it with a wrap, then gave the guy his aftercare instructions.

Finally, Nick walked him out, locked the door behind him, and killed the front lights. The shop had closed about an hour earlier. He'd heard Jeremy and Jess finish up with their clients, and Jess had left a while ago. When he returned to his room, he found Becca exactly where he'd left her, a faraway look in her eyes. The moment his gaze landed on her, she blushed. He stopped in his tracks. "What is *that* about?"

"What?" she said, playing it off.

"Horrible. Liar. Remember?" Crouching in front of her, he rested his hands on her thighs. "What's the blush about?" He gently squeezed her quads.

Her gaze brushed over his face, lingered on his lips, and fell to his hands on her legs. "Just thinking."

He tilted his head to catch her eye. "That sounds promising."

Becca chuckled and shook her head. "I was just wondering what it felt like to get a tattoo."

"It differs by placement, pain threshold, size, how much color," he said, watching emotions run over her expression that had nothing to do with curiosity. She was turned on. He'd put money on it.

"And I was wondering . . . if I ever decided I wanted one, if you'd do it." She looked at him from under her lashes.

He stroked his thumbs back and forth along the insides of her thighs and fought the urge to strip her down right here and now . . . for some ink and a whole lotta other things. Her muscles flinched and clenched under his touch, and the fact that he was maybe making her a little crazy turned his cock to steel. "In a heartbeat, sunshine. You just name the place and time." What he didn't say was that the thought of *any* other man putting his mark on Becca's skin made him feel more than a little violent.

She licked her lips and squeezed her thighs together. And that simple flexing of muscles had him wanting to tear her jeans off and bury his face between her legs until she was panting and writhing and screaming his name. Like this morning.

Much as he'd told himself all the reasons to resist his attraction to her, facts were facts. He needed to be there for her—to protect, comfort, support. And he needed the redeeming light of her sunshine on his body, his heart, his soul. God, he just wanted her. Right or wrong.

Her fingers reached out and slowly dragged along his bottom lip. Masculine satisfaction roared through him at the desire in her eyes. He leaned in, wanting to taste her again.

Knock, knock, sounded against the doorjamb.

Rixey turned and found Jeremy standing in the doorway with some papers in his hands. Frowning, he turned the sheets around in his fingers and held them up. The sketch artist's drawings from this morning and Louis's sketches of the Church tats. "Someone want to explain why and how you have pictures of these gang tattoos? And what, if anything, they have to do with the obviously unhappy reunion of your team?"

Chapter 18

*B*ecca looked from Jeremy to Nick, unsure what to say. A small sense of *Oh shit* slithered through her belly, because Jer's questions made it clear Nick hadn't filled him in on what was going on. Whatever his approach to this, though, it wasn't for her to say. "Maybe I should—"

"Stay," they both said.

She lowered back into her seat. "Ooookay."

Nick quickly cleaned up his table and supplies. "Here's the deal," he said. "You know about as much as you should probably know. Becca thinks she might've seen a tattoo like one of those on the guy who grabbed her." He washed and dried his hands.

Jer scoffed. "Nick, these are gang tats. And not just any gang. The Church is about as bad as they get. Drugs, guns, prostitutes, you name it. What the hell?"

"How do you know so much about them?" Nick's eyebrows slashed down.

"There are dozens of gangs in this city. They all use tattoos for identification. Most of them have guys do it in-house, others find tattoo parlors and sorta claim them for their gang. I never knowingly do a gang tattoo, but that means I have to be familiar with what they look like and who they represent."

Damn, his brother was smart. Nick nodded, leaned against the counter, and crossed his arms. "Interesting, but I want to keep you out of this, Jeremy. You hear what I'm saying?"

"I think you're the one who's got a problem with his hearing. Whatever this is"—he held up the papers again—"you need to stay way clear of it."

Lips pressed in a tight line, Nick landed his pale green gaze on her, and she hated that her situation might cause tension between them. Bad enough Jeremy was already mad at Nick for being late.

"I can't," Nick said. "*We* can't." He nodded to Becca.

Jeremy turned to her, and she saw in his face the moment it clicked. Her stomach squeezed. "The Church has your *brother*?" When she didn't answer fast enough, he plowed forward. "What are the cops doing?" His face went pale. "Oooh, shit a fucking brick." He dug his hand into his hair and flicked at the piercing on his lip. "*This is why your team is here*?"

Nick gave a tight nod.

"Why . . . what are you . . . ? I—"

"Cops involved in this are dirty, Jer. And that's the last fucking thing I'm telling you." Nick slipped the pages from his brother's hand.

"What the hell are you talking about? I don't deserve to know you're playing Rambo out of my house?"

Becca rose, guilt sloshing into her stomach. She hadn't just crashed into Nick's life, had she? What if she'd brought danger right to Jeremy—and Jess's—doorstep?

Ears back, tail down, the puppy came to the doorway behind Jeremy and whined. After a moment, she laid down with her head on her paws against Jer's foot.

"You *deserve* to know it all. But the less you know, the better. So you're *out*." Nick slashed a hand through the air, as if the debate had been decided.

Jeremy shook his hair out of his eyes and glared. "I'm not some fucking kid, Nick. I'm a thirty-one-year-old man. At the very least, you should've told me so I could keep an eye out for any kind of trouble. I may not be a soldier, but I could help—"

"You're right. And maybe I should've said something more sooner, but we didn't really know what we might be dealing with until this evening. And we're still not a hundred percent sure. You're not a kid. But here's what you *are*: you're a businessman, you're an employer, you're a homeowner. You have things to lose and people who count on you."

"And you don't?"

Nick stepped back and tossed the papers to the seat of a chair, then scrubbed his hands through his hair. They both had the tendency to do that, and she might've found the similarity endearing if it hadn't been a reflection of their shared frustration right now. "A lot fucking less than you."

The bottom dropped out of Becca's stomach. He didn't think he had anything to lose? Her and whatever they were or weren't aside, how could he think that about himself? If Jeremy hadn't been there, she would've run across the room, grabbed his face, and told him—

Jeremy's hands fisted. "You sonofabitch. You and Katherine are the last family I have on this earth. Don't you dare talk about yourself as if it wouldn't matter if something happened to you. It would matter to me."

At the strain in Jer's voice, tears pooled in Becca's eyes, and she looked to the ceiling to pinch them off.

Nick's shoulders sagged and his voice had a sudden strain to it. "Jeremy—"

"I remember what it was like to get that phone call. You know, the one that said my big brother was in critical condition in a hospital following surgery to repair multiple gunshot wounds to the back. Been there, done that, burned the motherfucking T-shirt. I couldn't do anything about that. I couldn't help. But this? Now? I can. And you're goddamned straight gonna let me."

For a few tense minutes, they faced off across the room, arms crossed over their chests, pale green eyes narrowed and blazing. She wondered if they had any idea how similar they looked or, really, how much alike they were as men. Both strong, both protective of those they cared about, both stubborn to a fault. In that instant, Becca realized she didn't just like Jeremy, she cared about him, too. And she could've hugged him for the way he cared about Nick.

She released a breath and stepped toward them. "Please don't fight. I'm sorry," she said, voice tight, sadness parked at the back of her throat.

"I don't want to fight," Jeremy said, expression stormy. "And don't feel like you have to apologize, Becca. I'm not mad at you. If my brother was missing, I'd go to hell and back to find him, too." Eyebrow arched, he eyeballed Nick. "But I also don't want to be shut out."

"Jesus, Jeremy," Nick said, scratching at the scruff on his jaws. "I'm trying to protect you. Simple as."

"It's a flawed premise, bro. If this situation gets worse, you don't think that has the chance of affecting me whether you tell me all the details now or not?"

"God . . . *damnit*." He pounded a fist on the roll-away tabletop. "Shit we're doing, we are breaking the law. Do you understand what I'm saying to you?"

"You're my brother," Jeremy said.

"And you're mine."

"Knock, knock," a voice said from behind Jeremy. He jerked around as Shane stepped alongside him. "Sorry to interrupt. Uh . . ." Shane glanced between the Rixeys. "When you're done down here, we have some things we wanted to talk about."

For a long moment, the tension was so thick it almost changed the physical composition of the air. Nick shook his head. "Shit, I didn't want this for you."

"And I appreciate that," Jer said, crossing the room. "But brotherhood is a two-way street. You have to let me walk it with you."

Nick blew out a long breath that ended in the word, "Fuck. All right." He shook his head. "All right. Then let's go see what's up."

"No regrets, remember?" Jeremy knocked his fists together side by side, and for the first time, Becca saw what the block lettering on the backs of his fingers said. Reading across his knuckles from his right pinkie to his left, the letters spelled out *N-O-R-E-G-R-E-T*. Sometime she'd ask him the story behind that tattoo.

The air was suddenly lighter, easier to breathe, and Becca had the sense that whatever had just passed between them was bigger than this moment, this conflict, this situation. Nick just nodded.

As the guys moved around the space turning off lights and making sure everything was locked up, Nick gave Jeremy the quick highlight reel of the past days' events to bring him up to speed. She hovered at the door with Shane, waiting for them to finish.

"They okay?" he asked, genuine concern shaping his handsome face and filling his intense gray eyes.

"I think so. I don't know. I didn't realize Nick was trying to keep Jeremy out of it."

Shane nodded. "If I had a brother, I'd have done the

same damn thing." Something flashed through his expression—something dark he quickly masked.

"You have any siblings?" she asked.

A storm moved in over his face, furrowing his brow and making the angles of his face severe and unforgiving. "No."

It was the most loaded use of that two-letter word she'd possibly ever heard. But everything about his demeanor said, "*Topic closed*," so she let it drop. "I'm going to take the dog out before we go upstairs," she said, patting her hand against her jeans.

"We're done anyway," Nick said. They made their way into the stairwell, and Jeremy double-checked that the door to Hard Ink locked behind them.

Becca pushed out the far door and let her girl do her business. The guys stepped outside with them. "You can go up. We'll be right there," she said.

"Air feels good after being inside all day," Jeremy said. Becca couldn't have agreed more. A soft breeze shifted the cool night air around her. The soft caress on her arms was relaxing, like it was blowing the difficult parts of the day away, just right on off her body.

"What's the dog's name?" Shane asked after a minute.

Nick and Jeremy looked at her, then each other, and burst out laughing.

"What?" Shane asked. "What's so funny?"

She just shook her head, glad to see them moving past the fight.

The guys apparently needed the release, because they quickly moved on from laughter to sputtering hysterics. Jer was actually crying. And every time Nick managed to get himself under control, he burst out again.

And man, that laughter was deep and throaty, so damn sexy. The dimple was carved a mile deep into his cheek, and laugh lines curved up from the corners of his eyes.

She wanted to grasp his face in her hands and kiss him until he was panting and gasping for breath for an entirely different reason.

"Here's what you need to know," Becca said, distracting herself from the urge to jump Nick just as the dog returned. "Her name's *not* Cujo, it's not Killer, it's not Tripod, or Three-Speed, Trinity, Skippy, Hoppy—"

"Sneezy, Dopey, Grumpy . . ." Jeremy managed, cracking himself up again.

"It's also not Shiiiii-looooooooh," Nick mocked.

Oh, my God, they were all the way over the deep side. Becca rolled her eyes and stepped back inside.

"Uh, okay," Shane said as they started upstairs, the Rixeys having now devolved into teenaged giggles. Who knew two such big guys could make those high-pitched sounds? "What about Eileen?"

"What?" Becca said, frowning at Shane. "You're just as bad as—"

The uproarious laughter from behind her made her turn around. Nick had taken a knee on the stairs, and Jeremy was hanging on the railing.

"Ei . . . Ei . . . Ei-leen," Jeremy gasped. "Get it? Perfect."

"No, not perfect. Her name is not Eileen." Becca bit back a smile at their hysterics.

Nick heaved a deep breath and opened his mouth. Not to speak, but to *sing*. "*Come on, Eileen. Oh, I swear what he means, at this mooo-ment, you mean eeeverything.*"

Becca put her hand on her forehead and gaped. Nick Rixey was down on his knees singing an eighties anthem to her while laughing and holding his stomach. And it was the sexiest freaking thing she'd ever seen or heard. Even around the ridiculous hilarity, there was no question the boy could sing.

And then the other two idiots joined in.

Out of nowhere, a howling sounded. Becca looked

around and found the dog sitting at the very top of the steps, head back, snout pointing to the ceiling, howling in long, loud *ahwoooos* like she was singing with them.

The door to the gym swung open. "What in the fucking hell?" Beckett asked, Easy and Marz coming out right behind him.

Shaking her head and succumbing to laughter herself, Becca started up the steps. "I broke them. Sorry."

Beckett eyeballed her like she had three heads. Right. Because *she* was the crazy one in a roomful of men singing, "Toora, toora, to loora, ay," at the top of their lungs.

"Hey," Marz said, sinking into a crouch. "This is my kinda dog. What's it's na—"

"No, no, don't say it!" she said.

Behind her, all three men said, "Eileen" in chorus.

"All right, Eileen." Marz scooped her into his arms and stood up. She licked his cheek. "You and me are going to get along just fine." He looked over his shoulder. "Now, come on in, assholes. I've got us a plan." He disappeared inside.

Becca's shoulders sagged. "Her name's not Eileen," she called, but she had a sneaking suspicion that none of them heard her as they all bustled into the gym in a rush.

TEN MINUTES LATER, everyone had calmed down and they stood in the back corner of the gym around Marz's makeshift computer desks, fashioned out of two eight-foot-long folding tables positioned to form an L. Becca scanned her gaze over his setup.

He had three laptops hooked to a series of cables and boxes she couldn't identify, plus the smallest printer she'd ever seen. Charlie's hidden note and the gang booklet lay open near one computer, and pages of notes and printouts lay this way and that. An empty pizza box sat on the floor behind the desk, and a row of diet Coke cans added a splash of color to the array of electronics. It looked like the desk of someone who had worked in this space for *years*.

He took a seat in the center like a king holding court and dropped the puppy—whose name was definitely *not* Eileen—to the concrete floor. "Beckett and Shane filled me in on today's field research, and I've scanned most of this book on the Church organization and done some additional research of my own. We are talking some bad-ass shit here." He looked around the group. "Don't let the word 'gang' make you discount their level of organization, their strength, or their discipline. In the past two years they have destroyed, disbanded, or absorbed three other gangs, expanding their territory substantially. They run eighty percent of the heroin trade in the city, do a fair amount of arms dealing, and appear to have a lot of officials in their pockets. The Church has a sophisticated recruitment system in place and a constant inflow of members. This is organized crime with a capital *O* and a capital *C*."

"Man, I didn't know shit could be stacked this high," Shane said.

"Got any *good* news for us?" Nick asked from next to her. At least she wasn't the only one who seemed to think the situation seemed more and more impossible. Her stomach flip-flopped when she imagined what their odds were against an organization like that.

"For operational purposes, maybe," he said, waking up the laptop with the largest monitor. Some of this equipment they'd bought today, but some he'd brought with him. "We're working on the assumption that the tattoo Becca saw on her assailant belongs to a Churchman. Yes?"

Becca nodded, so frustrated with herself that she couldn't be definitive when so much hinged on that damn tattoo. "I'm pretty sure, but in fairness I can't say with total certainty."

"Mind if I see that?" Jeremy asked, pointing toward the gang booklet. Marz passed it over.

"The fact that the hotel maid associated Charlie's abductors with being heroin dealers adds another piece of circumstantial evidence," Nick said.

Marz nodded. "Agreed. Well, then, I propose this lead is worth investigating further until we have something more to go on. It's gonna take me a while to see if I can work this bank info. Everyone good with that?"

Easy held out his big hands. "You know where I stand. If there's a chance this is who has Charlie, it makes sense to learn everything we can as soon as we can."

"I'd rather be doing something than sitting around Fort Living Room," Shane said. "Besides, we need to figure out the link between this gang and Merritt, assuming there is one."

Beckett nodded, crossed his big arms, and leveled a thoughtful gaze at Marz. "We're on board. What is it you have in mind?"

Anticipation sent a shiver down her spine. She glanced to Nick, so appreciating his reassuring smile. She couldn't begin to express how grateful she was that he was with her in this.

Derek was suddenly a flurry of activity. His fingers flew over the keyboard in front of him for a moment before he shoved a pile of papers aside to clear space on the desk. He slapped down four pieces of paper. "Church has four known front businesses." He tapped his pointer finger against each sheet as he spoke. "A barbershop, a shipping business and storage facility, a storefront church, of course, and a strip club."

"How original," Easy said, leaning in with the other guys around the table's edge to see what the pages said.

Becca glanced to Jeremy, who'd hung back beside her to study the book like he was trying to catch up to speed.

He gave her a small, crooked smile that told her to hang in. It was pretty clear he and Nick were cut from the same good-guy cloth.

Marz pointed to the laptop monitor and shifted sequentially through live images of buildings, headlights flashing across the screen as cars passed by. "I found traffic cameras that give us a visual on three of the four. The barbershop is in the corner of a strip mall, and I haven't been able to find an eye in the sky on that. Yet."

"Shit, dude, is there anything you can't hack?" Beckett asked, admiration clear in his expression.

"Heh. I live for challenge. I propose we put boots on the ground and check each of these out. At the very least, we can plant the electronic surveillance devices we picked up this afternoon and acquire firsthand info on interior physical layout, guard presence, and any special security systems you might be able to identify. Maybe one of you can sex up a waitress at the club and see if she's heard anything about a missing guy that might've found himself on the wrong side of the Churchmen." He aimed a smile at Shane, and everyone else's gazes slid his way, too.

Shane's answering grin was smug as all hell. "You know I'd make any sacrifice for you assholes." Becca bit back a laugh, but then her mind conjured Nick doing the sexing up of some scantily dressed dancer . . . and that was so *not* funny.

She studied Nick's strong profile, jaw tense, eyes narrowed, shoulder muscles bunched. Every inch of him was all business, and it was so sexy. The thought of anyone else's hands or lips on him didn't just make her jealous, though her brain buzzed with displeasure. Despite how recently they'd met and how much they still had to learn about one another, her soul looked at this harshly beautiful man and thought, *mine*. It wasn't even a conscious thought, really, more a reaction to the intense connection this crazy situation had forged between them. Not to mention a bone-deep wish. She wanted him.

It was that simple and that complex.

As she watched him make plans with his team, her chest suddenly constricted. Because she realized she was looking at someone who had the power to send her flying or crashing from the heights. And, *oh God,* the more they talked about the possible risks at each of the locations, the more her gut clenched with the understanding of just how much danger they were in, and how much more they might yet face.

And he doesn't think he has much to lose.

Becca nearly gasped at the memory of his words. She had to tell him. He had *her.*

Murda cut away from the group, pulling her out of her head. "I'll be right back," he yelled, boots echoing off the hard floor as he double-timed it toward the door.

"Probably only need two or three men for this," Marz said. "I figured I'd stay here to make sure the bugs were coming through loud and clear and look for additional cameras on our hot spots. Too much testosterone traveling together might raise suspicion with these guys. And someone should stay with Becca. Who's up for some recon?"

"No offense, Marz, but I've been your computer bitch all damn day, so I wouldn't mind a boondoggle," Easy said with a laugh.

"I'll stay with Becca," Nick said, giving her a smile that just hinted at the dimple.

Shane pointed to himself. "You just voluntold me I should go for the sexin' up."

"Dude, I got that shit covered, and then some." Easy winked, and Becca couldn't help but chuckle. The black Under Armour shirt he wore highlighted every dip and ridge of his muscles. Saying he was impressively built was a gross understatement. No doubt if he and Shane walked into a bar, every other man's arm in the room would grow cold as the women all drifted their way.

"All right, this doesn't need to turn into a jack-off contest," Marz said with a chuckle.

Geez, good thing she didn't embarrass easily. The people she worked with—doctors and nurses alike—could be some of the most humorously crude people she knew. The high-stress environment of the emergency department demanded the release. If people weren't having sex in the on-call room, they were at least joking about it.

"Prepare to be impressed, Marz," Beckett called, returning to the gym. "I have toys." On the edge of the table, he laid out an oversized tablet with antennae sticking out and several small cell-phone-sized devices.

"Aww, man," Marz said, picking up the camera like he was Gollum discovering the ring.

"What is it?" Becca asked.

Beckett crossed his arms. "An X-ray camera with see-through-the-wall technology. Can determine a person's location, speed, and direction through walls as thick as one foot. It's essentially a radar system that measures changes in WiFi wave frequency. It's so sensitive, it can tell the difference between an inanimate object and a person's breathing pattern."

"This has got to be a pre-market prototype, Beck. You gotta have some good friends doing R&D work. Or are you into testing equipment for law enforcement?"

Beckett smiled. "Let's leave it at good friends. Here's what I was thinking—for all of these locations, humans on the main floor make total sense. But this might allow us an eye into the nonpublic spaces of these buildings. If this picks up an identifiable human target, as indicated by breathing patterns, but it remains stationary, *that* could be our prisoner. Not foolproof by any means, but maybe another way to rule these locations in or out for further investigation." He grinned at Marz. "I knew you'd appreciate it."

"I want to procreate with it." He winked at Becca, and she adored how easily he could make her smile. "Sorry. I get a little overexcited."

She just held up her hands and chuckled. Didn't want to touch that with a ten-foot pole.

"Well, you'll get a chance to play, because it can send a feed back to your computer, so you can start analyzing the data if you want," the big guy said. "Just sync the devices."

"Damn skippy, I want." Marz rubbed his hands together and dove into setting up the scanner.

Beckett picked up the cell-phone-like devices. "And I brought a couple GPS trackers, too. If we see any vehicles that seem worth tracing, I can attach these and they'll send an alert to my phone any time the target vehicle moves. Might lead us to other likely stash spots if these turn up empty."

Easy settled a plastic bag on the desk. "We also have burn phones for everyone. So grab a cell and let's take a minute to program in each other's digits." They all reached in and took turns announcing and programming numbers.

Color her impressed. She never doubted they'd know what they were doing. But imagining it and seeing it were two different things. "You guys are like MacGyver, except instead of paper clips, pocket knives, and rubber bands, you have really cool electronics."

Everyone except for Marz let out a groan. His face totally lit up. "MacGyver was a god among men."

Easy rolled his eyes. "Dude, MacGyver had a mullet."

Marz held up a hand. "I refuse to hear you. Becca, between your three-legged dog and your MacGyver reference, you are officially my favorite person in the room right now." And there he went, earning another smile from her.

"Hey, I brought toys." Beckett's indignant expression was almost comical.

"Fine," Derek sighed. "It's a tie."

Becca smiled at Murda, and he threw her a wink. "Please be careful," she said, her throat suddenly going tight.

They all nodded and reassured her. Nick stepped in close, his arm against her shoulder. "Watch your sixes out there," he added. "And thanks." Something seemed to pass between Nick and the rest of his team, an understanding perhaps. Becca still didn't understand the latent tension that undergirded most of their interactions, and she was glad to see a bit of détente setting in. Even if it was only temporary, there was too much at stake for all of them for old conflicts to get in the way now.

"Just let me know what order you want to hit the locations, and I'll play along at home." Marz waggled his fingers over his desk. "Just remember that the strip club closes at three a.m. That's probably the only one you'll be able to get into at night, so make sure you get inside."

"Oh, we will," Shane said.

Easy scooped up the paperwork and bag of electronic bugs and shoved Shane toward the door. "Get your southern ass moving, McCallan."

Beckett pocketed the GPS trackers, tucked the scanner under his arm, and knocked twice on the tabletop. "Luck."

"Luck, hell," Easy called. "Carpe scrotum!"

When they disappeared through the door, something almost like peacefulness settled over the cavernous gym. It was like someone turned down the volume on a radio. Becca let out a sigh, because it was very likely the quiet before the storm.

"Hey, Becca," Marz said. She turned her gaze toward him, surprised to find an unusually serious expression on his face. "I know I cut it up a bit. Just want you to know it's not because I'm not taking this seriously."

A warm pressure filled her chest. If she had one thing going for her in all this, it was the complete certainty that she and Charlie were in the best possible hands with Nick and his team. "I never would've thought anything else, Derek, but thanks." Her stomach growled, embarrassingly loud. Marz cocked an eyebrow. "Am I the only one starving?"

Nick squeezed her shoulders from behind. "No. I could eat a horse. Let's go grab some food. Probably be a while before any intel starts arriving."

"Yeah, go eat. I chowed earlier. My babies will keep me company," he said, stroking a hand over the big laptop.

"Jeremy?" she asked.

He'd been unusually quiet since they came upstairs. "No, I ate earlier, too. Mind if I hang here, Derek? I'm curious how all this works."

"*Mi casa es su casa.* Well, I guess that's literally true, isn't it? Pull up a seat."

Jeremy swung a folding chair around and sat on it backwards.

Nick wrapped his arm around Becca's shoulders and they made their way across the gym. "Come on," he said. "I'll whip you up some of the meanest reheated pizza you ever had."

Chapter 19

When he finished his slices of pizza, Rixey watched Becca nibble at the crust of the single piece she'd eaten. Not sleeping, not eating, and under a lot of stress—it was a recipe for getting sick or breaking down. "I know what you need," he said, slipping from the bar stool.

She gave a small smile. "What's that?" The sleepiness in her gaze gave way to something a whole lot more engaged. Her eyes dragged over his body, trailing heat in their wake.

Rixey wanted to throw his idea out the window, but one need at a time.

"Chocolate ice cream." He grabbed the tub of double chocolate fudge brownie from the freezer and proudly presented it to her. It was the same half gallon she'd chosen the other night, when they'd wound up boxing instead, and kissing . . . His cock twitched against his fly at the very fine memory.

Her face brightened, dispelling some of the shadows hanging around her eyes. "Chocolate ice cream is a proven remedy for almost anything that ails you. Medical fact."

"I knew you'd see it my way." He gathered bowls and spoons and dished out two mounds. "Wanna move to the couch?"

"If I do, I might fall asleep."

"Then I'll hold you." He hadn't even thought to say the words. They were just out of his mouth before his brain caught up. But, damn, he felt their rightness down deep. Meeting her gaze, he absolutely adored the affection that filled her baby blues. He grabbed their desserts and nodded her over.

"Well, I could hardly resist that." She slipped off the stool, rounded the back of the big leather couch and sank into the middle.

"Good to know." Sitting again reminded him that his weapon was still in the back of his jeans. The bite of it was reassuring. And, anyway, he wasn't leaving her right now to deal with it. Not when she was looking at him like she was. It wasn't just desire he saw, but also comfort and gratitude and concern.

She adjusted her position to sit cross-legged facing him, her knees brushing against his hip and thigh. Her little moans and sounds of enjoyment as she tasted a scoop of the chocolate reverberated right down his body and pooled in his groin. But, for now, this was just about seeing her sated in this most basic of ways. And it was enough.

He swallowed a big bite of sweet, smooth ice cream and forced his mind to still long enough to really savor it. *Damn, that's good.* Ice cream was the single biggest food he'd missed while on deployment, and even after all these months back in the world he still couldn't get enough. He wasn't sure whether he or Jeremy had the bigger sweet tooth, but part of their survival kit included a freezer full of the sweet stuff. He took another bite.

Fact that he didn't *only* want in Becca's pants? That was a real gut check about where his head—and his heart—really were, wasn't it?

"Are you worried about the guys at all? Being out there?" she asked, stirring the ice cream to make it smooth.

"No. These guys are the best. They know what they're doing. They know how to take care of themselves. And you shouldn't worry, either." It was mostly true. The only thing that might've made him worry less was being out there himself so he could have their backs. Once, he'd been their second in command, but none of that mattered anymore, and this wasn't the Army. Besides, they all had jobs to do tonight, and he was content to do his. Events of the past few days proved Becca needed protection, and Rixey suspected she might be feeling a bit more fragile than she was letting on. No way the shock of Scott's destroyed guitar was far from her mind. Not with how devastated she'd been at the sight of it.

Her bowl sagged into her lap. "I'm sorry about what happened with Jeremy earlier." Chin down, she ate another spoonful.

"Don't be. Wasn't your fault." How could anyone look sad with a mouthful of ice cream? Going against instinct—and habit—Nick decided to distract her with the truth. "Twelve years in the Special Forces taught me to keep things tight to the cuff. Living that lifestyle, you become accustomed out of practice and necessity to be fully honest with only the close circle of your brothers on the team. I hadn't realized until tonight that even though

I've been in the real world for almost a year, I've kept Jeremy on the outside all this time."

He stuffed a heap of dessert between his lips to force himself to stop running his trap. Soon he'd be telling her that he'd also realized he'd lost too many damn people from his life to be *pushing* people away now. That included Jeremy.

And it included her.

One thing still tripped him up, though. He hated that he couldn't tell her the truth about her father. He didn't want to lie to her, but he also didn't want to hurt her. Learning that someone you loved wasn't the person you thought could be devastating—especially when that person was someone fundamentally important to your life. Nick knew that anguish firsthand. Realizing that the commander he'd looked up to for so many years was a liar and a manipulator and, really, damn close to a traitor to his country had ripped a part of Rixey's heart out and shaken his faith in the sacred ideal of the brotherhood of arms. Bad as that was, he could only imagine how much worse it would be to learn those things about your father, and then not be able to confront him because he was already dead.

But Charlie knew *something,* so one way or another the truth was coming out. And maybe whatever her brother knew could get them around the restrictions of the damn NDA. Every moment until she learned what her father'd done, he was complicit in a lie of omission. And that fact sloshed like battery acid in his gut. Because no matter how unworthy he felt, he could no longer deny that he wanted her. The taste of her this morning hadn't nearly been enough. He'd known that shit at the time, too. Now he wanted to make sure he didn't do another thing to make her question where she stood with him.

Not when she stood at the center of his newly realigned universe.

A universe where he could see himself as being important again, as having a mission, as having a purpose. And, the thing was, the realignment had done more than make him fall for a girl; it had made him reconnect with and value parts of his life he'd been neglecting—his love of art, his brother, his team.

Last year, his losses had been catastrophic. That was incontrovertible truth. But he'd actually made it worse by pushing what he still had away.

And Becca had been the one to hold the mirror in front of his face and make him see the light.

His sunshine.

"Want some water?" he asked, hoping she didn't hear the gruffness in his voice as he got up.

"Sure."

Heaving a deep breath, he crossed to the sink and busied his hands with the simple task. He'd take anything right about now to distract his brain from all the churn and burn.

"Here you go," he said, returning to her. He downed half his glass in one long swallow and wished it was something stronger.

When they finished their ice cream, she stretched and put the bowls on the dark, distressed coffee table. Her sigh was equal parts fatigue and satisfaction. He'd helped ensure one, now he could assist with the other. "Come here," he said, opening his arms.

With a smile, Becca turned, knees facing the back of the couch, and laid her upper body across his lap so her head hit his shoulder. The feeling of her laying on him was warm and tempting, especially with the little purr of contentment that spilled from her throat. But it was also just really frickin' peaceful. And, man, peace wasn't something he'd had a whole lot of lately. Hell, not for his whole adult life.

Nick shifted down just a little, holding her close, and let his head fall back against the leather. *This couldn't be any better.*

"I need something else," she said, shifting against him. Head on his stomach, she looked up. And her eyes were on fire.

"What's that?" His cock was pretty sure it knew what she needed, if his sudden erection was any guide.

"You'll say no."

Rixey ran his fingers through her hair, the word yes already on the tip of his tongue. "Try me."

She pushed her body down until her face lay in his lap, and then she mouthed him through his jeans, eyes slanted up at him.

He sucked in a breath, and his hips rocked into the touch. "Becca."

The denim allowed through only a hint of the heat from her mouth, but just the thought of it scorched him with lust and need. Her teeth grazed over the length of him, teasing until he knotted a hand in the soft length of her blond hair.

"I want you in my mouth," she said.

Aw, fucking hell.

His brain ran a calculus of the likelihood of getting caught *here* versus the ability to pull his cock away from her lips. Marz wasn't moving from his computers anytime soon, though. And Jeremy had made the cardinal mistake of asking how his equipment worked, so he'd most likely be caught in a Marz vortex for a good long while. And then she unzipped his jeans and pulled his hard-on out in her soft hand, and all those thoughts blew away like smoke in the wind. She bathed the length of him with a long, wet lick. And, damn if she didn't keep those blue eyes on him like she knew how much pleasure he'd get from watching her tongue him.

And he did. The sight of her mouth on his cock would *never* get old.

She pushed up on her elbows, swirled her tongue around his tip, and then engulfed him in a slow descent that ended with his head buried in the back of her throat. His hands flew to her hair, half of him wanting to hold her there and thrust deeper, half of him wanting to yank her away before this was over in about thirty seconds.

The other reason getting caught probably wasn't an issue—this morning aside, his abstinence from everything but his own hand for the past year meant he wasn't likely to have very frickin' much staying power. She withdrew in a torturous hard suck of his flesh that very nearly proved the point.

Goddamnit.

"Becca, you are going to make me come in about ten seconds," he said, awe mixed with a bit of embarrassment in his voice. Jesus, she was really fucking good at this.

She pulled off long enough to grin up at him. "Good. I want you to come."

Swirling wetness over his head, she lashed him with her tongue before sinking down once more. This time, the pace wasn't slow, but the fast swallow and suck was every bit as torturous. Maybe more. Because his body was barreling toward a cliff's edge he had no hope of avoiding. Her silky hair fanned over his lap and he tangled his fingers in it, guiding her head as she devoured him. Heat and pressure and mind-blowing sensation congregated in his balls, hung there until he was holding his breath.

"Christ, Becca, I'm coming. I'm . . . fucking . . . coming." Dizziness tossed his conscious mind to the corner and he groaned and thrust into her mouth as she sucked down everything that he gave her. The orgasm drained the tension out of his muscles until he was boneless against the leather. Except, miraculously, he was still so goddamned hard she could take his head to the back of her throat when she indulged in a few more lingering sucks.

His. Fucking. Turn.

Without a single word of warning, he pulled her off him, tugged the denim over his cock, and flipped her into his arms. Her swollen lips and flushed face and surprised laugh ricocheted right down his spine and ensured his erection didn't deflate by even an inch. He hauled them off the couch, refusing to acknowledge his protesting back, then stalked down the hall, kicking the office door shut with his boot.

In his room, he came to the bottom corner of his big bed and tossed her to the mattress in the darkness. She screamed and laughed as she bounced against the messy covers, still rumpled from how they'd left them this morning.

Damnit all to hell, but that felt like a million years ago. He removed the gun from the back of his jeans and settled it on the nightstand as he turned on the lamp. Her eyes found him immediately, and she smiled.

God, she was so damn pretty. And the way she looked at him sent him soaring.

Sometimes you plodded through life with nothing changing from one month to the next no matter how much you yearned for a revolution to erupt beneath your feet. And sometimes your whole world imploded and rebuilt itself in a matter of seconds. In the past, those instantaneous changes had almost always ignited with pain and loss.

Not this time.

This time, a woman had performed the simple act of walking through his front door. She'd sent his life spinning off on a whole new trajectory of rebuilding. Reclaiming. Maybe, even love.

Returning to the foot of the bed, Nick found that

Becca's gaze was equal parts humor and heat. Hands behind her calves, he hauled her toward the edge of the bed, undid the fly of her jeans, and tugged them over her hips. She lifted her legs, helping him remove them, and a twinge of pain shot through his back again as he yanked them off.

Rixey didn't mind the discomfort. It was a drop in the bucket compared to the soul-deep pleasure he felt, and, anyway, he was used to it. But it reminded him that she'd been injured. "Shit, Becca. Did I hurt your side when I threw you?" He leaned his upper body between her thighs until he hovered over her, reminding him of the fast frenzy of this morning.

She stroked his cheek with soft fingertips. "No. It's not too bad. But thank you for thinking to ask."

Relief flowed through him, drawing him to taste her. He leaned into her slowly and kissed her. And, damn, he could still taste himself in her mouth. It was a fucking rush, knowing she'd pleasured him so freely, so selflessly. His hand skimmed up her belly, tugging at the cotton and caressing her breasts. She arched into his touch, allowing him to pull her shirt to her throat. "Lift," he whispered, and then he removed it altogether. A flick of his hand behind her back bared her completely to his gaze.

Jesus, she was beautiful, soft perfection. Natural and real. With lots of curves and peaks and valleys and hidden places for him to explore. Her hands fisted in his shirt and dragged it up his stomach. With one hand, he reached over his shoulder and hauled it over his head.

And then he was on her. Kissing her mouth in urgent, aggressive twists of lips and tongue. Sucking and nipping down her neck and collarbones to her breasts. Teasing and tormenting her nipples. Becca writhed under him, her fingers plowing into his hair and trying to grip the short length. He'd actually worn it longer in Afghanistan to blend in with the locals, so he wasn't opposed to grow-ing it out again just so she could really pull it. The biting tugs against his scalp fucking turned him on because each one reflected her pleasure, her desire, her slow slide into abandon.

Easing onto his knees, he kissed her stomach, her hip bones, the inside of one soft thigh. "Put some pillows under your head, sunshine, because I want to watch your face." He waited for her to comply, a small, sexy smile curving her lips, and then he slid his hands under her thighs, guided her knees onto his shoulders, and stroked his tongue through her wetness. Her sweet taste and her ecstatic cry rocketed down his body, turning his cock to steel and making him yearn to get in her. But not before he drank in her pleasure.

Alternating flicks and circles with flat sweeps of his tongue, he explored and tormented her. He penetrated her with one finger, then two, remembering what she'd seemed to like this morning and drawing out her arousal until her hips bucked and thrashed and her hands fisted in the sheets. He strapped her down with his forearm and sucked her clit into his mouth.

He'd thought her beautiful before, but her face was a total stunner when she wore that mask of pleasure—eyes hooded, almost like she was drowsy, mouth open, and lips wet.

"Nick," she rasped. "Don't stop."

He smiled against her, stopping the furthest thing from his mind, and redoubled his efforts, licking, sucking, fucking her with his fingers. A long, low whine ripped from her throat as her muscles tightened around him, and then she was holding her breath, shaking, coming on his hand and mouth. The moment her body stilled, he withdrew, shoved down his jeans, and then cursed a blue storm at the laces on his boots.

She laughed, and he pretended to scowl at her as he finally got his feet free.

"Think that's funny, do ya?"

Grinning, she nodded. "I like you eager."

He threw the jeans and boxers somewhere behind him. "Eager's my middle fucking name when I'm around you." Nick retrieved a condom from the box he'd opened only this morning. Standing between her spread thighs, he rolled it on. "You are going to feel so good," he said, looking her over and loving every damn thing he saw. The tousled blond hair, the flush on her face, and the beautiful feminine curves all called to him, but it was the adoration in her eyes that most got to him. It sent him flying to the heavens with a feeling of completion, and it threatened to splinter him to pieces because he'd never fully deserve it.

A moment of doubt flickered through him, stilling his hand on his cock and rooting his feet to the floor. *Goddamnit.*

Becca shoved the pillows further up the bed and scooted backward, her hands reaching out to him. "Come be with me," she said.

Like she knew. She knew he'd gotten stuck there at the edge of the bed.

Her words drew him forward until his knees were between her thighs and his hands were braced on either side of her head. "Are you sure about this?"

She combed her fingers through the sides of his hair. "Completely."

Thank God. "Good, because I want you so damn much." He kissed her, took his cock in hand, and guided himself to her entrance. "Aw, damn," he groaned as he pushed inside. Hot. Tight. Wet. He pulled out and sank back in, gaze on her face, watching her struggle to keep her eyes open as he rocked in and out of her core.

Her short nails bit at his neck and shoulders, and then

he settled his weight fully upon her. Skin on skin. The connection wasn't just physical. Not for him. And the emotion in her eyes told him not for her, either.

Nick buried his face in her neck and grasped the top of her head with one hand. God, he needed to get closer, deeper, as far inside as she could take him. His hips withdrew and plunged forward, rolling to drag pressure against her clit. She grasped his back and moaned in time with his thrusts and rocked her hips to meet his. Even as his lower back started to ache, she was still the best fucking thing he'd ever felt. He'd pushed through it this morning, so he could do it again. He flipped a mental bird at his injuries, because no way was he missing out on a moment of this experience, nor shorting Becca even an ounce of pleasure.

"You okay?" he rasped against her ear before kissing the delicate shell of skin.

Her chuckle was deep and throaty, and drew his gaze to her face. She leaned up and kissed him. "I've never been more okay in my life."

He grinned, identifying with the sentiment and feeling it slip into the dark places in his soul and light them up.

A sharp twist of muscle in his back made him suck in a breath and clench his jaw. He gritted through. Leftover soreness from his fight. He was going to kick Beckett's ass for making him think of the guy during sex.

"Hey." Her hand smoothed over his forehead and cheek.

Opening his eyes, he found concern mixing with arousal in her expression. *Damnit*. He kissed her, hating the thought of anything ruining their moment.

"What's the matter?" she whispered against his lips.

"Not a damn thing."

She pushed on his chest, and he frowned. But she was smiling, a bit of mischievousness in her eyes. "Turn over," she said. "And sit against the headboard."

"Ma'am, yes, ma'am."

Rixey pushed the pillows upright and settled against them, relief flowing into his back at the change in position. He couldn't think on that long, though, because she straddled him and sank down onto his cock in one torturously good slide.

One hand on the headboard and one on his shoulder, she rode him, her core sucking him in, her clit rubbing against his stomach, her nipples dragging against his chest. He skimmed his hands up and down her back, grabbing her hips and thrusting deeper when he couldn't stand the nearly nonexistent distance between them.

"God, Nick, I'm going to come again."

The words shoved him a giant step toward his own release. "Good. I want to feel it." He latched on a nipple, sucking and tugging and teasing with his teeth. She moaned and tossed her head back, her body arching against him and the tips of her hair tickling his hands on her hips.

Her muscles squeezed, a slow, sure clamping down on his cock that had him growling low in his throat. "Yes, sunshine. Come all over me."

She sank all the way down on him, taking him in to the balls, and ground her hips hard and fast against him. Fingers digging into her sweet ass, he rocked her hips forward and backward on his dick, grinding her clit against his stomach.

And then she was coming, groaning, milking his body with her release. Her arousal flowed over him, hot and slick, and he lifted her hips and slammed her down, once, twice, three times. His orgasm was an out-of-control freight train tearing down his spine.

"Fuck, Becca," he gritted out as his cock erupted inside her. He thrust deep, rocking his hips as his mind and body went to pieces. And then he wrapped his arms around her and buried his face in her chest.

BECCA'S HEART BEAT so fast she was almost dizzy. And it wasn't just because of the incredible sex or the multiple orgasms, though those had been bone-meltingly good. It was because everything about Nick—his touch, his smile, the intense emotion in his eyes—all insisted she wasn't alone in this crazy, whirlwind connection. Which was really, really good. Since it was really freaking likely she was in love with him.

She might've questioned how she could feel something so deeply for someone she'd known for only a couple of days, but Nick had been with her every step of the way through the worst moments of her life. She felt a bond with him she'd never felt with anyone else.

The loneliness, the emptiness, the sense of dislocation she'd felt as, one by one, she'd lost nearly every member of her family? They were mostly gone. When they found Charlie—because they *would*—she'd be totally whole again.

And it was all because of Nick.

She wrapped her arms around him, one around his back and the other around his head, and held him tight. Words sat on the tip of her tongue, and she had to press her lips to his soft hair to keep them from spilling out. She didn't want to come off like a lovestruck teenager. Even though inside she kinda felt like one.

He kissed the skin above her heart and pulled back, and then he kissed her. Soft, sweet, worshipful kisses that sent a sheltering cocoon of warmth over her skin. She loved him all affectionate like this.

Slipping his hand between them, he said, "Better deal with this. Be right back."

She rose off his lap, hating to let him go. He gave her one last kiss as he removed the condom and walked across the room. The dragon on his back seemed almost alive as it moved over his muscles.

Her gaze lit on the full mass of scar tissue on his left hip and upper butt cheek. She'd have to find a way to broach how much pain he'd been in a few moments before. No way she was asking in the middle of sex and risk making him feel bad, but for a moment distress had been clear on his expression.

Her gaze dragged downward. More tattoos adorned his legs, but she could only make out the line of black and blue nautical stars on the outside of his right calf.

Man, he was a fine sight, scars and ink and all. "Nice ass," she said, her mouth running away with her thoughts.

The laughter he unleashed was the sweetest thing.

Grinning to herself, she settled against the pillows, still warm from his body. He reappeared from the hallway a few moments later, hint of a grin on his lips. Back in bed, he crawled in over her and came to rest with his head on her stomach, his arms wrapping underneath her back.

She ran her fingers through his hair, and his expression was pure contentment.

"What's the tattoo on your left leg? I could make out the stars, but not the words."

"It's says, 'All Gave Some, Some Gave All.' "

Her fingers kept moving, as if his words and the sentiment behind them didn't lodge a knot in her throat.

A few moments later, he shifted his hips like he was trying to get comfortable. Then again, he was lying on his stomach, which he'd told her bothered his back. "Hey, Nick?"

"Hmm?"

"Can I ask you something?"

His eyes flew open, the lashes tickling her stomach. "Always."

"How much did your back hurt?"

He released a long breath, his eyebrows making his displeasure at the topic clear. "You could tell?"

She gave him a little smile. "Only because you made a face. Not because of anything you did, which was all amazing, by the way."

The corner of his lip quirked up. "I didn't even think . . ." He shrugged his big shoulder. "Being with you today was the first time since . . ." He pressed his face into her stomach with a groan. "It was probably just because of the fight with Beckett."

Wait. Was he really saying she was the first person he'd had sex with in over a year? "The first time you had sex since you were shot," she finished for him.

He rested his chin on her stomach, and his eyes were a shade less confident than usual. "Yeah."

Inside, she was jumping up and down at the news, but she didn't want him to feel any more awkward about it. "Could be the fight. The counter dug into you pretty hard. But, if it's not, next time we'll just find the position that feels the best. Kama Sutra says there's over sixty of them, so I bet we can find a few."

"Next time, huh?" he said, his expression filling with humor and promise.

She smiled. "Mmhmm."

"I like the sound of that."

"Me, too." She dragged her fingers over his shoulder for a moment, then she met his gaze. "But you gotta tell me if something hurts. Okay? The last thing I want is to hurt you."

He nodded his head, digging his chin into her belly and tickling her. She flinched and laughed, but then his expression went serious. "I want to apologize for this morning," he said.

Becca traced a design against his skin. "What happened this morning? Did I do some—"

"No. It wasn't you at all. There's shit that happened in Afghanistan that I can't tell you about, and I haven't made peace with it. It blindsided me this morning and sent me to a dark place."

Her heart squeezed. "I can't imagine everything you dealt with over there. Just know you can talk to me. Okay? Even if it's to tell me you need some space."

He kissed her stomach and nodded, his eyes ablaze with emotion.

"Can I tell you something else?" Nerves had her stomach doing a loop-the-loop, but she couldn't let this go unsaid.

Nick arched an eyebrow. "Okay."

"What you said to Jeremy earlier . . . I just wanted to tell you it would matter to me, too. If something happened to you. It would matter to me a lot." A sting pricked at the back of her eyes, and she blinked it away.

He rolled onto his side and stroked his fingers over her breasts, her stomach, her thighs. Light, teasing touches meant to explore and comfort rather than to arouse, although just being in his presence accomplished that. He kissed the valley between her breasts and whispered, "So beautiful." And then he was quiet, seemingly preoccupied with her skin.

Had she said too much? It didn't seem like she'd made him uncomfortable. Maybe he just didn't know what to say? Becca sank back into the pillows and watched him look at her. Such a gorgeous man.

"Would you let me do something?" he finally asked, voice low and suddenly serious.

She smiled. "Probably."

"Be right back." He pushed off the bed and disappeared into the hallway again. What was he up to? When he returned, he had a fistful of pens.

"What are they for?"

He crawled in bed next to her, then met her gaze.

"I want to draw on you. Bad." Even in the dim light, his eyes blazed, his expression intense and so damn hungry.

Heat shot through her body, sending a tingle of thrill through her core. "Okay," she whispered.

"Skin markers." He held up five pens. "Nontoxic. They'll wash off. Eventually." He winked and laid the pens in the crook of skin where her thighs met. "Don't drop them."

They were cool against her still-heated flesh. She chuckled, but his enthusiasm was sexy as all hell. "What happens if I do?"

"I'll have to go exploring for them." He picked the black marker and uncapped it.

"And this is a disincentive?"

His deep chuckle puffed against her belly as he leaned in and drew a long line down the left side of her rib cage. God, she loved the sound of his laugh. "Don't move, now."

Which of course made her want to lean up to see what he was doing. She laced her fingers together to fight the urge to play with his hair or stroke his shoulders. "I wanna see."

"No, you just feel. For now. Trust me." More lines.

"I do." As the pen traced over her skin, a line here, a curve there, a bit of shading all in one place that was really hard to sit still through, she watched him work. Nick's intense eyes and angular face and big hands were all incredibly masculine. It made his artistic eye and the softness of the pen against her skin so much more intriguing.

And it was so freaking arousing.

The whole time he drew, her nipples were peaked and

straining. Dampness grew between her legs. How she could think of sex again after just having two amazing orgasms, Becca didn't know, but she was tempted to drop the pens between her legs just to see what he'd do.

He scooted down the bed and drew on the side of her belly, over her hip, and onto her upper thigh. Trading out pen colors, he added to the drawing in yellow and blue and red. As his hands and eyes and ink moved over her, she became more and more certain she wanted Nick Rixey to tattoo her for real, to put his mark on her exterior the way he'd done inside. Maybe not today or tomorrow, but someday.

It was one of the most sensual and erotic moments of her life.

"There," he said. "All done." He flicked his tongue over his bottom lip.

Heart kicking up in her chest, she asked, "Do I get to see it now?"

Nick stood and pulled her off the bed, his cock fully erect. "Full-length mirror behind the bathroom door." He chucked the pens into his nightstand drawer and followed her.

Her arousal spiked and was so much more noticeable as she walked. She was trembling with lust and anticipation. In the bathroom, she flicked on the light and stepped inside the small undecorated space, then let Nick in behind her before she closed the door.

She approached the mirror, Nick shadowing her. A guitar. He'd drawn an almost impressionist guitar down her whole right side, with the head and tuning pins just beneath her breast, the fretboard a long line over her ribs, and half the rounded body curving over her belly and hip. Extending from the joint of the neck and body was a single golden wing.

Tears sprang to her eyes. "It's beautiful, Nick. Can I touch it?" She met his scorching eyes in the mirror.

"Yeah? Yes, you can. It won't smear."

Becca traced her fingers over the lines. What an incredibly thoughtful thing he'd done for her. She'd wondered about getting a tattoo, and he'd given her a way to actually see it on her skin. Not that she'd start with one this big, but still. He knew what the image meant to her . . .

Jesus, she loved this man.

She leaned back against him and held his hand to her belly when he hugged her in. "Thank you."

"You're beautiful no matter what, but that is so damn sexy." He tilted his hips into her ass, his hard cock nudging her cleft. "I want to fuck you and watch how the ink moves on your skin." She moved to turn toward him, but he grasped her shoulders and held her in place. "Right here. Just like this."

She nodded, her heart pounding so hard she felt it beat under her skin everywhere. Paper crinkled behind her, and he tossed a condom wrapper on the counter by the sink. He nudged her ankles apart and stepped in close. In the mirror, she watched as he clutched her hip, bent his knees, and entered her from behind.

"Oh, God," she cried, feeling him fill her. A strong arm wrapped around her chest and he grabbed her breast. She clung to his forearm, holding him to her. And then he was moving, hard and fast, her back arched, his grip providing leverage, their gazes colliding in the mirror.

"Beautiful Becca," he rasped in her ear. The hand on her hip reached between her legs, forcing him to hunch around her as he thrust. His fingers pressed small, tight circles over her clit until she was panting.

In the mirror, his gaze alternated between her face and her body, and she understood why. Their reflection was so freaking hot. His muscles surrounding and guiding her, the tattoo on his bicep and the ink on her abdomen catching the light as they moved together.

The orgasm slammed into her out of nowhere. "Oh, God, I'm gonna come again," she said, and then her body detonated. Her nails dug into his arm and her knees went soft.

He held her tight. "Fuck yes, me too," he groaned, hips slapping into her. Three final, hard thrusts had his cock pulsing.

Their panting breaths echoed around the small space. She turned in his arms and threw herself around him tight. Her wetness on the condom pressed against her belly, but she didn't care. Emotion was on the verge of overflowing, and she had to let some of it out.

Nick petted her hair and hugged her back, and for a long moment they stood there, just holding one another.

A few minutes later, she yawned and tried to hide it, but he chuckled. "I wear you out?"

"Don't sound so smug," she said, grinning because it was true. She pressed a kiss to his chest and looked up at him. "Besides, I'm not complaining."

Nick disposed of the condom and kissed her. "Good." Taking her hand, he led her back to bed. The digital clock on the nightstand read 2:04. "You should go to bed for a few hours. Morning will be here too soon at this point."

"What about you?"

"I'll be back in a bit. Thought I'd go see what Marz's heard from the guys or if they're back."

She nodded, wanting to stay with him. "Okay, I'll come with you."

"No, you sleep. If something important has happened, I'll come back and get you." He kissed her on the lips. "Promise."

As tired as she was, Nick must've been, too. "But if there's no news, come back to bed with me. Okay?"

His smile brought out the dimple. "Count on it."

While he redressed, she spent a few minutes getting ready for bed, then she let him tuck her in. Sitting on the edge, he leaned in and kissed her. "Sweet dreams, sunshine."

"After that, no doubt." Question was, would her dreams of them being together after this crisis passed come true? His silence after she'd admitted she cared for him rang loud in her memory. His eyes and his touch said he shared the feeling, but maybe she was misreading them.

With a laugh, he turned off the lamp and left.

BECCA CAME AWAKE on a gasp. "Nick?" she said. In the darkness, the clock glowed the numbers 5:18. The lamp confirmed what her instincts had already told her; she was still alone.

The guys must be back by now. Right? Then again, Nick promised he'd wake her if something important happened.

Taking another moment to wake up, she rubbed her face and stretched. Here and there, her muscles twinged with delicious, little aches from their lovemaking, and she didn't mind one bit.

Indulging in a quick shower, Becca's mind started racing. What had the guys learned? What new challenges would the day throw at them? Would they find Charlie today? God, how she hoped.

She dried quickly, careful of her guitar drawing even though he'd said it wouldn't smear, and dressed in jeans and a baseball-style T-shirt that was one of the most comfortable things she owned. Hair still damp, she threw it into a ponytail and stepped into her sneakers.

The rest of the loft apartment was quiet, and she wondered whether that was because everyone was asleep or over in the gym. The living room was empty, so she slipped out into the stairwell and crossed to the opposite door.

Voices sounded from inside as she entered the code into the keypad and pulled open the door. She only took half a step inside, unsure what she was walking into. The door rested against her shoulder.

"Jesus, Nick. All of this is her father's fault. So she can damn well participate," Shane yelled. The words shoved away the last of her sleepiness. What the hell was going on?

"That's bullshit," Nick raged back. "She has nothing to do with what her father did. It's not her fucking fault the man was a goddamned criminal."

Criminal? The walls of the huge space sucked in on her, her brain repeating that word in Nick's angry voice. Why would he say that? Her heart pounded against her sternum.

"Guys," Marz said, standing up from his desk chair.

Shane didn't back down one bit. "Stop leading with your dick and think strategically—"

"Guys," Marz said louder, looking right at her. Her fight-or-flight instinct kicked in, and she had to force her feet to remain planted and not run away from whatever was happening here.

"What?" they both yelled.

Marz nodded to where she stood frozen in the doorway on the far side of the gym. And then five pairs of male eyes swung toward her.

Chapter 20

*S*hit," Rixey bit out, crossing the gym in what felt like one giant leap. "Becca." Not like this. She wasn't supposed to find out like this. *Goddamnit.*

She stepped all the way inside, letting the door click behind her. "Why did you say that? About my dad being a criminal?" Disbelief and hurt colored her expression. Pleading filled her eyes, and it shredded him. "Why would you say that?"

Heart in his throat, he reached for her. "Becca—"

"No." She batted his hands away. "What was my father's fault?"

Panic stalked around the edges of his mind, but Rixey refused to let that fucker have a way in. He gestured toward the guys, resignation a weight on his shoulders. "Okay. Come sit down."

Her eyebrows slashed down over stormy blue eyes as red climbed up her cheeks. "Just tell me what you meant."

His mind raced a moment too long with a response, apparently, because she pushed past him and marched to the corner where his team stood, their gazes alternating between the pair of them. Nick hustled after her. When the truth came, it *had* to come from him or she'd never forgive him. Maybe she already wouldn't.

Christ, they'd made love—and that's exactly what it had been, not sex, not fucking, not some fling—they'd made *love* and he hadn't been honest.

She faced off with the team. "Somebody man up and tell me what the hell is going on."

"Becca—"

Nick glared at Marz, and the man ate whatever words he'd been about to say. When the call had come in on the reward phone line that had led to this fight with Shane, they'd already agreed to Nick's appeal to trust Becca with the truth once they recovered her brother. Finding Charlie didn't necessarily mean the Merritts' troubles were over. Not if their enemies were still looking for whatever had led them to toss both their apartments. Moreover, Charlie would hopefully be able to corroborate some part of their story anyway. And if he was the one talking about whatever his father had been into, the NDA became moot as a reason for continuing to withhold the information.

Gauging the temperature of his team, it was clear from their gazes and their nods they thought she should know. And that was enough for him. He hadn't wanted to hurt her, especially the more he'd gotten to know her, but that ship had sailed. And fuck the goddamned NDA. If he was going down, it wouldn't be with this secret standing between them.

Shoulders braced and feet apart, Nick heaved a breath. "I'll tell you everything."

Arms crossed, she slowly turned toward him. Her gaze told him to get to it.

Unsure which knife to throw first, the words tangled on his tongue. "Shit, Becca, I'm sorry. Your father . . ." He shook his head. "For five years I served under him. Frank Merritt was my mentor. The kind of soldier I wanted to be. He loved being out in the field, leading men and making a difference. He could've gotten cushy on a base somewhere, but he stayed with his team. And I respected the hell out of him for that."

Damn, it wasn't easy admitting how much Merritt had once meant to him. He kept his eyes on her, not wanting to see the guys' inevitable reaction to his next words. "Frank was dirty. He had some black op running on the side—"

She blanched. "What? No. My dad would never—"

"Let me finish." Rixey raked at his hair. The scowl looked so out of place on her face, and *God*, he hated that he'd put it there. "For months, I'd noticed little things. How he started to go off on his own for meetings. Afghan farmers—new to all of us—who seemed to know him. Supposed last-minute changes in orders while on counternarcotics missions, including the day our convoy was ambushed."

The men knew all of this. And, damnedest thing was, after the fact, they'd all opened up. He hadn't been the only one to pick up on some of Merritt's oddities in behavior. But they'd all admired him so much that not one of them had believed what had been right before their eyes. Until it was too late, and half their team was gone. All this time that he'd beaten himself up over seeing but not believing what had been going on with Merritt, he'd forgotten that the others had experienced the same thing. His brain had piled all the blame on himself, when it wasn't any of their faults. Somehow, he hadn't had these insights until now.

"Go on." Anger, sadness, and suspicion clouded her expression and made him want to go to her. But everything about her posture screamed *Hands off,* and it parked a Humvee-sized ball of regret right in the middle of his chest.

He shook his head, his gaze skating over the empty gym equipment, and he heaved a breath. "We were transporting a huge quantity of seized opium. In our area of operation, there were two drop locations, but we almost always used the same one. Right before the convoy got underway, Merritt said we had to drop at the alternate location. About halfway there, out in the middle of BFE, we hit a two-truck roadblock that shouldn't have been there. I was in the tail gun truck and hung back. It didn't feel right. And your father was too reassuring on the radio, like he knew it would be okay. When, *damnit,* that shit is never okay over there." He scanned his gaze over the group.

Silent support radiated from all the men, shoring him up to finish the tale.

He scrubbed his hands over his face, the scruff there now pronounced. "SOP when a convoy stops is fives and twenty-fives. Gunners do five-meter scans in all directions. Soldiers dismount to secure the territory twenty-five meters out from the convoy. Your father told us to stand down. Fucking ridiculous, because a stopped convoy is a sitting duck for a grenade launcher. But your father got out of the truck and approached them like he didn't have a care in the world."

As he spoke, the blood slowly drained out of Becca's face. But now that the words were spilling, he couldn't stop them. You could've heard a pin drop as he drew a breath to forge on.

"The ringleader of the roadblock—an Afghan police commander we'd never before seen—shook your father's hand, then said, 'I have a message for you: death finds all traitors.' The man shot him point-blank. After that, the shit hit the fan." Rixey easily recalled the barrage of reports through his headset, the gunfire, and the pounding explosion of the point vehicle. "The front trucks were trapped when a grenade disabled the third truck. The team bailed from the vehicles, taking cover and returning fire. Insurgents went after the transport vehicles without checking their cargos, like they knew exactly which ones to take. Easy put two rounds in the police commander's gut. I think that's the only thing that kept them from staying until they picked every last one of us off."

Becca took two steps backward and sagged into a folding chair.

"After they left with the opium, six of us were still alive, though four were shot to shit. Shane did his best to keep us from bleeding out while Easy got one of the gun trucks up and running. By then, Zane was gone. We radioed for backup, but we were on the road again before anyone showed up."

"The casualty notification officers said he'd died in a routine checkpoint incident," she said in a shaky voice.

"That's the official word," Shane said, voice tight, expression dark.

"But what you're saying is . . ." Becca swallowed, hard, the sound audible across the distance that separated them. "That he led you to that roadblock with . . . what? The secret intention of turning over those trucks of opium to terrorists?"

She put the pieces right together, didn't she? Nick just nodded.

"But . . . why? Why would he do that?"

"There's a fuckton of corruption in Afghanistan," Marz said, elbows on the desk and hands fisted together. "Opium's a persuasive mistress. The local police are on the take. Upwards of forty percent of them in some regions test positive for the drug. Hell, among our own forces, positive drug tests for opium have increased more than tenfold since we've been over there."

She spun toward Marz. "The Army was my father's life. You think he would sell you out to make money off the drug that killed his oldest son?"

No one responded. The deafening silence was an answer in itself.

Nick cleared his throat, memories forming a thick knot. "When we got back to base and were stabilized, they immediately started in on interrogations. It became evident pretty damn quick they were investigating *us* rather than the incident. Our suspicions about your father were roundly shut down to the point where we were threatened with prosecution if we continued to voice them."

"They ruined our records, Becca," Murda said, leaning against the wall, his expression lethal, his tone like ice. "Every man in this room had exemplary service records. Look at them now and you'll find a long list of disciplinary problems and hints of dereliction of duty, supposedly reported by your father. Makes it look like we're trying to discredit his leadership to clear our own names. Someone was in on this with your father, protected him while he left us swinging."

Her gaze dropped to her lap, where her fingers knotted and unknotted.

"They forced us out on other than honorable charges," Shane said with barely concealed rage. He stabbed a finger into the table. "Made us sign nondisclosure agreements in order to stay out of prison. It's a permanent mark on our records that will never go away."

Nick had to hammer home the point. It was his only shot at getting her to forgive him. "Those NDAs are the main reason I didn't—couldn't—tell you the truth. But

I also didn't want to hurt you. And, shit, how could this not hurt?"

Becca kneaded the muscles in her neck and shook her head. "I don't know what to say." A single tear trailed down her cheek. Her glassy blue eyes cut to Nick. "Who was the message from?"

"What message?" Nick asked.

"You said the police commander gave him a message. From who?"

Wouldn't he like to know. It was one of the pieces of the puzzle that screamed corruption. "We don't know. But apparently Charlie stumbled on something that might help us answer questions just like that one."

Becca rose to her feet and closed the distance between them, her movements stiff, her sad blue eyes spearing him. "You promised to be honest with me. To treat me as a partner in this."

He shook his head. "I promised to tell you everything about our investigation to find Charlie. And I have."

"Bullshit, Nick." Anger burned away the sadness from her eyes. "You're splicing hairs too thin to be cut. Correct me if I'm too blond to follow, but this *story,* if it's true, is fundamental to finding my brother. *If* my father was working with some bad guys and Charlie found that out, then those bad guys are who probably took him, broke into our houses, and tried to kidnap me, right? Same investigation."

"I wanted to tell you, but the NDA affected more than just me. Breaching it risks all of our freedom, not just mine." His brain latched onto another part of what she'd said: *Story*? Becca thought he was telling a *story*. His chest cavity filled with crushed glass. "Are you saying you don't believe me?" He held his arms out. "You don't believe *us*."

"Yes, I do. I mean, I think . . . *shit,* Nick. This just

redrew the map of my world. I don't know what the hell to think right now. Okay?" Her voice cracked. "It feels like losing him all over again." Silent tears fell, and her expression filled with utter disappointment. "You asked me to trust you," she whispered. "And I did." Becca shook her head. "God, Nick, we just—" She gestured toward the door.

We just made love. Damnit, Becca, I know. The truth of the words sliced into him on a cellular level. He understood her anger. It was hard to accept any reason for being lied to by someone you love.

If she even loved him. Or ever could, now.

"So, what is it that Shane wants me to participate in?" she said in a monotone voice. She turned toward his teammate.

Sonofabitch. She was shutting down, and he was losing her. He felt it down to his bones. And as much as he wanted to drag her back to his bed, beg her forgiveness, and do any penance she required to make it up to her, he couldn't. Because they had a time-sensitive lead hanging over their heads.

And a fight to finish about how to pursue it.

Shane looked over her head to Nick.

"Don't look at him. Look at *me*. Tell *me*." She planted her hands on her hips.

Shane's eyes narrowed, but he started talking. "Man who says he attempted to abduct you called through the reward line and asked for a meeting with you this morning. He knew about the pinkie, so he seems legit. We're supposed to call him back at oh seven hundred to set it up."

Life filtered back into her voice. "This is good news, right? If he knows about the pinkie, he probably knows where Charlie is."

"Maybe," Nick said, stepping beside her. "But it could just as well be a setup to grab you."

"Still, it's worth learning more, isn't it?" She scanned her gaze over the group. "Unless the scouting you did last night turned up something useful?"

"We reconned four locations," Beckett said, pushing off the wall and giving her an appraising look. "Two were completely negative, two beg further investigation. We've also got bugs in place at the strip club, one on the bar and one on the stage. We couldn't access any private spaces, though, so we'll see what they yield."

"See," Marz began, pulling up a series of images on his computer. Grainy schematics appeared with small groups of blinking red dots. "In both locations, Beck's scanner identified stationary humans in basement rooms. In the first location, three. In the second location, two. This was at the shipping facility and a strip club."

"What does that mean?" she asked, leaning in.

"Possible prisoners." Beck braced his hands on the desk and studied the pictures. "Or not. It's hard to say for sure without more intel."

"Which our caller might be able to provide, depending on what the hell he really wants." Shane's voice didn't hold its earlier eagerness for the idea, which helped keep Nick's blood pressure from exploding off the top of his head. "But it means putting you out there. There's no way he's going to allow you to bring along a guard detachment. He's going to put demands and parameters on the meet, Becca. One will certainly be that you come alone."

"Oh." She visibly deflated, shoulders sagging, gaze dropping to the desktop.

Oh? No, more like, *Holy fucking shit*. Guy who tried to kidnap her wanted to meet alone. No. Just no. "It's too dangerous," Nick said.

"You guys would find a way to keep me safe," she said, with an implicit trust that tore at him. "So, if I'm game to do it, that's the end of the conversation."

"Becca—"

"Stop. Just stop. You don't get to dictate what I do or don't do." She arched an eyebrow at Nick, and he got the message loud and clear. He'd lost any right he might've had to an opinion about her life. Rixey fought the urge to rub at the ache splintering the left side of his chest. "Charlie is my brother. If doing this will help bring him home alive, then that's all I need to know." She looked at Shane for guidance, and that absolutely slayed Nick. "What do you think?"

"I think Nick's right about the risk," he said, throwing Rixey a bone. "But recon didn't tell us as much as we'd hoped, and this meeting could make the difference, depending on why he's asking for it."

Easy settled a hip against the edge of the desk. "Maybe he wants to make a trade? Or sell some information?"

"It's like a damn multiple-choice quiz right now. I'll pick D: all of the above." Shaking his head, Marz leaned back in his chair.

"One way to find out, right? We call." She surveyed the men, and Nick followed her lead. Maybe she didn't know them well enough to see it, but to a man they wore a new respect for her in their gazes. As much as he hated the idea of hanging her out there as some kind of bait, he admired her courage and willingness to help. To be part of the team. Everyone nodded, including him. He could totally get behind making the call. "Okay, then. What time is it?" she asked.

"Six forty-two," Marz said.

She nodded and released a long breath. "So, we call at seven o'clock like he asked and go from there."

WELL, BECCA GOT what she wanted. Which was why she found herself standing alone in an open-air picnic pavilion on the edge of the Canton Waterfront Park three hours later.

A yuppie neighborhood with a party reputation, all of Canton was probably still hungover and in bed, which meant she was the only one in the park. Good for their daytime op, a little scary as she stood here now.

She wasn't really alone, though. The team was stationed all around her. Miguel and Shane were hiding in plain sight. They were readying Miguel's powerboat down at the dock, like they were heading out to fish on the beautiful spring Sunday morning. Miguel had actually been the one to suggest this location, reasoning he could drop them off by water, which the gang wouldn't likely expect in case they were lying in wait. And, if the team could grab the guy, taking the boat out on the water would give them privacy to interrogate him. Nick, Beckett, Easy, and Marz had taken up hiding spots around the park. Even though she couldn't see them, she trusted that they were there for her.

That knowledge didn't keep her heart from pounding in her chest or her scalp from prickling, but it gave her the courage to stand and wait to meet the man who'd held a knife to her ribs and attempted to kidnap her.

The man who said he could tell her where Charlie was and what she had to do to get him back.

That had been enough for Becca. For the rest of the team, as well. Even Nick had begrudgingly admitted it was a critical lead, even if he hated the idea of her being out in the open by herself.

Nick. God, the story he'd told about her father. If she let herself think about it at all, nausea flooded her gut. Becca paced the length of the pavilion, twigs crunching beneath her sneakers. Part of her wanted to reject the idea that her father was anything but the hero she'd always believed.

What they said he did made absolutely no sense. None of it squared with the man she'd known and loved her whole life.

Except . . . now that the logic of the team's story had time to gel with what Charlie claimed and the reality of their situation, she was ashamed that she'd succumbed to a moment of knee-jerk defensiveness and made Nick question whether she believed in him. She'd just been so blindsided.

If only Nick had told her the truth sooner.

Damned NDA. The agreement made the team's freedom contingent on keeping quiet. On an intellectual level, she totally got why Nick hadn't said anything. But it didn't keep her heart from feeling a bit bruised. Here she was talking about her father like he and Nick were old friends, never having the first clue that he hated her dad with a passion. Believed to his core that Frank Merritt had ruined his life. Certainly explained the frigid shoulder that first day, didn't it? And it explained why the team had been standoffish toward her while they'd been more friendly toward Jeremy and Jess. But all along, she'd been clueless.

Becca turned to stare out at the bright sparkle of the Inner Harbor. Two wide-winged gulls swooped low over the water. A part of her heart wanted Nick to have trusted her despite the NDA. They'd made love, for God's sake. That didn't earn her a bit of extra trust and respect? Then again, she'd been the only one to ever actually voice feelings in this whole thing. Maybe she was putting the cart about forty-two cart-lengths before the horse, and Nick's feelings weren't anywhere near as pronounced as her own. That would certainly explain why he wouldn't have wanted to take a chance on telling her.

Given all that was at stake, for him and the four other men who shared his secret, she really shouldn't blame him.

So, fine. Whatever. Becca would just have to pull up her big girl panties and find a way to deal. Nothing could bring her father back. Her hurt feelings didn't matter—only finding and rescuing Charlie did. The rest of it would get worked out later. Or it wouldn't.

Pressing the button on her smartphone revealed the time to be 9:54 a.m. Guy should be here any minute. Fingering the charms on her bracelet and shifting from foot to foot, she did a three-sixty scan of as much of the park as she could see from the pavilion, which was located at one end of the open expanse of green with decorative pathways and surrounding trees. All the time she'd lived in Baltimore, she'd never once been to this little gem right on the water. Something told her that after today, she'd never want to come back, either.

Are you out there, Nick?

Forcing herself to take a calming breath, she pressed her palm against the Glock 19 handgun Nick had insisted she carry—not that she minded. Small and lightweight, she had it concealed in a small holster tucked inside her jeans on her right hip. She dropped her hands to her sides. Checking that the Glock was there was a dead giveaway that she was carrying. She straightened her shirt to make sure the gun wasn't printing through the material.

Tires screeched against pavement. Becca whirled toward the parking lot bordering the park on the other side of a narrow driveway and a line of trees. Through the new spring leaves, she could just make out a dark SUV cutting diagonally across the mostly open spaces. Her heart leapt into her throat, but she kept her eyes straight ahead. It was critical she not do anything to give the impression she wasn't alone.

God, how am I going to do this? Just breathe, Bec. This is too important to screw up.

Right. As long as her lungs kept operating, she'd be fine.

The truck whipped into the driveway about twenty feet in front of her, the drive that also led to the boat put-in and dock where Miguel and Shane were pretending to be Sunday fishermen. Score one for the good guys—getting her attacker in this space was one of the things they'd hoped for. It was why they'd chosen the pavilion as their rendezvous point.

She recognized the driver right away. In her mind's eye, she saw him crossing the staff break room. It was definitely the same man. And, thank God, he'd come alone.

Eyes drilling into her, he got out of the idling truck and crossed the grass looking like the gangster he apparently was—baggy jeans, hoody, chains at his neck. But, geez, he'd been beaten to hell judging by the bruises and cuts on his face. Every moment of this situation was more surreal than the next.

"That's close enough," she said when he reached the edge of the sidewalk that ringed the pavilion. Becca retreated behind a picnic table, placing a barrier between them.

He glared but stopped on the sidewalk. "So we meet again."

"Well, I wouldn't say we've met, since you know who I am, but I don't know you." Her gaze dropped to his hand, but she couldn't get a good look at the tattoos there from this angle.

His brown eyes narrowed. "All you need to know is I'm the one who can help get your brother back."

It sounded too good to be true. The breeze blew strands of hair loose from her ponytail, and she swept them away from her eyes. "What is it you want?"

"To know how your bro put two and two together."

Becca nearly groaned and her hands fisted. She had no more patience for bullshit mystery. "What the hell is that supposed to mean? Don't play games with me."

"Charlie found something that was supposed to be hidden, and we need to know what led him to it."

"How am I supposed to find that out?" she asked, a chill running down her spine despite the nice morning.

The hint of a smile played around the corners of his wide mouth. "I was thinking about that . . ."

A scuff. Rubber on concrete. Goose bumps erupted across her neck as she turned.

Time slowed to a crawl, and everything happened at once.

Two guys stepped out of the trees and entered the far side of the pavilion. Both had guns.

Panic had barely welled up inside her as one screamed and fell to the ground for no apparent reason. The other bolted but, just as suddenly, crashed to the ground with a shout and a cry. Could Beckett's silencer be the cause? The punks writhed on the grass, but one of them returned fire, the gun's report echoing loudly under the pavilion's roof. Becca instinctively crouched down, hands cradling her head. Her gaze whipped to her attacker.

Expression absolutely livid, he stalked around the table with a gun pointed at her head. "Not getting away this time, bitch."

She backtracked the opposite direction, her hand reaching for her gun.

His roiling gaze tracked the movement and he lunged.

Becca took off across the concrete, catching her shin on the blunt edge of a bench in a flash of pain. The stumble slowed her, and he grabbed her ponytail. Her head wrenched back, nearly taking her off her feet. Suddenly, her air was gone, his arm trapping her in a tight chokehold that had her clawing and gasping. Nearby, footsteps pounded on the earth. The team.

They'll get to me, they'll get to me, they'll get to me in time.

Above her, the bright blue sky filled with little pin-points of light as the guy's arm compressed her windpipe. And her medical training meant she knew she had mere seconds before blacking out.

Voices. A scuffle. A shove from behind. Then she was free and on the grass. Gulping down air, she rolled onto her hands and knees, blinking and shaking consciousness into her head.

Two bodies slammed to the ground ten feet away from her. Nick had come out of nowhere and taken the guy facedown. Now he was jamming the business end of his gun into the man's meaty cheek, drilling his knee into his back.

Through the mask he wore, icy-hot green eyes cut toward her.

"I'm okay," she gasped, remembering not to use Nick's name, one of the instructions they'd given her by way of preparation. When he didn't look away, she nodded. "I'm okay." Last thing she wanted was for him to be distracted by worry.

Beckett knelt behind the gangbanger and shoved a black hood over his head. The guys removed their masks, meant to protect their identity from the Churchmen. She was the only one who didn't need one, given they'd already seen her.

"Come on," Marz said, appearing beside her. He helped her to her feet and steadied her when she wobbled. "We have to move. Fast."

"Look," she said, pointing. The tattoo on the back of the baddie's hand was definitely the cross and tower symbol.

"Other two are secure where they dropped," Easy said, jogging up behind them with a handful of weaponry. He pulled off his mask and stuffed it in his pocket. "I called nine-one-one, although I should just let 'em bleed out."

He reached into the driver's side door of the SUV, killed the engine, and came back out with the keys jingling in his hands.

Nick produced a thick plastic zip tie. He secured the attacker's hands behind his back, grabbed his bicep, and forced him to his feet. "Please give me a reason to pull the trigger," Nick growled, digging the barrel of his gun into the man's back. Hand on his arm, Nick pushed him forward.

Guns drawn, they moved as a unit, gazes constantly scanning. Even with Becca and their prisoner in the center of the group, Nick's men very clearly moved in a synchronized formation as they walked down the drive to the boat they'd all arrived on, though now moored further down the waterfront. Even as he kept a handle on her attacker, Nick planted his body next to hers. Relief, admiration, regret for their morning fight. Love. The urge to tell him all of it flooded through her, but it would have to wait.

Luckily, the park remained empty and the trees provided cover from the neighboring parking lot. Ahead, the white fishing boat rumbled to life. They walked across the wood planking, the boards moving slightly under the weight of the group. Marz helped her step down into the boat, and Shane guided her to the empty seat next to Miguel in the central cockpit. In just a few seconds' time, the team was all aboard. Easy took a position on the wide rear wall, watching their tail, while the rest of the guys bustled their captive toward the open space at the front and forced him to the floor.

"Ropes are clear," Shane said.

Miguel pushed a lever forward, easing them away from the dock. Their speed felt excruciatingly slow, but then they passed a buoy with a No Wake sign and she understood why. "Harbor police ahead, gentlemen, just play it cool," Miguel said.

Sitting on the V-shaped benches built into the boat's bow, Shane, Marz, and Beckett reclined against the walls like they hadn't a care in the world.

Miguel pasted on a smile. "Smile and wave, boys and girls."

The police boat wasn't particularly close, but its captain waved. They waved back. Becca blew out a breath, adrenaline from the scuffle at the pavilion making her shaky now.

"You okay, kid?" Miguel asked.

She nodded and pulled loose strands of her hair from her face. Thought about how good an icy bottle of water would feel on her raw throat. Nick's team was being so quiet that she felt she should be, too. In fact, tension radiated off the men. Easy had his gaze peeled off the stern of the boat. The guys seated up front appeared braced for a fight, muscles rigid, eyes on a constant scan. Nick was on top of the guy on the floor, gun still jammed in the man's back.

Thankfully, Canton was close to the mouth of the harbor. They passed Fort McHenry on the right, the historic site that inspired Francis Scott Key to write the Star-Spangled Banner, and then they were out into more open water. Miguel picked up speed. It was a beautiful day, no waves or wind, and the fishing boat glided gently through the dark green-blue water as they passed Baltimore's industrial areas and boatyards, then went under the last bridges that officially marked their entry into the Chesapeake Bay.

"Open water, gentlemen," Miguel called over the twin engines. "Coming right up." He pushed the lever forward again, and the boat shot out over the calm bay.

Becca wrapped her arms around herself and hugged tight. It wasn't cold, but her bones rattled in her skin, her throat ached, and her head throbbed. Now that they had the guy, how were they going to get him to tell them what they needed to know?

Chapter 21

$\mathcal{R}$age and a healthy dose of deadly intent flowed through Rixey's veins. What he'd most feared had very nearly come to pass—Becca being hurt, kidnapped, or worse. This motherfucker had manhandled her. Twice. At this point, he'd happily bathe in the guy's blood and dance on his bones.

"Check him for ID," Nick said, still using his weight to make sure the asshole didn't try to get cute.

Shane and Marz went through his pockets. "Bingo," Marz said, lifting the guy's cell phone and a black leather wallet. He flipped the billfold open. "Hello, Mr. Tyrell Woodson. I'll just hang onto these." Marz slipped both into his pocket.

From his position on the deck, Nick didn't have a good visual of their location. He glanced up to Shane, who gave a tight nod, confirming they were out in open water.

"Start. Talking," Nick growled, giving an extra shove of his gun into Tyrell's kidney.

"Fuck you," the punk said.

Rixey heaved the guy's upper body off the floor and slammed it back against the fiberglass. "Wrong answer," he said as groans spilled out from under the hood. "We know you work for Church. Tell us why Church is after the Merritts and where Charlie Merritt is being held."

"I'm not telling you shit." He struggled under Nick's grip.

"Since you're going after his sister, I'm guessing Charlie said something similar, huh? What did you do to try to convince him, I wonder." He glanced to the team surrounding him. "Masks. I want Tyrell to see what I'm about to do." Bracing his feet against the boat's motion over the waves, he grabbed his full tactical face mask from his jacket pocket and slipped the thin black fabric over his head again. The other men did the same, leaving only their eyes uncovered. "Grab his arms and legs." Rixey pulled the blade free from his ankle holster and cut the plastic band binding the man's wrists.

Asshole struggled momentarily, but Shane, Marz, and Beckett made quick work of restraining him and flipped him to his back.

Kneeling, Rixey spared a glance to the cockpit. Becca had moved to the gangway next to the cockpit, in full view of their interrogation. He really wished she wasn't watching this, but she deserved to know everything they learned.

Marz tapped on Nick's shoulder and held up his iPhone. "Video," he mouthed.

Nick nodded, waited for him to indicate he was ready, and ripped the hood off their captive. Bruises and cuts covered his dark skin, like somebody had beat the shit out of him. Rixey was momentarily jealous that someone had gotten to this piece of shit first. Breathing so hard his lips puffed out on each harsh exhale, the banger's bulging eyes skittered here and there and squinted as he attempted to focus on Rixey kneeling above him.

"I open my mouth, I'm as good as dead," he squeaked, sounding more like a piss-scared teenager than a bad-ass banger.

"You're already as good as dead." Beckett's voice was icy cold as he restrained an arm.

"As soon as your friends back at the park tell anyone you were taken, they'll know you're damaged goods." Nick grabbed his jaw and turned it this way and that. "Judging by your face, I'd say someone's already not too happy with you." The guy sputtered, but Nick didn't have the patience for bullshit. Not now. Holding the blade up, he studied it for a long moment. "What were we talking about before? Oh, right. What you did to try to make Charlie talk. Anybody here remember what they did to him?"

"No. No, man. That wasn't me," he spluttered. Shit. A dark stain spread on his pants. The acrid scent of urine whirled through the sea air.

"Well, what part have you played in this?" Nick flashed the blade. "Attempted kidnapping. Twice. We know that much."

"I . . . I . . ."

"He needs some encouragement," Beck said.

Rixey nodded. "He does, doesn't he? Slide his hand over here."

"What?" Tyrell screeched. "Okay, okay, I was in her house."

"What were you looking for?" Nick asked, whipping the blade against Tyrell's throat and wanting to spit in his face. Put a gun in the hand of a guy like this, he was tough shit. Strip him of it, and he was a big fucking sissy.

"I don't know. I was just told to toss the place. Me and one other guy. We was just there to do the damage."

"But there was someone else looking for something."

"Above my pay grade, man. I swear."

Fine. Probably true. Nick changed tactics. Just for the fun of seeing fear cloud Tyrell's eyes like it had Becca's. Nick moved the knife. This time, down to dig right into his navel. "Where's Charlie?"

Tyrell shook his head against the deck. "I'm not sure."

Nick dragged the guy's beefy hand in front of him, held his wrist tight against the deck, and wedged the edge of the blade under his pinkie nail. "Where's Charlie?" he said again, voice deadly even.

Tyrell grimaced. "I don't know. I don't know."

"Not good enough." Nick exerted enough pressure to inch the blade under the nail. Tyrell gritted his teeth and tried to hold in his reaction, but the nail was beginning to separate from the skin. Blood slowly pooled.

"He was at a storage facility," he nearly screamed.

Now we're getting somewhere. Jackwad had no way of knowing they'd already found the facility he referred to. Nick withdrew the knife. Jesus, didn't take much to make him squeal, did it? "Explain. Do it right the first time or I'll rip the nail right off. And I won't stop there."

"They were holding him at a storage facility. But I heard they were gonna move him. Okay?" he blurted out.

"Move him where? And when?"

Tyrell whimpered.

"Screw the nails. I'm going for the whole finger. That's what you did to Charlie, right?" Nick pushed his weight down on the back of Tyrell's hand and pressed the blade into the little space where the finger met the knuckle joint.

Tears leaked from the asshole's eyes. Seriously? This was the kind of douchebag terrorizing Baltimore's streets. Just a big fucking bully.

"I heard . . . I heard . . ." he gasped. "Sometime today. Company's com-coming who wants to see him."

"Moving him *where*?" Rixey exerted a little more pressure on the blade. It was clear the threat of violence was enough with this guy. Didn't do a lot to assuage the vengeance Rixey wanted to rain down on him for the bruises he'd put on Becca's beautiful body, though.

"That's all I know. Moving him to see some BFD company boss wants to impress. And I don't know who the company is. Been real hush-hush. I swear."

That shit didn't sound good at all. Who the hell from outside Church's organization would want to talk to Charlie? And why?

"I forget anything?" Rixey scanned over his team. Negative reactions all around. "I think we're ready to take out the trash, then. Hey, Capitán?" he yelled to Miguel.

"Yo!" Miguel said.

"What kind of water temperatures we got out here this time of year?"

"Aw, damn. High forties, low fifties at best."

Nick shook his head. "Well, shit, Tyrell. I dump you out here like I want, you'll be hypothermic in an hour."

Tyrell's eyes rolled back until only the whites showed. "No, no drowning. Man, please."

"What exactly are you going to do to make it worth my while to leave you alive? Because I don't want to have to fucking deal with you again. You understand me?" Nick planted the business end of the knife into the soft skin under his jaw.

"Yeah, yeah, yeah. I'll stay away. No more. I'm out."

Nick nodded to Marz. "Well, just to make sure that's true, why don't you show Hollywood here that you could make him a star?"

Marz turned the phone around, a moving picture of the

guy blubbering about Charlie's location playing on the screen.

"I even *think* I've seen you. We even run into each other at the grocery store. Just once. And I'll make sure Jimmy Church gets a copy of this. Understood?"

Sniveling now, Tyrell nodded.

"Find us a drop-off, Capitán," Rixey called over a sudden gust of wind. The boat came around, causing Nick to slide on his knees. Beck grabbed his arm until he regained his balance. Rixey gave him a nod, digging how slowly but surely the team was coming back into itself.

The coordinated response to the unexpected development of Tyrell's buddies showing up was a perfect example. From their appearance until Nick had this shithead on the ground was about ninety seconds. About forty-five seconds too long for him, given what had happened to Becca. But it was almost like the team had picked up where it had left off. Except for their six missing brothers. That shit could never be made right.

"ETA five minutes," Miguel called. Hanging onto the railing, Becca made her way back to her seat.

"Roger that." Soon the roar of the engines dulled and the boat slowed, allowing the waves to rock the boat more than they had at higher knots. Nick stood, saw where they were, and grinned under the mask. Priceless. A man-made hexagonal island in the middle of the bay, not far from the mouth of the harbor. He gave a thumbs-up. "Masks in the rear," he called.

Easy slipped his on in one smooth motion, while Miguel fumbled with his for a minute.

When they were all secure except for Becca—whose appearance the banger unfortunately already knew—Rixey hauled him off the floor with the guys' help. "Okay, Tyrell. We'll get you as close as we can, and you can attempt to jump to dry land. Worst-case scenario, you get a little wet, but you'll survive. Ride's over."

"What? You can't leave me out here." His expression was almost cartoonlike with disbelief.

"I can do anything I want." Nick shoved him to starboard.

Miguel guided the boat in close to the wall, but he had to stay about three feet off to keep from getting pushed into it by the waves.

"Off you go," Rixey said, regret that he couldn't rid the world of scum like this once and for all feeling like a rock in his stomach. But even though they no longer wore the uniform, they couldn't go total vigilante without risking the loss of a vital part of themselves—the guiding principle of doing the right thing. In this situation, the right thing just happened to require some questionable means. He didn't relish that fact, but there it was.

Tyrell stepped up onto the boat's wide ledge. "Fuck," he yelled, and jumped.

Miguel didn't need to be told to gun it. He got underway again before any other boaters happened by.

"I'll fucking kill you!" Tyrell roared from the retaining wall of the small island.

Nick laughed and waved a hand. And then they were hauling ass back to shore.

"What say I call the harbormaster and let them know Becca's attacker's waiting out at Fort Carroll Light?" Miguel asked.

"Roger that," Nick said, tugging off his mask. Everyone followed suit. Nick squeezed by Beckett, slipped down the side of the cockpit, and stepped in front of Becca's tall chair. Hair windblown, cheeks flush, eyes wide, she was so fucking beautiful it hurt.

Those baby blues glassed over and she threw her arms

around his neck. "I'm sorry," she said. "I'm sorry about this morning."

Aw, shit. Relief nearly took him to his knees. His arms came around her. "Sshh, sunshine. You don't owe me an apology. If anything, I'm the one who should be saying I'm sorry."

She shook her head against his neck. "I believe you. I hate it. I hate that this is the truth of my father. I hate what happened to you. But I believe you. And I know you couldn't tell me. I understand." She trembled against him.

He pulled back and gripped her face. That she'd come to him with belief and understanding heated parts of his soul he thought might never again be warm. "We're okay? Can you forgive me?"

Eyes wet and uncertain, she said, "Yes. Can you forgive me, too?"

"It's not even a thing." He kissed her. Right there in front of everyone. Guys hadn't missed a fucking thing anyway. They already knew Rixey was way the hell into her. And making things right with Becca was more important than whatever pussy-whipped comments this might earn him later. "You okay?" he asked, bending to look at her throat. For a moment, his gaze went hazy. The skin was scratched and red.

"It's sore, but it's okay." She patted his chest, a silent request for him to step back, and then she slipped off her stool. "I need to do something."

"Okay," he said, not sure what . . .

She made the few steps to the stern, where Easy sat on the back corner, and said something Nick couldn't hear over the wind. And then she hugged him. Easy's arms came around her slowly but hugged her back. And then they were nodding to each other.

Nick had no clue what she was doing. She squeezed his

hand as she passed him, heading to the bow. And she repeated the same action with Marz, who wore a big goofy grin afterward. With Shane, who was visibly moved, and finally with Beckett, whom Nick'd never seen hug another person before in his life.

Over his shoulder, Nick asked Easy, "What did she say?"

The guy stood up, gave a nod of respect that shone in his eyes, and looked at Rixey. "She said she's sorry for her father. That she'll do whatever she can to make up for it. And that she believes us." Easy's voice was strained as he spoke.

No one had apologized for what had happened to them. No one had offered to help. And no one had said they believed them.

Except Becca.

He looked toward the bow, where Beckett was leaning down to hear something she had to say.

And that was the moment Nick knew unequivocally he was in love with Becca Merritt.

BECCA LAY NAKED on her side, her body intertwined with Nick's. His strong arms surrounded her, and the heat of his skin sank deep.

They were all going a little crazy having to wait the day to go after Charlie. But the storage center was open to the public until six on Sundays and located in a high-traffic strip. The team didn't want to risk civilians or exposure to themselves if the op went bad. And the strip club—*the* place in Church's empire that seemed most suitable for entertaining and impressing—didn't open until seven on Sunday evenings, and it would be significantly easier to search if they could go inside as customers.

So they were going out at seven on the dot. In the

meantime, they ate, slept . . . in her and Nick's case, made love, too.

Each hour that passed ratcheted up her terror that something would happen to Nick tonight when they went after Charlie.

She snuggled into Nick and pressed a kiss against his chest. Words had been parked on the edge of her tongue since the minute he'd accepted her apology on Miguel's boat. But she wasn't sure if voicing these overwhelming feelings welling up inside her would give him strength or prove a distraction.

And she was scared enough for him, because the dual assault on the storage center and the strip club meant their numbers were halved.

Which terrified Becca beyond belief.

Not just for Nick, whom she loved.

But also for the men who were all that remained of the brotherhood he'd cherished his entire adult life. Becca had no illusions that her apology to each of the guys made everything all right. It would take a lot more than words to undo her father's damage. She had to find a way, though, because she felt the weight of that responsibility like a second skin she'd never be able to take off.

Beside her, Nick stretched and yawned, his body coming to life all along the length of hers. They'd made love earlier, but he was hard against her stomach, and she wasn't complaining.

Sliding her thigh up the outside of his, she reached between their bodies and grasped and stroked his cock. He moaned low in his throat, a sound that added to the wetness growing between her legs from the feel of him in her hand and her not-at-all-accidental rubbing of his head against her clit.

"Put me inside you," he whispered.

A thrill shivered over her skin at the gravelly command. Becca dragged his head through her folds, tilted her hips, and guided him inside.

"Oh, Jesus," he said against the top of her hair.

She leaned her head back and kissed him. As their tongues twirled and lashed, he hooked his hand behind her knee and used the leverage to fuck her. The strokes were punctuated, hard thrusts, snaps of his hips against her clit that drove her wild and pushed her almost immediately to the edge.

His mouth stole her breath. His touch stole her heart. And his cock stole her sanity. Becca came. He swallowed her cry and whispered sweet encouragements as her body clenched and writhed.

"I'm coming," he groaned. "Oh, Becca, shit." Nick yanked his cock free, stroked it with a tight fist, and came all over her belly. "I'm sorry," he panted. "Didn't mean to forget." When the strain of his orgasm melted off his face, his eyes were so bright, so free of the shadows she'd seen that first day.

Her heart squeezed. "It's okay. I liked it. I'm on birth control anyway."

"Good to know." Pushing into a sitting position, his gaze raked over her. She looked down herself, wondering exactly what he saw when he looked at her. Two ribbons of cum painted white stripes over her belly button. "Goddamnit, I'd kill to draw you right now. But it's getting late." Nick twisted to look at the nightstand and groaned.

"What time is it?" she whispered.

"Almost five." Only two hours.

Her stomach dropped and she took a deep breath. Unthinkingly, she drew her fingers through the wetness on her belly and noticed his eyes flash to the movement. She did it again, on purpose this time, wanting to distract both of them from the awaiting reality. She smeared the liquid over the curved line of the guitar body still drawn on her side.

"That's so fucking sexy, Becca." He grabbed her hand, pulled it to his mouth, and kissed her knuckles. "But stop before I end up hard again and have a case of blue balls for the rest of the night. Stay right there." He winked and swung off the bed. A moment later he returned with a warm washcloth, and he bathed her stomach. It was the sweetest thing.

The pressure of emotion for him made it hard to breathe. She had to tell him. Who knew what the night would bring? And no way she could let him go out there without knowing he mattered to her. Not just a lot. But as much as anyone ever could. "Nick?"

His dimple came out as he looked at her. "Yeah?" He tossed the cloth to the nightstand.

Nerves almost making her light-headed, she forced herself to sit up. When he settled next to her, she stroked her fingers over him, his shoulders, his chest, his sides, and met those beautiful eyes. "I love you," she whispered, her breath catching. "I just need you to know. I'm completely in love with you. And I—"

"God, Becca." He cupped her face in his big hands. "I love you so fucking much I can barely breathe." He kissed her, a consuming, devouring physical connection that wrapped them up in a moment in time that was just for them, into which nothing could intrude. She'd remember it for the rest of her life.

The kiss gentled, and then they were embracing. Just holding one another. "I love you," she said. "I want you to remember my voice saying this while you're out there tonight. I love you."

He stroked her hair and kissed her temple. "I could never forget."

Finally, they had to get up. Dress. Her, in a pair of yoga

pants and a sweatshirt, him, in black jeans, a T-shirt, his gun holster—a double one, this time, and a sports coat that covered it. He looked so freaking hot, and it nearly brought tears to her eyes because— No. She wasn't even thinking it.

He knelt at a safe in the closet and loaded up on weapons—two handguns, various knives, extra clips of ammunition. Each addition ratcheted up her anxiety because it meant he was expecting a fight.

Nick held her hand as they walked out to the kitchen and met up with Shane and Easy, sitting at the bar eating leftovers. Jeremy leaned on the other side of the counter and nursed a beer.

"Beckett's over with Marz," Shane said. "We should run through an equipment and weapons check."

"Agreed," Nick said. "Gimme five to choke something down."

"Take six," Easy said with a smart-ass smile.

"Want me to make you something?" Becca asked. He shook his head and gave her a quick kiss. No way she could eat right now, so she settled against the bar next to Jeremy and bumped his shoulder. "Hey."

"Hey," he said, his gaze heavy with concern. Jeremy was upset he couldn't participate in the assault, but he'd only handled a gun a few times in his life, and the guys had reluctantly voiced concerns about his readiness for what they might be walking into.

"I'll sit on your lap later if you want," she said, referring to his T-shirt: *I'm not Santa, but you can still sit on my lap . . .*

That quirked a grin out of him. "My lap is open to you any time, babe. Ow." Nick cuffed him on the back of the head and he flinched. "Santa." Jer pointed to himself. "The Grinch." He pointed to Nick. "You choose."

Becca laughed and the guys joined in. Nick shoveled

some pork fried rice down his throat and tried to pretend it wasn't funny. But she could see the truth in his gorgeous eyes.

Fifteen minutes later, they were back in the gym again. Her eyes widened at the arsenal getting pulled from duffel bags and cases. Handguns. Rifles. Tasers. Ammunition. Headsets. Radios. Other things she couldn't identify and honestly didn't want to. Turned out each of the guys who'd driven here—Shane, Beckett, and Easy—had come prepared for the worst.

And now here they were.

"Why do you all have all this?" she asked.

Beckett looked over his shoulder. "Security is my line of work. But ever since I got back from Afghanistan, I've been preparing for the day the shit rained down again. Had to come sooner or later."

"I've always been a collector," Shane said. His gaze dropped to a duffel. "After last year, it became more than a hobby. It seemed smart to be prepared for whatever had come at me before to take another swipe."

Easy nodded. "What they said. In a nutshell."

The only thing lined up on the floor that didn't make her stomach hurt was a huge professional-grade trauma kit that made hers look like a child's toy—one of Shane's contributions to their new supplies. Nick had explained that Shane had medic training, and knowing the man was equally capable of healing as killing added a new layer she couldn't help but respect.

For a few minutes, Nick, Shane, Beckett, and Easy silently checked their weapons and filled their holsters. Metallic clicks and snaps filled the air. She sat with Jeremy and Marz in a semicircle behind Marz's desk.

Suddenly, Marz shoved up from his chair. Not-Eileen yelped awake from where she'd been sleeping at Marz's feet. "This is bullshit."

"What?" Nick asked.

"I'm coming with you." The sounds of their weapons checks ground to a halt.

Beckett shook his head. "We need you here, Marz."

"No, you don't," he seethed.

"Derek, man—"

Marz glared at Beck. "Don't you fucking say one word about my leg. I'm as capable as any of you." She hadn't known Derek long, but Becca absolutely believed him.

The big guy held up his hands. "I was just gonna say we need you to run the op with the cameras and scanner intel."

"Jeremy can do it," Marz said, crossing his arms.

Jeremy bolted upright in his seat, and Nick froze. "What?" they both asked.

Marz perched on the edge of the desk and looked at Jeremy. "I spent three hours teaching you this equipment last night during their reconnaissance mission. By the time he went to bed," he said, addressing the other men, "he could recite it in his sleep. Jer knows what to do."

"Uh, I don't know," Jeremy said, shaking his head.

Nick crossed to the desk, intense gaze focused on his brother. "Can you do this?" he asked. "Because we could use Marz in the field."

A lump lodged in Becca's throat.

Jeremy tugged his fingers through his hair and nodded, then he rose to his feet. "I can do it. I'll do it."

Nick rounded the desk and extended his hand, but when Jeremy accepted it, Nick pulled him in. Seeing the brothers embrace was almost more than Becca could take. As much as she missed Scott, she couldn't imagine Jeremy learning he'd lost his brother, too. She dropped her gaze to her lap and fought back tears. They clapped each other on the back, then Jeremy was beside her again.

"I might throw up," he whispered to her.

"Me, too. We can hold the bucket for each other." He chuckled, but she was only half kidding. Becca rose to her feet. "I've made a decision."

Nick's brows cranked way down. "You're not coming with us."

Her jaw dropped open, and she planted her hands on her hips. "First of all, that's not what I was going to say. I know a lot of things. One is that I know nothing about how to do what you're about to do. But, second of all, if I wanted to come, there'd be nothing you could do to stop me."

He crossed his arms and cocked an eyebrow at her, his gaze filled with heat and amusement. Nick bowed his head. "Please, then, continue."

"What I was *going* to say is that we have *got* to stop eating nothing but takeout. Tomorrow night I'm going to make a big meal of everybody's favorite comfort food. So decide what you want and I'll go to the store in the morning." Because they'd all be coming back. And they'd all sit down around a table together and give thanks that they'd made it through, like the family they were. Or were becoming. She simply wouldn't accept any other outcome.

A lively conversation erupted about what their choices might be. Laughter and groans of approval rang out. Nick came to her and dropped a kiss on her forehead. "You just told them you believed in them again. Thank you."

She nodded and found herself blinking a lot for the fifteenth time.

A few minutes later, Miguel walked through the door to the gym. He'd been here so often, Nick had given him the codes. "I'm back. And I'm ready to go," he called.

Nick scratched his head. "Uh, Miguel."

He held up a hand. "Don't 'uh, Miguel,' me, son. I did shit like this for twenty-five years on the force. You're understaffed to take on something this big. You need me."

He threw a challenging look up at Nick. The two of them facing off was almost comical, as Nick had a good five inches on the older man.

"I'd be proud to have you," Nick said, extending a hand.

From that moment on, Becca's gaze couldn't stay off the clock as it inched closer and closer to seven. At the windows, the sky went dark, another indication that it was time for them to go.

And then they were ready.

Marz gave some last-minute advice to Jeremy, who sat sheet white at the computers but was nodding and nailing the answer to every question Marz asked.

Nick came right up into Becca's space and, without a word, buried his hands in her hair and his tongue in her mouth. It was the kind of kiss that could change a woman's life. She just prayed it wasn't the last one he ever gave her. He pulled back, met her gaze, and said, "See you in a few."

As the six men crossed the room and threaded their way through the gym equipment, Becca called out, "Be careful, you guys. And good luck."

Without looking back, Shane raised a hand and waved. "Ain't no thing but a chicken wing."

One by one, they all disappeared through the door. And her heart dropped all the way to the floor.

Chapter 22

$\mathcal{B}$ecca's nerves had her tapping a tuneless song out on the desk, and Jeremy's skin still hadn't regained its color, but at least his voice was calm as he responded to the guys' radio transmissions. It was quite possible that they were the two most stressed-out and scared people on the face of the planet.

There were two teams. A-Team consisted of Nick, Shane, and Easy going to the strip club. B-Team consisted of Beckett, Marz, and Miguel going to the storage center. In place of real names, they all had call signs. Nick was A1, Shane A2, and so on. Jeremy's sign was Eileen. Marz's brilliant idea.

"B1, there are two cars in your target's parking lot," Jeremy said into his headset as he glanced between the traffic camera images on side-by-side computers. Otherwise, the U-Ship-n-Store appeared empty. But they weren't using their location names over the radios, either.

"Roger that," came Beckett's voice. Marz had routed incoming audio through the computer speakers so she could hear it, too. Sitting on Becca's lap, the puppy tilted her head back and forth with each new transmission, like she followed along.

"A1, you've got a packed house already." Jeremy wasn't exaggerating. Confessions was located in a long brick building that had probably once housed a store or business. The large lot at the side was crammed with cars, and the valets were hopping.

Nick's voice crackled through. "Roger."

"Eileen, this is B1. We have an ETA of three minutes. Any status change?"

"No. Two cars. No obvious interior lights."

"Roger."

"A1 to Eileen, ETA is two minutes to our target."

Becca's stomach did a nauseating loop-the-loop. The guys had decided a coordinated dual assault was necessary to have the best chance at rescuing Charlie. Because if they did them sequentially and the first one failed, that would allow Church time to move Charlie and defend himself. The downside to the coordinated strategy was each team only had three men.

Against however many Church had.

"B-Team is on location."

"Okay," Jeremy said. "I mean, roger that."

Becca rubbed a circle on Jer's back. "You're doing great," she said. "Don't worry about using the right words. They'll understand."

He blew out a breath and nodded just as another transmission came in.

"A-Team is on location."

"A1, B1. Be advised, both teams are on location." Nick and Beckett both acknowledged the information.

On one monitor, B-Team ran across the darkness of the storage center parking lot and flattened themselves against the side of the building. On the second monitor, Nick, Shane, and Beckett approached the strip club's front door just like any other guys heading out for the night. Becca covered her mouth with her hand, her gaze hanging on every detail of Nick's body. And then they disappeared inside.

On the side of the storage center, two men huddled at a side door while the third—Miguel—kept a lookout. Then the door was open and they disappeared from the screen, too.

Jeremy heaved a breath. "There go our eyes. Damnit."

For long minutes, nothing. Eternity came and went as they stared at the motionless buildings. Not even the bugs the guys had planted helped them because the blaring music inside the club drowned out everything else. So there was nothing for Becca to do but wait.

Then a line of cars crossed in front of the strip club, eased through the narrow aisles of cars in the lot, and went around to the back. Becca's heart tripped into a sprint. Could that be the "company" arriving? Or Charlie? Or, of course, it could be totally unrelated.

Jeremy had seen it, too. "A1, be advised. Three cars just arrived at your target and drove immediately to the back of the building."

"Any other details?" Nick's voice was deadly calm, an odd contrast to the base beat pounding in the background.

"No." Jeremy covered his mouthpiece and glanced at her. "Couldn't make out any passengers because of the glare off that streetlamp. Could you?"

She shook her head, wishing she could see more than

the narrow view these cameras allowed. What was happening?

Suddenly, chaos crackled through the speakers. "Eileen, we are taking fire. Repeat, B-Team is taking fire." Loud pops and cracks pierced the background. "Tell A-Team to move their asses."

"Oh, my God," Becca said, her hand trembling against her mouth. The puppy whined and sniffed at her face.

Jeremy's voice was tight as a whip. "A1, this is Eileen. B-Team is taking fire. Repeat, B-Team is taking fire. B1 says to move your ass now."

RIXEY PRETENDED TO sip his beer and watch the G-stringed dancer grind against a pole. "We have two situations," he said as casually as he could to project over the ear-shattering music. "B-Team is under fire."

"Shiiit," Shane bit out.

"And?" Easy asked, muscles so tense his grip was likely to break the bottle in his hand.

"Three cars just arrived out back," Nick said, throwing the dancer a smile like he was paying attention. She slithered toward him on hands and knees, her bare and very fake breasts swaying as she moved. Hoping to send her on her way, he tugged a dollar from his wallet.

Whipping her long black hair over her shoulder, she pushed up onto her knees and gestured for him to slide it under the side strap of her thong. Fighting back aggravation, he did it, hating the thought that any other woman would be on his skin when all he wanted to feel, smell, and touch was Becca. Especially after she said she loved him.

The dancer crawled away toward the next dollar donor.

"We should check out those cars, now. Too coincidental given today's intel," Shane said.

"Slow and steady, gentlemen," Easy said, voice an even keel. They all got up. "Half the guys in this place are carrying. Let's not give them a reason to draw. This way toward the back."

Nick had noticed it, too. Flashes of weapons under people's jackets. Printing through clothing. A few unconcealed carries, too. It was an OK Corral gunfight waiting to happen.

Easy led the way toward a back hallway. Unsurprisingly, a real meathead of a guy in a Confessions T-shirt blocked the way.

"This area's private," he said in a deep voice.

"Well, that's a good thing," Easy said, a scowl on his face. "Because we're *company,* and we don't want our business all out in the open."

Nick held his breath and kept his face a blank mask. Fucking Easy and his titanium balls. Precisely what had kept them alive on that dusty road that day.

The guy frowned and looked around like he hoped no one had noticed his faux pas. "Of course. Sorry, sir. Uh, welcome." With his tree trunk of an arm, he held open the fabric-and-beads curtain.

They stepped through and the curtains closed behind them, leaving them in a dim hall that ran the length of the club.

Shane's gaze met Nick's, and it was filled with all kinds of *I can't believe that just worked.* Nick nodded.

When Shane turned around, he walked right into a leggy, long-haired redhead. "Whoa," he said.

"Oh, my God, sir. I'm so sorry." She shook her head and dropped her gaze to her spiky pink heels. "Please. I'm sorry."

"No harm done, darlin'." He smiled at her, turning on the southern charm.

Impatience crawled through Nick's veins. They didn't have time for Shane to flirt, even if this girl was the most natural-looking female he'd seen since they arrived. No five-grand implants for her. Not that he was looking. It was just that she appeared too real for this place. He cleared his throat. A wordless *Come the fuck on, McCallan.*

"Say," Shane said to the woman. "We're company and we got turned around when we went out to the bar. Any chance you know which way everyone went?"

"Uh." Back pressed to the wall, nipples showing through her gauzy pink teddy, she glanced both ways down the hall, like she was checking no one listened. What the hell was she so scared of? Did Church knock his dancers and waitresses around? Wouldn't that be the perfect little irony, given the ridiculous name of this place? "Well, some went to the private party room down that way, and some went downstairs with, um, the sick guy. I'm supposed to be getting him some food."

The sick guy. Rixey's gut rang out a three-alarm code telling him that was Charlie Merritt.

Shane grinned. "That's where we're headed, too. Gotta message to deliver." He winked. "Just downstairs?"

She nodded. "On the left."

"You were very helpful . . ." Shane smiled expectantly. Boy, this guy could pour on the charm. Woman was skittish as hell, but he played her like a marionette, moving her along from one thing to the next like he held the strings.

"Crystal," she said. "You're welcome, sir."

"Maybe I'll see you around."

"Okay." Her smile was nervous, and the minute Shane stepped back, she bolted down the hall.

They went the opposite way toward the back door and, apparently, the basement steps.

"You see how fucking scared she was?" Shane asked.

"Yeah. Job well done, though. My gut says 'sick guy' is our guy," Nick said in a low voice.

Easy heaved a breath. "Now that I know the rendezvous, I'll bring up the car. I'll be outside this door in five." He glared at them. "Don't fucking get shot. There's only room in the car for one slacker to lie down at a time."

"Roger that," Nick said as Easy disappeared out the door. "Come on." Nick and Shane went slowly down the steps. Voices echoed from below.

Static sounded in his ear. "A1, A3 just crossed the parking lot on foot?"

Nick pressed his com button. "Yes," he whispered.

"Roger," Jeremy said. Damn if his bro wasn't hitting this out of the ballpark. Pride over how Jer had stepped up formed a warm ball in his chest.

They reached the stairs at the bottom, and Rixey shoved every other thought away. One door on the left, two on the right toward the far end of the long hall. Crystal said the sick guy was in the room on the left. Nick hand signaled to Shane to prepare to enter. They donned masks.

The door flew open in front of them. "Who are—" The overgolded black man predictably went for his gun.

Rixey didn't let him get that far. He punched him in the throat, which ensured the man grabbed there instead of his gun, didn't scream, and was momentarily incapacitated. Guns drawn, they rushed him into the room and pushed the door shut. A quick visual sweep found no cameras.

Rixey swiped Doorman's feet out from under him with a kick. He fell flat on his back, breath exploding out of him.

"Freeze," Shane ordered two teenagers who'd been hunting and pecking away at their cell phones on a cushy couch. "Toss 'em down. Nice and slow. Now, hands up. Don't be stupid." They sprawled onto their stomachs.

When Doorman's gaze cleared, it landed on Nick's gun pointed right at his head, and he froze.

"A1, be advised that A3 is in wheels coming around to the back of the building." The volume of the games playing on multiple TVs made Nick press the piece to his ear.

Ah, great goddamned news. "Roger. We got a ride."

"Go," Shane said, nodding at the door just past the boys.

Nick crossed the rec room and, gun drawn, pushed open the door. He cleared the room in a sweep. A blond-haired man lay on a bed with messed-up blankets. Jesus, he was pretty damn close to the spitting image of Frank Merritt. Just much younger.

They'd found Charlie.

"I got him," he said over his shoulder, elation filling his chest for Becca. Damn, it was going to feel good to bring her brother home for her. "Eileen, do you copy? We have him."

Crouching beside the bed, Nick scanned for injuries and found plenty. Cuts, bruises, badly chapped lips, sunken-in eyes, a ball of bandage around his right hand. Nothing obviously critical, which meant they could deal with it back at Hard Ink.

Charlie moaned, his eyelids fluttering.

"Becca sent me, Charlie. Can you hear me? You're with friends."

For a moment, Charlie's eyes seemed to focus. And then it was gone again. Rixey was going to have to hump him out of there. He dragged him to the side of the bed, pulled his arms over his left shoulder, and hiked him up from a dead squat. Nick's back screamed. Shit. Tall and lanky as Charlie was, he wasn't light. Things were gonna get dicey if they hit any resistance on the way out.

Charlie over his shoulder, Nick came out of the bedroom to find that Shane had been busy. Doorman and the teenagers lay bound and gagged.

"Let's go," Nick said.

Shane palmed the doorknob and counted to three on his fingers. He pulled it open, cleared the hall with a nod, and started up the steps.

They were halfway up when a shadow fell across the opening at the top.

Sonofabitch.

The easy way was always mined. Of course, in this case, the easy way was the *only* way. No fucking chance Nick was getting this close to bringing Charlie home only to have it all go to shit fifteen feet from the exit.

A willowy figure carrying a tray appeared at the top and took one step down. Crystal. Her eyes went wide. "They're coming. There was a call." She retreated as they kept going up the stairs. "I have to scream now, and you have to hit me."

"*What?*" Shane asked, echoing Rixey's own thoughts.

"If you don't, they'll know I helped you. And I can't . . ." Agitation overtook all her delicate features. "You have to. Please." Apology in her eyes, she screamed at the top of her lungs. "Please."

"Pretend to fall and cradle your stomach." Shane swung like he was punching her.

She dove, her head and back hitting the wall and the tray of food flying.

They bolted through the door.

Aw, thank fuck for Easy. He had his rental SUV sitting right there, back door open. Shane dove in first. Nick flipped Charlie off his shoulder, and Shane hauled him in. Rixey's ass was still flapping in the breeze when Easy peeled out and men exploded through the door they'd just come through.

Gunshots erupted in a barrage that sprayed the back of the SUV.

Shane and Nick went flat, covering Charlie, who was completely out now. Probably for the best.

More gunfire again. The back window shattered in a hail of glass.

"Do whatever you have to do to avoid a tail, man," Nick called.

"On it."

Shane groaned. "Motherfuck."

"What?" Nick asked as Easy tore out of the lot, cutting off traffic and sending oncoming cars into tailspins that luckily blocked the road.

"I'm hit." Shane pulled a handful of blood away from his right shoulder. "Flesh wound, I'm pretty sure. Sonsabitches."

"You need a hand?" Nick asked.

"No, goddamnit," Shane said, cussing up a blue streak under his breath. Yeah, he was good.

Nick scanned out the back window. Course that would've been too easy. Two SUVs had gone offroading onto the sidewalk around the cars blocking the road. "We have company."

"Yup," Easy said.

"A-Team, vehicles are in pursuit. Do you have everyone?" came Jeremy's voice.

An occasional round was still hitting home on their rear end.

Grabbing his gun, Rixey lowered the passenger window and leaned his upper body out enough to line up a shot. He pulled the trigger, and the first tail swerved and lost control, crashing into a parked car.

"Get us gone, E," he hollered.

They ran a red light, which Rixey only realized after the fact when cars went screeching sideways in their wake. He approved. But the damn tail still wasn't giving up. The road opened into two lanes lined with clubs and bars and restaurants, and traffic picked up. Couldn't damn well shoot now. Nick sat heavily in his seat just as Easy cut across two lanes of traffic and made a right turn at the last possible minute.

Rixey careened into Charlie and Shane, whose injured shoulder slammed into the door, sending off more colorful curses.

The turn-and-slide didn't stop there. Easy took the first left. Right again. And then another right, taking them back in the direction from which they'd come. No sign of the tail. Had they lost him? Nick kept a vigilant gaze out the back. Easy took the next left to cut across the city from east to west, continuing to zigzag to make sure they were tail-free. But he kept his speed down and drove carefully. Last thing they wanted was to get stopped by a cop for speeding or running a red light. Not when they were in the free and motherfucking clear.

Rixey blew out a breath and sagged against the seat. It might've been the first time he'd fully breathed in fifteen minutes. "Everybody okay?" He got two affirmatives, and hit his com button. "Eileen? This is A1. We have the package. I say again, we have the package."

"They have him," Jeremy said.

Some sort of static filled Nick's earpiece for a moment, then Becca cried out, "You have him? You really have him?"

Man, the joy in her voice made him feel ten feet tall.

"Yeah, sunshine. I'm bringing him home."

Chapter 23

$\mathcal{B}$ecca had been sitting by Charlie's makeshift bedside for eight hours, willing him with everything inside her to wake up long enough to let her know he was really okay.

Before they'd even returned to Hard Ink, Nick had given her a rundown of the injuries already identified: dehydration, probable broken ribs, multiple cuts and contusions, burn marks, infection in the amputation sites. They'd cut off two of his fingers. The macabre list went on and on, forcing her to detach from the idea of him as her brother long enough to treat him as a patient. Her attempted abduction proved they couldn't trust hospitals to be safe right now.

Somewhere along the way, B-Team had met up with A and escorted them back. Marz had been shot three times in his lower right leg—the one with the prosthesis. His jeans were literally Swiss cheese, but otherwise B-Team had escaped the firefight at the storage center intact.

By the time both teams returned home, Becca and Jeremy had set up a trauma station using a table from the tattoo parlor and the supplies from her and Shane's packs, which thankfully included IV fluids and antibiotics. Shane had helped her treat Charlie, and then she'd patched up Shane's GSW. Thank God he'd only been grazed.

Once she'd done everything she could for Charlie, and thanked everyone, and welcomed them home safe and sound, she'd broken down in Nick's arms.

After Charlie'd had two bags of saline and a bag of IV antibiotics, the guys had brought a mattress into the gym from the apartment so he could be moved off the firm table without jostling him too much.

She'd been sitting in this chair almost the entire time since then, alternating between sleeping against Nick, who sat beside her, staring at Charlie and willing him awake, and playing with her bracelet until she drove herself crazy with the jingle. She finally took it off and laid it at the foot of the mattress.

She wasn't alone. Every member of the team had sat or slept around her and Charlie.

If she hadn't already known before then, she knew exactly why Nick Rixey loved every one of these people. Becca didn't know how she'd ever repay them.

Actually, yes she did. She and Charlie had to help them clear their names.

Another hour passed, and Becca fell asleep on Rixey's shoulder again.

"Becca? Hey, wake up, sunshine."

Eyes still unfocused, she lifted her head. And realized she was looking at an awake but very groggy Charlie.

She flew from her seat, eased to her knees, and leaned against the mattress. Unsure where to touch him that didn't hurt, she stopped short. "Charlie. Thank God. I'm so sorry," she said. "You were right. And I'm sorry." Lightly, she brushed the mop of blond waves out of his face. He always kept his hair longish—it used to drive their father crazy—but he usually kept it pulled back in a ponytail.

He shook his head, his movements sluggish. "No worries." Typical Charlie. "Thanks for not giving up on me," he managed.

"I would never. Do you hear me? Never. I love you."

"Me, too, sis." The swallowing sound he made was hard and rough. "I would kill for a Mountain Dew."

She laughed. "How about some water to start."

He grunted but took a long draw from the cup she held. "Where am I?" he asked, eyes darting over the rough industrial space of the gym.

"A friend's house," she said for now. But she smiled at Rixey, and he winked.

Charlie's eyes scanned around the gathered group. Everyone had gotten up when she'd said his name. "The Colonel's team," he stated, using the name he'd called their father for years. It was like he'd recognized them right off. "And some other dudes," he said, eyeballing Jeremy and Miguel.

"How do you know us?" Nick asked. "I'm Nick Rixey, by the way."

Charlie nodded. "My dad had some files on a thumb drive. Just personnel records, like patrol schedules and fitness reports, and stuff." He shrugged. "I was able to patch together the names of most of the team."

"No shit? There were fitness reports?" Marz said, looking at the other guys. "That'll give us Merritt's own copies to challenge the official records. Oh, I'm Derek DiMarzio, by the way. Any chance you still have those?"

"Yeah. I still have the drive."

Becca sat on the edge of the mattress. "How, Charlie? Your place was tossed. So was mine, actually."

He frowned and shifted like he was trying to get comfortable. "Thumb drives are hidden inside the wall of a motel I stayed in." Holy crap. One of the ones they'd gone to, presumably.

Wide-eyed, Nick stepped to the edge of the mattress and looked down on her brother. "Can you start from the beginning and tell us what you found, what Church's guys are looking for, and why you told Becca to find me?"

Becca looked between the two men she loved most in the world. Her heart ached for Charlie to know something that might help the team.

"Water again first, please?" Charlie said, reaching out. The guys all edged closer as he drank. He passed the cup back to her. How she wished she could do more for him. "Two months ago, I got a letter from a Singapore bank in the mail. It was addressed to my father at my apartment, which was frackin' hilarious because he never once stepped foot in my place and wouldn't have trusted me to handle his affairs. Letter said that per the account holder's request, notification was being sent because of prolonged inactivity on the account. It'd be closed unless the account holder contacted them within ninety days." He met Becca's gaze, his blue eyes so like their father's. His whole face, really.

"The bank wouldn't give me the money or any other account information since my name wasn't on the account and I didn't have the passcode, even though I explained the account holder was dead. I even sent a copy of his death certificate, but they kept denying me. So I hacked in. Every single deposit was made by the same depositor. A company, presumably, called WCE. They deposited twelve million dollars."

She gasped. Curses and mutters went around the room. God, there it was in a numerical value. What it had taken for her father to throw away everything he'd ever valued. The price put on the lives of Nick's six comrades who'd died there on a dirt road in Afghanistan. It made her nauseous. "That's what the 12M stood for in the note you hid in my jewelry box?" She reached up a hand to Nick. His expression was a storm about to open up. He sat down and kept his fingers intertwined with hers.

"You found that? Yeah. When things started getting dicey, I needed to make some copies of the info. I put it in Mom's necklace, too, but I lost it."

"I found it at a motel. How did you get the necklace, though?"

A sheepish expression came over his exhausted face. "I broke into your back door. Needed to hide some stuff without you knowing."

"Charlie! I thought I was going crazy! What else did you hide?"

"Two of my laptops are in your basement crawl space."

Becca shook her head, completely overwhelmed by Charlie's story.

"Back up. What is WCE?" Marz asked.

"Never did find out. As soon as I started searching for it, attacks against my firewalls began. Someone must've set up a tracer alerting them of searches for that set of characters and was trying to figure out who was doing the searching. So I started moving locations. Lasted for a while. Until it didn't." He shrugged. "Guys who held me were hot as hell to find out how I'd learned about WCE, but I didn't say a word. Figured they were going to kill me either way."

Pride and sadness roared through Becca. How courageous he'd been. Her gaze dropped to the bandages on his hand. And how he'd paid for it. The guys were looking at him with a new respect, too.

"Well, hell, good to know about the tracing. Before I start hitting the bank information, I'll make sure the IP address is buried so deep no one can track it back to us," Marz said.

"Marz is their computer expert," Becca said. Marz and Charlie exchanged nods. She could totally see them getting along.

"In addition to digging into WCE, I dug into my father in Afghanistan. That's when I noticed that in the few accounts of the ambush I could find, they made it sound like everyone had died, when DoD records I later hacked trying to learn more indicated there were survivors. And the fitness reports in your official records don't match the ones I have on the thumb drive. The circumstances of the Colonel's death didn't add up. Seemed like you might be an ally in getting to the bottom of it all," he said to Nick.

"Jesus," Beckett bit out. "Do you realize how scary him and Marz would be together."

Charlie frowned. Marz grinned.

Charlie pushed his hair off his face and yawned with a grimace. "The Colonel was on the take from somebody. Big time. Someone with the power to trace my digital signatures and to grab me off the street. So it wasn't just any Joe Schmo. It has something to do with heroin. Main and most lucrative economic activity in Afghanistan plus main drug trade of the Churchmen equals way too coincidental when you're talking that kind of coin . . ." Charlie broke off, his gaze fixated and then narrowed at the end of the bed where Becca had discarded her bracelet. "What's that?" he asked, pointing at it.

"This? It's a bracelet Dad gave me for my birthday last

year." She grasped it. "Kinda funky for his taste, but . . ." She shrugged.

He frowned. "Can I see it?" She handed it to him, and he spread it out on his lap. "Bec, these charms . . . this is binary code."

She leaned in. "What do you mean?"

His eyes went wide, and the other men stepped closer. "I mean, zeroes and ones. Binary code. Someone have paper?"

"Holy shit. He might be right," Marz said, handing him a legal pad and a pen.

"Oh, never mind." He held up his wrapped right hand.

"Tell me what to write," she said, taking the pad. He read out the code, and she wrote it down. "I can't believe I've been wearing some kind of code on my wrist for the last year." She'd thought that once they had Charlie back, everything would make sense. But the situation was as surreal as it had ever been.

"Write it down this way, too," he said, turning the bracelet around and reciting the string of zeroes and ones backward.

"You think this is the passcode you mentioned?" Nick asked.

"Not this, but maybe the decimal equivalent. Which the Colonel would've known I could figure out. Damn, the guys who held me kept asking about the passcode, too. And here you might have been wearing it on your wrist all this time. God, if they'd known." Charlie's voice hitched. Shaking his head, he grasped the notepad and focused on the numbers, frowning. "This way it reads . . . 631780." He dragged a finger along the second line of numbers. "And this way . . . 162905."

"Shit, he's right," Marz said as he brought his laptop over. "You just converted that in your head?"

Charlie shrugged.

"Why all the cloak and dagger, though?" Becca said, frustration welling up inside her. "If he was going to send us information, why not just be straightforward about it? Do you think he was trying to sneak us access to that money? Because, God, I wouldn't want it."

"Problem is, the bank passcode is a seven-digit number. I found that much out," Charlie said. "These are six. It's not for the bank after all."

"What the hell does the bracelet go to, then?" Nick asked, tension rolling off him. Becca squeezed his hand, exhaustion making it hard to keep up with all this information.

"Jesus," Shane said. "Charlie's story raises as many questions as it answers."

Charlie yawned and grimaced. "God, I feel a lot like death warmed over."

"Take these," Becca said, handing him some pain medicine and water. He drank it down, and Becca was so grateful he was okay. Thankful to these men all around them.

Nick turned, his intense gaze raking over each person. "This isn't over. Whatever this is, it's just beginning."

Beckett hammered his finger into his palm. "Who or what is WCE? How was Merritt connected to them? To Church? What were they looking for when they ransacked both your houses? Who was the 'company' tonight at the club? What do these codes go to? When will they strike again, because you know they will. The list of what we don't know goes on and on."

You could almost feel the consensus build in the room around them.

"I want my honor back. My reputation. My career," Easy said from where he sat on a bench press. Blazing dark eyes flashed, and he gestured to the group. "Only way that happens is if we stay together and follow the leads wherever they go."

"Fuckin' A. I couldn't agree more," Shane bit out. "There's something here. And it just might lead to redemption."

Beckett stepped forward, shoulders tense, expression dark. "We did nothing wrong. It's time we take back what was stolen from us. Count me in."

"Shit, yeah. I'm prepared to fight," Marz said.

"What are they—"

"Whatever your father was into," Nick interrupted Charlie, "someone or some group was powerful enough to cover it up and blame the ambush on us. We were all discharged and discredited. Every member of the team who survived the attack had served ten or more years in the Special Forces, and someone just took that the fuck away." Becca rubbed Nick's back, hating the anguish layered beneath the rage in his voice.

"You can count on me," Charlie said. "There was never any love lost between me and the Colonel, and I have my own vendetta against the Churchmen now." He held up his bandaged hand.

Becca's heart ached for everything everyone in the room had lost. It was already so much. And it might not be over. "You can count on me, too. After everything you've done for me, I'd do anything for each of you."

"And me," Miguel said. "I know I'm not part of the team, but I'm invested now."

Jeremy stood up. "You're my brother," he said, pointing at Nick from across the group. "I'd stand with you no matter what you're up against."

Every man in there agreed. Whatever had happened between them in the past, their bond was forged anew in that moment. Becca swallowed around the lump in her throat.

Nick nodded and got to his feet. "All right, then. The Hard Ink Special Forces Team is hereby stood up." Chuckles went around the room, releasing a bit of the tension. "And I'm proud to serve with each and every one of you, including Miguel, Jeremy, Becca, and Charlie. We'll take our friends where we find them, and each of you has proven yourself." Approving murmurs followed.

The puppy jumped on the mattress.

"Cool dog," Charlie said. "Heh. We match," he said, waving his hand. "Three legs, three fingers. What's her name?"

The guys tried and failed to restrain their laughter. Everyone looked at her, and Becca just shook her head. How could she possibly choose anything else after "Eileen" had successfully run the operation to rescue her brother. The guys were attached to the silly name. Truth be told, so was she. "Her name's Eileen."

"What?" Shane asked, a grin on his face. "Seriously? I named her?"

"No, man. I'm the one who sang the song," Nick said.

"But I'm the one who said Eileen . . ."

The squabbling devolved from there until they were singing again. "Sorry," she said, leaning in to kiss Charlie's cheek. "I'll get them out of here so you can sleep. It's the middle of the night." She brushed his hair back again. "I'm so glad you're back."

Charlie nodded. "See you in the morning."

Simple words she'd feared she'd never hear again. She blinked back tears—nice that they were tears of joy for once. "All right, ya hooligans. Either be quiet or get out so Charlie can sleep. Nurse's orders." Slowly but surely, the party broke up. Everyone protested sleep, but really they were all two or three days overdue.

Nick slipped his hand into hers as they crossed the gym. She looked back over her shoulder, and Charlie's eyelids were already sagging. Eileen curled up in a ball by his side.

Quietly, Becca and Nick got ready for bed and crawled in together. His arms wrapped around her and held her tight to his chest. "I want you to stay here," Nick said.

Becca tilted her head back. "What do you mean?"

"I mean, I want you to live here with me. Not just because your house isn't safe and all this is going on. Because I want you by my side. I'm a better man with you. And I want to be there for you, too, every day and every night. Charlie's welcome, too. No matter what, you're family now to me. I love you, Becca."

Hearing him say it would never get old. Emotion lodged in her throat. How, in the midst of the worst crisis of her life, had she gone from being utterly alone to finding a whole new family and the love of her life?

"I love you, too, Nick. And I don't want to be anywhere but here."

"God, sunshine, that's the best news I've ever heard."

Becca smiled and reveled in his soothing touch. She hoped with everything she was that she could keep being the light and warmth in his life, because the anchoring weight in her gut told her things could very well get worse before they got better.

"Where'd you go?" he asked, kissing her neck.

"Nowhere, Nick. I'm right here with you. No matter what."

Acknowledgments

As they often are, this book was very much a group endeavor. Nick Rixey's world came to life around a birthday dinner table, as great friends and wonderful authors Stephanie Dray and Christi Barth helped me brainstorm the series plot. With the help of Jennifer Schober, those rough ideas took shape into something much more ambitious than I expected—but also hugely exciting. And then my wonderful editor, Amanda Bergeron, entered the picture, helping make this writer's dream come true. Without these four women, I never would've had the chance to meet Nick, Becca, and all the other wonderful characters at Hard Ink Tattoo.

Bringing the story to life on the page was one of the most challenging things I've ever done—and one of the most rewarding. I absolutely could not have accomplished it without the constant cheers and encouragements of writer friends Lea Nolan, Joya Fields, Christi Barth, and Stephanie Dray. Christi went way, way, way above and beyond by critiquing the entire manuscript with lightning-fast speed and incredible insight. And Stephanie, too, offered a critique that pushed me to make the story better.

Amanda Bergeron offered wonderfully thoughtful and engaged editorial guidance and challenged me to go deeper into the characters and the story. I can't thank each of them enough.

I also need to offer a special thanks to my husband, Brian, and daughters Cara and Julia for putting up with an MIA wife and mom while I escaped to the world of Hard Ink. This book would never have been finished without their devotion and support, and it means the world to me.

Finally, I offer thanks to Laura's Heroes for everything they do, and to the readers, who welcome characters into their hearts and minds and let them tell their stories over and over again! –LK

Special acknowledgment to the following readers who suggested dog names I used in the book:

Sadie: Cathe Green, Michelle Wilson, Dawn Howell Tinari, Kelly Ridgely DeLeon, Alison Gail Rush

Georgia: Sheri Vidal, Sara Long Butler

Phoebe: Julie Cooper Barber, Polly Greathouse Coffy, Amanda Brown

Shiloh: Nancy Lux-Nicholson

Trinity: LaVerne Clark, Carrie Marcinkevage

Hopalong: Amy Villalba

Tripod: Linda Eisenberg

Cujo: Carlyn McGill

Ilene: Laura Stein Bubley

Eilene: Panera friend Elicia Brand Leudemann

Clover: Joanne O'Meara, and Hope: Amy Villalba, Hayley Reynolds, Crystal Sworden, Grace Zamora, Christina Mesmiller, were other names I wanted Becca to consider, but there was just too much going on! Thanks to the nearly two hundred people who suggested names for Becca's puppy! You guys rock!

**Can't get enough
of the men of Hard Ink?
Good news, they return with**

HARD AS YOU CAN

in March 2014!

*Five dishonored soldiers
Former Special Forces
One last mission
These are the men of Hard Ink*

*E*ver since hard-bodied, drop-dead-charming Shane McCallan strolled into the dance club where Crystal Dean works, he's shown a knack for getting beneath her defenses. For her little sister's sake, Crystal can't get too close. Until her job and Shane's mission intersect, and he reveals talents that go deeper than she could have guessed.

Shane would never turn his back on a friend in need, especially a former Special Forces teammate running a dangerous, off-the-books operation. Nor can he walk away from Crystal. The gorgeous waitress is hiding secrets she doesn't want him to uncover. Too bad. He's exactly the man she needs to protect her sister, her life, and her heart. All he has to do is convince her that when something feels this good, you hold on as hard as you can—and never let go.